Treasure of the Ancients
BOOK I

TREASURE

I0685950

OF

EGYPT

Copyright © 2011 Barbara Ivie Green

Second Print Edition
ISBN-13: 978-0615526768
Texas, USA

www.barbaraiviegreen.com

This is a work of fiction. Names, characters, places, and incidents are either the product of the author's imagination or are used fictitiously. Any resemblance to actual persons, living or dead, events, or locales is entirely coincidental.

Use of this ebook is limited to personal, non-commercial use. All rights reserved, including the right to reproduce, display, broadcast, or republish in any form including, but not limited to, distribution or storage in a system for retrieval. No transmission, publication, or exploitation of the ebook in part or in whole is permitted without the prior written permission of the author, Barbara Ivie Green. This book may not be resold or uploaded for distribution to others.

Barbara Ivie Green

For my husband,
Shelby.

For bringing laughter
into my life,
and making me believe
in heroes.

Acknowledgments

My profound thanks to two dear friends, Dugie and Marsha, for being the best readers one could have; my sister, Diane, for her comments; and my mother for her unwavering support and insights. Also, I thank my daughters, who continue to be my inspiration; I couldn't have written this without you.

Special thanks to Mishael Witty at woweditor12@gmail.com for her amazing editing skills and to Tina, Karl, Bryden, and Peggy for their help in making my dream a reality.

Treasure Map

Chapter 1

London, England, 1863

The taverns beside the wharf were busier than usual, Alec noted as he stepped from his coach and looked up at his driver. "I don't expect to be here long."

"Aye, m'lord." Porter nodded as he eyed the street. "I'd be keepin' an eye out for the riffraff. No tellin' who's lurkin' about on a night like this."

"I'll keep that in mind," Alec said, amused by Porter's concern as he turned to survey the entrance of the Boar's Head. From the sound of it, the gaming hell was already in full swing. He watched as three young blades walked out the double doors, jovially hitting one another on the back, their anecdotes alluding to a night already well spent.

Ah, the young, Alec thought as he walked into the smoke-filled tavern, they'd be lucky to wake with only a hangover and not some other affliction.

The music from the quartet on stage mingled with the gaiety of the crowd as he assessed the room. His brow lifted slightly as a woman in a scarlet gown approached him, her generous favors barely concealed by the tight corset she wore.

"Hello, 'andsome. Would ye care for some company?"

Alec favored her with a lazy smile. "Just a whiskey tonight, love." He cradled her elbow as she turned to fetch his drink. "And bring it from the bottle, not the well."

"Aye, luv," she said breathlessly, tripping over herself as she left.

He knew he'd been blessed with the kind of looks that women desired. He also knew how to use them to get what he wanted, in this case a drink that wouldn't kill him when he awoke on the morrow.

Alec turned his attention to the crowded room once again. He hadn't visited this particular establishment in years, yet it was exactly as he remembered, down to the smell. Cheap perfume and cigar smoke hung in the air.

He hadn't missed anything, it seemed, with the exception of the lovely young dove dressed in canary yellow, swinging from the ceiling. Alec stood for a moment, watching as she swept over the crowd from her high perch.

The new attraction had drawn quite a crowd. Calls from the men below were enough to entice the girl to show more of her nicely turned ankle. Her actions were met with cheering applause as she leaned back in the swing and laughed. The movement only succeeded in exposing more of her shapely calf.

A large woman belted out a bawdy tune on the stage as the audience roared with laughter over her suggestive lyrics and comical gestures. No wonder Samuel wanted to meet here tonight; it was his kind of place. . . . They were only missing the elephants, Alec thought with amusement as he glanced around the room, filled with a collection of ruffians, rakehells, and even wilder women, for some sign of his friend.

Just then, he heard a woman's sultry voice at his side before she brushed up against him. "If you're looking for company, darlin', you're in luck. I'm right here."

Alec couldn't help but show his amusement as he smiled down at the lovely redhead. The green of her eyes matched that of her dress, while the red rose tucked into her décolletage matched her reddened lips.

Noting the direction of his gaze, she pressed her body further into his, rubbing her hand along his chest.

Alec's smile deepened. "Actually, I was just thinking to try my luck at the tables."

"Well, then, follow me, darlin'." She moved to grasp his forearm. "I know just the table where we can both be comfortable, and I promise you'll get lucky."

"Leavin' so soon?" The woman in the scarlet gown pouted up at him as she held out his glass. "Sure I can't change yer mind 'bout that?" she said, claiming his other side.

"Hhmm," Alec responded to their combined assault with good humor, "a most delightful offer. Perhaps later." He accepted the drink, using it as an excuse to extricate himself from both their grasps. As he did so, he expertly slipped a coin into her cleavage in return for it.

"We'll both be dancin' the cancan later, if you'd like to watch." The woman in green swiveled her hips.

"Tempting ladies, truly, but for now. . . ." Alec gifted his would-be seducers with another smile, showing the dimple in his cheek as he left them.

"He's a right 'andsome one, 'e is." The barmaid in red sighed, while the one in green nodded wistfully.

Obviously, there was no peace to be had this night, Alec thought with some derision as he headed to the back room. He was simply being hounded by women. As it was, he'd already escaped a crowded ballroom where the debutantes had practically mauled him, and now this.

Normally he enjoyed the attentions lavished on him by the fairer sex, but tonight he was simply tired of it, which was why he now sought the sanctity of the game room, where he could relax without being accosted.

As Alec passed under the tall entry arch, he noticed an opening at one of the tables. Crossing the short distance, he approached the players. "Gentlemen, care if I join you?" he asked.

A man with a bristled mustache answered, "By all means, good man. I was beginning to think that play would be cut short with no takers. Lord Campton's the name, and this chap here is Lord—"

"Bristol," the man seated across the table finished with a nod.

"Monsieur Blanoiś," the Frenchman sitting to his right offered up with a dignified nod of his head.

An older gentleman with a walking cane moved to stand for his introduction.

"Please stay seated, sir. No need for such formality." Alec hid a wry smile. Even in a den of iniquity, the older set were such sticklers for protocol. It never failed to amuse him.

"Lord Langston." The older man leaned back, settling himself once again.

Alec introduced himself as he took his seat and play resumed. It didn't take long for him to evaluate the competition. Bristol's mustache twitched when he bluffed, while Campton drummed his fingers lightly on the table. The Frenchman's dark eyes gave very little away, yet his mouth tightened into a thin line when the cards turned against him. The old lord was the hardest to discern. The man revealed nothing, not even when he'd lost ten thousand pounds in a single hand.

Strands of the rousing, yet forbidden, cancan drifted back from the main salon as the cards were dealt once again. Alec could feel the tension in the Frenchman sitting next to him as he sipped from his drink. The man had lost a considerable amount in the last hand . . . his lips had thinned to near vanishing.

Alec looked at his hand briefly while the old lord placed his wager.

"I'll see your bet and raise you five thousand." Bristol met the old man's bid.

Alec could feel the anticipation mount as he considered the other players. Lord Campton straightened his handlebars as he drew upon his pipe, while Bristol nervously strummed his fingers.

"I'll see that and raise it ten." Monsieur Blanoiś sat back, swirling the contents of his drink.

Alec watched the Frenchman over the rim of his own glass, noting the subtle changes in his attitude. He looked like a man who believed his luck had finally changed.

More than one man in the room took notice as the stakes became considerable. Several ladies had even braved the back room, joining the crowd that had gathered around the high-stakes game.

Alec glanced at his own cards briefly before placing several notes onto the center. "I'll see it and raise it twenty."

The old lord surprised everyone as he slid the near fortune in front of him into the center of the table. "One hundred thousand pounds," he announced.

An audible gasp was heard throughout the room as the old man remained leaning forward in his seat, showing the first sign of emotion since Alec had sat down at the table.

"Forgive me. I didn't expect play to be so deep this evening." The Frenchman gestured with his hand as he explained, "I will have to sign a note."

"You've a voucher for only half that amount," Campton raised his voice as the Frenchman signed the card. "How is it that we know you're good for it?"

The Frenchman's eyes sparkled dangerously in the low light. Though he kept a tight lid on his emotions, Alec wouldn't have been surprised if he called the Englishman out over the slight. "I have signed the note," he countered indignantly.

"Do you have collateral to back this up?" the older gentleman asked.

The Frenchman took his time considering his next words. "*Oui*," he finally said. Reaching inside his coat pocket, he pulled out a rolled-up piece of parchment. He leaned forward dramatically, holding it up for all to see. "This, gentlemen, is a map leading to the greatest treasure known to man." With an action bordering on reverence, he slid his note for one hundred thousand pounds inside the scroll and placed it in the middle of the gaming table. "I use it only as collateral."

Alec raised an eyebrow in response. From where he sat, it looked to be nothing more than a mottled old scrap tied with a leather string. It took considerable effort to hide his amusement over the man's bet.

"What else do you have?" Lord Campton scoffed, drawing even more interest from the other tables. He sat back with a smirk on his face that even his large mustache couldn't hide.

"You can't be serious." Lord Bristol shook his head. Snickers were heard throughout the room in response to his words.

"I stand good for it, I assure you. I have the funds," Monsieur Blanoiś insisted as he waited for his offer to be accepted.

A woman's high-pitched trill could be heard above the din. "That's what they all say," she snorted heartily. The crowd's raucous laughter mingled with the music in the background.

Lord Langston interrupted the commotion by holding up his hand. "I will accept it as such." There was a loud murmur among those watching.

Bristol threw his cards down and shook his head. "Too rich for my blood."

"I'm out," Campton muttered, sitting back in a cloud of smoke.

Alec eyed the crowd that had gathered before slowly counting out the desired amount and sliding it toward the pile. "Call."

The floor itself bounced in rhythm to the pounding feet of the dancers in the other room as Lord Langston placed his cards down. A full house, three aces and two kings, stared up from the table. The whole room buzzed with anticipation.

The Frenchman could hardly contain his exhilaration as he triumphantly spread out his hand. It was a straight flush, starting with the eight of clubs and ending with the queen.

There was a murmur of excitement from the onlookers who pressed forward to catch a glimpse. The winnings in this game alone would be a source of legend, let alone the cards being played to earn it. The Frenchman leaned forward to collect his prize. There was only one hand that could beat him, and those odds were astronomical.

"One moment, please." Alec leaned forward, stilling the man's hands over the pile. Slowly he turned his cards over, displaying a royal spade flush, ace high. The tension in the room exploded as the audience gasped in surprise. The Frenchman sat back, muttering to himself as Alec leaned forward to collect his winnings.

"It's a raid!" a man called from the hall outside.

Laughter in the main salon quickly turned to shouting as the gaming room became flooded with fleeing patrons, their screams filling the air. "Run! Run! It's a raid!"

Alec stood and quickly gathered the rest of the pile before him, stuffing money into his pockets as men pressed toward the door.

"I'll see you in the morning to settle my debt," the Frenchman shouted as he was caught in the throng and whisked away.

Alec looked up to see the old gentleman watching him calmly as he sat back comfortably in his chair.

"You'll probably never see him again," Lord Langston remarked, seemingly serene amongst the chaos. "I'd be happy to purchase the note from you. After all, I was the one who pressured you to accept it."

Alec was surprised by the gesture as he fingered the old scroll thoughtfully. The old man was probably right, he realized. The Frenchman was probably hightailing it out of the country as they spoke. "That, I believe, is why they call it gambling," Alec said as he tucked the map inside his coat. Tempted as he was to accept the old man's offer, he couldn't bring himself to do it.

"Suit yourself," the older gentleman said as he took a cigar from his pocket and nipped the end.

The whistles of the police grew louder as the room emptied. A flash of white from the corner caught Alec's eye, and he turned towards it. He recognized the barmaid who'd brought him his drink earlier, though her ensemble now consisted of a short skirt and petticoat, the white frills of which had drawn his attention.

"Over here, luv. Quickly." She beckoned to him as she opened up a secret panel in the wall.

Alec considered the older gentleman again. "Could I assist you in leaving?"

"Son," he rolled the cigar in his mouth, "at my age, I'd have to try hard to convince them I'd been up to something other than playing cards."

Alec smiled at his wit. "I bid you goodnight, then," he said before turning towards the woman who still waited for him.

As the police drew nearer, Alec stepped inside the hidden passage, aware that it could very well turn out to be a trap. They were immediately enclosed in darkness as the woman slammed the false door closed behind him.

"Follow me," she whispered after lighting a taper.

Bent over in the cramped space, Alec received a face full of fluff on several occasions as he trailed closely behind her. At last, they came to a door where they could stand. She paused, breathless, before it, trying the handle with little effect.

"Allow me," he said, reaching past her to take hold of the handle. Obviously well used, the concealed door slid soundlessly on well-oiled hinges. Hidden behind dense foliage, it opened, not into the alleyway as he might have guessed, but into a walled garden. The woman at his side quickly extinguished the light as she crossed to the opening to peer out into the street.

"I'll be damned," Alec whispered in surprise as he joined her. They watched the bobbies chase several people down the alley. Even more amazing to him than his escape was the sight of his coachman just rounding the corner. He chuckled; Lady Luck was definitely on his side tonight.

He looked down at the woman who stood in the doorway. In the streetlight, she looked much younger than before. "You deserve a reward," he whispered.

She pressed her breasts into him, turning her lips up to his for a kiss. Instead, he reached into his pocket and pulled out several bills, placing them into her hand. "For saving me," he said with a wink before running across the short expanse of grass towards his carriage.

"Laws, guv!" she cried in surprise as she counted the huge sum she'd been given before tucking it into her décolletage. "Sure you wouldn't care for a tumble?" she called after him.

He had no idea the total, but he'd probably just given her several thousand pounds. Of course she'd be inviting him back, Alec thought, somewhat amused as he climbed aboard the slow moving coach to the oblivion of the police down the road. "Just like old times, eh, Porter?" he hollered over to his driver.

"Aye, that it is, m'lord." Porter was hardly surprised by the new arrival as he steered the carriage clear of the paddy wagons. "Home, sir?"

Alec nodded as he opened the door and settled himself inside. Sitting back against the tufted seat, he sighed. *Could the night be any sweeter?* Not only had he won an incredible sum with the hand of a lifetime, but he'd also managed to win a treasure map.

A map to the greatest treasure known to man. . . . It was intriguing, to be sure. Alec removed the scroll from the inside pocket of his jacket, rolling it in his fingers. The old man's interest in buying the map had certainly piqued his curiosity. Absentmindedly, he tapped it against the palm of his hand before putting it back.

As he alighted from the carriage, Alec handed Porter a handsome tip. "Well done, my man," he complimented him as he headed to the front steps of his town house.

"The missus will be right 'appy, m'lord." Porter smiled as he pocketed the notes.

Alec let himself in, having dismissed his butler earlier in the evening. It was customary when he knew a late night was in store. Although it was still early by some standards, the clock in the foyer showed half past two. He shrugged off his coat as he headed toward his study, thinking a glass of brandy was just what he needed to wind down before bed.

Whack! Wood splintered next to his face as he opened the door to the darkened room.

"What the hell?" He ducked as a fist slammed into the side of his head from the other direction. The blow knocked him against another man, who tried to wrestle his arms to his side. "Not without a bloody fight, you don't," Alec growled, surprising the thug with his strength and speed.

He raised his arms, despite the man's efforts to restrain him, and quickly jabbed with his right. Though he could barely make out their forms in the dim light filtering through the window, the blow connected with the man's throat.

As the ruffian went down, the man behind Alec seized his arms again. He struggled against the strong grip as another looming figure succeeded in connecting a punch to his ribs. Alec felt the air leave his lungs as he doubled over. The bastard must be wearing brass knuckles, he'd hit him so hard.

Alec sucked in air, reared back, and kicked out at the man in front of him. The impact sent both him and the man holding him back into his desk. Several items scattered to the floor as they fought. Alec rolled free of the man's grasp just as a candelabra crashed down next to him.

Alec blocked another blow from the heavy base then reached out to twist the candelabrum free. Tearing it out of the assailant's grasp, he swung it hard, feeling it connect. The man grunted and staggered back. He was about to swing it again when a vase struck him in the back. It bounced off and hit the floor, shattering into a million pieces.

"That was my grandmother's vase," Alec ground out as he turned and hit the man square in the face. "An antique," he kicked out, sweeping the fool off his feet, "from the Ming dynasty!" The man hit the bookcase, sending several volumes to the floor.

From the corner of his eye Alec saw the outline of a chair as it came towards him. Snatching it in midair, he spun around and tossed it in an arc, sending it crashing against the wall. Unfortunately, he barely had time to cover his head with his hands as a small table broke over his back. The blow sent him staggering to his knees.

With catlike stealth, Alec shifted to his feet, reaching inside his boot for the knife he kept there. He straightened, prepared for the next attack.

BOOM! A shot rang out in the dark.

Plaster rained down on Alec from the ceiling. His ears were still ringing as he watched the scoundrels throw open the window and flee into the night.

"Are you all right, m'lord?" Sims asked, standing in his nightshirt before the open door.

Alec shook the debris from his hair as a candle was lit. "So it seems." He replaced the knife before standing. "What the hell took you so long?" he asked, looking around at the devastation.

Sims cleared his throat. "Sorry, m'lord. I thought at first you'd brought home an especially spirited female."

"Bloody hell!" Alec ran a hand through his hair.

"Should I call the constable, sir?" Sims asked.

"No," Alec replied, looking over at his butler, who was normally the picture of decorum. He had to hide a smile. With his hair standing on end, Sims looked like he was the one who'd just come from a fight. "I don't think they'll be returning anytime soon."

Alec spied his coat where it had fallen on the floor. He picked it up and shook it out. The bills it had once held lay strewn across the debris. With a slight groan, he tossed the jacket to the side as Sims dutifully started picking up the mess.

"Leave it until morning," Alec said tiredly as he sat down in his large leather chair. "You can pour me a brandy before you go back to bed, however."

"Very good, sir," Sims replied, handing him the drink, along with the decanter.

~*~

"Bloody hell!" Samuel looked around the study in surprise. "What happened in here?"

The expletive woke Alec with a start and he groaned, leaning forward. Damn, he hadn't meant to spend the whole night in the chair. He winced as Samuel threw open the shades, flooding the room with bright sunshine.

"I thought I'd find you surrounded by your booty, but not quite like this." Samuel laughed as he surveyed the mess on the floor.

"Booty?" Alec blinked up at him, shading his eyes.

"It's all the talk this morning." Samuel grinned from ear to ear. "You raked in quite a sum, I understand, along with a treasure map."

"Too bad you missed it." Alec grimaced as he rolled his shoulder. "Where did you disappear to after the Chesterfields' ball? I thought we'd agreed to meet at the Boar's Head."

"Sorry about that. I was tied up." Samuel raised his brows suggestively.

"Figuratively or literally?"

"That woman is relentless, I tell you." Samuel grinned mischievously.

He'd known better than to ask. Alec brought up his hand and rubbed his neck, while Samuel rambled on. Damn, he was sore. It must have been the table they broke over his back, or the cracked rib, or the sucker punch to the face, he thought, feeling the tender area around his eye.

Samuel glanced over, noticing the slight bruise Alec now sported. "I'm surprised that anyone could get the best of you."

"Who said there was only one?" Alec looked up at him with his good eye.

"Hmm," Samuel responded as he started picking up fistfuls of money and arranging them into piles while Alec poured himself another drink.

"How much should you have here?" Samuel asked with interest. "The rumor mills said you raked in at least three-fifty."

"Really?" It was Alec's turn to be surprised.

"You mean you don't know?" Both Samuel's brows shot up. "The game of the season, it's being said, possibly decade . . . and you didn't even count your winnings?"

"I was busy." Alec gestured to the utter chaos.

"Two hundred thirty-four thousand," Samuel whistled when he finished the tally. "Not including, of course, the infamous note and treasure map for another one hundred. How much do you think they got away with?"

"I doubt they got anything." Alec watched the liquor in his glass move as he rolled it. He did a quick tally in his head. "The winnings came to about two hundred fifty. I gave several bills to one of the tavern wenches and tipped my driver."

"You gave a strumpet sixteen thousand pounds?" Samuel snorted in surprise. "Holy hell. . . . You were busy."

There was no use explaining. Alec shook his head slightly. Samuel always came to his own conclusions, anyway.

"What *will* your fiancée say when she finds out?" Samuel feigned shock.

"What fiancée?" Alec narrowed his eyes on him.

"The one your mother all but proposed to in your stead."

"Hell," Alec groaned. "What else is the rumor mill saying?"

"Oh, that one isn't just a rumor. It's one of the bets that has been placed in the ledger at White's," Samuel said, speaking of the book into which patrons of the gentleman's club recorded their wagers.

"I suppose you've added one of your own?"

"Of course," Samuel supplied with a grin. "I bet that you leave the country within a fortnight in order to avoid the whole affair." He chuckled, enjoying Alec's awkward set of circumstances.

"That sounds a bit extreme." Alec irritably fluffed the cushion at his back, stabbing at it with his fist. "You seem to be enjoying this a little overly much."

"I am," Samuel said frankly. "You, my friend, have only just discovered the joys of a meddling mother, whereas I have had one for years."

Alec couldn't argue with that. Ever since Samuel had lost his father to an early death, his mother had practically smothered him. Alec hadn't had any idea just how frustrating it was before now. He downed the brandy he'd just poured with a single swallow.

"Is this it?" Samuel's voice was one of awe as he bent to pick up the scroll sticking out of Alec's discarded jacket.

Alec looked up with one eye slightly scrunched. "Indeed."

"What is it to?" Fascinated, Samuel pulled it out. Alec shrugged his shoulders in response. "You mean you didn't even look? The greatest treasure of mankind, and you didn't even look?" Samuel shook his head in disbelief as he unrolled the scroll.

"Well?" Alec asked from his chair as Samuel studied it. "What does it say?"

Samuel looked up with a blank stare, then turned it around for him to see. It looked like a sundial with chicken scratch all over it. "I believe you've been taken."

"Let me see that." Alec stood, snatching the document from Samuel as he started to laugh. "Hell," Alec swore as he looked at it, not in the least bit amused. It was bloody unlikely he was going to get one hundred thousand pounds for the damn thing.

"Well, I certainly don't envy you on this one either." Samuel held up the largest piece of the ceramic vase.

"It wasn't too bad." Alec remembered the hit he took as one of the thugs broke it over his back.

"It will be when your mother finds out about it."

"Hmmm," Alec reflected.

"Maybe you can glue it . . . or leave town," Samuel hedged.

"Although I'd love to help you win your bet, I think I'll be staying." Alec sat on the corner of the desk, looking at the drawing on the map.

"What's that there?" Samuel pointed to the back of it.

Alec flipped the parchment over in his hand. On the other side was another set of drawings, and these looked Egyptian.

"Aha!" Samuel stooped over, picking up two pieces of paper from the floor. One was the voucher from the Frenchman, while

13

the other had more strange writing with a line of fine penmanship beneath it. "This looks like ancient Greek." Samuel looked up. "Wait, I recognize this. It's been taken off the other side of the map."

Alec turned the map over. Across the bottom was a line of the same ancient script. "My ancient Greek is a tad rusty." He looked over at the note Samuel held. Beneath the Greek letters was another language. "How's your French?"

"Better than yours," Samuel said before reading it aloud. "What has four legs when it is born, two as an adult, and three when it dies?"

Alec rolled his eyes. "What does it really say?"

"That is what it says." Samuel looked suitably annoyed.

"Are you serious?"

"Quite."

Alec groaned.

"It must be a riddle." Samuel looked up with excitement.

"More like a joke, if you ask me," Alec grumbled irritably. "One that I am to bear the brunt of."

"Not necessarily," Samuel replied thoughtfully as he turned the note over. "Look, there is more."

"I don't think I can take any more."

"It appears to be a poem." Samuel cleared his throat before reading:

O Golden One, the lady of Heaven.
I worship her majesty, I give adoration to Hathor
I called to her, she heard my plea. She sent my Mistress to me.

"Do you think it's another clue?" Samuel looked up excitedly.

"A clue that someone is greatly disturbed, perhaps." Alec glanced at him with a raised brow.

"Ah, yes." Samuel nodded. "Seems your Frenchman was quite desperate for companionship. Either that, or he took his love of money quite seriously."

Chapter 2

It didn't take Alec a great deal of effort to locate the townhouse that Monsieur Blanoiś had let out for the season. As the carriage drew up in front he couldn't help but wonder if the old man's prediction would prove to be right, and the Frenchman wouldn't be there.

"It's not dilapidated. That, at least, is a good sign," Samuel noted as he surveyed the building.

Alec gave him a quick glance before alighting from the carriage. Samuel had insisted that he accompany him on this errand. Quite frankly, Alec doubted that he could have stopped Samuel. He seemed more interested in the outcome than Alec was himself.

"I can't believe the ol' codger said he'd buy it from you, and you didn't take him up on it." Samuel shook his head in disbelief as they walked up to the door and rang the bell. "What were you thinking?"

Alec almost wished he hadn't told him of the old man's offer. "There wasn't a great deal of time in which to make—" he started to say as a constable opened the door.

"Yes?" the man asked gruffly.

It certainly wasn't the welcome Alec had been expecting. "I am Lord Alecsian Rothchild Brighton, the Third, and I've come to collect a debt that Monsieur Blanoiś owes me." He handed the officer his card. "I was told I could find him here."

The constable took it, and then nodded. "He's here." He surprised them further by adding, "But good luck collecting it, the poor bastard shot himself last night."

Alec raised a brow at this information as the constable motioned for them to enter. He looked over at Samuel, whose expression mirrored that of his own.

"Maid found him this morning," the officer informed them as they followed him to the salon where the body lay. The dead man was still where he'd fallen, slumped back on the sofa, the gun in his hand.

"Poor bugger." Samuel glanced down at the body. "Rotten luck, ol' boy," he whispered to the side for Alec's benefit.

Alec couldn't agree more. It was highly doubtful that the older gentleman from last night's card game would buy the note now. It was most unfortunate, especially for the Frenchman. "Are you sure it was suicide?" he asked, watching as the constable made some notes in his report.

"Unfortunately, you're not the first creditors to show up since I have been here this morning." The constable looked grimly over at the deceased man. "I can't see as how it's the easy way out, though." He scribbled on a tablet of paper he held, holding it out to them. "According to his maid, this is the name of his solicitor."

"Thank you, you've been most helpful," Samuel responded when it seemed Alec was too preoccupied to do so himself. Taking the paper, he nudged Alec to get his attention.

Alec accepted the note and nodded his thanks. "We'll see ourselves out. Good day." Once outside, he turned to Samuel. "Did you happen to notice anything unusual about that?"

An expression of surprise registered across Samuel's face. "You mean, other than the dead man?"

Alec gave him a look of annoyance. "There was damage to the chair next to him, and I also noticed an impression left on the carpet from a table that used to be in front of the divan he was on."

"Really?"

"I also spotted a piece of broken glass behind the chair in the corner." With a grim expression, Alec looked over at Samuel. "That's not all. The gun he used was in his right hand."

"So . . . ?"

"Last night at the table, I noticed that Monsieur Blanoiś was left-handed." Alec glanced meaningfully over at Samuel. "I'm beginning to wonder if the Frenchman had some visitors of his own last night."

"You think he was murdered?" Samuel paused in his step.

"Possibly. . . ." Alec continued on as the coroner's wagon pulled up in front of the house.

Samuel rushed up beside him, speaking in a hushed tone. "And you actually think there might be a link between this and the men who attacked you?"

"I can't say. I thought, last night, they were after the winnings."

Samuel nodded in agreement. He, too, had assumed as much. He remained silent until they were back inside the carriage. "Tell you what," Samuel said, tearing his eyes away from the townhouse as the carriage pulled forward, "I know a man that may be able to tell us something about your map."

~*~

They arrived at the British Museum of Antiquities shortly after noon. "How is it that you know this man?" Alec had to duck his head as they entered the offices in the rear.

"He was a friend of my father's," Samuel said just as an older man with thinning hair approached them.

"Samuel, what a delight to see you. Come in, come in. Sit down," he said while ushering them into a room filled with objets d'art and other artifacts. The desk in the middle of the room was covered with books and sheaves of paper, piled in no discernible order.

Samuel made his way around the clutter to the other side of the desk. "Thank you for seeing us, Sir Richard."

"My pleasure. Tell me, how is your mother doing?"

"She's wonderful, taking in the waters at Bath this season."

"Good, good. Delightful woman."

Alec and Samuel exchanged a quick glance. He apparently knew a side of Samuel's mother they were both ignorant of.

Alec shook his hand as introductions were made. Sir Richard seated himself awkwardly behind the desk with a groan. "Leg seems worse on rainy days like this. Growing old is not for the faint of heart, I tell you."

17

Alec and Samuel took chairs on the other side. Once they were seated, Sir Richard leaned forward. "Tell me, what can I do for you?"

"Well, it's actually for my friend here. He recently acquired a document of considerable value, and we were wondering if you could shed some light on its contents for us."

Alec retrieved the scroll from his jacket and placed it on the desk.

"I'll do my best." Sir Richard carefully unrolled the parchment, studying it for several minutes. "Hmmm."

Both Alec and Samuel looked at each other again when nothing else followed.

After several minutes of intense scrutiny, Sir Richard looked up at them over the small glasses perched on his nose. "You know, this reminds me of some of the writings in Bombay where I served under your father, as it were. You know those days were—"

Thirty minutes of reminiscing later, Alec and Samuel were finally able to get some information.

"Cuneiform, an ancient script that gave birth to Arabic and Latin, actually all of the Semitic—"

Another fifteen minutes passed as they were given a lecture on the origins of the written word, which did at least explain the chicken scratch.

"It's most unusual that this has been written in a combination of cuneiform and hieroglyphics," Sir Richard was saying, "but how I do digress, when what you wanted to know is what this map refers to."

"So, it is a map?" Samuel shot forward in his seat.

"Yes, yes. Drawn in an old style that existed before maps, as we know them now, were ever made."

Another fifteen minutes passed as the history of cartography was dissected. By the end of it, Samuel had shifted position to lean back in his chair, affecting a pose that was as close to nodding off as Alec had ever seen.

"What do you make of the Egyptian writings?" Alec inquired before he too succumbed to a dazed stupor. Another lesson on hieroglyphs ensued, but at least this time he gained some answers.

"This indicates a tomb." Sir Richard pointed to a symbol. "See the lock over the foundation with the sacred scroll and reed?"

Samuel leaned forward again. "Does it say who it belongs to?"

"There is a cartouche next to the figure."

"Whose is it?" Samuel craned his neck to see over a pile of papers.

"Well, this symbol, ⌒ indicates a woman, and this one, depicts a throne. But this here—," he tapped the five-pointed star with a circle in the middle with his finger, "hmm. . . . Just a moment." He groaned as he stood, busily searching through the large bookshelf behind him.

"Yes, yes, here it is. I thought I recognized it." He placed the book he'd collected on the desk and took his seat. On the page was another five-pointed star with more strange writing. "It's the symbol for the goddess Seshat, the goddess of writing."

"Seshat?" Alec raised a brow. "Never heard of her."

"Well, its use is metaphorical. It would have been used for a queen who symbolically represented the goddess."

"Cleopatra?" Samuel supplied eagerly.

"No, I don't think so. This appears to point to a queen from a much earlier period, one who would be linked with the goddess. Though Cleopatra did adopt the goddess Hathor as a symbol. . . . Here we are." He pointed to the other cartouche at her feet. "It says S'ba."

"Haven't heard of her either," Samuel mumbled.

"Does it say where?" Alec leaned forward.

"No, but it does have some very compelling clues. These lions, which are facing away from each other, are depictions of the earth god, Aker, and guardians of the underworld." Sir Richard then indicated the writings above each. "This one says *akhet*, while the other says *pet*."

Alec glanced over at Samuel with an expression of disbelief as the older man continued to interpret the ancient dialect.

"Interesting, very interesting," Sir Richard muttered, speaking more to himself than to either of them.

"And what does that mean, exactly?" Samuel couldn't hide his smile. "In English."

"Oh, yes." Sir Richard cleared his throat. "Horizon and sky, as it were."

"Really," Samuel curiously said, "that's fascinating."

"And this here," Sir Richard ran his finger over an eye on the right side of the lions, "is the all-seeing eye." He paused briefly. "If I'm not mistaken, it says, 'the image of Wedjat, the powerful one '."

"Now that is interesting." Samuel nodded as the scholar pointed to the left side of the map.

"This, I believe, is a symbol of the cat." Sir Richard looked up to see he had both men's attentions. "It says . . . 'Where the cat arches over the door'."

"Where the cat arches over the door?" both Alec and Samuel repeated simultaneously.

"Yes, indeed."

"But does it say where?" Samuel leaned sideways for a better view.

"Well, as I said, there are some compelling clues. If I had to make an educated guess. . . ."

"Yes?" Both Alec and Samuel pressed.

"Egypt."

Again, Alec and Samuel exchanged glances. Alec raised a brow as he considered the older man. Sir Richard was obviously not one to go out on a limb.

"Ah. . . ." A smile flickered at the corners of Samuel's mouth. "Is it possible to narrow that down some?"

"What I'd really like to do is keep this overnight and let a colleague of mine have a look at it. He's a specialist trained by Champollion himself."

"Splendid!" Samuel slapped his hands to his knees, noticing as he did that Alec was shaking his head. "I mean, we'll be keeping it with us," he quickly amended.

"I understand completely. He'll be here tomorrow, if you'd like to bring it around," Sir Richard offered. "But I feel it would be remiss of me not to mention that there appears to be some type of warning attached," he added gravely.

"Warning?" Samuel abandoned his seat altogether to get a closer look. "You mean a curse?"

"This little sparrow here is an ominous sign indeed."

"Really?" Samuel eyed the drawing skeptically. "This little bird is the portent of doom?"

"Quite literally, the interpretation is to bring evil," Sir Richard informed them.

"What kind of evil does it speak of?" Alec leaned closer as well.

"Again, I really think you should speak with my colleague. He is much better versed in these writings."

"Any help you could give us would be greatly appreciated," Alec encouraged him.

With a sigh, Sir Richard leaned over the parchment again. *"i'nhw swsty.sn hr m'h't—"*

"Uh-hum," Samuel coughed, clearing his throat meaningfully.

Sir Richard glanced up over the rim of his glasses, fixing him with a troubled gaze. *"O' the living upon the earth who pass by this tomb,* it warns, *keep a distance,"* he restated before glancing back down. *"We call upon the one that sees all, the great lord of the west, to bring evil in the form of death."*

"I say, that is rather bleak, isn't it?" Samuel could not help but be amused by the older gentleman's dour expression.

"That is not all," Sir Richard continued gravely. "It goes on to say that whoever opens the tomb without the keeper shall perish in spirit, never to rise again."

Apparently unconcerned with the curse, Samuel leaned closer, his eyes sparkling with curiosity. "The keeper, you say?"

"This is ominous indeed." Sir Richard looked up from the document, his expression grim. "You see, to die was one thing to the Egyptians. But to die in spirit was essentially the worst curse they could possibly imagine."

"Does it say anything else about the keeper?" Samuel stared down at the map with avid interest, choosing to ignore the warning.

Sir Richard looked over at him wearily and sighed. "I'm not entirely sure, but I believe this says that life ⚲〰 opens ☐✕ the door ⟤."

"Life?" Samuel rubbed his chin as he considered it. "How intriguing. A real puzzler, then. isn't it?"

"Indeed," Sir Richard remarked as he sat back in his chair. "I could recommend a very good archeologist, though it will be difficult to get a permit for a dig. . . . Blasted French!" He slapped his palm against the desktop. "Ever since Auguste Mariette was made Conservator of the Monuments, they've all but sewn it up. Not to mention the Suez—"

The topic did wonders for his exhaustion, Alec noticed. "I'm not sure we'll be doing anything at this time," he said quickly before he was forced to spend an hour listening to another dissertation on the heated subject.

"Well, that is, of course, advisable. After all, chasing after something of this nature can be," Sir Richard fixed him with his steady regard, "a waste of a lifetime."

Something in his eyes made Alec wonder if he was speaking from personal experience. "Sound advice." Alec tucked the scroll away as he stood, shaking his hand.

"I'm sorry I could not be more precise," Sir Richard apologized.

"You've been a *wealth* of information." Alec inclined his head. "My thanks."

Sir Richard seemed pleased by the praise and turned to Samuel. "Give my regards to your mother."

"Yes, sir, I will." Samuel took his hand once more.

~*~

"Good grief, I thought we'd never get out of there." Samuel's relief was obvious. "I'd forgotten how long-winded some of my father's old cronies could be."

22

Alec adjusted his collar up as they left the building. The fine mist had turned into a drizzle that was threatening a downpour. Thunder rumbled in the distance as they crossed the plaza to the waiting coach.

"Ghastly weather, if you ask me." Samuel climbed inside the carriage, pulling his coat closer around him. "I don't know about you, but I'm in the mood for someplace warmer.

"Home, Porter," Alec called up to his driver, who'd pulled his hat down low against the weather. He received a nod in response.

Samuel lost little time in haranguing him once he sat down opposite him. "You mean to tell me that you're not interested in finding this tomb the map speaks of?"

"I was actually of a mind to find the *ol' codger,* as you put it, and ask if he is still interested in purchasing it."

"I think that ship has sailed, now that the Frenchman is dead, don't you?"

"Could be." Alec shrugged noncommittally.

Samuel retrieved a flask from his inside pocket and took a nip. The carriage bounced slightly as they pulled forward, causing the liquid to slip down his chin. "Blasted roads! You should see about your springs." He withdrew a handkerchief. Not one to be offset so easily, he pressed his argument while wiping at the spill. "I say we sail over to Egypt and have a look for ourselves."

"I thought you wanted to go over to the Americas and run the blockade," Alec reminded him, although Samuel seemed inured to his sarcasm.

"I did, but that idea pales in comparison to looking for lost treasure, don't you think?"

"I think your mother would cuff herself to your person if she knew you were considering either one."

"Don't start," Samuel warned. "At least she hasn't threatened to go down on one knee and propose in my stead."

"Touché."

"C'mon, man. Just think of it!" Samuel sat forward, unable to suppress his excitement at the idea. "The tomb of a great queen just begging to be opened. Imagine ... Egypt ... sand dunes ... dancing girls ... harems. I tell you, it's the opportunity of a lifetime, ripe for the picking."

"Yes, and all we have to do is find where the cat arches over the door . . . somewhere in Egypt," Alec commented with more than a dose of cynicism in his voice.

"Well, if it were easy, it would have been found already," Samuel responded optimistically as he cupped his hands around his mouth. "Hello, are you hearing me? It's the chance of a lifetime, Alec."

"Quite." Alec lifted a brow. "You're telling me that you are willing to risk eternal damnation of your soul for a little entertainment."

"C'mon, you don't believe that any more than I do," Samuel scoffed as he glanced out the window. "I say, when did you move?"

Alec regarded the passing view with little interest. It appeared they were heading out of town, rather than toward his townhouse. "Hmm, there must be some traffic on the main road Porter's going around."

"I can understand bypassing a few roads, but the entire city?" Samuel craned his neck to see in front. "I don't see any—"

Knock—knock—knock. A series of dull thuds sounded in the carriage.

"What the bloody hell is that?" Samuel turned in his seat, having felt the vibration of the knocking through the back cushion.

Alec opened the shutter to the driver's box and called out to Porter.

"Hhaa!" the driver yelled in response, cracking his whip. The carriage lurched forward as the horses were driven to a greater speed.

Alec turned back to Samuel with a look of annoyance.

Surprise registered on Samuel's face. "I believe we're being shanghaied."

"It certainly does appear that way." Alec looked out the window. "We also have some company." There was a man standing on the footman's rail.

Samuel stole a quick glance out his side. "I'll be damned. I suppose it wasn't your springs, after all. There's one on this side as well."

Knock—knock—knock.

"That is no doubt your driver locked in the trunk in back," Samuel remarked as Alec pulled the secret panel in the floor up, revealing a pistol and several knives.

"Well, that's certainly more like it." Samuel rubbed his hands together eagerly as Alec handed him an old flintlock pistol. He eyed it critically, turning it in his hand. "I'd rather have those." He picked up the pair of throwing knives, giving Alec back the gun. "That is, if you don't mind." He grinned.

"Suit yourself."

The men readied themselves at either door.

"On the count of three . . . One . . . Two . . . Three!"

The doors sprang open as Alec and Samuel jumped to the rail on either side. Their surprise was short-lived, however, as both highwaymen already had pistols aimed at them.

The man facing Alec fired his gun. The bullet whizzed past, splintering the open door behind him. Alec pulled the trigger of his own weapon. The man cried out as he fell from the carriage, a deep crimson mark spreading out from his shoulder.

The driver turned at the sound, using the whip against Alec. The leather strap wrapped about his forearm. Alec pulled against it as he climbed. The action caused the carriage to veer toward oncoming traffic before straightening.

Samuel pressed himself against the other side to avoid a lamppost as they careened past. The other man on the back rail raised his gun, squeezing the trigger. The shot went wide as a vicious jolt rocked the carriage, its wheel finding the depth of the gutter before erupting back out. The carriage rocked crazily as the horses surged forward.

Scrambling to hold on, Samuel elected to drop the knife so that he could grab the door. "Bloody hell!" he swore when his feet were dragged alongside. He struggled to hold onto the window casing as the man in the rear once again pointed his weapon at him. The blackguard fixed him with a malicious grin as he took aim.

"Ah, c'mon!" Samuel breathed. It was bad enough that he had his hands full hanging onto the door so as not to fall beneath the wheels, let alone being in that precarious position while looking down the barrel of a gun.

Alec managed to wrestle the strap free from the driver. With the bullwhip in his hand, he slashed out at the man holding the gun on Samuel. The highwayman pulled the trigger just as the lash of the whip wrapped about his wrist, yanking the gun out of his hand. Samuel checked his vitals, breathing a sigh of relief.

Alec kept the whip stretched taut, pulling the man's arm up over the top. Taking the knife from his belt, the man cut the leather strap. The sudden loss of tension almost cost Alec his grip on the rail. He caught himself just in time, pulling himself up onto the roof.

"*Khod el Kharita!*" The driver shouted back at the man in the rear. The other man stopped his advance toward Samuel and climbed up after Alec instead. Alec dove onto the driver, wrapping his arm around the man's neck from behind. He managed to unseat the driver before the other man was upon him.

Shouts from the street were accompanied by flying chickens and cabbage as the carriage careened up onto a sidewalk. People jumped out of the way as the horses plowed through the market.

Samuel lost his footing for a second time as a cart of melons smashed into the side. "Aw, not again!" He grabbed the top of the door, swinging wide into the street as he held on.

Alec was pulled backwards as the other man wrestled his arm free and threw a punch. He had to release the driver to block it.

The driver grabbed the reins and proceeded to increase the breakneck pace. The clatter of the cobblestones under the horses' hooves mingled with the outraged screams of the vendors.

The man had Alec in a choke hold as they rolled backwards into a sitting position on the roof. Alec pulled at the arm about his neck with both hands to no avail. Changing tactics, Alec leaned forward, and then, in a quick motion, he slammed his head backwards, smashing it into the bastard's face.

The carriage swayed as it hit a bend in the road, sending it up on two wheels careening around the turn. Samuel was forced to either climb the door or be ground into the pavement. He pulled himself up until his foot found purchase on the window casing.

Alec sucked in air as the dazed man's grip slackened enough for him to free himself. The odd angle threatened to send both men sliding off the slick surface of the roof. Alec managed to grab the back of the driver's seat with one hand as the carriage tilted.

Though his nose was bloodied, the man recovered enough to hold onto Alec's legs in an attempt to stop his slide. With his legs dangling off the side, the man tried to find purchase on the door that Samuel was perched on. He kicked out, managing to get a foothold for a brief second before his weight caused the door to swing away from him.

Samuel rode the door toward the driver, who lashed out at him with a fist. The force of the carriage settling back down on all four wheels sent the door backwards again just as Samuel returned the driver's punch.

Alec managed to free a leg from his assailant's hold and kicked out, smashing the man in the face with his boot. His grip slipped further down Alec's leg as he kicked out again for the door until he dangled over the side, clinging only to Alec's boot.

The sound of the horse's hooves changed as the carriage started across a bridge. The ground disappeared from beneath Samuel as the door once again swung wide. His eyes widened when he looked down and all he could see was the water far beneath him.

Alec wiggled his foot. *Damn it! Of course it has to be my favorite pair of Hessians,* he thought with irritation as the boot slipped free.

"Aaugh!" the man yelled as he dangled over the side of the bridge.

Samuel clung to the door as the man slid past him, grabbing for air as he dropped to the water below. He kicked the side of the carriage, pushing the door away so that it swung toward the driver once again. This time he managed to get a foot up on the seat as the driver lashed out at him. Alec was quick to pull the highwayman back, punching him in the side of the head as he did.

Samuel let go of the door with one hand and grabbed the rail, pulling himself up onto the box. Filling the newly vacated seat, he picked up the reins just as the open door collided with a streetlamp on the other end of the bridge, ripping it from its hinges.

"Whoa!" Samuel pulled back on the reins with all his might. The horses responded by slowing their pace from the reckless gallop.

Alec wrestled with the driver, landing another punch that sent him falling backwards, sliding off the back. The man hit the trunk on the way down and rolled onto the pavement. Alec watched as he staggered to his feet and hobbled off down a side road.

"Whoa," Samuel called to the horses again as he pulled on the brake, bringing the carriage to a stop. He looked over his shoulder at Alec, who was standing on top of the roof, watching the man disappear from view. "Are you going to give chase?"

Alec looked down at his bootless foot. "Damn it all to Hell!" He ran a hand through his hair in frustration. "I don't know about you, but I'm beginning to think someone is after the map."

"I'd say it's a certainty." Samuel grinned up at him with satisfaction. "In fact, I'd go so far as to say it's an absolute certainty."

Alec raised his brow in question. "And why is that?"

"Because of what the driver shouted back there."

"And what did he say that makes you say that with absolute certainty?"

"He said," Samuel's smile widened, "take the map."

Knock—knock—knock. "Hell," Alec swore as he climbed over the seat. "I'd better get Porter out of that trunk."

"You do that." Samuel chuckled. "He'll no doubt want a raise after this." He brushed off his sleeve, straightening his jacket. "I'm also thinking you should put the map where it will be safe."

"It is safe where it is," Alec grumbled as he jumped down.

"I meant safer for me."

Chapter 3

Alec walked through the doors of White's three hours later. Having just spent the greater portion of that time making a grand show of depositing the map within the Bank of England's vault, he was more than glad to finally be finished with the performance.

Handing the doorman his hat, he signed the ledger, noting Samuel's scrawl several names up. Good, he was actually where he said he would be for a change.

Alec walked past several gentlemen as he crossed the great room with its dark paneling and leather chairs. He found Samuel seated in front of a window reading from the societal page of *The Tatler*.

"Any news of my engagement?" Alec asked jokingly as he sat down opposite him.

"Now that you mention it . . . yes."

"You're kidding, right?"

"Actually, no. Look." Samuel turned the paper over to show him a small caricature of several ladies of the ton. It depicted a row of debutantes lined up in front of an older woman, who looked suspiciously like his mother. She was assessing them critically through opera glasses. In the distance, one could see a gentleman's tailcoat and heels running in the opposite direction.

"I take it that is supposed to be me."

"I think they've captured you quite nicely." Samuel chuckled.

Alec shook his head as he picked up the paper and studied it. "The woman has gone too far."

"Speaking of women. . . . How did it go with 'the Old Lady of Threadneedle Street'?" Samuel used the Bank of England's moniker. "Think they bought it?"

"I did everything but wear a sign. If anyone was watching, I'm sure they were left with little doubt as to what I was doing." Alec tossed the social rag back to Samuel and picked up the latest issue of *Lloyd's List*.

"Speaking of which, here are the real one and another copy I made." Samuel handed him an envelope. "Nicely played with the fake, by the way."

Alec nodded and slipped the envelope into his coat pocket as Lord Spencer walked up smiling. "Brighton, St. Clair." He greeted them. "Congratulations on your big win."

"Thank you." Alec inclined his head.

"I've got to run now, but perhaps you will tell me all about it tonight at the Worthingtons' ball."

"Not much to tell. The cards were in my favor."

"Nonsense. Besides, it would be a highlight to what promises to be an otherwise dreadful evening." Lord Spencer leaned closer, whispering conspiratorially. "We must stick together at these things, you know." He nodded sagely before taking his leave.

"You're actually considering going to the Worthingtons'?" Samuel looked over at him as if he'd lost his mind.

"Why?" Alec raised a questioning brow.

"Because the lovely young woman in the front of this line," Samuel said, pointing to the cartoon, "is Miss Angelina Worthington, that's why."

Alec picked the paper up once again. "I was wondering who the object of my affection was supposed to be."

"Lords Brighton, St. Clair," Lord Lindsey acknowledged them as he approached. "I hear congratulations are in order."

"Luck of the draw."

"Well, she is quite lovely."

Puzzled, Alec looked up at him. "Who is?"

"Why, your fiancée of course, I heard that you'll be announcing your engagement at the ball tonight."

Bloody hell! Alec's eyes flared in outrage. "I can assure you that I have no intention of doing any such thing."

"Of course." He gave him a conspiratorial wink. "You want to keep it hush-hush."

TREASURE OF EGYPT

Alec waited until the older man was out of earshot and then turned to Samuel. "That's it!" He tossed the paper to the side and stood up. "Pack your bags, we're going to Egypt."

Samuel slapped his hand against his thigh. "Exceptional idea, if I do say so myself." He watched as Alec stalked away. "You mean *now?*" he hollered after him.

"You have a problem with winning your bet?"

"I. . . . No."

~*~

Alexandria, Egypt, 1863

Good Lord! What *is* that smell?" Samuel wrinkled his nose at the foul odor that permeated the air. A cart of entrails and fish heads passed them. "Never mind." He coughed as he continued to walk with Alec down the dock to where their luggage was to be off-loaded from the steamship, *The Great Eastern.*

"Absolute marvel, isn't it?" Samuel looked up at the huge smokestack. "I still can't get over how quickly we traveled here. Just imagine how long that trip would have taken us just a few years ago. I tell you, we're in the wrong business."

"And what business is that?" Alec sidestepped a young boy peddling hats. "English lords with nothing better to do than gallivant around the Egyptian countryside looking for exotic species?"

"I don't see why we can't pose as merchants, rather than as part of a scientific expedition. Especially now, with the Suez being built, trading with India will be a snap. Just look at all this." Samuel looked around at the busy port.

"I think the key word here is *pose.*" Alec gave him a sideways glance. "And I thought we agreed that doing research on the indigenous wildlife would create less interest than having to grease the wheels of trade."

"I think we may have missed out on the opportunity to make a king's ransom."

"And here I thought we were looking for a queen. If you'd rather not. . . ."

31

"No, no. I'm in, come hell or high water."

"Let us hope it doesn't come to that." Alec had to sidestep another man, who cut across his path with a basket laden with fruit.

"I do hope we can find better accommodations now that we're on dry land. I still can't believe they put us next to the engine room." Samuel sniffed again as he ducked to avoid the fruit. "Why," he continued, "you'd think, on a ship of that size, they'd have been able to offer better with five minutes' notice. My ears are still ring—" He was cut off as a cart bumped into him from behind. "Hey, watch it!" he called out, tripping forward.

The cart in question stopped short, sending the one directly behind it out into the crowded walkway to avoid a collision. Several pedestrians scattered as yet another cart, this one containing coal, tipped over, spilling its load. The small boy with hats ran straight into Alec in all the commotion. He nearly fell over as Alec straightened him up.

"So sorr-eh, sir-rah," he cried as he found his footing and took off again.

"Take a better look next time," Alec called after him as he checked his pockets. "Bloody little urchin!"

The boy glanced behind quickly before breaking into a run.

"That little thief!" Alec shouted as he ran after the boy. Fast on his heels, Alec reached out to grab him, but the boy darted under another cart.

Samuel was on the other side and caught him by surprise. "Got him!"

The boy managed to wiggle free of his grasp.

"Slippery little. . . ." Samuel lost his hold.

They both chased him down a side street, taking the corner at an all-out run. Alec's fingers brushed against his vest. The boy turned quickly, eluding his grasp once again as he darted down a smaller side alley.

They both went straight in after him. It opened into a courtyard with a dozen men kneeling around a center pit playing a game with pebbles and shells. They fell silent as the boy came to a stop on the other side of the group, clinging to one of the men.

"*Abu, Abu, el-Afareet!*" the young boy called to his father.

"Uh-oh." Samuel stayed a hand in front of Alec. "Sorry, our mistake," he called out, backing slowly away.

"Hell if it was!" Alec growled.

Ssh-LING. The sound of several swords being unsheathed rang out in the small area as the men stood.

"RUN!" Samuel shouted as he turned.

"Unbelievable!" Alec bit out as they charged.

They rounded one corner and then another, knocking down several carpet hangings as they desperately tried to stay ahead of the dozen men chasing them. They darted inside an open archway, hugging the wall inside the darkened interior, as several men raced by.

Waiting until the last man had passed their hiding place, they snuck back out, trying to retrace their steps through the maze of twisted alleyways.

"*Ukaf!*"

They heard the cry to halt as they turned the corner. They dashed through another small archway and ran toward the rear. Three old women looked up, startled from their weaving as both Alec and Samuel practically stumbled over themselves in an effort to stop.

"*Taiyib matakhafsh,*" Samuel whispered, telling them not to be afraid as he pressed both palms together in front of his head and bowed, begging their forgiveness.

Instead of being afraid, one of the women started to chuckle, shaking her head. "*Inglizi howadji.*"

Alec looked over to Samuel who mouthed, "English tourists," for his benefit.

They could hear the band of men searching shop-by-shop outside. Two of them came back into the interior of the alcove where five old women worked on their weaving. Ignoring them, they began to search the corners, behind the wall hangings and baskets.

One of the old women stood and shooed them. Calling for help, she picked up a broom and began to aggressively sweep them away. They left, continuing their search further down.

"*Shukran.*" Samuel breathed a sigh of relief as he removed the scarf from his head. He thanked them again profusely as Alec pressed gold coins into each of their palms. They smiled toothless grins, biting the pieces with what nubs they had left.

Sitting on the floor, rather than pillows, both Alec and Samuel began removing the bundles of spun wool the women had piled around them to hide their size.

Alec climbed out of the hole he was in, unwrapping the shawl they had wound about him as he went. He felt a sharp point in his back as he rose to his full height. Apparently help had arrived.

He looked over at Samuel, who already had his hands held high, and slowly raised his own. Alec wished fleetingly that he'd let the others capture him as the old woman cackled. The sound grated up his spine right to the knifepoint in his back.

"*La, la, Inglizi howadji.*" She laughed again as she spoke to the owner of the knife digging into his skin.

Alec had learned enough from his book of interpretation to know that "*la*" meant "no". He had no idea what else she had said, but he did feel the pressure on the knife release some as the old woman showed off the gold coin he'd given her. She came close, jabbing him with her crooked finger, pointing to the coin, then to the one behind him.

He didn't need that translated. Handing over another coin, Alec slowly turned to see a middle-aged man with his wife and children behind him.

"It's her son and his family." Samuel came forward. "Let me ask them if they can help us safely to the docks."

A transaction was agreed upon, in which Alec was made to hand over the rest of the money he had on his person. They followed the son through the back of the shop with the others close behind. He led them not twenty paces to the front of the building which conveniently opened onto the docks.

Alec looked at Samuel with irritation. He'd just given the shopkeeper a king's ransom in exchange for a brief walk through his damn store. The smiling family cheerfully waved them away as they quickly closed the doors behind them.

"Well, he did say to come back anytime." Samuel's attempt at subtle humor didn't lighten Alec's mood as they turned to leave.

"No doubt." Alec glowered at him. "I've just given the man a year's pay for the privilege of walking to the front of his bloody shop."

"Yes, but we are safe."

"Safe?" Alec raised his brow in a sideways glance. "We were just robbed by a little boy, three old women, and a family of rug makers."

"Yes, but safely."

"Yes, well, I do hate to be in real jeopardy while being fleeced of my coin." Alec ran a hand through his hair in exasperation. "And how is it exactly that they didn't take any of *your* money?"

"I told them you were my servant."

"Your servant?" Alec snorted indignantly. "And they believed you?"

"I said you were my bodyguard. You *were* rather hostile-looking."

"Hmm!" Alec snorted again.

"I told them it was your job to hold onto the money. It was below me to handle such trivialities."

"Next time," Alec's voice held a warning, "you get to be my servant."

"As you wish," Samuel said as he bowed mockingly. "My liege."

~*~

Alec stood before the mirror in the hotel room and scraped the straight razor across his cheek. He dipped it in the water basin and tapped it, scraping another swath of cream from his jaw.

"You're up. Good." Samuel barged in the room without knocking. The suite they had managed to find was the best the hotel had to offer, despite the fact it had only one bed. Samuel had taken the couch.

Alec looked at him in the mirror as he continued shaving. Samuel was in his usual good spirits as he plopped onto the divan by the window. "Down at the bar—" he started.

"You've already been to the bar?"

"Why yes, and I've found us the perfect dragoman."

"*Drago*-what?"

"Dragoman. That's what they call guides around here. Anyway, he's already gone to make all the arrangements to acquire a felucca—"

"*Felucca?*"

"A sailboat. We're going to meet up with him and the *Reis*—"

"The what?"

"The *Reis* . . . the captain," Samuel paused, "are you doing this on purpose?"

"Yes."

"Why?"

"Because I'd rather you spoke English."

"I've hired us a guide. We're going to meet him and the captain of the boat at noon."

"Well, why didn't you just say so?"

"I did," Samuel replied irritably. "God, but you're a whiner in the morning."

"Tell me," Alec looked at him in the mirror, "how do you really feel?"

"Lord!" Samuel exclaimed in exasperation as he stood up and crossed the room to his luggage. Pulling out a large map of the area, he spread it out on the bed. "He said he knows of a temple in the western desert in which they once worshiped the cat goddess Bastet."

"You didn't tell him about the map?" Alec looked up him in alarm.

"No, of course not, I simply said we were looking for a rare species in the region. Look here." He pointed to an area on the map of the Nile Valley and surrounding desert. "According to the chap we had decipher the map before we left England—"

"Sir Richard?" Alec mumbled as he shaved his upper lip.

"No, the other one, Sir Richard's colleague, Professor Wheaton," Samuel said, glancing up. "You remember, Champollion's understudy. The one I was lucky enough to track down just before we sailed."

"Oh yes, the reason you were late getting to the ship, and the reason why we had to settle for the steerage compartment next to the engine room," Alec specified as he rinsed the blade.

"Blame that on me, why don't you?"

"Uh-hmm."

Samuel shrugged, disregarding Alec's opinion as he took out his notebook. "Let us review what we know, shall we?" He looked down at his notes. "There is the curse, we know of that." He turned the page. "Then there is this bit about the chosen one of Isis, born of S'ba, the beloved of Amun, the true and pure voice, the justified, the revered one before Osiris, lord of two lands, living repeatedly and enduringly." He took a deep breath, looking up at Alec. "How they did tend to go on." He scanned down the page further. "Ah, here it is." He looked briefly up with excitement. "It tells of a temple, 🏛 belonging to a goddess, 🏛 the revered one, 🏛 before 🏛 the sacred lands 🏛 of the west 🏛."

"Uh-hmm," Alec mumbled his understanding as he trimmed up his sideburns.

"Well, considering what both men have told us, I think we've found it."

Alec toweled off and turned to face him. "Really?

"Yes, really."

"Because I'd *really* hate to be *taken* on another short walk, if you get my drift."

"Don't worry about a thing. I'll fix everything. Trust me," Samuel promised as he compared the map to the notes he'd laboriously written in his diary. "You know, I actually think that I'm beginning to understand these writings.

"Take this symbol, 🏛, for instance. The square box depicts an estate, 🏛 and the pennant represents a god. 🏛 See, a house of god . . . a temple. And, of course, the front of the lion, 🏛, means in front of, or before. Simple logic, if I do say so myself."

"What about this one?" Alec asked pointing to another hieroglyph. 🏛

Samuel scanned his notes. "The circle ⊜ is a ball of string or placenta. And this one, ⏣, is a cow's rib cage, and, of course, the reed."

"What is it for . . . an ancient recipe for bovine pâté?"

"Actually, no, it means revered one."

"Yes, I can see the logic there." Alec raised both brows in exaggeration.

"Alright, so some of it defies logic, but look here." Samuel pointed to the cat. "These characters actually spell out m, and iw. What say you about that?" Samuel stared at him as though he were a simpleton when he didn't respond. "M-iw." He waited. "As in mew. . . . You still don't get it? Honestly." He sighed heavily. "Cat . . . meow?"

"I get it." Alec stared at him humorlessly as he pulled on his pants. "Can I at least get dressed before you start haranguing me?"

Samuel stood, closing the map inside his book with a snap. "Did I mention you are an absolute delight in the morning?" He gave Alec a look of irritation. "I'll be down at the bar if you need me," he added before closing the door behind him.

Alec joined him a few minutes later, looking more like a lawless man from a penal colony than an English lord. He'd opted to forgo the overcoat, which left the gun belt and knife strapped to his thigh exposed. His vest was open over the loose lawn shirt he wore.

"Good God, man!" Samuel's brows shot up when he saw Alec. "I thought we were supposed to be going on a scientific expedition."

"I just don't want to be confused with the prey anymore." Alec patted one of the revolvers he wore at his side.

"That should do it."

"Where is our guide?" Alec looked around at the other patrons.

"He isn't allowed in this part of the hotel."

"No wonder the people here hate the English."

"Don't blame us. The Turks are the ones in charge." Samuel swallowed the last of his drink. "We're to meet him at the boat. It's set to sail in an hour." He then turned and ordered a few more bottles. "For the road." He grinned. "What with the Zulus threatening war and making it difficult for the caravans to travel, it could get a little dry. Not to mention that most of the peasants are Muslim. It could get very, *very dry.*"

Samuel turned back to the attendant. "Have it sent here," he wrote down the information, "along with our things." The man nodded and waited patiently.

"Ah, yes." Samuel handed him several coins. "*Baksheesh.*" He looked over to Alec after handing over the generous tip. "And you thought we wouldn't have to grease the wheels of trade." The man bowed happily and left them.

"I've done nothing but since arriving," Alec remarked sarcastically. "How did you hear of an uprising. . . . And how, pray tell, does something that is happening half a continent away have any bearing on whether or not you can obtain alcohol?"

"It's as I said. The caravans bring it across the desert, but with the Suez scheduled to open in a few years, that's all about to change. All those British colonies to the south in Zululand now stand to make a fortune. Trade," Samuel continued on, even though Alec was barely listening, "is where the next fortunes are to be made."

"So you've said," Alec sighed, "although it doesn't answer my question."

"Oh, well, that. . . . It may surprise you to know the kind of information you can glean from *fahddling* in a bar . . . even before eight in the morning." He grinned.

"*Fahddling?*" Alec gave him a sideways glance. "Do I want to ask?"

"Gossiping." Samuel stood up. "There is a place around the corner that comes highly recommended. Let's go get something to eat. I'm starving."

~*~

Samuel swiped at the flies hovering around his plate of mutton. Alec joined him on the mat, sitting cross-legged before a large bowl of steaming couscous.

"Why can't a civilization as old as this one discover the benefits of a simple chair?"

"Why don't you ask them?" Samuel eyed the large man in back, who was slicing off hunks of meat with a cleaver. "They look like they'd love to explain it to you."

Alec looked over at the man who'd been watching them since they'd arrived. "At least this time I'm dressed for the climate," Alec commented as he returned the cook's icy stare. He adjusted the knife he had placed in his waistband so he could bend more easily.

"Ah, here he comes," Samuel said as the server approached them. "Do you want anything else?"

A fork, Alec thought with rancor as he pulled out the small book of interpretation he'd been reading. Opening it, he pointed to the mutton and asked for another plate.

"Ah, hell," Samuel groaned.

The man turned angrily from him and shouted to the man in the back. The cook shook his fist in the air and hollered something in return. Several more men with sharpened cutlery emerged from the rear joining the server up front.

"What? I did nothing but order another meal of mutton." Alec seemed surprised by the uproar as the man shook his fist at him.

"Actually, you implied that his mother is a goat." Samuel sighed with regret.

"I did no such thing!"

"He's demanding restitution."

"Of course he is." Alec gave Samuel a look of irritation. He handed over the book of interpretation, pointing out the phrase he had used. "Tell him it was a mistake."

Samuel reiterated. The large man yanked the book away and skewered it with a sharp pole he'd been waving. He then placed it in the hot coals, where it began to smolder.

"Ah. . . ." Samuel looked over at Alec when nothing else was said. "I believe he still wants payment."

"I figured that."

The waiter complained vehemently, shaking his hands while pointing to Alec.

He stood up, his height giving him some advantage over the shorter men. "Tell them I will pay *only* for my meal."

Samuel spoke to them again, gesturing with his hands for them to calm down as he rose. The large man argued against Samuel as the server stood behind him.

"Sorry, they are insisting you pay for the insult as well."

"Tell them I have at least a dozen reasons as to why that's not going to happen." Alec placed his hands on his revolvers. A few men shrank back as he stared them down.

Samuel looked at him for a moment. "Alright, if that is how you want to play this out." He opened his own jacket, revealing two more revolvers, one on each side of his gun belt. "Make that two dozen." Tossing enough coins to cover their meal onto the mat, he issued the challenge.

The large man raised his cleaver threateningly. Both Alec and Samuel drew their weapons in response. The men froze . . . waiting.

"Perhaps now would be a good time to back out of here," Samuel suggested.

"That's probably the wise thing to do." Alec nodded as they started to slowly back out of the shop.

As soon as they were out the door, the cleaver the large man had held sank into the wood pole of the awning outside with a thud, missing Alec's shoulder by an inch.

Alec's expression hardened as he narrowed his eyes on the large man and fired. The clay pot above his head exploded, scattering grains into the fire below. Smoke quickly overcame the small area, billowing out of the storefront.

"Let's get out of here!" Samuel called as the men started pouring out into the street, pointing at them angrily.

"Agreed!" Alec shouted as they turned and ran towards the docks.

Several men chased after them as they hightailed it to the boat that was preparing to set sail. As they ran, they called out to the captain of the ship, waving to get his attention.

The guide noticed them first. The captain at his side issued several orders and started pulling up the rope fastening the boat to the dock. Several of the hands aboard ship readied the sails, sending them up the mast. They billowed out as the wind caught hold. The ship creaked under the strain of the open canopy as it surged forward. The guide waved at them to hurry, shouting as the ship separated from the dock.

Alec and Samuel reached the end of the pier and jumped, launching themselves across the widening gap. They landed on the deck as the angry men who'd chased them crowded together at the end of the dock, shouting and shaking their fists.

Samuel turned and waved at the group with a smile on his face. "That was close," he gasped, trying to catch his breath.

Alec started laughing. "Yes, but we still have our coin." He smiled while tipping his hand in farewell to the large man who stood, waving his fist at him.

Chapter 4

Somewhere near the Southern border of Egypt, 3 months later

Alec removed the rocks covering the watering hole they were lucky enough to have found. Reaching down, he scooped the water up with his cupped hand and drank thirstily. The liquid slipped down his dry throat as he swallowed. It might be the foulest water he'd ever tasted, but it was wet. He moved to the side to allow Samuel to drink.

"Aaughhh." Samuel collapsed to the side once he drank his fill. "I can't believe—"

Crack! The sound of musket fire reverberated as the dirt a few feet away from him sprayed up from the shot.

"What the—" Samuel started and turned around. "Ah, c'mon!"

"Bloody hell!" Alec swore as he looked up to see several men on horseback descend from the hills. Swathed in black, they looked every bit like a swirling bevy of blackbirds swooping down to prey upon them. Several more shots rang out as they approached.

"And just when I thought being in the middle of the desert without a guide was bad enough," Alec remarked cynically as he moved to stand.

"Well," Samuel said as he stood beside him, waiting for the welcoming party to arrive, "at least we didn't die of thirst."

Alec raised his brow at his friend's attempt at levity. Funny . . . Laughing was the last thing he felt like. In fact, returning a little gunfire was a temptation. He stood with his legs spread slightly apart, a hand resting on the handle of his gun.

Samuel eyed his stance warily. "Why don't you let me try talking to them first?"

Alec eyed him skeptically. "So far . . . that hasn't worked out too well for us, has it?"

"Alright, I admit it. It was I who hired the dragoman to guide us into the desert. Can we drop it now? It's not like I also contracted him to steal our water and leave us here to die."

Alec raised an eyebrow in a sideways glance, then looked back at the small army of Arabs that approached them. "It doesn't look like I have much choice."

"It's no doubt, just a show of strength to gain tribute for crossing their land."

"You mean highway robbery!" Alec practically swore as he pulled a hand through his hair.

"I believe they see it more as a tax. It's the way of the land for these desert nomads. Just let me handle it."

The warriors continued to fire their weapons in the air as they circled, tightening the gaps as they closed in on them. Even the Arabian horses they rode stomped and flared their nostrils angrily as they came to a halt before them.

Samuel spoke up but was immediately silenced by a harsh command from their leader. As a group, they unsheathed long, curved swords and "invited" the "intruders" to accompany them or pay the price that their trespass demanded . . . death.

"It seems we're going on a little ride," Samuel interpreted.

"Uh-huh."

"It also seems they want our weapons."

"Of course they do."

~*~

They were escorted to a solitary enclosure on the outskirts of an encampment. Nestled against a rocky outcrop, the many large tents blended in with the sun-bleached sand. They hadn't been there long when an elder from the tribe arrived with an entourage, seeking counsel with "The Man of Tongues."

"This shouldn't take long," Samuel said before leaving Alec to pace the small confines of the tent with nothing but a table and chair for company.

TREASURE OF EGYPT

What the hell was I thinking? Alec thought as he trod upon the sand-covered carpet. The flea-bitten scrap was starting to show the effects of his angst. Several rolls had appeared, tripping him at every turn.

Bloody hell! Why *had he allowed the lure of treasure to get him caught up in another of Samuel's wild schemes . . . one more ludicrous, idiotic, ill-conceived. . . .* "Damn!" Alec dragged a hand through his hair in frustration.

He sat down on the old, rickety chair that was placed in the center of the small tent. He hadn't seen anything but cushions or hard ground to sit on in weeks, yet there it was. It creaked under his weight as he tested it by rocking slightly back and forth, but it held, even when he propped it back against the center post and placed his feet on the table.

To sit helpless as Samuel controlled his fate was worse than torture. Truth be told, the discomfort of having his sweat-soaked clothing stick to his body in the veritable sauna was comforting, in comparison.

Much to his annoyance, his awareness of that fact was punctuated by a fly that kept buzzing around him, in spite of how many times he waved it away. It must have become aggravated at being trapped inside with him, for it repeatedly rammed itself into the canvas walls. Alec certainly understood its distress. . . . He too had felt like battering his body against the fabric in frustration.

"For the love of God, how much longer is this going to take?" Alec groaned, listening to the sounds of the busy workday as they drifted on the wind. Lord only knew how tired he was of watching the shadows of the guards as they patrolled outside the tent.

He was momentarily distracted by the children who dared come near the enclosure, but a stern warning from a guard sent them running off in the other direction. He listened to their laughter as it faded into the fabric of the camp.

Visitors must be a rare sight for these people, he realized. Hell, the last one probably brought the ancient chair.

As the sun rose higher, the village quieted, leaving him all the more impatient. The conclusion that they must rest in the heat of the day did occur to him, along with the thought that it offered a slim chance of escape. Though the idea of searching every tent in broad daylight for Samuel was ludicrous, he still entertained the idea as he leaned his head against the pole.

The sight of the sun's rays filtering through the fabric ceiling, perfectly framed by a water stain, would forever be emblazoned on his memory, that and the fly which continued to make its rounds. It was while he was debating whether or not to aid the insect in its escape that the hum of his fellow cellmate was drowned out by the murmur of a large group of people approaching.

Astonished, Alec stood and moved towards the entrance. Skimming the fabric of the door, he parted a slit in the opening and spied out. The sight shouldn't have surprised him as much as it did.

Far from resting, as he'd thought, the whole village was headed his way, the entourage led by none other than Samuel, his step spry, a smoldering cigar clenched in his teeth. By all accounts, he looked like the proverbial cat that swallowed the canary . . . and that look never boded well, especially for Alec.

After a moment's deliberation, Alec decided to sit behind the table facing the opening. The noise, which had been rising to a feverish pitch as they assembled, quieted suddenly.

He didn't know which was more unnerving, being held in a tent isolated from everything, or being held with the whole population of the village outside holding its collective breath. He waited, ignoring the pull to find out what was going on.

An interminable amount of time seemed to pass before the flaps of his canvas prison separated and Samuel sauntered in with a flourish, grinning from ear to ear. His expression was somewhat distorted by the smoldering stogie wedged in one corner of his mouth.

Executing an elaborate bow, Samuel audaciously faced Alec, giving him an inconspicuous wink as he pronounced loudly enough for all to hear, "My king."

King? Alec narrowed his eyes. At least he managed to keep a bored expression on the rest of his face in response to Samuel's outrageous behavior.

"If you will?" Samuel motioned for a trunk to be brought in and placed before Alec by one of the guards. Ceremoniously, the trunk was opened for him, revealing several old books and bound sheaves of paper. The guard, obviously affected, respectfully stepped back from the surprising display of crusty old tomes.

"What is this?" Alec cautiously peered over the edge of the table.

"The trunk?" Samuel queried innocently, and then announced with his voice at a volume an opera singer would have envied, "'Tis the key to the city, oh great sultan."

He really should be on the stage, Alec thought as he watched Samuel bow before him, presenting a picture of courtly propriety for the benefit of the onlookers. Alec raised an eyebrow at this. "They live in tents, Samuel. They don't need keys." His voice held his irritation.

"Please, huh-hum. . . . Please, my king," Samuel intoned. Placing his hands together as if in prayer, he bowed slightly, as if to placate Alec. A pleading look entered his eye. "Truly Sire, the Gates of Heaven." He then lowered his voice, "Of paradise and our *freedom*." Samuel said the last bit with a slight warning. Taking another bow, he turned and motioned for his former jailer to follow him outside, closing the flaps behind him.

Alec couldn't believe they were buying this nonsense. He was not only surprised by his sudden coronation, but also by the bizarre turn of events that had led to Samuel ordering his former guard about.

What the hell was he up to? Alec wondered while Samuel was outside playing to the crowd. . . . And what could a large trunk of old, dilapidated books possibly have to do with it? At least the fly escaped, Alec realized, amazed that he was actually envious of it.

Samuel once again entered the tent, his backside reappearing as the curtain parted. He was turned facing the crowd outside, repeatedly bowing and waving his hand in circles before him as he stepped backwards. Once the flap closed, he turned, another of those grins splitting his face. "Ha, entirely too easy. my friend, like taking a pebble from a beach," he practically crowed while dancing a little jig.

"Don't suppose you'd like to fill me in," Alec motioned to the trunk on the floor, "on precisely which pebbles you are presently stealing from these people?" Alec's voice at least held the authority of a king.

Barbara Ivie Green

Samuel had the sense to, finally, stop jigging. He mumbled, "Umm . . . sor-rey, Alec."

Was that a hiccup? Alec's eyes were riveted to the spot where his friend stood. Was he drunk? By God, yes! The fool had definitely been drinking, and quite a lot too, for him to be slightly off-balance. Alec pulled a hand through his hair in frustration. Unbelievable!

"I mean, hum-hmm. . . . Sorry, Your Majesty." Samuel's eyes gleamed with merriment. Alec's narrowed at the appellative. Samuel cleared his throat, his look not nearly as contrite as his words. "It's not easy to negotiate with these people. Why, they have to toast every little point in an agreement."

Alec's throat had never felt so dry.

"And what little '*points*' have you been agreeing to," Alec deliberately questioned with a heavy accent on the word, "while your '*king*' has been relaxing here in these luxurious accommodations?" He could feel his temper rising as he indicated the small space with his hand for emphasis.

"It's all rather hard to explain."

"Humor me," Alec replied without much of any. "Do you have any idea how long this day has been?"

"Truly, I'm sorry. I thought it would be a short meal, but the courses just kept coming. Sheik Allehbaba Kazirrah really knows how to pack it in."

Alec groaned at the news. "Samuel!" he intervened, "I haven't eaten since yesterday morning!"

"Oh, well, as to that." Contrite, Samuel came forward. "You must be starved." He then proceeded to pull a flat bundle of food from his sleeve.

Alec thought it was the understatement of the year.

"I'm not sure this will help. It might be slightly smashed." Samuel smiled apologetically as he handed over the pilfered scrap of cloth, flopped the lid of the trunk closed, and settled himself onto it.

Alec unwrapped the dry bit of crusty flatbread and eyed it dubiously. Was he really that hungry? He looked up into Samuel's hopeful face and took a bite.

Crunch! "Dry" might have been putting it mildly, he thought.

48

Samuel looked pleased nonetheless and quickly started running down the events as Alec chewed. "You won't believe it, but. . . ."

It was always the "buts", Alec realized as he listened.

"I have procured us three camels, two tents, cooking utensils, you name it. We have all the foodstuffs we need to complete our journey," Samuel took a breath and then continued, "and a guide, a guide that not only knows the way, but can also speak several languages. He even reads the ancient writing of the Babylonians." He tapped on the trunk with his finger as if to indicate the vast knowledge of the guide.

There's that "but" again, Alec noted as he listened.

"Not only all that, *but* she can cook too. Well, that may be an overstatement, *but* it doesn't matter. All that matters is that all of our property has been restored to us, even the rifles."

Another "but" . . . She? Did he say she? Alec questioned his own hearing.

The thing with Samuel's explanations, Alec had learned through the years, was what he didn't say or, more appropriately, what he avoided saying. That, and what he said quickly, and the last part had definitely come out in a rush.

"Except the horses," Samuel was saying when Alec returned his attention back to him. "Horses, as you know, don't do well without water. They have a tendency to expire."

"You purchased all of that from the sale of our horses?" The skepticism in Alec's voice could be heard even with his mouth full.

"Well, no. . . . We—"

"What, exactly, is in the trunk?" Alec interrupted.

"The trunk. . . . Well, yes, the books," Samuel paused, considering, "it's representative of a payment of sorts."

"Payment?" Alec asked through the dry breadcrumbs in his mouth, his mind still on the rushed part of Samuel's explanation. The guide, there was something to that, he realized. "What else did you sell?" Alec wondered briefly if his friend had sold him into slavery. No, that couldn't be it. He was the *king* in this little farce, even if Samuel's face held a sheepish, if not guilty, expression.

"What did we buy?" Alec asked, feeling that he was getting closer, especially by the look on Samuel's face. "You bought the girl!" Alec exclaimed, and knew he was onto something. "You bought a slave?" A dusting of crumbs flew out of Alec's mouth as he spoke.

"Well, no, not exactly. . . ." Samuel brushed the crumbs from his shirt. "It's more a bond."

"Indentured servant?" Alec asked incredulously. He was starting to feel extremely anxious about his friend's behavior.

"It's more a bond of . . . matrimony, a dowry if you will." Samuel waxed philosophical, gesturing with his hands.

"You're going to marry the girl?" Alec knew he was wrong even before he asked it.

"No, you are!"

Cough. "Aahh." Alec literally inhaled the breadcrumbs after that revelation, choking on them.

Samuel, being the helpful *friend* that he was, jumped up and started pounding him on the back. "It will be alright, perfect. . . . Really," Samuel alleged while he continued the beating. "All we need to do is get her back to England. That's it." He added the last part as if it were the easiest thing in the world, or as if it made the slightest bit of sense.

Tears welled up in Alec's eyes as he choked. The burning sensation was almost as intense as his outrage.

"It's not like I didn't try to change it." Samuel looked suitably horrified as Alec glared at him. "They'll kill us if we don't take her, and, and," he stuttered, "they wouldn't allow her to go with us unless she was wed. Hell, it's death to propose anything else. An unwed woman traveling alone with two strange men is unmentionable here, not to mention back in England. Well, it's not death, but. . . ."

"Enough!" Alec coughed. The beating Samuel was giving him was bad enough without having to listen to his rambling. Alec swung an arm around to stop the poundings and stood. The chair caught him in the knees as he teetered. His foot becoming trapped within the wrinkled folds of the carpet was just as ill-fated. Unable to regain his balance, he landed hard against the post. There was a slight creak before it gave, and then the whole tent came down on top of their heads.

TREASURE OF EGYPT

With a loud *Whoosh!* the tent was leveled, sending both men sprawling. Samuel was the first to recover.... With his body shrouded in canvas and his arms flailing, Samuel managed to navigate to the entrance. Like a moth struggling from its cocoon, he emerged with his hair slightly askew, but none the worse for wear.

It must be the drink, Alec surmised as he watched him through the tunnel of fabric Samuel had left behind. The drunkard staggered slightly, holding his arms out for balance while blearily squinting at the audience assembled before him. The part of the group that Alec could still see seemed only slightly surprised by the mishap, almost expectant. None dared move.

Alec struggled under the canvas as he cleared the post from his path. Unfortunately, once he was able to take a step, he collided with the damn chair again and tripped. Cursing, he managed to stand and, with a great tearing noise, rent the fabric, throwing off the remaining pieces of canvas as he did.

Breathing heavily from the exertion, Alec stood before the stunned tribe, the knife that he normally kept hidden in his boot in his hand. A murmur of alarm erupted from the crowd as they eyed him cautiously.

Samuel, quick to appease the mounting tension, raised his hands and shouted, "Yes, yes, we have a deal. He'll do it." Then, remembering himself, he repeated it in Arabic.

A heavyset man, swathed in brilliant robes, stepped forward in the crowd, a relieved smile on his face. Though Alec's understanding of their language was paltry, at best, he understood the large man as he said something to the crowd about being saved from the plague by Allah and the English king.

That would be a reference to him, Alec realized. Either that, or he was the plague. He continued to puzzle it through as the man spoke.

When the sheik finished addressing his people, an incredible sound arose, bursting forth like a cacophony, a full orchestra, or a million crickets. The women of the group started a high-pitched *"la, la, la, la,"* which the men accompanied with a lower *"ya, ya, ya, ya,"* interspersed with *"whoop, whoop."*

Alec watched, slightly alarmed by this odd catharsis.

"It's how they celebrate. They're pleased," Samuel added for his benefit. "Either that, or it's how they mourn their dead." He made this last comment more to himself than Alec.

"What?" Alec's ears perked up with that aside.

"I said they're pleased. Look, they're celebrating."

"Uh, huh."

"What?" Samuel innocently replied.

"Nothing." Alec shook his head. *Unbelievable!*

Rifles fired off from the crowd. With a start, both he and Samuel ducked while looking for the source. Several men of the tribe had begun jubilantly firing their rifles into the air.

"See, they're not aiming at us." Samuel grinned back at him as he pointed skywards.

Chapter 5

No sooner had the group of villagers stopped cheering than three camels appeared, laden with supplies. Their rifles were mounted, and the trunk, which had been delivered to the tent, was retrieved and loaded onto the back of the largest beast.

Alec watched, somewhat surprised at all the commotion. It was almost as if they were afraid he'd change his mind, and they couldn't act quickly enough to get them to leave. Not only was that strange, but the whisperings he'd overheard definitely put him on edge.

Infuriated, Alec glared over at Samuel. "What happened with paying tribute?"

"With what, our good looks? Well," he amended, "your good looks."

Alec narrowed his eyes. "You actually find this amusing, don't you?"

"C'mon, you know the captain took nearly half of what I had, and the guide took the rest, along with the water he stole. What was I to do, offer them a note?"

"Yes, damn it!"

"Do you really think any of these people would be familiar with an English bank note?" Samuel's gaze raked the crowd. "Look around, they're practically living in the Stone Age. I don't believe these people are aware of anything other than sheep, sand, and swords."

The only thing Alec could see was the elderly man who'd come for "the man of tongues" earlier, beckoning him. "What now?" he groaned, looking briefly over at Samuel. *Man of tongues,* indeed, he'd like to cut the damn thing out!

"I believe he wants you to stand over there for the ceremony."

Alec seriously doubted a walk to the guillotine could be worse. He had to fight a strong impulse to run the other way as he crossed the short distance and stood before the old man. Samuel followed closely behind and stood at his shoulder.

The elder of the tribe opened his arms to the heavens and spoke several phrases that Samuel translated.

"He's asking Allah to bless your union."

Alec barely heard him through the rushing of blood in his ears as he too offered a silent prayer up to the heavens, but apparently God wasn't listening, for everyone remained as they were, and the earth did not open up and swallow anyone, least of all him.

A disturbance at the other end of the crowd, however, did catch his attention. A wide path was cleared for a figure covered from head to toe in black. The men especially shrunk back, giving the ominous apparition a wide berth.

Was this some kind of ceremonial dress? Alec wondered as she approached. The other women had brightly covered skirts and scarves. The whispering again came to mind. Perhaps she had some kind of ailment . . . leprosy?

"Ah. . . . Here comes the bride." Samuel spoke cheerfully at his side.

Alec fixed him with a cold stare and mouthed, "I'm going to kill you!"

"You're the one who wanted to be *king,* remember?"

"What the hell does that have to do with this?"

"Well, they certainly weren't going to marry her to your servant." Samuel innocently pointed to himself.

Alec rolled his eyes with a groan. He'd known when he said it, that it would come back to haunt him, but not quite like this. "I'm still going to kill you," he hissed through clenched teeth. He received a glare from the elder, who put his hand up for silence, as the woman came to stand before him.

Alec could actually feel her next to him; his skin crawled with the awareness of her. His hands went unconsciously to his side, feeling for pistols that were no longer there. With booted feet rooted into the ground, he looked more like he was prepared for a gun battle. He'd certainly prefer one to this.

Far removed from any wedding ceremony he'd ever imagined, this one matched his mood. The atmosphere was somber, reminding him more of a funeral than anything else, especially with the bride completely swathed in layers of black.

The elder produced a scarf, which he looped over each of their wrists. Alec was just grateful he didn't actually have to touch her and risk contamination. A few words were spoken, and the scarf was removed. It was fairly painless, considering he'd just been shackled.

The crowd remained strangely silent, almost afraid, as if they were waiting for the heavens to roll back and for God to smite them. And now that he considered it . . . why not? It's not every day you marry off the *Plague of Egypt*. No wonder they were waiting for lightning to strike.

It was no longer difficult for him to sort out the words that Samuel had elected not to translate. Alec threw another disgusted look at the man. Marrying him off to no less than the *Plague of Egypt* had to top just about everything else he'd ever done to him. Despite the provocations, this little stunt went beyond the pale.

"There you are," Samuel pronounced as a woman bearing a plate laden with an assortment of meats and fruits came towards them. "Your wedding feast has arrived."

"You mean last supper?" Alec's voice was flat as he waved it away. "You actually think I could eat after this?"

Samuel shrugged his shoulders as he grabbed a handful of dates before she turned away. They both watched as the *bride* went to stand before an old woman. They spoke quietly, then embraced.

"Look on the bright side." Samuel popped a few dates into his mouth. "If that old crone is her mother, she might be as old as the hills herself."

"And exactly how is that the bright side?"

"Well, you won't have to run very hard to get away from her," Samuel mumbled around a mouth full.

Alec fixed him with an icy stare.

"I'll just go see what's taking so long."

Left alone, the prickling sensation of being watched intensified as Alec scanned the crowd. It didn't take long to find the source. The leader of the blackbirds was standing back from the crowd, and though there was no discernible reason for it, his rage was palpable, his face a mask of barely concealed malevolence.

It was curious that the man would be acting this way over a plague. The untimely arrival of an *English king* had definitely not been to the man's liking. Alec found himself wondering if he'd disrupted a love match and would have to surrender his bride. . . . He could only hope so.

The only problem with that solution was that, with the way his luck had run lately, they'd have to kill him in order to free her from their nuptials. "Bloody hell!" Alec swore, expecting a challenge to ensue any moment. *Great, just great!* His jaw tightened with impatience as he waited.

"Time to go," Samuel called.

"Finally," Alec sighed with relief as he turned away. He climbed on top of the kneeling camel as Samuel tossed him a sack containing his weapons.

"Like taking a pebble from a beach. . . ."

"If you never said that again, it would be a good thing," Alec warned through clenched teeth as he placed his guns in his belt and then searched the sack for more. "Where's the ammunition?"

"Ah, I believe it has been loaded onto the camel with your bride. Something to do with keeping the peace, I believe."

Alec snorted in response.

As they left, the tribe started jubilantly cheering once again. The trilling of the women blended with the whooping and hollering of the men. Alec made it a point to keep an eye on the leader of the blackbirds, especially when shots were fired into the air. The man fixed him with a black stare before he turned and stalked away.

It was a warning . . . or worse. The look had definitely held a promise of dire consequences, though what they might be he could only imagine. The only thing Alec knew for sure was that he'd had enough of these people.

Alec prodded his camel forward, glancing at the tent he'd been forced to stay in all morning. He could almost laugh at the irony. He, the "king," had been left to swelter in the heat, while Samuel, his "servant", had been received with the aplomb of a visiting dignitary. Not that he could have known at the time, baking as he'd been in the canvas oven with five guards to ensure he stayed there.

He felt some vindication that the damn thing had been leveled. The tent now looked as though it had been run over by a herd of elephants. It wasn't nearly enough compensation for the indignity of having been held captive within it, or the debacle of what had transpired afterward, all of which he blamed one person for . . . Samuel.

Alec watched as the idiot waved goodbye to the cheers of the tribe who'd followed them out of the camp. *Escorted* them, was more like it.

~*~

Alec wiped his sleeve across his brow and adjusted the brim of his hat. It was not only as hot as Hades, but he was also fairly certain the large expanse of desert they rode toward looked like Hell, as well, which was why he was amazed to find that he was viewing the bleak vista as a reprieve from his ordeal, rather than a dire circumstance. In fact, he welcomed it with open arms.

He and his two companions rode single file with several yards distance between them. Riding in the middle of the exodus, Alec felt no desire to close the gap between either of the two. In truth, he preferred to avoid both of them for as long as possible.

He stole a quick glance back at the apparition who now followed behind him. *How could my life have taken such a drastic turn?* Alec wondered as he watched the woman perched atop her camel, not sure why he couldn't seem to shake the tingling awareness of her that set him on edge.

"Bloody hell," he groaned, turning back around. He couldn't for the life of him think of a worse fate. How could Samuel sell him out like this? *Hell!* He reminded himself he should count it lucky he hadn't been sold into slavery.

Well, actually. . . . Alec's eyes narrowed on his friend's back as he rode before him. The turncoat *had* sold him into slavery, just of a different kind. Especially when one considered that the whole reason for coming to this god-forsaken country was to avoid getting married.

Alec made a promise to himself right then and there. If he should ever get out of this predicament, he would return to

England, assume his responsibilities, and never again listen to that ill-begotten. . . . Seeking an adequate description, he glanced at the figure ahead of him swaying precariously on his mount. The *traitorous bastard* could barely stay seated on the camel he rode.

Alec sure as hell was never letting him *handle it* ever again. He glanced back again at his current "*wife,*" *The Plague*, and shuddered. She reminded him of a crow with her black garments flapping in the breeze. Hell, all the responsibilities he'd avoided thus far in his life were preferable to this.

Strains of a little ditty that Samuel was entertaining himself with drifted back on the wind. There was nothing Alec would like to do more than strangle the man right now. The fool had even let his hat fall back from his head, exposing his face and reddish-blonde hair to the bright sunlight.

The idiot would have sunstroke before long, and Alec wasn't even a bit inclined to save him from it. A small part of him actually wished it on him. *Hell!* He was only amazed it hadn't happened yet. It would have been among the highlights of this journey.

What a fool he'd been. He should have sold the piece of scrap to the old man at the card table for five quid, instead of traipsing out into the middle of the desert to avoid his fate.

He felt like a puppet being toyed with. First the pressure to marry, and now the burden of finding a way out of that state. Alec could just imagine the look on his mother's face if he were to introduce *The Plague* to her as his wife. The thought actually lightened his mood, until he turned around again.

"Oh, God," he groaned. He certainly had a better understanding of the saying: *When choosing your demons, the known is better than the unknown.*

Alec blew out an exasperated breath as he faced the front again. The only thing left to him, it seemed, was to find out exactly what Samuel knew about the predicament he'd placed Alec in. If nothing else, he wanted to get a few things clarified.

He urged his mount forward, easily catching up with the drunken idiot. "Did you know they called her *The Plague of Egypt?*" he whispered loudly.

"Ho-ho, I'm impressed." Samuel nodded. "Your understanding of their language is much improved since we started."

"You're not denying it," Alec accused.

"Come now, Alec, you really believe that?" Samuel looked at him with all the surprise his reddened eyes could muster. He was teetering on the back of the camel, the effects of the strong drink still apparent.

Watching him, Alec wondered for a moment if he would lose his seat, then a thought occurred to him. "This is because of the dancing girl in Amsterdam, isn't it?" he charged.

"What?" Disbelief registered on Samuel's face. "Really, Alec, I'm appalled you'd even think so. I happen to like bearded ladies."

"You married me off to *The Plague of Egypt* to get even. Admit it."

"No." It was a statement, not a denial, more like a denial to admit denial.

Alec's eyes narrowed as he considered him.

"Besides, I told you not to think of it as a marriage." Samuel waved his hand in the air as if mimicking nothing, a paltry nothingness at that. "For God's sake, man, it's merely an act of transport. Once in England, you can simply annul it, if that is even necessary." He paused, as if contemplating the merit of this new idea, and then continued. "I'm not sure the heathen practices of this country are even acknowledged by the laws of our courts. Unless, of course . . . no."

"Unless what?" Alec said, picking up the conversation where he'd left it. He was truly exasperated now.

"Just don't, you *know?*"

"No, I don't *know.*" Alec became increasingly concerned that he did, indeed, know what his friend was getting at.

"C'mon, man, you *know!*" Samuel leered at him. "*Consummate it.*" He chuckled as he urged his mount forward, putting space between them, his laughter drifting on the wind.

"Bloody hell!" The expletive was heartfelt. Alec glanced at the figure completely swathed in black that rode behind them and cringed. *Oh, God! How can this be happening to me?*

Urging his mount forward, he chanced yet another glance back at the woman riding behind him, *his bride*. His only recollection of her during the ceremony was that she was shoulder height, didn't appear to be too heavy under all that covering, and that he'd been glad he hadn't had to touch her and risk catching any diseases.

That was it . . . all he could remember of his *wife,* he thought disparagingly, and now he was married to a bundle of shoulder-height black cloth with the plague. *God help me*, he thought, as he tried to recall more. It was as if his memory had been encased in fog. Perhaps it was trauma, or maybe sunstroke?

~*~

The sun beating down on him was merciless, and, despite the breeze, the smell permeating the air was god-awful. Alec was a little surprised that the stench emanating from the camel he was riding wasn't attracting vultures.

The hulking beast seemed to read his mind and bellowed at the insult. In all fairness, he allowed, smelling his shirtfront, that he might be partially responsible for it. What he wouldn't give for a bath or some shade! God, this land was ruthless, he thought disparagingly as he swallowed a sip of bitter water from the sheepskin flask he carried.

It was almost as hard to swallow as what Samuel had done to him. Alec still couldn't believe how the bastard had sold him out, and to think . . . he'd actually been relying on Samuel's ability to charm a snake, which was why Alec now felt as though he'd been ensnared in its coils.

Alec continued to scan the horizon for a sign of the tribesmen that he feared would follow them from the camp. Dark shimmers seemed to dance in the distance as waves of heat played with his vision. It seemed he could conjure up the dark images wherever he looked, the illusion made worse by the prickling awareness of being watched.

Of course, he thought, looking back at the woman, *I am being followed by a demon straight from Hell.* Perhaps that was why he couldn't shake the feeling.

They had ridden in an easterly direction for hours before it occurred to Alec that their "guide" was following them, while

Samuel, who was sleeping bowed over in the saddle, was leading them.

"Bloody hell," Alec swore. Could anything else possibly go so glaringly wrong? What an idiot he was to take so long to notice. It must be the strain of the day. He hadn't eaten anything but a mouthful of dry bread and, Lord knows, most of that he'd inhaled, literally. He felt lightheaded from the heat and had a sharp twinge in his neck. That he'd been repeatedly peering over his shoulder at *The Plague* certainly hadn't helped.

Cursing under his breath, Alec rode forward and nudged Samuel. The braggart didn't stir, just plopped his head back and emitted a loud snore.

"For the love of God!" Alec leaned over and shook him.

"Aaugh . . . yeah, that's it, love," Samuel murmured in his sleep.

Alec immediately released him in horror, leaving the sleeping man swinging crazily in the saddle. He reached over and caught Samuel by the shirtsleeve before he fell. Forced to practically haul him up by one arm, he yelled as loudly as he could while seriously contemplating strangulation, "Samuel, wake up!"

"Huh?" A bleary-eyed Samuel looked up at him. "Oh, hi, Alec."

The fumes from his breath alone were enough to intoxicate someone. Alec choked and held him at arm's length.

Groggily, Samuel smacked his dry parched lips together. "I don't feel so well."

"Good!" Alec smiled as he placed him, none too gently, back in the saddle. "Listen, we need to talk to our . . . *guide* about where the hell we are!"

Mystified, Samuel looked over at him. "Well, why then don't you ask her?"

"Because, idiot, I don't speak the language!" Alec snapped.

"What, you're not English? Aahh. . . . I told you that our guide speaks English. Could it be that the bashful groom is just scared?"

What the hell was the lunatic raving about? *When did he tell me?* Alec wondered. Was he referring to that fast explanation he gave before dropping that little tidbit about marrying the . . . The Plague?

"You told me she spoke several languages, you bastard, and conveniently abstained from mentioning English." Alec eyed him with more than mild irritation. "And for the record . . . I'm not scared of anything!" he added menacingly.

"Yes, but English is a language," he pointed out as Alec turned away from him in disgust. Samuel laughed to himself, served him right. That would teach Alec to set him up with a woman with more facial hair than the two of them put together.

The continuous sway of the camel stirred his stomach. "Uugh. . . . I don't feel so good," Samuel moaned.

Alec rode back towards the *guide* with purpose. It was well past time he took control of this situation. Just one question *plagued* him. How in the hell did a man go about asking a woman for directions?

"Do?" Alec's voice squeaked. How the hell had that happened? His voice hadn't done that since adolescence. "Umm . . . hmm," he cleared his throat. "Do you have any idea where we are?" The moment he spoke, he realized the harsh comment possibly could have been better phrased. He winced at his own words.

"Yes." The voice was silken, a soft caress.

He was taken aback by the effect it had on him. He felt desire rush to his loins. *Unbelievable!*

How in the hell could he react like this? *C'mon, man*, he said to himself. *This is the crow with the plague, remember?* He'd been out in the sun too long. One incredibly short word, uttered with the most erotic accent he'd ever heard, and his insides turned to mush. Well, no, quite the opposite, in fact, his breeches felt tight. "Bloody hell!" he cursed softly.

"Hum-um," he cleared his throat and tried again. "I've noticed that we've been traveling without benefit of direction. If you know where we are. . . ." He paused, aware he sounded like a complete idiot. This wasn't what he had intended when he decided to take charge of the situation. "Where are you taking us?" he blurted out.

"There is a small oasis at the base of the hill just over the rise. We'll stop there."

Her voice was so smooth it washed over him in ripples. It was almost difficult to comprehend what she was saying. Didn't he have a question? Oh, yes. "Should you not be leading us there?"

"The camels know where the next water is to be found. They will lead us."

Like honey, her voice was like honey. What was he thinking? He shouldn't even think about consummating this thing. A crow with the plague, remember. . . . Camels? Well, hell, at least *now* he knew who was in charge. The damned camels! Alec turned and watched, astounded, as Samuel fell off his.

Unbelievable!

Alec stopped, looking down on the fool in disgust before dismounting. It took several tries to get the idiot back into the saddle, not an easy feat considering his state. "If you fall again, I'm just throwing you over the damn thing."

"I owe you one," Samuel moaned.

"You owe me more than one after today. . . . Trust me," Alec remarked as he straightened him in the saddle.

"Oh, have mercy. Stop shouting."

"I'm not shouting," Alec yelled a little louder.

"Oh, God," Samuel groaned. "I think I've been poisoned."

"Then someone beat me to it," Alec said irritably as he climbed back up on his own mount.

"Alright, I confess. I could have probably offered the sheik a note. It's just that the man was so desperate. It seemed the perfect solution at the time. Just please, *please* stop screaming."

"Since when did marrying me to *The Plague of Egypt* become a perfect solution?" Alec growled.

The only thing that prevented Alec from reaching over and shoving his friend off the camel was the sight of the oasis that appeared in front of them as they neared the top of the hill. It had at least fifty trees surrounding a pool in the center. A rocky hill rose up behind, creating a natural barrier from the harsh desert. It looked like a slice of Heaven. They both watched in wonder as the camels took them to the water's edge.

"Oh, thank God!" Samuel moaned as he slipped off the camel and fell face down on the grass that surrounded the water.

Alec left him as he was. He was doing well not to strangle the man right now. He certainly didn't need to tempt fate. Dismounting his own camel, he stretched his legs as his mount dipped its head and began to drink.

"Where would you like to set up camp?" the *voice* asked from behind him.

It sent shivers down his spine when he turned around to see the black-clad figure right behind him. "Aaugh!" The noise escaped him as he fought the urge to jump back. He tried to hide the slip by clearing his throat. "Ah, how about here?" His voice sounded strange, even to his own ears.

"I think we'll have a better night if we stay up on the ridge." She pointed to an area on the hill above them.

Her arm looked like a wing unfolding, with the scarves draped across it as she moved. He took another step away from her. The effect of her voice on him was at odds with the vision that she presented. The combination made his reaction all the more disturbing.

"We'll have a better view of our surroundings and fewer snakes to worry about while we sleep."

"You'll get no argument from me," Alec agreed.

"Me either." Samuel rolled over. "I think I'm lying on a snake."

"You are a lying snake." Alec stalked off.

Chapter 6

Alec lay back in the grass, his head and shoulders supported by the base of a large tree trunk. The aroma of something wonderful tantalized his nose. "Aahh." This was more like it. He folded his hands behind his head as he listened to his stomach rumble. The goat cheese he'd eaten when they started to unload hadn't kept his hunger at bay, and the scent of whatever she was cooking had his stomach growling in anticipation.

He looked up at the sky through the palm fronds high above him, surprised at the tranquil beauty. It certainly was not what he'd expected to find after his ordeal. He rolled the muscles in his shoulders as he made himself more comfortable. It had felt good to work them, even if it had been in an effort to remain calm.

He'd hauled everything the camels had carried up the slope, tirelessly working until most of his anger had dissipated. He'd set the tent up, avoiding at all costs anything to do with the woman. Samuel hadn't been good for much besides moaning.

Alec glanced over at his friend, who still lay in the grass. Now it seemed they were both doomed, Samuel to a horrid death from what he had consumed, and Alec to a different kind of plague altogether. Alec looked away. The idiot deserved to have some kind of bloody disease after what he did to him.

On cue, Samuel raised his head from his comatose state on the grass and sniffed the air. "What's that smell?" He winced. "Uugh . . . I'm going to be sick." He dragged himself weakly into the bushes.

Alec smiled at the sound of retching. "Serves you right!" he laughingly said in the general direction of the quivering bush. "I'm going to see if *The Plague* needs anything." The only response was a groan. Alec climbed the narrow path leading to the ridge.

She was sitting in front of a small fire, her back to him, but at the sound of his footsteps she adjusted her headscarf. By the time he arrived, she was completely covered. *Damn! What could she possibly be hiding?* he wondered as he crouched down beside her.

It was the closest he'd dared get to her since their arrival. "Smells marvelous." He inhaled deeply.

"Thank you," she replied softly.

Her voice washed over him again, the effect almost hypnotizing. He watched, almost paralyzed, as she reached out to stir the contents in the large pot. With morbid curiosity he looked down at her hands, afraid of what he might see.

Much to his relief they were not scarred or covered with sores. They were, well . . . perfect. He hadn't really noticed women's hands before now, but her hands were truly lovely. He also couldn't help but notice how they gripped the ladle, her fingers so delicate, her movements so gentle. He felt the stirring in his loins again. Bloody hell, what was wrong with him?

Do something else, man! Alec ordered himself as he stood, running a hand through his hair. "Can I help with anything?" he asked, glad that his voice held.

"I could use more water." She held a small clay pot out to him.

Alec spent his time walking to the pool inventing ways to get her to take the damn black covering off her head. When he realized what his mind was preoccupied with, he was appalled. What was wrong with him? You'd think he'd never seen a girl before.

He had to stop this nonsense. He busied himself with filling the pot, still so distracted by thoughts of the woman that he was surprised when the mound, face down in the grass, spoke up.

"I don't know if it's a good idea to leave her alone with the cooking," Samuel mumbled weakly.

"Why do you say that?"

"According to the sheik, she burned down the whole village one day when she was left to tend the cooking fires." Samuel rolled over so that he was splayed, face up, across the ground.

"Really?" Alec noted that, since Samuel had started to confess, it was like a river undammed, other truths just kept rushing out.

Samuel pulled himself up on an elbow. "They say she's like Medusa."

"Medusa . . . the one with snakes for hair?"

"That's the one. . . . Some say that if you look upon her, rather than turn to stone, the opposite will happen."

"The opposite?" Alec's brows rose.

"Yeah, the opposite," Samuel whispered conspiratorially, deciding to spill it all, "a man's *pride* will shrivel up."

"*Pride?*"

"You know . . . *Pride.*" Samuel glanced at him meaningfully.

"Oh, *pride.* . . ." Alec nodded his understanding. "And the sheik just offered up all this information while he was trying to marry the girl off."

"Hell no, why do you think I'm so sick?" Exhausted, Samuel wilted back into the grass.

Alec waited, not answering, and not sure at all that he could endure any more of Samuel's conscience clearing.

"I had to ply him with enough alcohol to loosen his tongue." Samuel thought to explain after a time. "Clever wasn't it?"

"Let me get this straight," Alec fumed. "You, *the guest,*" he paused for effect, "plied the sheik, our *questionable host,*" he waited as Samuel nodded in agreement, "with liquor, so that you could find out that the potential bride was a snake-haired pyromaniac who can shrivel the male member of any potential mate that looks upon her, so that you could marry her to . . . me?"

Samuel, who had been nodding slightly, stopped and tilted his head toward Alec. "No, it wasn't like that."

"Yes! Right, how clever of you!"

Samuel had the decency to wince at the words, or perhaps it was the volume Alec was now using.

"I'm going to kill you, not yet, however. I don't want to put you out of your misery. After you're feeling better, I'm going to slowly dismember you! How's that for clever?" Alec raised his brows and stared down at him.

"You don't understand. You're taking this entirely too personally," Samuel muttered meekly as he put his head back down.

Alec looked at the wounded expression that crossed his features. He couldn't believe Samuel was trying to worm his way out of this one.

"Every time the sheik would slip up, he had to make the pot sweeter, while I, on the other hand, made you seem all that more grand, a *king* among the elite. Why do you think we were given everything back?"

"I don't know, but thanks to you, *now* all I can do is extricate myself from this situation." Alec heaved a long-suffering sigh. "That is to say if that *is* the full extent of the problem. There isn't anything else I should know, is there?"

"Other than *The Plague*? No, that's it. I mean," Samuel sank back into the grass, "that's all the sheik told me." Though weary, he looked relieved, like a man that had just stepped out of the confessional.

"Well that, at least, is good news," Alec said, his tone not quite matching his words as he lifted the jug.

"I'm beginning to think that there is something to that curse," Samuel groaned.

Alec looked down at the wretch; the sun had turned his complexion as red as a ripe tomato. He could almost take pity on him . . . almost. A smile flickered at the corners of Alec's mouth. "That's not a curse. That's my prayers being answered."

Samuel groaned again, weakly pulling himself toward the bushes.

Alec's smile widened as Samuel left him. Now that was justice. With a lighter step, he returned to his bride, moving as stealthily as he could. Regrettably, she seemed to sense him and covered herself just before he arrived. *Damn!* If he could just get a glimpse of her, perhaps that would dispel his feelings of dread. Either that, or make them worse.

He stopped himself short as the realization struck. Good God, what had he been thinking? He didn't even know her name. There was only one thing he could do under the circumstances . . . introduce himself.

"By the way . . . I am Lord—" He paused. Perhaps he should have bowed and formally introduced himself using his full name as one would normally in the civilized world, but he just couldn't seem to do it while peering into the black shroud that faced him. It was starting to get on his nerves that he felt vulnerable when near this concealed woman. She could be old enough to be his mother, for all he knew. "Alec," he finished.

"It is nice to meet you, Lord Alec."

Her voice sounded surprisingly young, he realized with relief. "What may I call you?" he asked while trying to see through the black curtain that veiled her face.

"My name is Genevieve," she breathed.

A very un-Arabic name, Alec thought in surprise. Curiously he studied the black covering, trying to see beyond the veil, until she dropped her gaze.

Scorching heat hit his upper thighs. "Aaugh." He bent forward. The ladle had slipped from her fingers and splashed into the pot, splattering him with the hot liquid.

"Are you all right?" She reached forward to grab the swirling spoon and bumped heads with him, banging her forehead on his nose.

THUMP!

The sound of the impact seemed to reverberate in his head. With his hand up to his injured nose, he straightened. *Bloody hell!* It felt like she'd broken it. Fighting the tears that welled up in his eyes, he stepped back.

"I am so sorry. Did I hurt you?" She stood up and took a step forward with her hand raised as if to touch him.

With his vision blurred, the apparition in front of him looked more than ever like a large black bird as it approached. He took another step back.

She took another step towards him.

He took another three away from her.

She raised her arms, which looked more like great wings unfolding the further he leaned away. Unfortunately, he was teetering on the edge of the embankment. He tried to catch his balance, but it was too late. He stumbled, completing a backward somersault as he tumbled before finally coming to a halt some distance down the trail.

Alec stood abruptly and dusted himself off, acting for all the world like nothing untoward had passed. "Huh-um," he cleared his throat. "I think I hear Samuel calling. I'll just go check on him." He practically shouted in the silence while continuing to back down the trail away from her.

Samuel was smiling up at him when he returned to the pool.

"What?" Alec absently fingered his nose as he went to the water's edge. It was tender and felt swollen, but he didn't think it was broken.

"Nothing." Samuel's grin widened. "I didn't see anything. . . . I certainly didn't see you being manhandled by your wee wifey."

Alec glared at him before splashing water on his face. He couldn't fathom what had come over him. What a bumbling idiot he had been. Even if she *had* looked like a vulture with wings spread, it was still unlike him to run from anything, let alone a mere woman . . . *even if she does have the plague . . . and snakes for hair . . . and a withering glance.*

He really had to stop this. One minute he was fantasizing over her hands, and the next he was undone by the thought of her touch. The maddening need he felt to see her would be best squelched before he got more than he bargained for. He really had no interest in contracting a disease, or whatever else she had.

~*~

Alec leaned back against the tree trunk that he had claimed as his own and stretched his legs before him. Sopping up the last of the sauce with a piece of flat bread, he chewed with pleasure, despite his concerns. It had taken quite a bit of bravery on his part to take the first bite, but now he was glad he had.

It certainly wouldn't be the first time that a forced marriage had ended with the groom being poisoned. And, given the name his bride was known by, poisoning seemed all the more likely. Unfortunately, the only person who could have acted as food taster for him was out of commission at the moment.

Samuel was currently propped up against a tree, his face and hands slathered in a white paste, sipping on a concoction that she had prepared specifically for his condition. Considering he was now sitting, that said at least *something* good about the cure. By the expression on Samuel's face, it didn't appear he was enjoying the taste much. Alec had to smile at that.

Alec glanced over at the woman, who was now reluctant to be near him. He couldn't blame her, especially since he'd run from her like a schoolboy. He wasn't even surprised when she'd set the plate of food down on the blanket, rather than hand it to him directly. She was probably afraid he'd run off again, he thought with embarrassment.

After that, she had retreated to sit by herself a short distance away. Alec watched her as she finished her meal. Much to his consternation, she had the ability to eat with that damn scarf on. With one hand she'd hold the veil away from her face and slip food right up under the edge with the other, where it disappeared.

Alec cleared his throat. "Thank you, Lady Genevieve. The meal was wonderful." He hoped the awkwardness he felt wasn't apparent, especially when she only nodded in response. It was like talking to a damn wall.

It appeared she wasn't going to forgive him for his rather hasty and humiliating departure. He wasn't about to mention it in Samuel's company. It was bad enough he'd witnessed Alec's fall from grace.

Samuel decided to join the living then and asked, "Genevieve? You don't say?" His tone was surprisingly jovial as he continued in his usual flare. "What a lovely name." He glanced towards Alec. "Just like your grandmother's. What a coincidence."

He gave Alec a conspiratorial wink before favoring the black shroud with his delighted attention and continued. "Please forgive me, fair lady, my deplorable manners, and allow me to introduce myself. Lord Samuel Augustus George St. Clair the Third, at your service. But please call me Samuel, dear. My friends all do."

Here he goes again. Alec threw his eyes heavenward in mute dismay. That was another thing about Samuel, Alec bemoaned, shaking his head. He actually confused himself with a ladies' man.

"I would like nothing better than to bow over your lovely hand, but I seem to have lost the use of my legs." Samuel grinned.

Genevieve giggled at his audacity.

Encouraged, Samuel continued in his usual stride. "As soon as I'm able to stand, I should very much like to remedy that."

Alec interrupted the debaucher before he could sign for her first dance. "It would be a good idea to get some rest before we set out tomorrow. We're already starting to lose the light. Perhaps you could *help* by bringing up the camels."

"I'm truly sorry, Alec," Samuel feigned regret, "but I'm weak as a wee bairn. Should I even be able to stand, I truly doubt that I'd be up to much."

Alec graced him with a look of annoyance as he stood. Gathering the blanket that Genevieve had placed the rinsed dishes in, he hoisted it up like a sailor's sack.

Genevieve stood, offering to help the useless sod as he attempted to rise, which help, Alec was disgusted to see, the sot accepted with a grin on his face. The invalid even leaned against her for support, oozing charm all the way up the hill, thanking her on and on for saving his life. Alec had to fight the urge to make that statement fact as he walked behind them.

He would have liked to have broken Samuel's scrawny neck by the time the idiot was situated in front of the dying embers of Genevieve's cooking fire. Instead, Alec returned to the oasis to collect the camels; fed up with the other man's foolery, he felt the need to get some fresh air.

Before he could leave, however, Genevieve stopped him. "Lord Alec." He turned toward her but kept his distance as she spoke. "Thank you for bringing up the dishes."

He was struck yet again by the woman's incredibly sultry voice as he nodded. Had she been born to seduce a man simply with the sound of it? Then wilt him with the sight of her? That thought came to him unbidden. He had to stop these absurd ideas, he warned himself. The very idea was ludicrous. He was a man of science, for God's sake, a man of the modern world, not one of these superstitious barbarians. Besides, she certainly seemed to have the opposite effect on him.

~*~

Camels were, Alec decided, the most stubborn, cantankerous, ornery beasts he'd ever had the displeasure of meeting. He decided to urge the largest one up the hill, hoping the others would follow, but it wouldn't budge from the water's edge. The damn thing would not cooperate, no matter what he did. He tried pulling on the reins and then pushing from the rear. He even tried to jump up and swing a leg over.

In response, the camel stepped to the side every time he tried to get a foot up. He chased it around in circles, hopping on one leg every other step until he actually managed to swing a leg up over the damn thing and pull himself up. The moment he did so, however, the beast just lay down in response.

Alec stayed in the saddle, rocking back and forth like a small child on the back of a great rocking horse . . . feeling like an even greater fool until the beast bellowed its discontent.

"Alright, you win! I'll get off, but only if you get up." Exasperated, Alec slid off, and, to his astonishment, the camel actually stood. He was amazed even further when the beast rewarded him for all his efforts with a large wad of cud, which landed squarely in Alec's face.

The damn thing spit on me. Unbelievable!

He wiped at the foul-smelling green slime dripping from his hair onto his face and eyed the ornery beast with suspicion. The fickle animal had returned to grazing, as if nothing had happened. From the direction of the camp, a whistle sounded, and a clucking ensued. To Alec's utter amazement, the three demon beasts merrily danced up the path toward the sound without further prodding.

Alec could do nothing but stand where he was, dripping with slime, and watch them go. He wiped his mouth with the back of his sleeve and did the only thing left to him. He dove into the water clothes and all.

~*~

"You're looking rather wet." Samuel greeted Alec as he emerged from the darkness. "I was starting to think I would have to see about your welfare."

Samuel still sat in front of the fire he'd managed to stoke, resting against a saddle. The blaze had died down some, but was cheery nonetheless, though the sight didn't improve Alec's mood. Samuel took a flask from his jacket and held it out to him. "You look like you could use some."

Alec nodded agreement but didn't take it. Instead, he sat down, pulled off a boot, and poured the water out. That done, Alec arranged the boot upside down near the fire and followed it with the other.

Samuel sat back with a nonchalant shrug and took a long draught from the flask. He shivered as he swallowed. "Aaugh."

"Are you sure you want to do that?" Alec asked, amazed Samuel could even stomach something like that after his ordeal.

"Hair of the dog, Alec, hair of the dog," Samuel quipped.

"More like the bite, if you ask me. Don't suppose you've seen any of our clothing recently?" Alec's voice was muffled as he stripped off his shirt and draped it over a nearby bush.

"Actually. . . . No. I believe I played the part of the suffering villain while you and the little wife set up camp." Samuel smiled at his own wit. "Our belongings are probably still tied to the horses we left behind." He chuckled. "Never knew I'd miss the stride of a horse so much. The thought of the ride that awaits me on the morrow makes me ill."

"No doubt, but I'm still in need of some dry pants," Alec muttered.

"I had no idea one could get seasick in the middle of the desert," Samuel continued, paying little heed to his friend's mumblings.

There was obviously only one other possibility as to where his pack could be. . . . Alec turned towards the tent and took a deep breath to fortify himself. What if he found himself the recipient of her unwanted attentions?

Alec was prepared to admit to being curious about her, but the idea of being chased around by the woman shrouded in black, all the while thwarting her advances, was the last thing he wanted to endure this evening.

"Would you like me to go ask her?" Samuel whispered. "It's the least I can do. I mean . . . I understand if you're afraid."

Alec gave him a baleful glance before walking towards the tent. Samuel's grin broadened as he watched him go.

Heavy-footed, Alec approached the enclosure. There was a soft glow emanating from within. He paused at the opening of the tent, feeling like a marauding bandit. It wasn't as if he were trespassing on a sanctified shrine, he admonished himself as he cleared his throat.

"Lady Genevieve . . . may I enter? I'm in need of dry clothing and was wondering. . . ." Alec explained in a rush. He certainly didn't want her to misunderstand his intentions.

"You may enter." Her soft, silken voice stopped him short.

Silenced by the invitation, he stood for a moment, took a deep breath, and opened the flap. Bracing himself, he stepped inside. . . . Dear God Almighty, he couldn't believe his eyes!

The vision that greeted him left him stunned and speechless. She was sitting beside an oil lamp which cast a soft glow about her features. He blinked in amazement. Never had he seen such perfection.

Her hair was of the bluest black imaginable. The long tresses cascaded down her back in shimmering moonbeams that ended well past her waist. Her large blue eyes held him entranced, light in color, yet fringed by the longest, darkest lashes he'd ever seen. Her dark brows were delicately arched, and her cheekbones were high, leaving a hollow below that only emphasized them.

Her jaw was strong and angular, yet it too only added to her feminine, exotic beauty. Her lips were full, lush, and ripe. She must have sensed his attention there, for she ran a light pink tongue across them as he watched. He stood entranced, feeling a strong reaction to her in his very core.

He couldn't for the life of him tear his gaze from her. His hungry eyes searched lower, exploring her sumptuous form. The area where her long, elegant neck met her delicately sculptured collarbone entranced him as he imagined kissing the spot. Her skin glowed with pearlescent highlights against dark, golden honey.

Her full breasts swelled above the tight bodice of the garment she wore, riveting his attention. It was modestly cut, but to his eyes it was the most sensual display he'd ever seen. The color of the material matched her eyes and sparkled iridescent in the flickering light.

He took a step toward her, drawn by an irresistible need as he watched her rise in a fluid graceful motion that only accentuated her femininity. His eyes flared at what the rest of the garment revealed, and his jaw dropped.

The bodice ended just above her midriff, leaving his eyes to feast on the flesh of her narrow waist. The skin of her belly glistened in the glow of the small flame beside her. The light only emphasized the filmy layers of diaphanous blue hugging her hips.

The goddess in front of him was made of sea mist and moonlight. He blinked his eyes and found the sense to close his mouth, despite the fact he'd just witnessed the birth of Venus.

"I say, Alec, does she know where your pants are?" Samuel called out.

Samuel's words were like a bucket of ice water, effectively breaking the spell Alec was under. He looked away, raising an arm as he did to run a hand through his hair.

Outside, Samuel sniffed his shirtfront, and then grimaced as he tested under his arm. "Could you see if she's seen my clothes while you're at it?" Samuel requested from his place by the fire.

"I seem to be in need of some clean clothes." Alec smiled apologetically.

She leaned over the pile of blankets in the center of the tent and pulled at the edge, exposing most of their belongings. "You learn to sleep on your valuables in this land." She bashfully returned his smile, and then, to his immense pleasure, turned and reached for one of the leather bags. Through the sheer material, she displayed the nicest bottom that he'd ever seen. "Is this one yours?" She looked back over her shoulder at him.

Oh, God! How he wished . . . desire shot through him . . . *Hell!* What was he going to do? She stood up with his bag in her hand, a beautiful smile on her lips. He wondered briefly if he dared to tempt himself by getting near her. *God have mercy,* he thought as he stepped forward and placed his hand over hers to lift the strap. The touch sent a jolt of awareness through him.

"Yes," he spoke softly, his face only inches away from hers. "It is *mine.*" The word was flavored with ownership.

"I say, Alec, does she know where *mine* are?" Samuel shouted again.

Of all the irritating . . . does he do it on purpose? Alec wondered in frustration. *That idiot could drive a man of the cloth insane,* he fumed. The mood had definitely been broken, and with that realization came the unbidden one that he shouldn't be attempting what he was.

"Thank you, Genevieve." Alec cleared his throat as he stepped away from her. Having retrieved his pack, he forced himself to turn away from her. It was one of the longest walks of his life as he left her and returned to the fire.

"I say Alec—" Samuel shouted again.

"I'm right here!" Alec grumbled, "Would you desist?" Cursing, he plopped down beside Samuel. "I think I could use that drink now".

"Got a look at *The Plague,* aye?" Samuel joked with a Scottish burr.

Alec's only response was to take a long, deep pull from the flask.

"That bad, huh?" Samuel tipped his head in commiseration.

All Alec could do was wonder at the heaven he had glimpsed in those amazing blue eyes and the torture his friend had unwittingly delivered him into. How in the hell was he going to keep his hands off her? Not consummate it. . . . *Damn!* He was only human.

"I'm sorry, my good man." Samuel sighed sympathetically. "Just remember, you can still have the thing annulled when we get back. We'll return the girl to her grandfather, and then you, my friend, can marry your mother's favorite debutante." As a by note, he whispered conspiratorially, "Ahh, she doesn't have to know I married you off to someone else, right?"

"Excuse me, Lord Samuel." Genevieve's sultry voice sounded from behind, interrupting their reverie. "I have found your bag."

Alec didn't turn around, but he could tell by the indrawn breath of his friend, that he had. Samuel was stunned into silence, something that Alec had never thought to see. The dumbfounded man stared after Genevieve as she returned to the tent. Alec dared a glance towards her, immensely relieved that she'd chosen to cover the outfit he'd seen with a shawl.

"You lucky bugger!" Samuel cursed him when he did find his voice. "You owe me one."

"I'll be sure to marry you off to the next plague we run into." Alec smiled into the night as the brilliant stars shone down on them from above.

Chapter 7

Genevieve plopped down on her make-shift bed with a huff, immediately regretting the impulse. Her backside had come in contact with something quite hard underneath the coverings. She pulled out the offending metal teapot and sat back down, fingering the handle absently.

She chewed on her lip as she considered the conversation she'd overheard. "So . . . he wants an annulment," she said softly to herself. She'd been afraid something like that would happen.

She remembered how he'd looked just moments ago, half-naked, his light brown hair made darker with the water, a strand curling rakishly across his brow as he stood watching her with his smoldering amber gaze . . . He had the eyes of a lion! Just the thought of it made her tingle all over.

"Aaugh!" She stood in frustration and crossed the floor of the tent impatiently. That scoundrel had another think coming if he thought she was going to let him take advantage of her! He probably wasn't even a nobleman . . . she'd probably just been married off to a fishmonger!

There was only one thing for it. She was going to have to stay away from him. The caress of his voice as she recalled it sent shivers down her spine . . . *As far away as possible*, she promised.

~*~

Splash!

Alec dove to the ground and rolled beneath the undergrowth near the pool. He remained still, his mind racing. He had awakened, sure that he was the first to do so. Samuel was snoring softly, and Genevieve was still within the tent. Wasn't she?

There was no way she could have passed him in his sleep and not awakened him. He had an uncanny ability to sense when someone was near, even when asleep. That left only one other possibility. They now had company, and friend or foe, predator or breakfast, he intended to find out who it was.

Using his elbows to propel himself forward through the tall grasses, he slowly neared the water's edge. Alec carefully stilled himself before the reeds that bordered the pond, waiting to make sure he had not been detected. Quietly, he peered through the tall grass which concealed him.

Nothing.

Alec was sure he had heard something. A bird shrieked its discontent over his intrusion and flew towards the upper palm leaf of a nearby tree. Even though he felt ridiculous skirting around in the undergrowth, he'd learned that it paid to be careful in this land. He stood, cautiously.

Genevieve surfaced and inhaled deeply, her arms making a wide arc to each side of her lithe form as she did. Settling back into the water, she cast out her body to float onto her back. Adrift in abandoned splendor, she sighed her content.

Alec dropped back into the reeds with the speed of lightning and the grace of a toad. *Holy hell!* What did she think she was doing out here all alone . . . NAKED!!!

He couldn't believe his eyes. Thank God she hadn't seen him. "Bloody hell," he swore softly. *What am I going to do?* he wondered, while struggling to keep his eyes from straying back to the lush figure in the pool.

Alec ducked even lower behind the tall grass, trying to tear his gaze away. He had to be rational, to think. Instead, he found himself gazing at her through the reeds like a love-struck calf.

What was wrong with him? He had to get the hell out of here without. . . . Just then the light notes of a whistled tune drifted to his ears. *For the love of God!* Alec rolled his eyes. Samuel was headed his way with his usual impeccably bad timing and was sure to discover him, or worse . . . her.

Alec scrambled from the brush in the nick of time.

Samuel, not the least surprised to see Alec groveling in the dirt, greeted him cheerfully. "Top of the morning to you, Alec . . . oomph."

No sooner had the words left his mouth than Samuel found himself flat on his back with Alec's hand firmly clamped on his mouth.

"Shhh!" Alec lessened the pressure of his hand. To his own ears, it sounded as though Samuel had practically shouted the greeting at the top of his lungs. *God, I hope she didn't hear.*

"What the hell are you doing?" Samuel mumbled through Alec's fingers.

Alec tightened his grip again. "Shhh," he whispered menacingly while dragging Samuel with him as he crawled away.

Samuel struggled away and rolled to face him. "What the devil has gotten into you?" he demanded. Alec had a look of desperation in his eye that sent a chill down Samuel's spine. Never had he seen him this out of sorts. "Are we being attacked?" Alarmed, his eyes darted from side to side. Alec didn't answer, but a very feminine voice from behind him did.

"Are you gentlemen alright?" Astonished, Genevieve came upon the prone men rolling in the middle of the path with some concern.

Alec grimaced.

With a knowing look directed towards Alec, Samuel rolled over and sat up with a cheerful smile. "Why, Alec, look who's here!"

Alec tried hard not to look. It was bad enough that the image of her beautiful, naked form would forever be burned into his imagination.

Samuel sprang to his feet. "Good morning to you, Lady Genevieve! I didn't know you were such an early riser, did you, Alec?" Samuel shot him another discerning glance while he dusted himself off and continued to carry on the sort of conversation one might have upon encountering a lady during a stroll through the park.

Alec moved to his knees much more slowly than his friend had. "Good morning," he mumbled miserably. It was painfully hard to ignore her wet tendrils of hair, the blue of her eyes, and how her damp robes clung to her perfect form.

"What on earth were you doing down there?" Genevieve asked.

"He tripped," Alec said at the same time that Samuel declared, "He fell."

"I mean . . . I fell," Samuel corrected.

"Actually," Alec asserted, "I came down here—"

"What he's trying to say," Samuel clarified, "is that he thought he might have seen a *podimus ichthyosis,* but the rascal got away.

"*A podimus ichthyosis?*" Genevieve repeated skeptically.

"Why, yes," Samuel rambled on, "it's a rare species of lizard related to the—"

"Samuel, please," Alec intervened, trying to stop him.

"He does so hate it when I mention his scholarly pursuits," Samuel persisted, stopping Alec from telling her the truth.

Alec got to his feet and rubbed the back of his neck uncomfortably.

"Not to mention all of the specimens he's collected for antiquity," Samuel added prudently.

"Well, I shall leave you two to it, then." Genevieve passed by them, a hint of jasmine in the air, before turning back. "I should very much like to help you find your lizard, Lord Alec. I believe I could make a very nice trap."

Feeling trapped himself, Alec ran a hand roughly through his hair. "Thank you, but that shouldn't be necessary." Before Samuel could dig him in any deeper, he tried to change the subject. "I think we should be leaving here soon and ought to start packing."

"I shall begin, then." Genevieve nodded, then turned away.

They both watched her as she walked up the path. Alec, now all too aware of what was under the black covering draped around her, wanted to groan in frustration.

Samuel leaned towards him conspiratorially and whispered, "Do you think she meant to begin packing or trapping your lizard?"

He was grinning from ear to ear when Alec looked at him with irritation.

"What?" Samuel implied innocence. "I'm quite sure she believed us." He looked down at the grass stains on Alec's trousers. "On the other hand," his gaze followed the wide path of matted grass behind him, "maybe not."

Alec looked down at the telltale signs of his travels off the beaten path which had stained his knees, and then at the broad trail leading straight to the water's edge.

Samuel clapped Alec on the back good-naturedly. "You should have seen the look on your face." He laughed as he turned away, resuming the bawdy tune he'd been whistling earlier as he headed off toward the water.

"Do you think there're any fish in this pond?" Samuel called out, his voice fainter with distance.

"Just the mermaids," Alec mumbled surlily, tortured by the memory.

~*~

Podimus ichthyosis! Genevieve thought with irritation as she climbed the embankment. "A lizard afflicted with horny, skinned . . . feet. My foot!" Latin was one of the many languages she'd learned as a child. She was chagrined to know that they obviously thought her an imbecile, to boot. What had they been up to? she wondered, and then to her horror she realized that *he* might have seen her bathing.

She hesitantly glanced back and caught Alec still staring after her. She quickly turned away. "Oh, dear!" This was rather awkward. She felt the blush staining her cheeks reach all the way down to her toes.

~*~

Alec took the time offered him to sharpen his razor as Genevieve packed and Samuel collected the camels. Alec had tried to assist her in packing, but it quickly became clear that he had no idea how to organize their many belongings back into the packs the camels carried. Too kind to be blunt, Genevieve had asked him to fill the water skins while she cleared the tent.

Alec was almost relieved he didn't have to stand and watch her, for he could not keep the image of her naked form from his mind. Every time she bent over, he remembered her leaning over to get his bag. And when she reached up for something, he could see her surfacing in the water. It was a hard, *hard* thing to watch and not respond as he'd like.

With Samuel actually being useful for a change, Alec had finished with his own chore and busied himself by pouring some water into a tin cup. Using a small mirror tied to one of the tent poles, he lathered his face and began to shave the week's growth from it.

Standing in his shirtsleeves, suspenders dangling from his waist, Alec was halfway through his routine when the largest of the camels burst through the camp, knocking everything helter-skelter. The tent bumped into him as it collapsed, knocking the razor from his hand.

"Bloody hell!" He was damn lucky he hadn't cut himself. "You'd think these people could at least make a tent that stands up." Alec voiced his frustration as he followed the noise.

From the other side of the billowing canvas the sound of Samuel's hollering mingled with the ringing of clanging pots. Alec lithely moved around the debris in time to see Samuel, dangling from the huge camel's side like a circus act gone awry, cussing at it in blistering terms.

Much to Alec's relief, Genevieve was unharmed and had actually managed to collect the reins of the rampaging beast. She was presently clucking gently to soothe the spirited animal.

Samuel disentangled himself from the stirrup and fell, none too gently, to the ground. Shooting to his feet, he proceeded to lambaste the towering demon. His reward was a large wad of cud like the one Alec had received in his face.

Samuel sputtered, "Did you see that?" Outraged, he turned to where Alec had come to stand by Genevieve. "I did nothing to this animal," he claimed with his arm raised, his finger pointing toward the beast.

"I highly recommend a refreshing dip in the pool," Alec responded calmly.

Samuel sputtered and might have said more if the slime hadn't been threatening his upper lip. Left with no alternative, he turned briskly and stomped away, his back rigid and his arms swinging stiffly at his sides.

Alec turned to Genevieve, noticing, as he did, the suppressed merriment in her face, not to mention the mischievous glint in her eyes.

Genevieve, in turn, looked at Alec and noted the half-lathered face, a missing sideburn, and a charming dimple threatening his cheek. She couldn't help it. She started to giggle.

At the sound of her delightful peal, he too started to laugh. Only as their merriment subsided did she once again gaze up at him. His breath caught in his chest at the sight of her upturned face and sparkling eyes.

Unable to help herself, she reached forward and dabbed a long finger lightly across his cheek, coming away with a creamy white froth she proudly displayed on her finger for him to see. "I think that you should finish what you started, Lord Alec."

Looking up at him, she smiled. The color of his eyes darkened considerably in response. Genevieve suddenly felt very shy, casting her gaze downward briefly.

God, this woman is beautiful, Alec thought as he stared down at her, his throat suddenly dry. Her words had him thinking of things he'd like to finish. Hell, the things he'd like to start. She was definitely put on this earth to tempt a man.

The camel saved him from further action as it bellowed its discontent while stomping its foot against the entangled rope, rattling the pots it had corralled. Alec was grateful for the interruption. He felt an overwhelming urge to enfold her in his arms and kiss her. He swallowed hard to keep his hands and thoughts in check. *Damn!* he groaned inwardly. He certainly had his work cut out for him if he was going to stay away from this woman.

"Oh, dear," Genevieve said, turning away. "It looks as though Cupid has had enough of this. I think his foot might be caught."

Cupid? Alec thought with surprise, trying to reconcile the name with the hairy beast as he went behind the animal and removed the offending rope. Even though its foot was free, the camel again favored its weight, the toe of its hind leg barely touching the ground.

"I think he may have hurt it." Genevieve's brow knit in concern.

Alec felt the animal's rear flank and carefully examined its ankle. "It doesn't seem broken."

"Oh, poor baby," Genevieve crooned. "We'll have to stay another day."

That thought gripped Alec with fear. He wanted as much distance between them and her tribesmen as he could get. He had a feeling it wouldn't be a good thing to run into them again. An odd sense of protectiveness rose up in his breast as he watched her. The sensation disturbed him more than a little.

Genevieve walked over to the tent and started sifting through the chaos with the great beast hobbling after her, groaning in misery. She produced several sweet dates from one of the sacks on the ground and fed the cantankerous animal while speaking softly to it.

Cupid, Alec realized, was almost as good as Samuel when it came to getting something he wanted. He watched in amazement as the beast nuzzled her for more of the sweet meat while resting its back foot solidly on the ground. In fact, Alec surmised, the surly animal might even be better at it than Samuel.

Alec smiled to himself. They weren't the only ones that knew how to get what they wanted. He walked forward and stroked the muzzle of the wily old rascal as he spoke. "He'll be fine. Look, he's already walking on it."

Genevieve looked at him doubtfully as she continued to soothe the great, hairy beast.

Alec then asserted his clever plan by saying, "He should be able to bear his own weight soon. We'll just have to ride double for a day or so."

~*~

Waves of heat shimmered in the distance. The desert, awash with the current, enveloped the riders as they journeyed across the white expanse. Genevieve hadn't realized it was possible for two people to sit together on the back of a camel and yet stay so far apart from each other. She had to stifle the urge to laugh at the sight. It actually appeared as though a large "V" was wedged between the men as they rode a short distance away.

Alec cursed his luck again. So much for thinking he could insist she ride with him. All he'd received for his efforts was Samuel's non-stop grumbling.

"I swear to God, if I ever set eyes on another camel after this, it will be too soon," Samuel groaned as he swayed with the animal's motion.

"What was that again about how horses don't do well out here?" Alec reminded him. "Something about how they have a tendency to expire without water?"

"And I'm sure you'll never let me forget that either," Samuel complained. "But you can't blame this one on me. It wasn't my dimwitted idea that left us in this situation. Couldn't you have come up with a better scheme to get her to ride with you than to convince her that the camel shouldn't be ridden?"

"Obviously my plan backfired."

"Oh, yes, the *plan*." Samuel leaned closer. "The *plan* was to find the tomb the map speaks of, yet now that we're here, you're suddenly hell-bent for England."

"No, the real reason I left was to avoid getting married, and since you rather neatly handled that for me, I am now fulfilling my obligation to take her back home."

"Oh, come on, what if we were to just show her the map?" Samuel hedged. "What harm could come of that?"

"We're through!" Alec looked back at him crossly. "The only place we're going is back to England."

"You're not even slightly curious?" Samuel attempted to goad him.

"No!"

"How can you say no when we haven't even shown it to her?" Samuel threw his hands up in dismay.

"We showed the last guide, if you recall, just before he stole our water and left us for dead," Alec retorted.

"Yes, but he obviously didn't have the foggiest clue how to read it," Samuel rushed on. "At least now we have someone who really may be able to."

"No!" Alec repeated sternly. "And no more buts, either."

"How can you say that, especially when we're right here?" Samuel demanded. "For the love of God, man, we can't just leave when we're this close."

"We're not close." Alec turned in his seat. "Not by a long shot! That damn map is so old, we're off by centuries. If we'd embarked on this journey a couple of millennia ago, it may have proved useful."

"It could still be here."

"Even if we knew where *here* is, it would still be impossible." Alec tapped his ear. "Haven't you been listening? It's too damn old. *Hell!* If the clues haven't disintegrated, they've almost certainly been swallowed up by the desert."

"What if she's heard the riddle?" Samuel said, choosing another route. "Didn't you think it odd that our last guide became so nervous after we asked him about it?"

"We're going back to England." Alec's voice was flat.

"No!" Samuel stubbornly declared. "You're going back to England. I'm staying right here."

"You can't possibly be serious," Alec said with censure.

"And why not?" Samuel asked, with the lack of it.

"Why not? For one thing, your mother would kill me if I returned without you."

"Don't give me that!" Samuel sputtered indignantly. "I'm a grown man. . . . Bloody hell! I certainly don't need you or my mother to protect me!"

Truly irked, Samuel fought the urge to clobber him; instead, he swung his leg over. "I believe I'd rather walk," he added stiffly before jumping down from the camel. "And don't forget the times I've saved your skin, Alec!" Samuel yelled after him.

"Damn it all to hell!" He'd be damned if he was going to stop for the lout. The hothead could just walk it off. The fool always did have a quick temper, Alec thought irritably. Glancing back, he was surprised to see that Genevieve had stopped to pick up the braggart.

"Why, that damn little sneak!" Alec swore under his breath.

"Unreasonable, bloody. . . ." Samuel was grumbling as he walked.

"It's quite a bit farther." Genevieve rode up beside the unlikely pedestrian. "Do you really want to walk?"

"Not especially," his surly tone surprised her, "but I could not tolerate my circumstances any longer."

Genevieve wondered what could have happened between the two. She'd seen the heat cause this type of thing before. Concerned, she offered him a skin of water.

He looked up optimistically. "Double malt scotch?"

"Sorry, plain old water," Genevieve responded lightly. "Take some. It will do you good."

Samuel eyed it dubiously, but took a swig of it anyway. "Aaugh, you're truly a saint, Lady Genevieve, to offer me anything but poison after what I've done to you."

Genevieve raised a brow at this. He seemed so sincere she couldn't help but ask. "What have you done, Lord Samuel?"

"What have I done? Why, the worst thing imaginable," he practically snorted. "I have done the most horrible deed conceivable." His expression was pained as he looked up at her. "Please tell me you'll forgive me for marrying you to that miserable, ill-begotten . . ." he paused, remembering himself, "Sorry."

Genevieve raised both brows in surprise at this and wanted to laugh. She was starting to see the ploy. No doubt, the *ill-begotten one* had put him up to this. She hesitated for a moment before saying, "You needn't say this on my account." She lifted her chin. "You needn't try to spare my feelings. I know that he intends to annul our marriage when we return to England."

Samuel practically fell over in surprise at her comment. "You do?"

He seemed so taken aback by her confession that she rushed on. "Yes, and I'm quite relieved too."

"You are?"

Genevieve fixed him with her steady regard. "Why, yes, I didn't know how to broach the subject myself."

"Really," Samuel responded with astonishment. "Does this mean that you'll forgive me after, all?"

"Of course," Genevieve stated with certainty. "Would you care to ride with me, and we can discuss it further?"

Samuel accepted gladly, listening to her as he climbed up.

"Actually," Genevieve continued optimistically, "I was rather hopeful that we wouldn't have to tell anyone back in England and avoid the annulment altogether."

Samuel's brows shot up in surprise as he seated himself. "I say, that is rather forward thinking of you."

"Well," Genevieve said, "considering it took place against the wishes of both bride and groom, I don't think it's legally binding."

He coughed uncomfortably. "You may be right."

Not wanting to beat around the bush any longer, Genevieve stayed her course. "Once we are back in Cairo, I believe that it would be best if I employ a female chaperone to accompany me back to England."

"You do?"

"Why, yes. It will solve all sorts of problems upon my arrival. Don't you agree?" Genevieve asked.

"I think it's a wonderful solution." Samuel nodded.

Alec had slowed his mount considerably, Samuel noticed, as they passed him. Alec gave him a look that bespoke of dire consequences. In response, Samuel waved cheerfully, mocking him with a sardonic smile.

Alec had had quite enough and rode up beside them. "Don't listen to a damn thing he has to say."

"Excuse me?" Genevieve responded anxiously.

Samuel threw his hands up in innocence. "What?"

"I know what you're up to, and it won't work!" Alec's eyes narrowed on the braggart.

"It won't?" Genevieve asked hesitantly.

"No! I'll not permit it," Alec stated vehemently, with his gaze fixed on the troublemaker behind her.

"But why in heavens not?" Distraught, Genevieve pleaded with him. "Surely you can't mean to keep it?"

"You'd have to find it first."

"Find it?" Confused, Genevieve looked from one to the other. "What are you talking about?"

Alec couldn't help but notice her perplexed expression. "What are you talking about?"

Samuel decided to spare them both and chimed in. "He's blathering about a silly old map," he said to Genevieve, then turned to look pointedly at Alec, "and she's decided to let you off easy, old chap, and forget you were ever married."

"What do you mean forget?" Alec demanded, looking toward Genevieve for an explanation.

"What map?" Genevieve asked in turn, looking to Samuel for hers.

Chapter 8

"Did I say map?" Samuel asked as he looked over at Alec, who was glaring at him. "Yes, well, apparently, it will lead us to an endangered cat." It was almost the truth.

"Cat?" Genevieve glanced back at him.

"Why, yes. It would probably surprise you to know that we are here on a scientific expedition." Samuel gave Alec a conspiratorial wink. "You know Alec has several degrees in zoology and physiology."

"Really?" Amazed by the information, Genevieve looked over to Alec, who seemed rather embarrassed by the praise. "So there really is a horny toad?"

"Lizard," Alec corrected.

"Yes," Samuel grinned over her head, "nasty little buggers." When Genevieve turned around, he quickly wrinkled his nose for her benefit.

"I take it that's not your specialty?" she said over her shoulder.

"I've been accused of worse, I suppose," he laughingly said. "Actually, I have a degree in mathematics, but I believe that I have a real knack for languages, especially those of love."

Alec shook his head and threw his eyes up in dismay.

Genevieve smiled as she watched him. "Do you have a degree in that as well?"

"He's an honorary linguist," Alec replied sarcastically. "And whatever you do, don't let him negotiate for you."

"Well, I never." Samuel smiled at the insult. "Why, you'd think he'd be grateful. It's not every day when a man is blessed by such beauty . . . and all because of my considerable skill in the art of haggling."

Genevieve laughed. "I was wondering how it was that you merited being married to the Plague of Egypt?" she looked over at Alec as she spoke. "Now I know."

"Well now, that is actually one of the good things he's done." Alec smiled, showing her the dimple in his cheek. "You should have been there when—"

"Alright, alright," Samuel interrupted. "I believe she gets the idea. But since you brought it up, I've been dying to know how it is that you became known by such a horrid name."

"It was actually meant to protect me," Genevieve confessed.

"Protect you from what?" Samuel asked, puzzled.

"Getting married."

"Well," Samuel snorted with a laugh, "that certainly backfired, didn't it?"

"It worked surprisingly well for eight years."

"Is that how long you've been out here?" Alec looked at the beauty who rode beside him with empathy.

She nodded. "It did keep me from becoming one of the sheik's many wives."

"Good grief." Samuel was clearly mortified. "I'm glad you found a way around that one. But, tell me, why did the sheik say that you caught the whole village on fire, and that you could wilt a man with a look?"

"The sheik is an idiot." Alec looked at Samuel as if the sheik wasn't the only one.

"It's actually true." Genevieve couldn't help but laugh at their expressions.

Alec coughed while Samuel sputtered. "It is?"

"Yes, well . . . partially."

"Which part?" Samuel asked despite himself.

Alec gave him a look that spoke of dire consequences.

"Well, the fire was a complete accident. You see, I had been left to tend the cooking. It was very smoky, and I thought, if I removed some of the grease, it would help. Unfortunately, I tripped, and it splashed onto a pile of kindling that was too close to the brazier. Before I could stop it, the pile burst into flame." She laughed at the memory. "I was so startled. I probably wasn't thinking clearly. I should have left the container of oil where it was, but I was afraid it would cause further damage, so I took it with me. I hadn't realized it was leaking as I ran to get help. The flames followed me everywhere until the grease had run out."

"Apparently, you ran quite far," Samuel guessed as he looked over at Alec with a brow raised.

"No, not really, just to the sheik's tent, where the meeting of the elders was being held."

"I'm beginning to see why he was so motivated," Samuel remarked, "but what about the other . . . thing?"

"Oh, that was Aura's idea. She's the old woman of the tribe," Genevieve clarified.

"Is she the woman you went to speak with after the ceremony?" Alec asked.

"Why, yes." Genevieve looked at him shyly, startled that he'd noticed. Glancing quickly away, she continued with the tale. "It's said she has the gift of sight. Of course, that's debatable. She is, however, quite the prankster. She used to tell little Habieb that, if he should continue to lie, toads would spring from his mouth. He didn't stop until he awoke one morning with frogs in his bed."

"She sounds like my grandmother." Samuel laughed.

"Aura decided that if she told the women of the tribe that, should a man get near me, he would suffer," Genevieve paused, "um—great loss to his—um. . . ."

"Oh, yes. . . . *Great loss.*" Samuel nodded in understanding.

"It wasn't until I was left to watch the sheep that the fib actually grew to biblical proportions."

"Why is that?" Samuel couldn't help but ask.

"The sheep fed upon a particular bush that I didn't know to keep them away from. As a result, they didn't go into season again for another month. It only proved the lack of male potency in my presence."

"Oh," Samuel expelled a breath, "is that why?"

Alec hadn't been aware that he too had been holding his breath until he let it out. Both he and Samuel exchanged a look of relief.

"Of course." Genevieve was taken aback. "You didn't actually believe that nonsense did you?"

"Of course not," Samuel announced at the same time as Alec denounced it saying, "No, no . . . I never entertained the notion." Again their eyes met over her head.

"Well, I don't know about you, but I've had just about enough of this for one day." Samuel stretched. "What say you, Alec? How about letting up on this grueling pace? It's not as though wild dogs are nipping at our heels."

Alec was surprised at how closely this described how he felt. He had been thinking about continuing till dusk just to put more distance between the tribesmen and themselves. Damned if he could shake the feeling of being followed.

"Just think of this lovely young lady's sensibilities," Samuel interjected when it looked as though Alec might keep on going.

"Oh, I'm fine, really." Genevieve reassured them with a nod.

"No, no. I must insist." Samuel inclined his head. "Look, there's a nice area over there by that rock that looks like an elephant." He pointed to one of the many rock formations that decorated the landscape. "Besides, I'm absolutely famished."

Alec took stock of their immediate surroundings. The occasional rock outcrop slowly gave way to cliffs that bordered the land in the distance. The sun was sitting lower on the horizon, creating long shadows from the towering structures.

"I think that crevasse in the rocks over there would be an even better spot. Plus, we'd have protection from the elements under the overhang." Alec pointed to the area, although he was thinking more about sheltering them from the human element, rather than the other.

"Excellent," Samuel readily agreed.

Alec wasted no time setting up the tent after they stopped. He created a small enclosure for her use by simply fastening a rope from each side of the rock walls and stringing a cord taut across the expanse. After that, he simply draped fabric over the line.

Samuel saw to the camels while Genevieve prepared a meal of dried meats, cheese, flatbread, and dates. She created a table by dragging her trunk onto a blanket and then placing the saddles around it for back support. All in all, it was quite comfortable.

~*~

"Ah, that's just what I needed." Samuel sat back with a sigh after he'd consumed a plateful. "Tell me, Genevieve, are you familiar with any of the ancient stories of this land?"

She nodded. "Some of them."

"Have you heard the story that tells of a Sphinx which stands guard over a city? In order for you to pass, she asks you a riddle. If you cannot answer it, she devours you."

"It sounds familiar." She thoughtfully nibbled on a date as she considered it. "What is the riddle?"

"What has four legs when it's born, two legs as an adult, and three legs when it dies."

Alec seemed to grow more annoyed with Samuel as he spoke. "Not this again," he groaned. "Genevieve, would you care for more figs?"

"Yes, please." She watched as he stood up.

"None for me, thanks," Samuel piped up, even though Alec hadn't offered him any.

"Promise me you'll not get bitten by the treasure bug too." Alec called over his shoulder as he walked away.

"Treasure?" She turned to look at Samuel with surprise, masking her sudden feeling of concern. "I thought you were on an expedition?"

"Well, we are. You see, the map tells of a sacred cat. It's far easier to show you," Samuel replied as he raised his pant leg, exposing the top of his boot.

Against all odds, the scroll that Samuel pulled out was none other than the one her father had on him when he'd been killed. Genevieve stared as he unfolded it and spread it out before them on the makeshift table.

"Where did you get this?" Genevieve barely recognized her own voice as she asked it. She leaned forward, studying the scroll before her, though it was hardly necessary for her to do so. She knew every line, every crinkle in the piece of parchment; that is, with the exception of the dark stain that now marred the upper corner. She could barely control her trembling when she realized what it might be . . . blood.

She felt her own blood drain from her face as she stared at the discoloration, which might very well have come from her own father. She took great care to control her reaction and discreetly folded her hands in her lap to conceal their shaking.

"Aaugh, well, that was Alec's doing." Samuel interrupted her thoughts. "He won it in a card game, of all places."

Alec, she noticed, was still busily rummaging through the food sacks.

Genevieve had to still her panic; she could feel her heartbeat racing in her chest. How could this be? Had all the years of hiding in the desert been for naught? She watched as Samuel mulled over the Egyptian writing on the one side. He then flipped it over, displaying the side with the seven-pointed star.

Samuel leaned forward, pointing to the drawing. "The circle within a circle in the center depicts the land with the ocean surrounding it." He glanced up to see if he had her attention.

She nodded her understanding, not trusting her voice.

Encouraged by her avid interest, Samuel continued by indicating the area at the top of the map, placing his finger between the two star points closest to the top. "This, of course, indicates north."

Genevieve raised her brows. Could they truly be this misinformed?

"Within the circles lie two long rectangles which cross in the center, forming a shape much like that of the letter 'I'. The small horizontal one on top," Samuel ran his finger over it, "represents the Mediterranean Sea, and the vertical one is the Nile River."

Genevieve watched, further amazed by his explanation as he pointed to where he thought the treasure lay. "Right here in the center," he said, placing his finger where the two rectangles crossed.

"How did you discover that?" Genevieve finally found her voice.

"It makes perfect sense." Samuel grinned up at her. "'X' marks the spot." Humor sparkled in his eyes as he said it. "Like all great treasure maps."

Genevieve forced a smile of her own before focusing down on the map. She didn't want him to see the turmoil within her own eyes. The area where he thought the treasure lay was directly in the center of the map, indicated by a red circle marked suspiciously with an "X" in the center of it.

"Actually, I had this translated by an understudy of Champollion himself," Samuel stated, obviously proud of the achievement.

They had it translated. . . . Oh, dear God! Do they know?

"It seems the circle with a cross inside it ⊗ is not only the hieroglyphic symbol for a city, but the place where the tomb is to be found."

"Do you know what city it is?" she asked, a frown furrowing her brow.

"Unfortunately," Samuel sighed, "that still remains a mystery."

She let out the air she had been unconsciously holding. *They don't know.*

"But there is a key," he added, searching through his jacket. Pulling a flask out of his pocket, he smiled sheepishly. "You just never know when it might come in handy."

From deeper within the pocket, he retrieved a small book. "Ah, here it is," he smiled, "just where I left it." With the look of a magician who had just pulled a rabbit out of his hat, he displayed his find. "In my notes, I have a symbol."

He'd opened his book and pointed to a collection of hieroglyphic symbols. "It is the symbol for life, the ankh."

Genevieve studied the page, seeing the precise drawings he had made on the paper. "And you believe that this is the key?"

"Yes, you see, it opens the tomb."

She swallowed, trying to make her voice sound as light as possible. "How does it do that?"

"I'm not sure, but I believe the answer lies in the mystery of the language itself. You see, first we have the symbol of the

Egyptian ankh, ⚲ followed by a jagged line, which represents water ∿∿∿ and sounds like 'n'." He glanced up at her. "The ebb and flow of life."

"This symbol here," ⊜ Samuel excitedly pointed to another symbol, completely oblivious to her turmoil. His finger hovered above the etchings, "The one that looks like a ball of string or," Samuel leaned towards her conspiratorially, "I have also heard that it may be a placenta."

"Excuse me," Genevieve raised her brows in dismay over his bizarre revelation, "did you say placenta?"

"Sorry, my dear, if I speak too candidly." Samuel seemed sincerely alarmed that his frankness might have shocked her sensibilities.

"Good heavens, no . . . I was just surprised," Genevieve reassured him.

He looked back to the page. "The *ball of string* is pronounced 'kh', as in Bach, the composer."

He looked up to her and smiled. "See, not only does this pictorially spell 'ankh', but, phonetically, it also depicts the word, 'n-kh', or 'ankh'. Brilliant, isn't it?"

She nodded wordlessly as she scanned the page. Samuel had written many symbols with their meanings next to them. Most of them were correct, she noted, with one exception, ◁ "T", which he'd labeled 'bun' or 'loaf of bread'.

It was indeed the symbol for "T", but it was hardly a sticky bun. She certainly wasn't going to argue the point, however, since it was in her favor that he was so confused. She watched as he went to close the book. "You are a very good artist. May I see it?"

Samuel looked mildly uncomfortable at her request. He cleared his throat, saying rather apologetically, "I'm sorry, Lady Genevieve, but I have many drawings from the temples of. . . ." He looked over to Alec as if he could be of some help. He wasn't. In fact, he looked to be avoiding anything to do with the map.

"I'm rather chagrined to admit to you that there is much here that would be. . . ." Samuel paused, trying furtively to put it delicately. He cleared his throat again. "Not for the viewing of young ladies," he finished uncomfortably as he placed it back inside his pocket.

Grasping at anything that might keep him talking, Genevieve smiled encouragingly. "Did you say Jean-Francois Champollion?"

More than willing to change the subject from the dangers of his diary to a safer one, Samuel responded with a certain degree of relief. "Why yes . . . you've heard of him?"

"I've been living in something quite close to isolation," Genevieve confessed. "I do, however, remember hearing something about his genius."

"But of course you must have known of him, how else would you know how to read all of this?" Samuel laughed as the obvious occurred to him. "Tell me, what do you make of it?"

Genevieve practically froze at his words. "Who told you such a thing?"

"Why, the sheik, of course." Samuel looked baffled. "He told me you were proficient in all the ancient languages of these lands."

"I'm sorry, Samuel, but you were misled." Breathing became difficult as she waited to see if he believed her.

Alec, having listened to their conversation as he rummaged through the bags, joined in. "That's perfect!" he laughingly joked. "She obviously doesn't know a thing about it." Alec seemed to truly enjoy Samuel's dismay.

Incredulous, Samuel sat back, stymied. "I can't believe he deceived me."

"It's about time someone pulled the wool over your eyes." Alec reveled in the information as he plopped down beside her, offering a plate of dried figs. "My hat's off to the man!"

Genevieve accepted a piece, if for no other reason than to keep her hands busy, her appetite having been squelched by the advent of the map. "Thank you." She nodded, looking at him. "I don't understand. If the map shows the city where the Nile meets the sea, shouldn't you be looking there for it?"

Alec shrugged while Samuel answered her. "Excellent question. I asked that of Champollion's understudy myself."

She turned to him. "What did he say?"

"Apparently these seven circles scattered throughout the map somehow place the 'X' in different locations." Samuel indicated seven circles that dotted the other side of the map.

"Oh, I see," Genevieve said.

"Really? Because I'm quite confused." Samuel's brow was furrowed as he looked down at the parchment.

She breathed uneasily. Had she said too much?

"Our last guide told us he knew exactly where it was located." Samuel briefly glanced her way. "Unfortunately, we now know that he duped us."

"He means left us for dead," Alec clarified, an edge to his voice.

"Really?" Genevieve's eyes widened with that information.

Alec nodded in answer as he threw up a date, catching it in his teeth.

It didn't appear she would get any information from him as she watched him chew. She looked back over to Samuel, who was still intent on the drawings. "I believe I have heard something of this riddle," Genevieve offered up, hoping he might reveal more. He looked up with interest as she spoke. "It's a fable from the city of Memphis. The answer being ma-"

"Man." Both Alec and Samuel finished at the same time.

"We actually managed to crack that one." Samuel smiled at her. "Man, who crawls when he is born, stands upright as an adult, and walks with a cane when he's old. We've been there, but the other clues didn't match. I was hoping you might have heard of another Sphinx, somewhere else."

"What other clues are there?" Genevieve asked.

"Where the cat arches over the door," Alec announced prophetically.

"Have you been to the Temple of Hathor, which is dedicated to the goddess Bastet?" It was the very least she could do . . . mislead them.

"No, I don't think we've seen it." Samuel pulled another map out and spread it over the table. "Where is it?"

"If I remember correctly, it is here." Genevieve pointed to an area north of the Temple of Karnak.

"I think we should add this to the list of possibilities." Samuel enthusiastically looked over to Alec, who rolled his eyes in response. "What?" Samuel eyed him defensively. "It's on the way back home."

"You actually think you're going to find it?" Alec assessed him critically.

"It's got to be somewhere." Samuel folded up the map.

"I think it might as well be on the moon," Alec countered.

Genevieve choked on the date she was chewing with that revelation.

Alec leaned forward to pat her on the back. "Are you all right?" he asked with concern.

She nodded. "Please excuse me, will you?"

"Of course." He stood to assist her. She flushed as he helped her up. The dimple in his cheek deepened as he noticed. She looked away shyly before taking her leave.

"She seemed rather choked up," Samuel whispered as soon as she was out of earshot. "Do you think she'll abscond in the middle of the night like the last guide?"

Alec looked over to him. "You don't ever stop, do you?"

"What?" Samuel replied. "I'm just trying to be careful, considering what happened the last time I showed someone."

"If that was the case, I think you'd find it far more effective if you just remained silent," Alec commented dryly.

"Where would be the fun in that?" Samuel bandied back. "You should calm yourself, Alec. You're like a clock that's wound so tight it's only a matter of time until you pop a spring." He sat back, taking his flask out for a nip. "You don't think she'll steal our water now, do you? Perhaps we should tie it to the camels."

"She just might leave with those too." Alec looked at him with irritation. "I know. . . . Why don't you tie it to your person?"

"Excellent idea, I'll do that."

Alec threw his eyes heavenward and shook his head in disbelief.

Chapter 9

Genevieve was sitting on a rock that looked out over the desert, watching the sun sink below the horizon as Alec walked up behind her. A full moon had already risen in the east.

He watched her for a moment, amazed at how breathtakingly lovely she was. "It's beautiful isn't it?" he said softly. She appeared to be in such deep thought that his words startled her. "Excuse me, I didn't mean to frighten you," he added quickly.

She looked up at him and smiled in relief. "Sorry, I'm not usually so easily startled."

The striking color of her eyes held him entranced for a moment. He had to give himself a mental shake before he spoke. "I was wondering if you would like some of the *kaf* that I prepared . . . to take the chill off."

"Thank you." She accepted the mug in his hands with a smile, then coughed after taking a sip. It had to be the worst concoction she'd ever tasted, and some of the brews that Aura had made were positively lethal. She managed to swallow the bitter liquid, giving him a weak smile.

"Too strong?" He stood awkwardly before her. "I'm sorry. You don't have to finish it."

She watched him drag a hand through his hair as he turned to stare out over the silvery landscape. He looked like a man with a lot on his mind. She wondered what troubled him the most, the map or their marital vows.

"Would you care to join me?" she invited, scooting over to make room on the rock where she sat. She knew she was playing with fire as soon as the idea occurred to her, but she needed some answers, even if it meant resorting to using her feminine wiles to get them.

"Yes, thank you." Alec smiled as he seated himself rather stiffly at her side, leaving several inches between them. One might think there was a ballroom full of matrons chaperoning them, instead of just the two of them beneath the light of the full moon.

A romantic scene . . . Genevieve thought, wondering how to best use it to her advantage. She'd no idea that she'd feel this insecure once she started to play the vixen. Pushing her fears aside, she mentally urged herself, *You can do this!* Women had done this since the beginning of time. How hard could it be?

She adjusted her position on the rock, making sure to allow her scarf to slip as she moved, exposing a creamy shoulder and just a hint of cleavage. "I was just wondering," she purred.

"I was just thinking . . ." Alec began at exactly the same time. "Ladies first," he said, turning towards her.

Awkwardly, the moment she looked into his eyes, all thoughts fled into the night. How did he do that to her? she wondered as she tried to fill the silence with something. She shivered instead.

"Are you cold?"

"A little, but I'm fine." She hesitantly glanced over at him, aware that he had nothing but his arms to offer for warmth. What was she thinking? It was going to be difficult to remain in control of this situation if she couldn't keep her head about her.

Alec reached forward and pulled her scarf back up over her shoulder in a purely platonic fashion.

Oh, bother! This was going to be harder than she thought. She looked out at the star-filled sky, plotting her next move.

"I wanted to talk to you about our *marriage*," Alec hesitantly started. "I'm glad you're agreeable to . . ." he paused, "to. . . ."

"You mean . . . forgetting about it," she added helpfully, watching him.

"Yes— I mean. It's not that I—umm," he cleared his throat. Alec had hoped to apologize for the circumstances in which they found themselves, though he was frustrated by his need to explain himself at all. Her eyes were far too expressive; he could see that his words pained her, even though she tried to hide it.

Damn! This was more awkward than he ever envisioned. He'd thought to forge a truce, though watching her in the moonlight was a savage temptation, especially when all he wanted to do was kiss her.

"I don't. . . ." He paused as he gazed down into her upturned face, she was so lovely. It had been hell to pull up her wrap when all he wanted to do was rip it off.

"Wish to be married?" Genevieve prompted as she quickly looked away.

"Right. . . ." Alec blurted out, realizing that his attempt at an apology was having a disastrous effect. He was so distracted by her that it was hard to think. He always seemed to make a complete ass of himself around this woman.

What happened to his ability to lie? He could have said something charming and had her in his arms instead. *No!* He silently berated himself. He could not afford to start something with her.

She spoke up, saving him from his inner conflict. "I am glad that you're agreeable to forgetting about our . . . marriage. I believe we can consider it annulled by mutual consent," she continued in a remarkably businesslike fashion.

It was amazing the strength of backbone the pain of rejection could create. *Just like a proper English miss*, she thought, embracing her heritage. *I have a stiff spine and an even stiffer upper lip.*

"I couldn't agree more." Alec, all too aware of the conflict within himself, couldn't help but wonder at it. What the hell was wrong with him? He should be happy that she was agreeable to forgetting about their marriage. *Right?*

He'd been staring at her throughout the conversation, but he was startled when she turned to look at him. Her eyes, lit softly by the moon, shimmered like pools. Alec wanted to kiss her now more than ever.

With her face turned slightly up towards him, Genevieve's lips beckoned. God, he wanted her. In this moment, under the stars, he wanted this woman more than any other he'd ever known.

"I'm relieved that you understand, and that you're not going to," she started to say before being distracted by the smoldering heat she saw within his eyes, "going to. . . ." Struck speechless by the longing she saw there, she could feel herself lean forward, drawn by the pull of his gaze.

Covering the rest of the distance between them, Alec's lips touched hers. His kiss was both soft and demanding. His arms enfolded her in an embrace that only succeeded in deepening his kiss. His lips urged hers to open, and his tongue caressed hers in intimate play.

With a groan, he pulled away from her, abruptly ending their kiss. Alec stood, dragging a hand roughly through his hair again. "I'm so sorry, Genevieve." He practically shook with desire. "Please forgive me. I just can't seem to trust myself around you."

Genevieve sat where she was, stunned again, utterly and completely speechless.

"You'd better go back," he whispered hoarsely before tearing his gaze from her and turning around.

She had been playing with fire, she knew, but she never imagined that his kiss would ignite her so. So much for seducing him for information. Why did she think she was up to the task?

She had the momentary urge to throw caution to the wind and go to him. Thank God she now had a stiff spine. . . . She practically ran away.

Holy hell! Alec expelled the breath he'd been holding after she left.

~*~

Genevieve was more than a little relieved that Samuel was already asleep when she came rushing back. She wasn't up to facing his scrutiny after her botched attempt to seduce her estranged husband for information.

She'd been hoping that a little flirting would loosen his tongue. It most certainly had, though not in the way she'd planned. Genevieve hated to admit it, but she was totally out of her league when it came to Alec.

What else could she do? The map had changed everything. Her lip caught in her teeth as she looked down at Samuel. He was sleeping in his boots. She let out a puff of air and looked about her. Separating him from the map would be problematic as long as he carried it on his person.

If only she had a scorpion, she thought mischievously. He'd be out of his boots quick enough then. Genevieve watched the unsuspecting man sleep for a moment longer. She had no alternative but to let him keep the treasure map for the time being; she had more important things to do than to attempt to remove his footwear.

Samuel had moved the trunk off the blanket so as to bed down where it had been. Strangely, it also appeared that he'd tied himself to the water bags. What a bizarre thing to do. She wondered at it as she carefully stepped around the area, where he snored softly, and began to slowly tug on the trunk's handle. It made a horrible scraping sound as she dragged it over a rock. There was no help for it; the trunk was too heavy for her to pick up.

Samuel murmured, rolling onto his side. Genevieve paused, waiting to make sure he was still asleep. She breathed a sigh of relief when he started snoring again. Good grief, the last thing she wanted to do was have to explain why she felt the need to have the trunk next to her all of a sudden.

Once he'd settled back down, she gently untied his rope and pulled the trunk past the water bags. Moving quickly, she retied the rope and then continued to slowly drag it toward the curtain. She was hoping to get it there before Alec returned.

It was surprising that Samuel could sleep through the racket she was making, but then again, everything seemed amplified to her ears. Her breathing alone sounded loud enough to wake the dead. His comatose state was probably due to the many nips he'd taken from his flask after dinner, she decided.

It took several more tugs on the trunk to get it safely behind the draped curtain. Genevieve waited, her ears still attuned for any noises made by either of her traveling companions. Once she was sure that she hadn't alerted anyone to her presence, she lit the small oil lamp and eyed the trunk she had worked so hard to haul inside with her.

What a difference a day makes, she thought, reminding herself that it was only yesterday morning that the sheik's guards had taken the trunk away and informed her she was to be married. It had been a shocking development, to say the least, but nothing compared to the turmoil of seeing the map again.

Winning it in a game of cards just might be the worst luck that she'd ever heard of, if that was indeed the truth. If they truly didn't know what they had, then they probably weren't even aware of the very real danger they were in.

If they did know . . . she blew a soft puff of air out as she considered it. She'd been plopped right into the thick of it, as they say, and she could not afford to let the trunk out of her sight, especially now that she knew what her companions were really after.

Kneeling down beside the trunk, Genevieve opened it, sifting through the books on top. Everything looked fine, even though they weren't exactly as she'd left them. The trunk had been jostled quite a bit lately. The book that mattered the most to her wasn't among these, anyway. She felt for the hidden latch and pulled it. A secret compartment in the lid opened up. She breathed a sigh of relief . . . it was still there.

Genevieve removed the old book reverently. She opened the back cover and gently lifted the edge, exposing a folded piece of paper hidden within the lining. She carefully unfolded it. It was an exact copy of the map that Samuel had shown her earlier.

Tucking the map back inside the cover, Genevieve set it aside and began to pace back and forth, so lost in thought she almost didn't realize that Alec had returned.

Concerned that he might need another article of clothing or something else entirely, she quickly placed the book back in the secret compartment and closed the trunk. She was careful not to make too much noise as she slowly dressed for bed and blew out the light.

Sleep, however, would not come so easily. Her mind kept returning to how it had felt to be in his arms . . . and to the feel of his lips.

~*~

Alec arose, aware that he'd barely slept, his back a painful reminder of it. Images of Genevieve had kept him awake the whole night. *Damn it all to hell!* He was never going to be the same after this. Last night when she'd left him, he'd been hard-pressed not to run after her, crush her to him, and kiss her as he wanted.

Oh, hell! He groaned, a scowl knitting his brow. She'd been like warm satin in his arms, her response like liquid fire when he'd kissed her. The kiss, however, wasn't the only memory that had tortured him all night long.

When he'd returned, she'd been pacing the area behind the curtain he'd unwittingly strung up. She might as well have not been wearing anything at all as the light from her lamp went right through the thin veils of her clothing while she undressed. *God help me,* he thought as he remembered the striptease she'd unknowingly treated him to.

"Top of the morning to y—" Samuel's morning greeting was stopped in mid-sentence as he looked at Alec's expression. "Oh, not so good again, I see."

Samuel looked around cautiously and then back at Alec. He seemed to be preparing himself for another attack, like that of the previous morning. "Where is she?" he asked cautiously.

"Relax," Alex looked over at him with irritation, "there isn't a pond to drown myself here." He moved from the small brazier that he'd been sitting by. "Help yourself to some *kaf*."

"Ah, no thanks." Samuel winced. The offer of a cup of Alec's brew was indeed a threat. "I think I'll stick with this."

Samuel did the unthinkable and uncorked a skin of water. Taking a large swill, he shivered all the way down to his toes as he swallowed. "Bloody hell, that's about as tasty as drinking from a pig's trough."

Thinking that the *kaf* might actually be better, Samuel picked up a cup and poured himself a good measure of the lethal brew. "Cheers!" He saluted Alec, who rested against one of the camel's saddles. It took Samuel a few more seconds to choke it down this time.

Desperate, he reached into his breast pocket, removed his flask, and took a swig. "Aaugh," he sighed after the generous libation, smiling at Alec as though the day was the brightest one he'd yet to see. He added some of the contents to the coffee, then placed the old, silvered container back into his breast pocket, patting it as if it were a loyal pet.

Samuel had a knack for finding the bright side of things. *An optimist to the bitter end*, Alec thought, feeling somewhat jealous of the ability. But, then again, he wasn't *plagued*. Damn him, anyway.

"What I wouldn't give for some crisp bacon and scrambled eggs right now," Samuel declared as he rubbed his hands together with eager enthusiasm, as if the meal that awaited them wasn't more of the dried meat and equally dry bread, topped off with some rapidly molding goat cheese.

Samuel shook his head, looking at Alec. It didn't take a genius to know there was something bothering him. Even appealing to his stomach hadn't been enough to get his mind off the girl. There was nothing else for it . . . Samuel tried goading the disgruntled man instead. "Or some real *kaf*," he pestered. That comment also failed to get a rise out of Alec. Something had happened last night, of that he was sure.

Alec looked as though he hadn't slept much. Samuel, on the other hand, had slept like a rock. "Aahh," he breathed a contented sigh while stretching. "What should we do today?" he asked with excitement, as if riding through the desert in the blistering heat wasn't their only option.

Alec at least responded, raising a brow to suggest the answer should have been obvious.

"That's what I thought you'd say," Samuel happily replied to his silent rejoinder with nary a care in the world. "C'mon, Alec, it can't be that bad. You were only gone five minutes . . . even you're not that fast."

Alec gave him a look that made it plain he wasn't amused.

Nonplussed, Samuel continued. "Guess what I found?"

Considering their relative isolation, Alec could hardly imagine. He raised both brows in response and replied irritably, "You found a horn-toed lizard?"

"No." Samuel's enthusiasm remained undaunted by Alec's surly response. "She *does* know how to read the ancient writings." He smiled smugly as Alec gave him his full attention.

"How could you know that?" Alec asked in a hushed whisper.

"I looked through the trunk last night while you distracted her," Samuel admitted. Though the way in which he did so made it sound as though Alec was a willing participant in his scheme.

"You what?"

"I looked through—"

"Yes, yes," Alec interrupted him in a whisper. "I heard you. I just can't believe you'd do such a thing."

"You can't? Really?" Samuel seemed surprised by Alec's look of disgust. "Ah, c'mon Alec," he rolled his eyes in response, "it's not as if you've never done anything like this before. After all, we've spent the better half of the last decade in the service of Her Majesty doing just that."

Why did Samuel have to choose *now* to be himself? *Damn it all to hell!* Alec fumed inwardly. The man had outdone himself this time. "Is it too much to expect you to know the difference between spying on the enemy and spying on a hapless female, who just happens to be under our protection?" He ran a hand through his hair as he stood.

Though Alec wished otherwise, he couldn't help admitting he was curious. "So what was in the trunk that made you think that she can read it?" he asked in a hushed voice, while giving the fabric wall a cautious glance.

Samuel grinned triumphantly. "It's filled with ancient writings." They were both whispering now.

"That is hardly proof that she knows how to read them." Alec, incredulous that Samuel had actually gone through her things, again ran a hand through his bedraggled hair. *What a debacle*, he fumed to himself. *While I am on the front line hard-pressed to be honorable, Samuel is in the rear, pillaging with abandon.*

"Then why drag that heavy chest everywhere?" Samuel pointed to the marks the trunk had left behind as if their existence was a mute testimony to what he was saying.

"Sentimental value?" Alec interjected, trying to deter Samuel's fervor. He knew from experience that it was always better to keep a rational mind when dealing with Samuel's talent for overdramatizing the facts.

"I tell you she knows how," Samuel replied adamantly before going to his bag to retrieve an old book from within. He came back to where Alec was standing with his pilfered prize. "Haven't you noticed the way she treats that old trunk?" Samuel whispered conspiratorially as he opened the book, showing Alec the writing of ancient Egypt. "It's as though it was filled with treasure."

"Oh, hell, you actually took one?" Incredulous, Alec stared as Samuel displayed one of Genevieve's crusty old tomes. "She's going to know you went through her things."

"She won't even know it's missing. *Trust me.* There are a hundred of these in that trunk."

The last thing Alec wanted to do was trust him. After all, it had been several conversations ending in *"trust me"* that convinced him it wasn't ever a good idea. Frustrated with Samuel's lack of scruples when it came to his desire to find the treasure, Alec took the book from him and closed it saying, "It's hardly proof . . . and even if it were, what difference does it make?"

"It makes all the difference," Samuel retorted, taking the book back. With as much indignation as a whisper allowed, he asked, "If it didn't matter, why would she hide her knowledge of it?"

"I can't imagine."

Samuel opened the book to the page he'd been studying. "Look here." He pointed to a symbol on the page that Genevieve had shown interest in the night before. "Why would she act as though it was new to her when it's right here?"

"I couldn't say." Alec's voice held as much disinterest as he was capable of inflecting. *Damn his hide, anyway!* His curiosity had indeed been piqued, but that hardly gave either one of them the right to go through her things. Samuel, true to form, however, seemed to be immune to his actions.

Alec could well imagine how Genevieve would feel about it. He had long since stopped questioning why he cared what she thought. Again, he pulled a hand through his hair in frustration. Tired of Samuel's obsession with treasure, and now treachery, Alec reached out again for the book and demanded in a loud whisper, "Let me see it."

"Yes, yes, of course," Samuel replied absently as he continued to scrutinize the page. It took a moment for him to look up and see Alec's expression. Surprised at the anger he saw there, he moved the book farther away from Alec's grasping fingers and eyed him warily. "Why do you want it?"

"So that I can return it," exasperation laced Alec's voice, "as any *sane* person would do."

"Are you implying that I'm not sane?" Samuel was taken aback, seemingly surprised by the insult.

"Was I too vague?" Alec asked dryly. "Look at yourself. You have just violated her privacy and stolen her property."

"Technically no . . . it was part of her dowry," Samuel disputed the issue. "I've merely stolen *your* property, and I would prefer the term borrowed."

"Then give me *my* book!" Alec lunged for it. "And technically . . . since my marriage has been annulled, so has my claim to her property."

"Then I call dibs." Samuel pulled the book back from Alec's grasp and placed it under his jacket for protection. "I think you should be rational about this. . . . Just look at yourself. Since when do you act this way over a woo—man?"

Alec grabbed Samuel by the shirtfront with both hands and lifted him off the ground. Samuel, still unwilling to let go of the book, used his free hand to hold on to it while he dropped his head and spun around. The tactic didn't work out too well. Alec had him in a headlock before his next breath.

Samuel was starting to turn an unnatural shade of red when Genevieve spoke up. "Am I interrupting?"

Alec groaned. He could only imagine what she must think of the spectacle they made. At least the book was still concealed inside the blighter's jacket. "No . . . not at all," he said lightly while loosening his grip on Samuel's throat.

"Good morning, Lady Genevieve," Samuel croaked while attempting to smile brightly at her. When he still couldn't shake Alec, he added in a hoarse whisper, "I say, Alec, loosen up, ol'chap. You've won the match."

Reluctantly, Alec let go of the hold he had him in.

"We're just enjoying some exercise." Samuel rubbed his throat, straightening his collar.

Alec decided it was best for now to go along with Samuel's explanation of events. The last thing he wanted was for her to find out what the idiot had really done.

"I was beginning to wonder if you'd spotted another specimen," Genevieve said as she observed the two.

"Oh, yes, the horny toad." Samuel smoothed out his jacket while he glanced sideways, his eyebrows slightly raised.

Alec returned the look with one of warning. "Lizard," he corrected.

"Sorry to disappoint, but none sighted today." Samuel turned back to Genevieve with a smile.

"Well, then, I'll just leave you two to it," Genevieve responded with a glimmer of déjà vu shading the morning's events as she left.

"Put it back." Alec pointed toward the tent after she had gone from view.

"Your wish is my command, my liege." Samuel bowed mockingly. "But if you think I'm riding double with you today, you've got another think coming." He walked toward the curtain, pausing before it. "You might want to watch for her return, since this is obviously important to you."

Chapter 10

Unfortunately for Alec, she did return before Samuel had finished. Damning his luck, he stepped forward, blocking the path. "Genevieve, may I have a word with you?"

"Certainly, Lord Alec." Genevieve accepted his invitation graciously as he led her farther away from her enclosure.

What is taking Samuel so long? Alec agonized. He hadn't wanted to talk to her privately, avoiding it at all cost had been his original plan, but fate had intervened. He certainly couldn't risk her catching the little thief in the act.

"Please, just call me Alec." He smiled, hoping to stall as long as possible. Uncertain what he was going to say, Alec cleared his throat, but before he could think of something, Cupid bellowed for attention. Thankful for the excuse, he guided Genevieve towards the camels.

"I think he wants some breakfast." She smiled congenially as they walked.

"Well . . . that's what I wanted to talk to you about," Alec said, grasping at straws. "I think Cupid is well enough to carry weight again."

Was he serious? This is what he wanted to talk to her about in private? She was sure he had wanted to talk about last night's kiss.

"A light load," he amended when she still hadn't responded.

Men, what confusing creatures! "Of course, I agree completely." Genevieve chose to focus her attention on Cupid, who was nuzzling her hand.

Alec was stalling for time and desperate for a topic that avoided any mention of kissing her. He couldn't keep his gaze from her full mouth as he watched her, or the feel of her lips from his thoughts. *Damn it!* He looked away from her; this attraction to her was almost too much to take. He cleared his throat again as the silence stretched. "I uh-m. . . ."

"Breakfast is ready," Samuel called as he approached, handing them each a portion of dried meat. "I thought that I'd cook." He smiled brightly at Genevieve.

"Thank you, Lord Samuel." Genevieve accepted the meager fare.

Alec stared hard at the man over Genevieve's head, his mute question understood. *What took you so long?* His glare was answered with a wide-eyed nod that said, *You wouldn't believe it.*

In unison, they took a bite of Samuel's offering, each of them taking comfort in the effort required to chew the tough meat to avoid further conversation.

Genevieve swallowed first and, to her dismay, started to choke on the morsel. Samuel was quick to offer her his flask as a remedy. Unfortunately, the fiery liquid only induced another spell of coughing. Alec went to get water, offering her some from a skin. She smiled her thanks, but declined nonetheless.

"Perhaps some of Alec's *kaf*," Samuel ventured.

She shook her head a little too quickly in response. "I'm fine, really," she choked out the words, her eyes streaming.

"I'm so sorry, Lady Genevieve, I didn't think my cooking would take your breath away," Samuel said in an attempt at levity.

"Don't worry. It seems to have that effect on everyone," Alec remarked, remembering the dry bread Samuel had given him.

With mock chagrin, his friend responded, "I am crushed."

"Hardly," Alec added dryly.

"Thank you." Genevieve nodded. "It was truly kind of you to . . . cook." She smiled weakly and then tried to change the topic of conversation before they were at each other's throats again. "I think we will be able to reach the river by noon if we get an early start."

Samuel practically jumped for joy at the news. "By noon? Did you hear that, Alec?" He clapped his friend on the shoulder good-naturedly. "And you thought we'd never see civilization again."

Admittedly, Alec had questioned it.

"I'll just go get ready then," Genevieve excused herself.

Alec waited until she disappeared behind the curtain that had so tormented him the night before. Turning to Samuel, he whispered, "What the hell took you so long?"

Samuel shrugged his shoulders. "Sorry, old man, but the blasted thing was locked."

"Bloody hell!" Alec tugged a hand though his hair. "So where is the book now?"

"Don't worry. It's back in the chest, just like you ordered." Samuel wore a crafty smile, priding himself on the fact that there wasn't a lock made that he couldn't pick. "But I did find something else," Samuel displayed another version of the treasure map, "inside a hidden compartment."

"Oh, no," Alec groaned over what the lunatic had done yet again. "Put it back!" he growled this time.

"I will." Samuel nodded, raising his hands in mock surrender. "I just wanted you to see it first," he whispered. "It was in a book filled with that ancient script."

~*~

The ridge they had been following all morning had merged with the Nile around noon. After a brief respite to let the camels drink their fill and to refresh their own water supply, they had continued along its banks.

Genevieve chewed on her lower lip, debating whether or not to ask about the map he'd shown her at dinner the night before. Samuel relieved her of the dilemma. "What did you think of our little map?" His eyes were bright with curiosity as he looked over at her.

His frankness took her by surprise and neatly turned the tables on her. She had wanted to be the one asking questions. It was her chance to quell some of his fervor, however. "I'm not sure. I've heard tell of many treasures buried here." She gave him a look of regret. "Unfortunately, I know that many men were lured into the desert only to be robbed of their wealth, as well as their lives."

"So you think we are on a wild goose chase, as Alec here does?"

She only hoped the pity in her eyes conveyed her answer.

"Ah, well." Samuel sighed, looking around at the hot desert. "It is indeed a land of mystery. Much like the map, it is at odds with itself."

"Whatever do you mean?" She was surprised by his comment.

"Take the climate, for instance. It's hotter than blazes during the day and freezing cold at night." He gestured with his hand as he spoke. "Even those that live here follow a philosophy of peace, yet there are some tribesmen," he leaned closer, "that seem awfully fond of their guns, if you get my drift."

She noticed he hadn't mentioned the map. Even though she felt she was being led by him in this conversation, she couldn't help herself. She had to ask. "And how, exactly, is that like the map?"

"Well, for one," he looked over at her conspiratorially, "half the map is dedicated to enticing one to enter, and the other half issues a dire warning if you do." He watched her closely as she responded.

"Really?" She smiled sweetly.

He nodded. "Why, yes, it quite literally invites one to descend into the tomb to view the splendor of everything good and pure on which the god lives. It even goes so far as to tell how to open the door." He watched as she nervously fingered the bridle. "Then, on the other hand, it promises death to anyone who tries without the *keeper*." Her eyes darted away from his when he looked directly at her. "See what I mean?" He grinned at her. "The land of contradictions."

The topic was quickly becoming uncomfortable, as was his close scrutiny of her. She glanced over at Alec, who rode beside her. He didn't seem to be interested in their conversation. Instead, he was looking around at the distant horizon. She watched him for a moment until he caught her glance and smiled. The brief contact made her heart beat faster. His behavior toward her had changed after breakfast. Just the memory of it caused her to blush.

He had asked to speak privately once again, even asked if she'd walk with him a while. They sat on the same rock as they had the night before, where he tried to find the words to apologize. It was only when Samuel came to tell them he was done putting things away that Alec visibly relaxed, his step much lighter as they walked back to the camp.

It was indeed the land of opposites, she thought. On one side of her was a man obsessed with the map, and on the other, one who was intent on avoiding it. Just as he was intent on avoiding her, though his eyes longed to devour her. Pushing the thought away, she wondered about another thing that had been puzzling her. "Tell me, Lord Alec," she waited until he gave her his attention, "if the map is yours, why is it that you don't carry it with you?"

"Yes, Alec, why don't you?" Samuel chimed in.

"Just Alec," he responded, smiling at her before looking over at Samuel, who was far too entertained by the question.

Samuel ignored him, turning to her instead. "You see, dear lady, he threw it away."

"You did?" She looked at Alec, surprised by the information.

"Why, yes," Samuel again answered for his friend. "The morning that we met you, we found ourselves in dire circumstances indeed. Our guide had disappeared two days before, taking our water with him. We had traveled for a time, trying to find our way, but we found ourselves all the more lost for our efforts. We were just about to give up hope."

Alec, she noticed, was beginning to look annoyed, while Samuel, who was caught up in the telling of the story, seemed immune to his censure.

"Alec blamed our situation on the map, you see, and threw it away in a tantrum a three-year-old would have been proud of." Samuel raised his eyebrows mockingly.

Alec, Genevieve decided, was definitely not amused.

"But, you see," Samuel paused, watching Alec's response, "it was because of this. . . ."

Alec exhaled in exasperation and stated flatly, "I did not have a tantrum."

"Like I said, it was because of this . . . sizable tizzy," Samuel restated, "that we were saved. I tell you, it was fate. The map blew right into the ravine below us, and behold . . . there it was . . . the water we'd been searching for."

Alec cast his eyes heavenward before looking at her. "I didn't have a tantrum or a tizzy. I simply threw it away."

Genevieve smiled her understanding. It was obvious that Samuel loved to get under Alec's skin whenever possible.

"Can you believe it? It practically landed right on the spring," Samuel continued. "I tell you, it's a sign."

Alec rolled his eyes. "A sign of your gullibility, perhaps."

"A sign?" Genevieve prompted.

"Yes, a sign that we were meant to find the treasure," he pointedly said to Alec before turning to Genevieve and saying, "Don't you see? The map has proven to be good luck after all. Why, it's how we found you."

"Well, I don't know about the map, but the last part I can agree with," Alec commented with a wink, showing her the dimple in his cheek as he smiled.

Ooh! Genevieve thought, disgruntled, *He's doing it again.* Talk about contradictions. One moment he's rejecting her kiss, then the next flirting outrageously with her. *What is the man up to?*

~*~

Samuel's low-pitched whistle was one of wondrous appreciation as they neared the colossal forms of four seated statues of Ramesses II, whose silent vigil guarded the entrance of the temple.

"Would you look at that!" he called back to Alec and Genevieve, who rode up behind him. Carved from the sandstone cliffs, and half buried by sand, four giant depictions of the great Pharaoh sat silently before them.

"It's the temple of Abū Simbel," Samuel said excitedly as he dismounted and walked up to the mound of debris that had collected before the great shrine. He seemed to grow smaller as he approached the mammoth figures.

The cliff itself cast a shadow across the lower portion of the hill, creating an ethereal effect upon the ancient carvings, which were bathed in sunlight.

Alec dismounted and came around to assist Genevieve, who still sat on top of the largest camel. He offered her a hand to help her dismount, just as he had earlier when he'd assisted her to mount.

The memory of it still surprised her. He claimed it was too taxing for Cupid to kneel with a sore leg, so rather than let her mount in the normal fashion, he'd assisted her.

Much to her dismay, Alec had placed his hands around her waist and slowly lifted her, watching her with hooded eyes as she rose above him. He'd then placed her on the saddle, his hands lingering on her hips as she shifted into the seat.

Genevieve could hardly believe how the heat of his palms had seared through the thin layers of fabric she was wearing. Shockingly, he had continued to gaze up at her with eyes that smoldered with promise. He'd given her that lazy smile of his that accentuated one dimple in his cheek.

Before she could respond, he'd turned to mount his own camel. Without looking back, he'd prodded the animal forward, leading the way into the desert.

What she might have done in response to his manhandling, had she not been so surprised by it, played through her mind all afternoon as they traveled. Placing a foot squarely in his chest and pushing him away was only one of the scenarios that had come to mind.

Alec now stood before her with his legs spread wide, his hands raised to assist her. The kiss was one thing. She'd thought then that he'd acted with innocent longing. Practiced seduction was another thing entirely.

Only the Lord knew where that devious little thought came from, but before she could stop herself, Genevieve pitched slightly more forward than necessary. Her unexpected weight fell against Alec, taking him unaware. His eyes widened in response as she then provocatively slid down the length of his body. Pretending to have lost her balance, Genevieve leaned against him a moment longer than necessary with her breasts pressed against his chest.

She herself was breathless by the effect and looked up at him shyly. Gazing into his heavy-lidded eyes, she smiled bashfully, then turned away. She was rewarded for her efforts with the sound of an exhaled breath of air that was quite gratifying.

Two could play this game, she thought with a mischievous smile playing on her lips as she led Cupid away.

TREASURE OF EGYPT

The little temptress! Alec watched Genevieve sashay away with her large demon beast in tow. He was playing with fire, and, God help him, he liked the heat.

"Alec!" Samuel called from the other side of the dirt mound. "Genevieve!" He appeared over the top and waved them over. "You've got to see this." He disappeared behind the heap of rubble, then reappeared a moment later. "And bring a lamp," he yelled before vanishing again.

Alec watched appreciatively as Genevieve led Cupid to a shady area. The other camels followed happily after the pair. He knew from experience how cantankerous they could be. Women and camels . . . two things in life he was sure he'd never understand.

Alec looked around. The shade from the cliffs and the water close by made the area a perfectly good campsite. Besides, with Samuel otherwise entertained, he might actually get some *alone time* with Genevieve, something he'd recently decided he would like.

Once the camels were unloaded and Genevieve had located a lamp, Alec invited her to join him. "Let's go see what Samuel has found." She seemed reluctant to go. He'd thought the excitement of exploring would appeal to her. Perhaps she was frightened by the idea. Either way, he didn't want to leave her alone.

"Come with me," he urged, taking the lamp from her. "We can't let him have all the fun." She looked a little doubtful. "I'll be with you every step of the way. I promise." He held out his other hand to her.

That's what she was afraid of, especially now that she'd seen the pile of stones left as a marker on the path.

"I wonder how much of this rubble is from Belzoni and his excavations," Alec commented as they began to climb the hill. "Can you imagine blowing something like this up?"

"No." Genevieve shook her head as she gazed up at the magnificent temple. "But, then again, some men will do anything to obtain treasure." She watched him carefully for his response.

He nodded in agreement as he looked up. "Those early archaeologists were a little too enthusiastic with their dynamite for my tastes. I'm glad that the new breed practices different methods."

Genevieve was most relieved when they made it to the top, and she could let go of his hand. How could his touch make her tingle all over . . . or turn her insides into mush?

She watched as he climbed through the entrance that was filled with the accumulation of mud and boulders from the river's flooding. Over the years, debris had partially blocked the opening that Samuel found.

Alec waited for Genevieve on the other side while she climbed through the entrance. Once inside, she could see that the mud had also filled the interior. Surprisingly, the ceiling was still so high that it loomed above them in the darkness, even with the floor artificially raised by the rubble.

Genevieve looked about her. There were eight more giant pillars of Ramesses along the walls of the great hall. He'd been portrayed as Osiris, god of the underworld, with his hands folded over his chest, holding the crook and flail. It was impressive, even in the dim light.

"It's a crime not to appreciate such beauty," Alec breathed as he watched her.

She glanced over, catching his eye before quickly looking away. She had the distinct impression he was speaking of her, rather than the elaborate interior of the temple. The attention he was lavishing on her was most disconcerting, making it almost impossible to concentrate on anything but the man next to her.

Samuel had cleverly set a mirror on the floor, reflecting the sun's light onto the five seated statues in an alcove carved into the back of the temple. The reflection on bright limestone made it appear as though the statues glowed, giving them a life of their own. He had his diary in hand and was busily sketching when they walked up behind him. "It's really something, isn't it?"

"Yes, it is," Genevieve answered, awestruck by what she could see in the darkened interior.

"Lovely," Alec said from nearby.

Genevieve again felt as though he'd spoken of her instead of their surroundings. Unsure exactly how to handle his advances, she busied herself with the lamp Alec had placed on the ground.

"They say that on two days of the year, the twenty-first day of both February and October, the sunrise pierces the darkness and

lights them up." Samuel continued to sketch. "With, of course, the exception of the one on the left whose face has been destroyed; he is the god Ptah, from the underworld."

"So he's been intentionally left in the dark, I take it?" Alec quipped.

"Just so," Samuel laughed. "I bet it's a grand thing to see."

"I don't think I'm interested in staying that long for the show." Alec stood looking at the statues for a few moments before moving away from the scene.

Genevieve's hands froze above the lantern when he leaned over her. Kneeling beside the lamp, she could feel his breath tickle her cheek as his hand covered hers.

"Here, let me help you with that," Alec whispered softly into her ear.

The effect of his words sent shivers down her spine as her head involuntarily tilted back, exposing her neck. She closed her eyes to it. How did he do this to her? All she wanted was for him to place his kiss where his breath had caressed her.

Afraid she might drop something again or embarrass herself in another fashion, she left him alone with the lamp and moved quickly away.

Swooping vultures emerged as the lamp flickered to life. The ceiling was edged with stars and painted in the center with the flying birds. She focused on the ceiling above.

"They say the vulture represents Upper Egypt and the goddess Nekhbet, while the five-pointed stars belongs to the goddess Seshat, the Keeper of Wisdom." Samuel said as he too looked up.

Genevieve chose to remain silent, turning her attention to the walls which were covered in scenes depicting Ramesses as a great warrior with his fallen enemies at his feet. Combined with the statues that guarded the passageway like sentries, it was a bit overwhelming.

"If they placed these here to intimidate, it worked." Alec placed his hands on his hips as he looked up at the figures. "Quite the show of power."

"The architects who designed this were certainly good at employing the gimmicks of the era." Samuel stopped sketching to

look up at it. "Colossal statues, glowing gods, and the flagrant use of the indigenous people's deities."

Genevieve nodded. "In a time when people believed the gods actually inhabited these stone images, it would have been daunting, to say the least." It was hard not to appreciate the artistry it had taken to create the beautiful interior, as well as its meaning, even if she did have to leave it. Excusing herself from the men, she left quickly, saying she had to attend to some personal needs. She only hoped that would be enough to afford her some privacy and keep the man from looking for her, at least for a while.

Climbing back through the entrance, she carefully picked her way down the hill until she stood in front of the pile of stones she'd seen earlier. Though it was not obvious to the casual observer, she could tell they had been arranged so that they would point toward the smaller temple.

Following their direction, Genevieve soon found herself before the large statues of Ramesses and his wife Nefertari that fronted the Temple of Hathor.

The two standing statues of Nefertari were flanked on either side by images of her husband Ramesses. She wore the double-plumed headdress of Amun with the horns of fertility around a large disk. Genevieve considered the round disk for a moment. It had become something of an enigma, its true meaning having been lost in the passage of time.

The debris from the river was not as prominent in front of the lesser temple. A few of the stairs leading to the entrance were actually visible. Genevieve climbed them until she stood beneath the giant doorframe. The late afternoon sun was partially obscured by the cliff face above. It was nearly impossible, standing in the bright sunlight, to see very far into the dim interior.

At her feet lay another pile of stones, arranged in such fashion that they could only have been done by one person. She stepped forward, entering the darkened temple.

~*~

As soon as Genevieve left, Samuel stopped sketching and looked over at Alec, who was still staring after her. "Tell me. . . . Have you completely lost your mind, or is there something I've missed?"

"What do you mean?" Alec, surprised by the question, turned around.

"You haven't exactly been subtle," Samuel replied sarcastically.

Alec raised a brow. "Oh, that."

"Is this about the treasure?" Samuel asked blatantly. "Or are you just trying to bed her?"

"No, on both counts."

"Then what the hell are you doing?" Samuel demanded.

"Keeping my wife," Alec informed him.

"What. . . ?" Shocked, Samuel stared at him for a moment. "Why?"

"Why not?"

"I can think of several reasons." Samuel told him. "Your mother, for one."

"That's the beauty of it. I will no longer be pressured to marry because you, my friend, have already solved my problem."

"Now, don't blame this on me." Samuel put his hands up as if he could ward off the implication. "I only did it because I knew you could get out of it."

"Well," Alec smiled, "I've decided that I don't want out of it."

"Are you insane?" Samuel couldn't believe his ears. "You must be, to even consider it. You've only known Genevieve for two days. It took you three years to decide to get a dog. Just think of the scandal."

"You're the one who's always saying I should stop planning everything and live with passion," Alec pointed out, "something about my clock being wound too tight."

"Would you listen to yourself? For God's sake, man." Samuel threw his hands up again, this time in frustration. "I was talking about a bloody holiday, not a lifetime commitment!" He looked at Alec as though he was half-crazed.

"You're right." Alec nodded. Samuel looked somewhat relieved that he was at least listening, until Alec continued, "I have not been one to rush up the aisle, but I've never known a woman who makes me feel the way I do when I'm with Genevieve." Alec paused, considering. "She makes me feel alive."

"Bloody hell! You're serious, aren't you?" Samuel groaned as Alec turned and started walking away from him. "Perhaps you should consider getting another puppy first."

Alec ignored him as he continued to climb over the debris at the entrance to the temple.

"Think, man!" Samuel called after him. "At least wait a whole week to decide?" Samuel watched him leave. "Of all the stupid," he muttered, "the fool has gone and done it this time." He turned back around, shaking his head in disgust. Looking up, he was surprised to see the hieroglyph right over the archway of the room he'd been drawing. Two lions facing outward with a disk in between them had been carved in the center over the door. "Well, I'll be damned."

Chapter 11

Genevieve paused in the doorway of the temple, waiting for her eyes to adjust to the dim light. Slowly, she moved forward into the room, whispering into the darkness, "Mother?"

A woman came forward from the interior of the temple, her black robes blended into the darkness around her, making her almost invisible until she was close. "Thank God," she whispered, hugging her daughter in a tight embrace. "I'm so sorry. I would never have gone to help deliver Tara's baby if I'd known Sheik Kazirrah would do this. I came as soon as I learned."

Pulling away, her mother looked at Genevieve with compassion-filled eyes. "Are you all right?" Her brow creased with concern. "It's been pure agony to think what you might have been forced to endure." She cast her eyes to the door and led her daughter farther inside for privacy.

"I'm fine, Momma." Genevieve followed behind. "Really." Her mother looked weary. Genevieve realized she must have ridden all night to beat them here.

"They didn't hurt you, did they?" her mother asked uneasily, looking as if she would burst into tears at any moment.

Genevieve smiled reassuringly, aware of what her mother was really asking. "No, Momma, they have been perfect gentlemen." Her mother looked unconvinced. "Really, I'm fine," Genevieve reassured her.

Her mother crushed Genevieve to her body again in a tight hug. Now that she knew her daughter was safe, her calm demeanor was starting to crack. "Please forgive me for leaving you alone."

"Momma, I'm all right. I'm not a child—"

"Genevieve?" Alec called from the doorway. He'd watched from the hill as she entered the smaller temple, surprised that she would go inside alone, especially since he'd thought her skittish about exploring.

Her safety wasn't the only thing that had been on his mind when he'd decided to follow her, however. His mind had been full of ways to woo his wife as he'd approached the temple.

The last thing he expected was to hear voices coming from within the dark interior. Concerned when she didn't answer, he called again. "Genevieve, are you alright?" His hand went instinctively to the handle of his revolver.

"Yes, Alec, I'm fine . . . just a minute," Genevieve called back, trying to keep him from entering. It was useless. Alec slipped the pistol from the gun belt he wore as he entered the darkened temple. She was about to go to him when her mother put a hand out to stop her. She turned back to her. "It's alright, Momma."

"No, Genevieve, there is more to this situation than you are aware of," her mother whispered cautiously.

As he approached his wife, Alec was surprised to see another woman with her. But for the obvious difference in their ages, they could have been twins; he turned to Genevieve for an explanation.

"Alec, this is my mother, Lady Sophia—" Genevieve began.

"That's close enough," interrupted a deep voice from behind Alec as a sharp blade was pressed against his back.

Alec had been hoping he'd never have to hear that particular voice again. He slowly raised his hands and looked over his shoulder to see the leader of the sheik's guards standing there, his black-clad figure silhouetted against the light from the entrance. Alec silently berated himself for letting his guard down. *Damn it!* He'd walked right into the man's trap . . . again.

The blackguard must have been standing beside the door when he entered, and if that wasn't enough to irritate him, the bastard could now speak perfect English. How things could have been different if he'd only known that little fact.

Alec decided to ignore the man and greet his new mother-in-law instead. "Lady Sophia," he said with all the genteel mannerisms he could muster. Bowing his head in acknowledgment, he introduced himself. "Lord Alecsian Rothchild

Brighton, the Third." He found himself wondering if he'd feel the steel of the Blackbird's sword before he was finished. "I am delighted to make your acquaintance."

The leader of the Blackbirds spoke up in response to his introduction. "You have something that doesn't belong to you."

Alec assumed that he'd been correct in thinking the man's hostilities stemmed from an interrupted love match. "Yes, well, as you will remember, your sheik married her to me." It was ironic to think that he'd have handed over Genevieve without a thought two days ago. Now the man would have a fight on his hands, Alec decided.

"The map," the warrior clarified, "where is it?"

"Right here," Samuel stood in the doorway, a pistol in his hand, "but I think you're mistaken. I believe we'll be keeping the map."

Unfortunately for Samuel, another figure emerged from behind him as he spoke, pressing a knifepoint in his back. "Or not . . ." Samuel finished as he felt the blade prick his skin.

The warrior was quick to take the pistol from Alec's hand when the balance of power had shifted back to him. He then stepped over to Samuel, relieving him of his weapon, as well, before pointing the revolver at his midsection. "Where is it?"

The silence became positively lethal when no one answered.

"It's in his left boot," Genevieve spoke up.

Her mother, Alec, and Samuel all looked at her as though she had just betrayed them. Her mother, especially, seemed surprised that she knew of the map.

"I should have killed you both when I first encountered you," the warrior said, a threat in his voice.

"You will not harm them," Genevieve told the menacing warrior. Turning, she appealed to her mother in a low voice, "Mother, please . . . I don't think they know what they have."

Sophia did not appear to be swayed as she spoke to the men. "The map is stolen property. You will return it to its rightful owner." With that she nodded to the guard, who unsheathed his curved sword. The unspoken threat was still ringing in the air when Sophia issued an ultimatum. "Give him the map, and you may leave with your lives."

Samuel looked over to Alec, who nodded. With agonizingly slow movements, Samuel bent to retrieve the map from his boot. Sighing in defeat, he handed it over to the man.

The warrior opened the parchment and looked it over, nodding to Sophia. He then motioned for Samuel to be brought forward. The man with the knife prodded Samuel in the back, encouraging him to move forward.

"Mother, this is not necessary," Genevieve insisted.

"Sorry, ol' chap." Samuel gave Alec a look of exasperation as he joined him. "I botched that rescue," he whispered with regret. He had thought to save Alec from himself before he did something irrational, not to mention irreversible. He'd never imagined it would turn out like this when he decided to follow the love-struck fool.

Samuel turned to see his unidentified assailant. "Well, well . . . would you look here." Surprise flashed across his face as he recognized the man in black. "Alec . . . It's our long lost dragoman, who stole our water and left us for dead. Come back to finish the job, did ye?" Samuel adopted an accent as spoke.

Alec's expression was one of annoyance. The muscle in his jaw clenched. "Don't encourage him." He quickly spoke up, afraid that the difficult spot they found themselves in could quickly escalate. The last thing he wanted to do was have a fight with the warrior and his henchman in front of Genevieve and her mother. "This can all be easily solved." He attempted to diffuse the mounting tension.

"The map is yours." Alec directed his words to Lady Sophia. "I give it to you gladly," he said, ignoring the fact they already had it. "I was unaware of its history." He gestured innocently with his hands. "Please, let us handle this like civilized people."

"If we weren't civilized, young man, you'd already be dead," Sophia stated, her accent crisply English. "Who sent you?"

"Sent?" Alec asked mystified. Genevieve's mother certainly had a way about her which brooked no defiance. He really wished he knew what she wanted or how to answer her without inviting bloodshed.

"Who is behind this?" Sophia added for clarity.

"I— am." Alec wondered what kind of reaction the admission would create.

"Who gave you the map?" Sophia's voice was sharp as she pinned him to the spot with her gaze.

Alec groaned inwardly. Apparently that wasn't what she had wanted to hear. His future relations with his mother-in-law weren't looking up. "I won it in a card game, back in England."

"At White's?"

"No," Alec answered, a little uncomfortable at having to admit he'd been in one of London's questionable gaming hells. It was not something one wants to admit to one's mother-in-law.

"Then where?"

She was ruthless, he realized. He'd have to confess. "At the Boar's Head." He cleared his throat. "It's—"

"I know what it is." She looked unimpressed.

Alec groaned inwardly. No doubt she thought him a gambling womanizer and a thieving treasure seeker. They were definitely off to a great start.

"And who, may I ask, placed it among the winnings?"

"A Frenchman by the name of Monsieur Blanois." Alec was unsure of the man he'd met at the tavern. It wasn't the type of place known for keeping records of their patrons. He decided to keep the news of his untimely death to himself for now.

"Who else was at the table?" Sophia continued her interrogation of him.

"There were four others. Lords Bristol, and I think the other's name was Crampton or Campton."

"You said four."

"There was an older gentleman at the table. I don't recall his name." She looked as though she wanted more information, anyway. He couldn't very well call him the Ol' Codger, as Samuel was fond of addressing him. Alec thought about what he could remember. "Silver hair, clean shaven, he tied his cravat in the old fashioned way . . . wore a signet ring on his left pinkie," Alec relayed, grasping at anything to satisfy her.

"Lord Langston?"

The name she spoke surprised him. "Why, yes. I believe that was it." Alec nodded, finding himself with a few questions of his own, though he doubted she'd answer if he voiced them. He continued to watch her carefully as she assessed him. He felt lacking under her scrutiny and actually breathed a sigh of relief when she finally spoke.

"Thank you." With finality, she turned her attention on the blackguard. "Akeim, we have what we came for. Let's leave these men to find their way home."

"Mother," Genevieve stopped her, "I— I'm not going back."

"We can discuss this at another time," Sophia replied sternly.

"No—we're going to discuss it now." Genevieve had never spoken against her mother before now. "I refuse to go back." She straightened her back, standing tall. "There is nothing for me there."

"Genevieve, I cannot keep you safe in England."

"Safe?" Disbelief registered across Genevieve's features. "Can't you see that I'm not safe here? What am I supposed to do? Wait to be foisted off on the next lost lord who happens by?"

"Ouch," Samuel said in an aside to Alec being referred to as a 'lost lord'.

"Even if I had to get married in order to leave, it was preferable to living the rest of my life out here in the desert," Genevieve continued.

"I didn't come all this way to leave you here, Genevieve," her mother stated firmly. "Nothing's been done that can't be undone."

"I'll not sacrifice—"

Her mother cut her off. "You're not the only one who's made sacrifices, Genevieve. I too had to wed so that I could be here."

Startled by the news, Genevieve glanced over at Akeim, who looked to be mildly uncomfortable at the revelation. "You're jesting." She turned back to her mother.

"No, I'm not." Sophia's tone was one of frustration.

"Ooh, that's a shame." Samuel smiled at Akeim's expense, receiving a menacing stare in return which was meant to silence him.

Both ladies looked over at the audience they had to this private conversation. Sophia added her next comment in a language she hoped none of the men would understand.

Samuel raised his eyebrows in surprise. "Oh-oh, that's not a good sign." He couldn't help but grin at the looks he received from both men, not intimidated in the slightest.

"And to think, here I was envying your wedded bliss." Samuel clapped Alec on the shoulder. He received another scorching look. He found this even more amusing and chuckled in response, enjoying himself immensely at their benefit.

Sophia, still speaking in another language said, "I will speak to the sheik when we return. He will never dare do such a thing again. I promise."

"*Nein!*" Genevieve shook her head. There was no way she was going to live out the rest of her life in the desert. Desperate, she did what she had never thought she would do to her mother . . . she lied. "Would you let your grandchild grow up without a father?"

Sophia looked suspiciously at her daughter, despite Genevieve's mask of innocence. "I thought you said he'd been a gentleman?" She glared at the man who had dared deflower her child.

Genevieve gave him a rapid glance before committing him to her mother's wrath. She hoped her mother wouldn't kill Alec because of Genevieve's her deceit. She said a little prayer before she lied again . . . "He was a gentleman . . . a married gentleman."

Responding to the ladies' glances, Samuel said, "Oh-oh, that certainly doesn't look good. Why, Alec, if looks could kill, I do believe you'd be dead."

"Like I said . . . don't encourage them," Alec commented dryly, feeling as though he could use a little air. It seemed that the tables had finally turned. Samuel could not understand what they were saying; whereas Alec, whose Swiss grandmother had taught him to speak her native tongue, was finally in the loop for a change. This meant Samuel hadn't a clue as to how close he'd actually come to the truth.

Sophia took a moment to digest the new information. "Even so, Genevieve, you may not be safe with him. You need to think about that when you consider your child."

Genevieve listened, not knowing how to respond. What was she to say of her fictitious unborn child's welfare, especially when she herself had worried over her own safety?

"We don't know anything about these men," Sophia continued with a note of anxiety in her voice, "except that they had the map and were able to find you."

"Which is exactly why we're no longer safe here," Genevieve argued, grasping at the leverage her mother had given her. "Please, let us go back home . . . to England," she pleaded.

Sophia reached out and put a comforting hand on her daughter's shoulder. "Akeim," she addressed the warrior, "I believe we'll be escorting these men to Aswan. Will you please further disarm them?" She noticed her daughter's look of panic, and then added insightfully, "Without doing them harm."

Genevieve relaxed visibly. She almost wanted to jump for joy but did her best not to look too pleased about her victory.

Akeim smiled menacingly as he pointed his sword at Alec. "You first . . . slowly."

Alec did as requested and tossed his gun belt and knife to the ground. Because he wore a thin lawn shirt and a pair of beige pants which fit him like a glove, it would have been noticeable if he'd carried more within his clothing. He looked down his person, implying as much with the motion.

Akeim nodded. "Now, empty the boots."

Slowly, Alec took out his knife from one boot and then a small pistol from the other, adding them to the weapons on the ground between them. It didn't sit well with him that this was the second time he'd had to give the bastard his weapons.

Satisfied, Akeim nodded toward Samuel. "Now you."

Samuel did the same as Alec, adding another two knives and a pistol to the pile. Akeim wasn't satisfied. Though Samuel was dressed much the same as Alec, he also wore a jacket with several pockets. Akeim motioned for him to empty them . . . three more knives joined the pile.

"All of them," he commanded.

With a sigh, Samuel reached up behind his neck and pulled a thin knife from his collar. Brass rings from an interior pocket fell to the growing pile, followed by three small throwing stars. He then looked towards Akeim with hands up, implying he was finished.

Akeim took the added precaution and turned to Alec once again, "Anything else?"

Alec shook his head in the negative.

Akeim sized him up. This one was either capable of defending himself without a weapon or was too cocksure, he didn't know which. The other was too slippery to trust either way. He pointed the sword to Samuel again and warned, "All of it."

Samuel rolled his eyes before pulling a straight razor from his boot. "That's it. I swear." He looked to Alec and added, "I feel as naked as a newborn."

"Don't give them any ideas," Alec told him, wondering if they'd be stripped down next.

~*~

The fire crackled between the two pairs of men sitting on opposite sides of it. They had just finished their dinner, which included a lizard and two snakes that had been roasted on sticks over the flames.

Samuel licked his fingers "Mmmm . . . snake kabob . . . what a rare treat." His voice was filled with sarcasm. "Would you care for another, Alec?" Samuel held a piece of the skewered meat up.

Alec shook his head as he continued to watch every move the warrior and the dragoman made. Having been used much like slave labor, dinner hadn't settled well with him. He and Samuel had collected the wood the river had washed downstream, as well as set up the tent for the women's use.

It was something he would have done anyway, but having to follow the dictates of the warrior named Akeim was enough to put him in a foul mood. He'd really like to be back in charge of his life and keep it that way for more than a day.

Alec had only a brief glimpse of Genevieve as she'd disappeared within the tent. Her mother's watchdog hadn't let either Samuel or him out of his sight, and now he eyed them over the flames. It was going to be another long night, Alec thought wearily.

"Well, I'll be damned," Samuel exclaimed as he examined his next morsel, "they do have horned toes." He showed Alec his find, amazed that the hind leg of the lizard actually sported several spikes that jutted out from its toes.

"Hmm." He took a curious bite. "Tastes like chicken. Sure you wouldn't care to try it?"

"You do realize that you've just managed to eat the only specimen we've actually seen?" Alec remarked.

"I take it that's a no." Samuel picked at his teeth. "It is a little gristly, if you ask me."

"I'll be sure to write that in my notes when I submit my findings."

Samuel slowly pulled out his flask and took a swig as the warrior monitored the movement. "Care for some of this instead?" He held the silver container out to Alec. When he declined, Samuel carefully replaced it, stifling a yawn. "I'm bushed." He stretched. "Yes, indeed. I think I'll hit the dirt." Taking a blanket, he made a place beside the fire.

"You do that." Alec kept his eye on the warrior who was still watching them. The man had the blackest eyes he'd ever seen.

"Look on the bright side." Samuel adjusted his bedding as he lay down. "At least your new father-in-law seems to have taken a shine to you."

"Yes, I'll sleep much better knowing he's watching over me," Alec commented dryly, seeing the man for the first time as his father-in-law.

Unbelievable!

Chapter 12

Alec awoke to find the warrior still watching him. Bloody hell! Did this guy sleep? The man didn't appear to have shifted his position in the slightest since Alec finally nodded off.

"I'm betting he sleeps with his eyes open," Samuel whispered from his place by the fire. "It's almost enough to give you the heebie-jeebies."

"More like nightmares." Alec sat up as Samuel stoked the fire. He really didn't think things could get worse until Lady Sophia joined them.

"Gentlemen," she stood before them, "I trust you slept well."

"Good morning." Both Alec and Samuel greeted her as they stood up.

If the black stares of the warrior and their former guide hadn't been enough to make one uncomfortable, being informed that she wished to talk to Alec about his marriage to her daughter certainly did. . . . It was remarkable how fast everyone else found another place to be. The guide disappeared first, closely followed by the warrior, who stepped twenty paces away. Keeping a close eye on them, he drew his sword and proceeded to sharpen it.

"It's good to know he keeps it nice and sharp," Samuel commented as he watched him. Catching the lady's eye, he too left, saying, "I'll just go see to the camels."

Alec remained standing, while his mother-in-law seated herself on a log by the fire, then he chose a spot opposite her.

"Tell me, young man," Sophia looked directly at him, getting right to the point, "what are your intentions regarding my daughter?"

Alec cleared his throat . . . Should he confess they had decided to annul the marriage? The truth would hardly get him what he wanted . . . and Genevieve had told her a much different story. It might make it easier to win the daughter if he could win over his mother-in-law.

"If she'll have me," he declared, "I intend to make her the best husband that I can possibly be."

"Would you put her happiness above your own?" Sophia asked sharply.

"Yes."

"What of her welfare?"

"I would die for her," he stated emphatically and was surprised to realize he meant it.

She watched him for a moment. He noticed a sadness enter her eyes as she finally spoke. "Let us hope it doesn't come to that." She started to rise.

Alec stood as well. "I'd like to ask a question of you, if I may?" he asked as she turned away.

She paused. "I'll not answer any questions regarding the map."

"How did you know that Langston sat at that table?" When it looked as though she was not going to answer, he continued, "I'm asking as a matter of safety. I'd like to know if he is a threat."

"I wish I could answer that," Sophia spoke softly. "My husband, Jonathon, died trying to protect us. It seems we were betrayed by someone close. Unfortunately, Lord Langston was very close."

"He died protecting the map?" Alec could hardly believe it when she nodded. "Why not just get rid of it?"

"It's not that easy," she sighed wearily. "As for your question about Lord Langston, the answer is, yes, he is very dangerous."

He waited for more, but there was no further conversation. She left him and went to speak with Akeim. Apparently she accepted what he'd said, for even Samuel remarked on the vast difference in their treatment from the warrior a little later.

"I don't know how you did it, but it seems to have worked," Samuel commented as he headed off toward the temple to do some more sketches. "Don't suppose you could offer him your firstborn son in return for our weapons?" He looked at Alec's expression. "No?" Samuel feigned regret. "I didn't think so."

Genevieve awoke to find her mother and Akeim sitting by the fire, talking quietly.

"Good morning, dear," her mother greeted her as she poured her a hot cup of *kaf*.

Genevieve accepted it and inhaled the aroma. "Mmm, thank you." It smelled delicious and tasted even better. She didn't know how Alec achieved such a bitter brew. Thinking of him, she looked around. Unfortunately, he was nowhere to be seen. She could see Samuel up on the hill busily sketching the exterior of Ramesses's temple, but there was no sign of Alec anywhere near him. She was about to ask after him when her mother spoke.

"Lord Brighton is down by the river fishing for our breakfast." Sophia smiled. "Why don't you take him some *kaf* and see how he's doing?"

Genevieve was stunned that her mother had actually suggested she find him. What had happened while she slept? she wondered, walking toward the figure she could see down by the water's edge.

After yesterday, she assumed Akeim would continue to treat the men as criminals. Something had happened . . . she just didn't know what yet. She looked back and received a wave from her mother. Something had *definitely* happened.

"Good morning," Alec called out to her as she approached. She smiled in return and held up his cup. He nodded. "Let me have another go at this, and I'll be right up." She stood on the bank, watching him as he slowly wound the net back into his arms.

She could see that he'd taken his boots off and set them on the shore. He'd also rolled up his sleeves and pants legs, but it hadn't prevented him from getting wet. In fact, his whole front was soaked from his efforts.

There was something about him that made her heart skip a beat as she watched. He looked like the wet Adonis who had entered her tent on their first night, only now he was playfully hauling in his catch. Somehow it made him even more appealing.

"Akeim didn't trust me with a spear, so it was the net or nothing." He smiled at her again over his shoulder as he worked. There was a flash of silver from a small fish that had become entangled within the netting. His eyes danced with merriment as he caught it in his hand and showed her his prize. It was only about four inches long, but he was acting as if he'd just hauled in Moby Dick. She felt a serious pull on her heartstrings as she watched him.

The fish wiggled free of his grasp and flopped back into the water. Alec lunged for it but lost his balance on the slick bottom of the bank and fell. With a splash, he hit the water, disappearing beneath the surface for a moment before reappearing. Struggling to his feet in the waist-high water, he looked over at her, shrugging his shoulders as she laughed. "If you think that was graceful, wait till you see me dance."

She envisioned him dancing across a ballroom floor, complete with a few toe-stomping steps. She wished she could see him dance. Truth was . . . she'd almost give anything to be the one that he held in his arms.

Genevieve felt her heart sink as she glanced back toward her mother. Sophia had been right. They knew nothing about him. She worried at her lip as she looked back toward Alec. He was so beautiful. She knew she was in trouble, despite her efforts to guard her heart from him. She was only falling deeper under his spell.

He caught her watching and laughed. "Don't worry. I'll catch another."

She smiled in return and watched as he gathered the net once again, tossing it high over the water. It spread out like a fan before dropping.

"That's the best one yet," he said in regards to his technique. "You should have been here for my first attempt. It dragged me right in with it after I tossed it." Alec motioned with his arm, so that she could see that he'd tied the net to his wrist.

He definitely wasn't a fishmonger, she decided, as the movement almost made him lose his balance. Once he had regained his footing, he grinned at her again, making light of his abilities.

She laughed as she watched him. He was actually rather graceful, she decided a moment later, as he braced himself against the current and rhythmically wound the net back in. The sinuous movement of his bulging muscles against his wet clothing might have had something to do with it. Her throat was dry by the time he'd gathered it up again.

He must have used every muscle in his body, she decided, having watched, spellbound, unable to tear her eyes away. Alec gifted her with another of his grins that showed the dimple in his cheek as he said, "One more time." She noticed the mischievous glint in his eye as he added, "Kiss for luck?"

His grin deepened at her surprised expression, but his eyes darkened with pleasure when she blew him a kiss. He threw his head back and laughed before he let the net fly.

Alec started rhythmically winding up the net again, "Would you look at that!" The water churned in front of him as he hauled it in. Caught within the line was a large fish. She was just relieved he hadn't hauled in a crocodile.

"Your breakfast awaits, my lady," he called proudly. "And the best part is that Akeim will have to clean it." He laughingly explained, "It was our deal, since he would not allow me a knife."

Excitedly, he gathered up the net, careful not to let his prize escape this time. Keeping the fish in the net until he was on shore, he strung it on a line, slipped his boots on, and flung the net over his shoulder.

He was breathing heavily from his efforts as he stepped closer, accepting the cup she'd been holding. He took a big swallow, "Mmm, much better than mine, isn't it?"

She tried to say something positive, but nothing came out.

"I'll admit that it's not my forte." Watching her as he was, his expression said his forte was something else entirely. He stood close enough to kiss her but didn't. Instead his eyes longingly caressed her face until they found her lips. "Thank you for the good luck kiss."

Genevieve smiled bashfully, casting her eyes down. Alec couldn't help but laugh at his beautiful, blushing bride.

~*~

Sophia watched as her daughter and Alec walked toward them. "What do you make of him?"

Akeim turned toward the couple at her question and groaned when he saw the fish.

Sophia raised her brows at his response. "That bad?"

"No, it's that I hate to clean fish." He nodded as Alec held up the catch for him to see. "He dares much," he said of Alec's action. "I am glad it is to him that she is wed, and not the other," he added as he watched the two.

"Why is that?" Sophia asked curiously.

He considered the question for a moment. "The one called Samuel is flighty and like the wily fox. I do not trust him."

"What of Alec?" she prompted.

"It does not appear that he mistreated Genevieve, despite what the sheik forced upon him."

"No, it doesn't, does it?" She was lost in thought as she continued to watch the young couple walk toward them. They were laughing at something and looked, for all intents and purposes, to be deeply in love. "Do you think he is safe?"

Thoughtfully, Akeim turned to her. "I think the lion has yet to bare his teeth."

Samuel, who was making his way down the hill, hollered over towards Alec just then, "I say, good catch, ol' boy."

Akeim rose as they approached from opposite directions, more from the long years of training than from thinking they were threats, though he wasn't of a mind to offer them an opportunity either.

"Fantastic! Look at the size of it," Samuel called out in appreciation as Alec held his catch up. "Hmm, I, for one, can't wait for a decent meal." He caught Akeim's eye. "Not that shish kabobbed snake isn't one of my all-time favorites." He laughed when Akeim gave him an unappreciative glance, in return.

Alec shook his head at Samuel's antics as he headed for a large boulder to set the prized catch upon. Irritating the warrior had apparently become far more entertaining than trying to get a rise from him. Under normal circumstances, he would have welcomed the reprieve. In this case, it might not be the wisest choice.

Alec lifted the net and placed it on the rock, turning slightly away from the task to look back at the group. He froze when he noticed all eyes on him. It wasn't their attention that made him stand deathly still. It was the knives flying in his direction. He let out the breath he'd been holding as they flew past him.

"Holy hell!" He turned in surprise to see what had elicited such a response. A large cobra withered a few feet away from him. The net he'd had over his shoulder had hidden it from his view.

Obviously, it hadn't kept the others from seeing it. All four daggers had struck their mark, two in the head, one in the neck, and another at the tail.

Akeim walked past him and pulled the blades out. The two in the head were returned to Genevieve and her mother. Alec briefly wondered at that. It appeared that there was more to her life in the desert than the usual pursuits of young ladies of the ton. Akeim pocketed the knife he pulled from the neck. He then looked at Samuel as he took the one from the tail.

"From my vantage, it was all I had to aim at," Samuel defended his target. "Pinned like that, it wouldn't have been able to strike," he continued, in response to Akeim's continued blank stare. "All right, I confess... I kept one," he threw his eyes heavenward.

Akeim tossed Samuel the dagger. "It appears then, that you have what you need to clean the fish," he remarked as he handed the catch to him. From his side, Akeim withdrew another knife. Holding it blade first, he extended it toward Alec, saying nothing. It was enough. Alec took his knife from Akeim and slipped it back into his belt.

His father-in-law then picked up the cobra and walked several feet away before he made quick work of skinning it. "It is good you like snake, Samuel. It appears to be on the menu."

~*~

Breakfast was over, and Alec and Samuel were breaking down the tent when Samuel leaned toward him. "You don't appear to be too upset that they've stolen the map, essentially fleecing you of your coin."

"Considering you have another map in your right boot, and I have one in my left, I can't see how they have actually stolen anything but the original."

"I meant, in theory. They have taken what is yours."

"Well, now that I'm married, what is hers is mine, and vice versa." Alec looked over to where Genevieve and her mother were working.

"It looks to me as if she's happy about your decision to keep the marriage," Samuel remarked speculatively.

"She doesn't know," Alec responded testily.

"Change your mind, or lost your nerve?" Samuel asked with a chuckle.

"Things have not exactly been in my favor." Alec briefly glanced over to where Akeim and the guide were talking. The dragoman returned just after they ate breakfast.

"Is it me, or have you noticed how Sophia seems to be in charge?" Samuel whispered quietly, changing the subject. "I don't know what you read in your travel manual, but I had the feeling, in this country, the men were supposed to be in control."

"Perhaps it's because she's of English nobility," Alec wondered. "Who did the sheik say Genevieve's grandfather was?"

Samuel shrugged his shoulder. "Some duchy up in Northumberland." Glancing over at the women, he added thoughtfully, "I think it's more than that."

Even though he rarely gave Samuel's ideas much credit, Alec had to admit that he might be on to something. He looked over to where Genevieve and her mother were packing up the cooking utensils.

"And what of that accent?" Samuel continued in a whisper. "Although they can both speak perfect English when needed, they have the most unusual accent."

Alec couldn't help but reflect on the first time he'd heard it as he watched her. Genevieve, sensing his attention, turned to look at him, smiling shyly. He returned the greeting in kind and had his head knocked sideways as Samuel tossed him a pack without looking. It landed in his arms as she laughed at the mishap. With another smile, she turned away.

It took another pack hitting him harder for Alec to realize it was not an accident the first time. He gave Samuel a look of warning, but his friend just laughed it off, saying, "Just saving a love-struck fool from himself."

Fortunately, their former guide didn't stay long, and when he left, it was to go in the opposite direction of the one in which they were headed. If Alec had to guess, he'd say the man had been scouting. Whatever the case, he was grateful he no longer had to tolerate the dragoman's company. He, for one, didn't appreciate it when someone tried to kill him.

Within an hour's time, they had loaded up the camels and were on their way, following the river towards Aswan. There was at least a hundred feet of bank exposed along the river's edge. Alec imagined that during the wet season the area would all be under water. That observation was evidenced by the lack of growth nearby.

Despite the lack of vegetation, the scenery was far more interesting than the bleak desert they had been traveling through. With the river on one side and high cliffs offering shade on the other, even the temperature seemed more tolerable.

"I've been meaning to tell you," Samuel spoke up from beside him. "I found the symbol of the double lion within the large temple . . . over the arch," he added meaningfully.

"I'm beginning to think there is one over every door," Alec murmured, not in the least bit impressed.

"When I went to check on the camels this morning, I also took the liberty of looking over the smaller temple," Samuel continued. "It too is very intriguing."

"Really?" Alec couldn't help but roll his head back as he sought fortitude for another one of Samuel's diatribes.

"Well, as you know, when Abū Simbel was first discovered, it made quite the stir. Ramesses had portrayed his wife as his equal by having the statues of the queen on the exterior of the temple as large as his."

Samuel scanned through the book lying open on his lap. "And, on the interior walls, she's shown being anointed by two goddesses. Something, as you know, usually reserved for only the Pharaoh."

"Actually, you're assuming that I know either of those things," Alec said, trying to hide his boredom.

"They also call her the Mistress of Two Lands. I'm wondering if this isn't our elusive queen," Samuel speculated.

Alec expelled a deep breath, afraid of where the conversation was leading.

"Look at this." Samuel held up the sketch he'd done of it this morning. "She's wearing the double-plumed crown, just like the figure on the map. I've also come to believe that it too means something."

"Like a feather in the cap means that one is a dandy," Alec joked.

"Exactly!" Samuel remarked.

Alec rolled his eyes. "Do you really think she would have led us right to it?

"Good point," Samuel said. "I guess this means that we can cross off the temple of Hathor that she recommended too." He shook his head with regret. "Well, at least we're narrowing it down."

"Hmm." Alec looked at him as though he were half-crazed. "Only ten thousand more to go."

Samuel chose to ignore him, saying instead, "I'm not going to rule out this place just yet."

"What of the other clues?" Alec watched as Samuel studied his drawings.

"Details, details," Samuel muttered. "There is another oddity. I mean, if Ramesses had such great love for his wife, Nefertari, why is there a whole stele dedicated to another of his wives, the daughter of the Hittite king, within her temple complex? In fact, it says he was bowled over by her and loved her more than anything."

"Why is that an oddity?" Alec couldn't help but ask.

"Well, for one thing, he was supposed to love his chief wife more than anything. She was considered to be beyond compare. After all, Nefertari means 'of beautiful face'."

"So he calls both wives beautiful, and you think it odd," Alec laughed. "I think the man had too many wives to satisfy, and it's a testament to the art of diplomacy."

"Speaking of wives," Samuel cleared his throat, "here comes yours."

"Mind if I join you?" Genevieve rode up beside them.

"Please." Alec smiled at her, obviously relieved to be saved from Samuel and his infatuation with the temples.

"Hello there, lovely lady," Samuel greeted her in his usual style. "Why, the sky itself pales in comparison to the blue of your eyes."

"I thought that myself the first time I gazed into them," Alec added when she looked at him. His eyes darkened with pleasure as he watched her.

Genevieve's gazed was trapped within his as he made reference to seeing her for the first time. She blushed as she remembered him standing before her, half-naked, devouring her with his smoldering gaze.

Samuel shook his head when he realized they weren't even aware of him. Waiting a moment for the two to come back to earth, he finally cleared his throat.

Genevieve broke free of Alec's glance and smiled apologetically at Samuel, noticing as she did that his journal lay open on his lap. She could see the sketches he'd drawn of the temples. "Those are lovely."

Samuel held it up so she could have a better view. "You really think so?"

"Yes, you've really captured the details." She nodded appreciatively.

"Here," he flipped the page to show an up-close version of the cartouche of Ramesses, "look at this one."

Samuel pointed to the page. "This, I believe, is the actual cartouche that Champollion deciphered when he first identified the ancient Egyptian language as being phonetic." He slid his finger over the symbols. "Ra ☉ mo 𓏠 sis 𓏤. The cartouche or ring that encircles it, of course, shows that it belonged to a Pharaoh."

He then flipped the page back again. "Take a look at these." He pointed to the decorative border of the temple. "I was just wondering at them. Why do you suppose there are baboons across the top?" He indicated the scenery around them. "Especially all the way out here in the desert."

"They say that baboons stay quiet until the dawn breaks," Genevieve supplied, "and then as the first rays touch them, they burst into a loud chattering celebration."

"Really?" Samuel gave Alec an *I-told-you-she-knew-more* look as she spoke.

"It's because of this that they have always been used to show homage to the sun god, Ra. The baboon, however, is also one of the symbols of the god Thoth." She glanced up at Samuel, interrupting a look he was giving Alec.

"Thoth? Isn't he the god of scribes?" Alec looked over to Samuel as if to say, *Even I know that.*

"Why, yes." Genevieve glanced over at him, interrupting yet another meaningful glance. She was getting the feeling there was another conversation going on that she wasn't privy to.

"But I thought he was the god of the moon," Samuel said as he puzzled it over. "They represent the sun and moon?"

"Like I said . . . it defies logic," Alec replied.

"What of the uproar caused by the statues of Ramesses's wife being the same size as his?" Samuel looked at Genevieve.

She shrugged slightly; there was really no harm in answering. "Actually, it is really very logical. When Ramesses brought the upper lands of Egypt under his control, the indigenous people already worshipped their own ancient goddess here. When he rebuilt on the site of the previous temple, turning that devotion towards his wife only served his purpose."

"Ah, I see." Samuel's gaze was one of triumph. Alec, in turn, rolled his eyes. She had known of the map, after all, so no real shock there.

Surprising them all, however, was Akeim's shout as he galloped past. "Follow me!" he commanded, urging his stallion to a greater speed. "We must find shelter now!"

What the hell is happening? Alec wondered. Was there a raging dust storm ready to overtake them? He chanced a glance behind them. There was certainly dust, but not from a storm. He could see half a dozen riders in the distance. It was evident from the dust churning up in their wake that the newcomers were riding hard in their direction.

Bloody hell! All they needed was to run into another marauding band seeking payment for trespassing. Alec looked over at Samuel, who was doing as he had just done.

"Here we go again." Samuel rolled his eyes as he caught Alec's glance. He then looked forward, swearing as Akeim left them in his dust.

Genevieve bent low across the back of her camel, slapping it with her reins as she shouted, "Shee-shee-shee." Her camel responded by leaping forward into a gallop.

Both men looked at each other briefly before emitting loud, "Shee-shees." Unlike Genevieve's camel, theirs loped in confusion until Sophia charged up behind them and yelled, "Hyaa!" The camels bolted forward in one of the craziest, most reckless, rides of their lives.

Up ahead, Akeim veered toward the cliffs. He was making a beeline for a crevasse that could be seen in the rock face. As the dust cleared, Alec saw more riders were heading towards them from the opposite direction.

They were trapped.

They had been channeled right into a narrow valley with the Nile on one side, too wide to cross, and the cliffs on the other, too high to climb. As Alec caught up with Genevieve, he could see the fear written on her face. He knew why. . . . Should he fail to protect her, she would be at their mercy, something he would not allow as long as he lived.

Chapter 13

"Don't shoot until I tell you," Akeim shouted over to Alec and Samuel as he tossed them the rifles he'd taken off their camels the day before.

Samuel caught his and kissed the stock, saying, "Hello, love. Did you miss me?" The Spencer rifle was his pride and joy. Alec had one as well, but his feelings weren't quite so involved.

The shelter Akeim had led them to had large rocks bordering the entrance, creating a natural defense. Behind that, an area at least twenty feet wide opened up. The crevasse continued beyond that, narrowing into a gap that was barely wide enough to get the animals through.

"I've sheltered here before." Akeim pulled two more rifles from his saddle.

"I take it this is not the usual welcome you receive," Alec remarked.

"Correct," was all Akeim said as he turned and walked away.

"Friend or foe?" Sophia asked Akeim, dismounting before her horse had come to a stop.

He shook his head as he passed her.

PING! A rock by Samuel's head splintered, followed a moment later by the distant crack of the rifle. "Inaccurate bastard," he shouted, as if the marauder could hear him. Looking over to Akeim, he shouted, "Well, that answers that question. . . . They are obviously friends of yours."

P-ting! Another shot hit the rock, followed by a softer *P-oing* as it ricocheted through the air. Several more shots rang out, sending everyone diving for protection. Small shavings of rock were spraying down on them as the area was pelted with fire.

"Duck, if you have a care for your head." Samuel turned to holler at the women behind him.

Akeim tossed Alec the pack containing their other weapons. Alec caught it and took out his revolver. "Where's the ammunition?" he asked, searching through the contents.

"Is it not there?" Akeim looked back at him in surprise. "Look in those packs still tied to my saddle," he suggested as he carried two muskets with him up to the front and knelt behind the rocks.

Alec tossed the pack to Samuel before he started searching through the sacks, untying several in his haste. The fishing net and several bags fell to the ground as he looked, but he found no sign of any ammunition. "Damn!" he swore, running a hand through his hair in frustration.

He went back to where Genevieve and her mother stood holding the reins of the other animals. "Did you find any ammunition when you packed?" Alec asked as he looked through the bundles tied to one of the camels. Several cooking pots hit the ground.

They both shook their heads. His eyes met, and briefly held, Genevieve's. He could see the worry she was trying to hide. He wanted to go to her, to reassure her, but there wasn't time. He had to duck as another barrage of bullets rang out, striking the rocks nearby. Staying low, Alec crawled back to the front of the crevasse, passing Samuel as he went.

"What . . . ? No ammo?" Stunned, Samuel watched as Alec crossed in front of him. "You've got to be kidding me," he grumbled. "I had a fortune tied up in those cartridges."

Samuel had assumed a prone position so as to avoid the bullets that continually flew overhead. "Bloody careless, if you ask me," he muttered to himself as he searched his numerous pockets for any stray bullets. Unfortunately, the few he'd found were for the pistol, rendering the rifle useless.

"Whose bright idea was it to empty the guns, anyway?" Alec yelled over the noise towards Akeim as he tossed his prized rifle to the side. Unable to do much else, he set about loading his revolver with the ammo he'd been able to find.

"Bloody hell!" Samuel swore as a bullet hit the ground inches from where he lay. "Bastard's aim is improving," he mumbled to himself as he scooted further back.

"Samuel," Akeim shouted from behind him, "there is an alcove down that passage. Take the women and the animals there for cover. If these men make it past us, I trust you to protect them with your life."

"Aye, aye, captain." Samuel touched his fingers to the brim of his hat in salute before scooting away.

Alec assumed sending him away was Akeim's way of shutting Samuel up. He'd used the tactic himself on many occasions. Alec joined him up front as the warrior peered over the edge, watching the men approach.

"I couldn't find any ammunition," Alec informed him as he crouched nearby. With regret, he set his own Spencer rifle to the side. Perhaps his feelings for the weapon were stronger than he'd realized, for he was sadly regretting its loss.

"They're going for a close fight," Akeim informed them as he tossed Alec one of his muskets and a pouch of gunpowder, along with a few of the remaining musket balls.

Alec nodded in understanding as he took the musket and began loading it. Glancing over at his rifle with futility, he pounded down the lead ball with a rod. Taking up the weapon, he positioned himself behind a large boulder. "I take it it's safe to return fire."

Akeim placed his own rifle between two rocks and pulled the trigger in answer. The sound exploded in the small cavern they had taken refuge in.

Alec found a niche of his own and fired, ducking back down before he could see the man fall. He reloaded and fired again, shouting to Akeim over the reverberating percussion, "I only have one more shot."

Akeim nodded as he discarded his rifle and drew out both his long, curved sword and dagger. The riders were closing in on them. Alec fired off his last shot as another musket ball blasted the rock above him. He pulled his revolver out and loaded it with two bullets that he'd found in his gun belt.

TREASURE OF EGYPT

Alec looked over again at his rifle, wishing like hell he could have found at least one bullet for the damn thing. Just beyond it lay the bags and fishing net he'd cast aside earlier. He holstered the gun and picked up the net. It wasn't much to work with, but he had an idea of how he could use it. He looked over to Akeim, who was waiting. "If it's a close fight they want, it's a close fight they'll get."

~*~

Genevieve and her mother led the animals single file through the passage, deeper into the crevasse. The high, twisting walls opened up to the sky above them, allowing light to filter down into the passage. Samuel followed behind them, dragging a very irritated Cupid behind.

"Not now, fella." He pulled at the cantankerous beast. "Look here, it's nothing to me if you want to go the other way," he warned as the camel jerked the reins.

About twenty feet back, the wind-carved channel opened up into another small nook that was big enough to corral the animals. The ravine they had been following continued further back, but it was too narrow to go any further with the animals. The shelter offered protection from flying debris, though the crack of gunfire echoed within the chamber.

~*~

Alec chanced a quick look over the rocks in front to see how close their attackers were getting. Though they had taken down a few with their muskets, there were still a dozen or more charging up the embankment. Some had dismounted, but it looked like most intended to attack on horseback.

Alec carefully gathered the net up in his arms. Crouching behind the rock, he readied himself. Akeim had a better view of the approaching riders than he did. Alec watched the shadows on the rocks for his cue.

Akeim jumped up with his long sword in hand and sliced through the air as the first horse jumped the boulder in front of him. The man cried out but fell silent before he hit the ground.

Alec let the net fly high overhead. The net plummeted, capturing two riders. The men struggled within the netting as another rider jumped the rock barricade. Alec withdrew his

153

revolver and fired, hitting him in the chest. The newcomer slumped and fell to the ground beside the body of the man Akeim had just killed.

He quickly glanced over to see Akeim fighting two of the marauders as a third approached. Akeim sliced the hand of one before engaging the next one. Alec found himself grateful they were on the same side.

Alec reached the men entangled in the net as another rider jumped the rocks, his sword already raised. The sharp blade he held came down in a deadly arc towards Alec, who lifted the struggling man in the net, using him as a shield.

The force of the blow jerked the man from his arms. Moving quickly, Alec grabbed the horseman's wrist before he could swing the blade again and yanked him from his saddle. He buried his knife in the man's chest as he lifted his gun to fire at the next rider to jump over the boulders.

The other man, caught within the netting, plowed into him from behind, knocking him to the ground. Alec's revolver went off, missing its mark. The man stood over him with his sword raised.

Alec rolled away from the blow that landed inches from his head, and then in the opposite direction to avoid the next. In his path lay Samuel's discarded rifle. He grabbed it, using it to block the oncoming blow. The sword hacked into the stock, barely missing his fingers. He twisted and rolled again, hoping to take the sword with him, but the man pulled the sword free as Alec moved.

The rider prodded his horse forward in an attempt to trample Alec beneath it. Trapped between the horse and the swordsman, he had no choice other than to ball himself up and cover his head with his arms for protection while he rolled to the other side.

"Bloody hell!" Alec swore as the hooves dug into his shoulder. He rolled over the metal pan that had fallen to the ground earlier and grabbed it, using it as a shield for his head. The only thing that he could see as he looked up were two men slipping past, heading down the narrow crevasse toward Genevieve.

No! his mind screamed as he watched in horror, so distracted that he had no chance to dodge the horse's hoof that hit him in the gut. His breath was forced from him in an explosion of air. "Humph," was all that came out as the air escaped his lungs.

~*~

They could hear the sounds of fighting as it echoed along the passage and into the chamber. Genevieve and her mother exchanged worried glances. The noise was almost too much to take. The animals danced in agitation as the women held tightly onto their reins.

The noise made when Samuel fired several shots down the narrow passage at the men almost caused the frightened animals to bolt.

Genevieve looked back at her mother, who was holding onto several of the distraught animals. The largest one was on the verge of throwing a king-sized fit. Sophia was doing her best to soothe Cupid when three dark figures emerged from the narrow crevasse behind her.

Genevieve could hardly believe her eyes. "Mother, watch out!"

Sophia swung around, letting go of the large beast when she saw the men approaching. She made her way to her daughter's side in the chaos, leaving the men trapped behind the disgruntled camel.

Samuel, who had been guarding the front, rushed back to them, placing himself between the attackers and the women. One of the men made his way around the angry camel, pulling his knife from his belt. Samuel raised his revolver in hand and pulled the trigger.

Click . . . nothing happened.

The damn thing was out of ammo. With disgust, Samuel threw the gun to the side and pulled out his knife, but not before their assailant had let his own dagger fly. Samuel ducked, hearing the knife strike the rock wall behind him. He loosed his own blade as he rose, hoping it would pierce the blackguard's heart. To his amazement, the man snatched the whirling weapon out of mid-air.

"Ah, c'mon!" Samuel breathed as he backed up, trying to shield the women from the man. Instead of throwing his knife, the man slowly withdrew his pistol, his sinister grin exposing the dark gaps in his decaying teeth.

"Impressive," cynicism laced his voice as Samuel pulled out a pair of throwing stars, "but can you catch two while you fire?"

The man's expression lost some of its arrogance as Samuel let the stars fly. His finger jerked on the trigger. Samuel was thrown backward as the bullet hammered into his chest. He fell, hitting the back of his head on a rock as he landed. The other man slowly slumped to his knees and then pitched forward onto his face. Both of the stars had found their mark.

Cupid bolted as the blast from the gun went off right next to him. The charging beast ran past Genevieve, barely missing Samuel in its escape back through the passage. She heard the men who were in the narrow opening screaming to get out of his way as she ran over to Samuel, who lay unmoving.

"Oh, my God!" Genevieve cried out as she bent over him. A dark stain spread out from the hole in his jacket. She looked up to see two men grab for her mother. "No!"

~*~

The horse that threatened to trample Alec reared up, giving him time to grab the breastplate of the saddle. He used it to pull himself off the ground. Raising his feet, he kicked out, striking the man who was standing beside it with his sword raised. Taken by surprise, the man was knocked to his knees.

As the horse reared again, Alec used the momentum to get his footing and jump up on the other side. He raised the pan he still held to block the blow from the rider's sword and grabbed the man's leg, pulling him off the horse.

Alec caught the man's arm as he fell and twisted, applying pressure to the man's elbow until he felt it break. The man cried out as Alec hit him over the head with the iron skillet before grabbing the sword from his useless hand.

The man he'd kicked ran at him with his sword raised. Alec barely had time to lift the sword he now held to ward off the blow. The dazed man joined the fray, a dagger in his good hand. They attacked Alec simultaneously from opposite directions. The swordsman's blade came down towards his head, while the other man jabbed his knife toward Alec's middle.

Alec swiveled, stepping towards the swordsman as the blade continued its descent. The sword barely missed him as it slashed down to the side of him. In one move, Alec wrapped his right hand over the man's forearm, trapping it while he bent forward, twisting to the side to avoid the dagger as it stabbed towards his center.

Using his momentum against him, Alec pulled down on the man's trapped arm. Crouching low, he flipped the man over his back to the ground. The dazed man was too slow to sidestep, and they landed in a heap as the other man rolled into him.

Alec heard a scream echo out from the crevasse. He tried to run for the opening but was blocked by the dazed one who had managed to stagger back to his feet. This man was unreal! Alec shook his head in disbelief. There had to be something in the pipe they smoked.

The man ran towards him with his dagger raised. Alec used his own momentum to toss him. The dazed one completed a somersault, ending against the rock wall once again, this time staying there.

Alec turned to see the swordsman charging towards him once again. This time he held not only a sword, but also a dagger in his other hand. He came towards Alec, holding the knife so that the blade pointed down towards his own elbow. The sun glinted off the sword as he raised it, cutting a wide arc through the air.

He met the man's blow with the sword he held. The assailant continued to turn, lifting his dagger with the intention of plunging it into Alec's heart as he came around.

Alec grabbed the man's hand as the dagger came down towards him and twisted it so that the blade continued, burying itself into the man's own stomach. Alec took the sword from his hand as he fell.

Holding a sword in each hand, Alec turned, slicing through the air so that both weapons were up, ready for the next attack. Akeim stood before him in a similar pose. They faced each other briefly before turning outward, their backs now guarded by each other's as they faced the remaining attackers. The last of them soon fell at their feet.

Genevieve's scream echoed from within the crevasse. Alec turned back towards the twisting rock passage and cautiously entered. He could hear the shouting of men as the two he'd seen slip past him appeared around the first corner, running at high speed with a rampaging camel at their heels.

As the man in the lead noticed Alec, he slowed, causing the man directly behind to collide into him, and they stumbled. Cupid trampled over them, followed by the rest of the crazed animals. Alec barely had time to jump out of the way before they reached him.

All Alec could think of as he pressed himself against the rock wall was the scream he'd heard. He had to wait until the frightened animals had cleared the passage before he could continue. He heard a moan as he entered the alcove. His heart felt like it leapt into his throat.

"Samuel . . . Samuel, talk to me." Genevieve knelt over his friend, who lay on the ground. Alec's gut twisted as he realized Samuel was actually down. He noticed Sophia standing behind them and was shocked to see three more bodies at her feet. She stepped over them as she went to Samuel, kneeling beside him.

"Oh, my God!" Alec groaned as he stepped closer, seeing, for the first time, the dark stain on Samuel's chest.

Samuel moaned again.

"Can you hear me?" Genevieve asked, worried.

Sophia checked the pulse at his neck and then opened his shirt. "Aaugh, my head," Samuel groaned, blinking his eyes.

Sophia spread his shirt wide. . . . Nothing. There was a bright red welt over his heart, but no blood. She pulled his jacket back to find a hole, and then dug inside his pocket.

"What happened?" Samuel blinked his eyes dazedly. "Did I at least get the bastard?" He tried to sit up, looking over to where the body of the man he had fought lay dead. He winced at the effort and settled back down, grabbing his head as he did.

"You're a very lucky man," Sophia said as she shook his flask. A rattle came from within the container as she handed it to him.

A bullet had ripped through one side of it and dented the other. He turned it upside down over his open mouth. A single drip splashed on his lip as he held it up. "Oh, no!" He groaned over the loss. He looked at the liquid that soaked his shirtfront. "Damn! What a waste," he moaned, dropping his head and hand in defeat.

Akeim entered and went back to the three men who lay behind them.

Sophia went over to him. "They came out from the back."

He examined the curved dagger of one of the men. "He is most likely a hired mercenary." Akeim's tone was one of disgust.

"You can tell from the knife?" Alec watched as he examined it.

Akeim nodded, showing him the design on the man's *khan jar hushan*. "This man comes from the region up north. You can ask him yourself in a moment if you'd like." He nudged the man with the toe of his boot.

"What happened back there?" Samuel seemed mystified once he'd sat up and spied the other bodies on the ground.

"You saved us," Sophia answered. "We're forever in your debt."

"I don't remember fighting those men." Puzzled, he rubbed his brow. "I only remember that one." He pointed to the man he had downed with his throwing stars.

"You have hit your head," Sophia remarked sympathetically. "It's not uncommon for men to perform great acts of bravery and forget them when they have suffered a blow to the head."

Alec crouched down beside Samuel and examined his injury. There was a huge lump on the back. "You're going to have a hell of a headache."

Samuel looked at Sophia suspiciously for a moment, but her face showed only empathy for his injury. "No," he said quietly to Alec. "I don't remember fighting those men. I remember . . ." He looked up with a frown.

"What?" Alec asked.

"Good God." An amazed expression crossed Samuel's face. "I think your wife and her mother can fly."

Alec rolled his eyes as he looked up at the two women. "He'll be fine."

Chapter 14

One of the men Akeim was standing over groaned, rolling his head from side to side. Akeim grabbed him by the front of his kaftan and half lifted him off the ground. The warrior's menacing stare was the first thing the man saw when he opened his eyes.

"*Allah a bah*—" the man started to holler, but was quickly silenced.

"Who sent you?" Akeim asked in rapid Arabic, shaking him.

The man looked as though he would not talk, but he found his tongue when Akeim found his knife. "The White Devil, the White Devil!" he screamed in a foreign tongue.

"I'm sending you back to hell with a message," Akeim growled as he held the man off the ground. "Tell the White Devil that the Black Serpent has risen."

The man's eyes grew wide with fear as Akeim took his weapon and hit him over the head with it. The man slumped to the ground beside his still unconscious companion.

"We are not safe here." Akeim looked back over his shoulder as he quickly removed their other weapons. "We must leave quickly."

"Well, that was all rather melodramatic," Samuel whispered to Alec as he tried to sit.

"Can you ride?" Alec knelt beside him.

"Yes." With a show of bravado, Samuel smiled. "Besides, it doesn't look as if I have much choice, does it?" He gave Akeim a sideways glance. "What with the White Devil and the Black Serpents on the loose."

Samuel accepted Alec's outstretched hand. Wincing as he stood, he held on to his head and leaned forward with a groan.

"Are you all right?" Alec watched him with concern, as well as confusion over his words.

Samuel nodded in response and winced again at the effort.

"Dizzy?"

"Not any more than after having had a bottle, a pint, and another bottle," Samuel replied with some levity. "I'll be fine, just let me get my bearings." He leaned back against the rock face behind him.

Alec looked over to where Genevieve stood. He could tell she was upset, though she was doing her best to hide it. He left Samuel and went over to her. He could see the shimmer of tears as he looked down into her beautiful eyes. Without much thought, he enveloped her in his arms and held her tight. Holding her close, he whispered against the silken strands of her hair, "It's alright now."

"I'm sorry," she sniffed. "It just reminded me so much of the day I lost my father."

Though she had spoken quietly against his chest, he heard her. Alec continued to hold her tightly until she looked up at him, her cheeks wet from the tears. "I'm sorry for your loss." He dried the moisture with his thumb as he gazed down at her. "You know I'd go to hell and back before I'd let anything happen to you."

Sophia watched Alec embrace her daughter. His actions convinced her of his feelings for Genevieve more readily than his words ever could. Genevieve would be safe with him. She quietly passed them and went to Samuel's side. "Here, let me help you," she offered, assisting him to stand upright.

He stubbornly tried to walk without her help, but she placed his arm over her shoulders for support when it became evident that he needed it. "You can ride with Akeim if you don't think you can keep your seat."

It was a dire threat, to be sure. Samuel stood taller after her remark. "I assure you, madam, I have suffered far more serious injuries than this and have yet to lose my seat on a horse. I don't intend to start now."

"Notice he didn't say camel," Alec whispered quietly to Genevieve, who was still in his arms.

"I heard that!" Samuel said indignantly.

They both chuckled, remembering his fall from grace. Genevieve smiled up at Alec. "Thank you." She sniffed.

"Come." He placed his hand gently on her back as they walked toward the opening together.

"I cannot believe you're letting them live." Samuel watched in amazement as Akeim tied the two men together.

"I do not commit murder, if that is what you are suggesting," Akeim told him as he completed the knot.

"Now you tell me!"

Akeim looked up at him. "When it comes to you, I will make an exception."

"Was that a joke?" Samuel looked over at Sophia in surprise. "Did the heavens crack, as well as my skull?"

Walking to the front, they all stood speechless for a moment as the bodies of the dead confronted them.

"Dear heaven," Sophia was stunned by the carnage. "This was a close call."

"We were very lucky," Akeim spoke solemnly. "I would not have prevailed against so many had I been alone."

"So the lion has teeth," she breathed.

"Indeed." Akeim gave her a brief glance before turning away.

"What lion?" Samuel looked around curiously.

"He speaks of your friend," Sophia enlightened him.

"Alec, a lion?" Samuel scoffed. "What is it about you and all these names? Demons, snakes, lions . . . ." He paused, considering it. "Just out of curiosity, what am I?"

"You are sneaky, like a fox," Akeim commented dryly before whistling for his horse.

"I'm not so sure I'm flattered by that," Samuel snorted, "especially since I so nobly sacrificed myself back there."

"I'm sure he meant cunning," Sophia amended diplomatically.

"Perhaps you would prefer being a sacrificial lamb." Akeim had an amused glint in his eye as he looked back at Samuel.

"More like a wolf in sheep's clothing," Alec, who had been listening, remarked.

"This is hardly the way to treat an injured man," Samuel moaned.

"Well then, you'll be really happy about this." Alec stooped to pick up Samuel's prized rifle and handed it to him. "Sorry. It was unavoidable."

"Augh, what has happened to you?" Samuel asked in dismay as he cradled the weapon, looking down at the cracked stock with a huge chunk missing.

"I'll replace it when we get back." Alec picked up his own rifle. "Or you may have mine."

"Just tell me it was worth the sacrifice." Samuel looked at him hopefully.

Alec rolled his eyes. "I'm fairly certain it saved my life."

"Well, then, I'll carry it proudly."

"I'll be happy to replace the stock," Alec offered.

"Nonsense. I shall display it on my mantle in a place of honor." He lowered his voice and whispered to Alec, "Besides, nothing excites the ladies more than a tale of bravery."

"I see. . . . Would you care to know how it happened, then?" Alec asked curiously.

"Not necessary. I'll improvise." Samuel grinned.

Akeim, who had been gathering weapons nearby, came over and handed Samuel a sword that had been broken in half. "You may have this for your trophy as well."

Samuel eyed the useless stub suspiciously. "Thank you, but no."

"Are you sure?" Akeim asked, a slight grin on his face. "You obviously need all the help you can get."

Alec chuckled, while Samuel grumbled. "Sure, pull one over on the stunned man. Not very sporting of you."

Akeim climbed up the rock to where his horse waited for him. "Gather up all their weapons," he ordered as he mounted his horse, "while I collect the animals."

"I say," Samuel complained after he had left, "who put him in charge?"

"I did." Sophia's voice brooked no defiance.

"Can't argue with that," he said quickly with a grimace toward Alec.

~*~

Alec looked over at the sun, which was sinking low on the horizon. They had been riding along the bank of the Nile for hours with Akeim scouting ahead, making sure their way was clear of danger. The threat of being ambushed and the need for constant vigilance made for an arduous journey, especially with the extra horses they were herding.

Calling a halt, Akeim finally dismounted. Alec and Samuel walked with him to the ridge of the hill. On the other side lay a fishing port that looked to have served as a center of trade for thousands of years. Akeim pulled an eyeglass from the pouch he carried at his waist. Keeping low, he used it to assess the village below.

"Well . . . do you see any of the devil's henchmen?" Samuel asked impatiently.

Akeim ignored his question and continued to watch the people of the small town as they went about their business. In response, Samuel gave Alec a look of exasperation.

Alec's father-in-law returned the telescope to its pouch and turned to eye them critically. "I think it would be best if we wait until nightfall to ride into town." He pointed to the terrain below. "We will herd the animals there, to that enclosure on the edge of it."

Alec nodded in response.

"I say we ride down there with guns blazing and be on our way," Samuel argued. "How many can there possibly be, anyway?"

"From what I could see, it appears that there are several men down there who are not fishermen."

"How many were there?" Alec looked back down at the village.

"See that encampment on the other side?"

"Yes." Alec nodded while Samuel tossed his hands in frustration that Akeim would answer Alec and not him.

"It wasn't there earlier this spring."

"There have to be at least a hundred tents down there," Samuel scoffed. "You actually think they are all in league with the White Serpent?"

"Devil," Akeim corrected. "I'd rather ride in under the cover of darkness and not find out the hard way." The warrior stood and walked back to where the women were sitting in the shade.

"I'm telling you, he's starting to get on my nerves," Samuel whispered.

"No offense," Alec shrugged his shoulder in commiseration, "but if I had to choose a plan at this time, I'd go with him on this one."

~*~

They quietly skirted around the buildings of the town after having left most of the animals in the pen. Akeim was first, followed by Alec and the women. Samuel brought up the rear. Each led their own mount, walking beside it, rather than risk riding through the streets.

A man, dressed more like a marauder than a fisherman, paused near the entrance of the alley they were hiding in. Much to their horror, he entered the dark passage and relieved himself against the wall. Belching loudly, he then expelled exhaust from the other end before continuing on.

"That was god-awful," Samuel declared in a whisper to the one near enough to hear him; Cupid snorted softly in response.

Akeim spied around the corner, then looked back, using his arm to signal the others to follow as he started across the street. They all slipped soundlessly into a storage building across the way.

"Wait here." Akeim turned to the others once the animals were settled. "I will go talk to the omdeh."

"The omdeh?" Alec looked over at Samuel for an explanation.

"The governor," Samuel explained.

Both Alec and Samuel followed him to a small side door, where they waited in silence to make sure the coast was clear. Akeim stood with his face pressed to the narrow opening as he looked out.

"Are you sure you don't want one of us to go with you?" Alec whispered behind him.

"It is best that I speak to him alone."

"I could help you make an excellent deal," Samuel suggested.

Akeim gave him a look of annoyance. "He does not care for foreigners."

"You have a lot in common, then," Samuel commented dryly.

"On this we agree." Akeim turned back to the street, monitoring the activity outside.

"Well, seeing as how I'm not going," Samuel continued, despite the man's chafing remark. "Could you see if he has any ammunition?"

"Anything else?" Akeim asked sarcastically over his shoulder.

"Now that you mention it, do you know if he sells whiskey?" Samuel goaded him. "I've heard some tradesmen are willing to make a deal."

"I am not here to buy you alcohol," Akeim told him with mounting irritation.

"I am willing to part with this," Samuel held out a purse of gold coins, "to aid in the deal."

Akeim briefly turned to see what he offered then turned back to the door.

Incredulous, Alec eyed the coins. "You mean you had this on you the whole time?" he whispered in disbelief.

"Of course I've had it on me. It's not like we've passed any banks."

"You mean you could have bought our freedom, and you didn't?" Incredulous, Alec stared at him.

"Are you really going to go back to that?" Samuel responded with a bored sigh.

"Yes!" Alec practically swore.

"I told you. . . . We didn't have enough on us to ransom a *nobleman*."

"And who told them I was a *nobleman*?" Alec growled in a low voice.

"Why are we discussing this?" Samuel groaned. "You've got the girl, and you've got your mother off your back."

"Don't change the subject. If I recall correctly, you recommended that I get a dog instead."

"Shh!" Akeim whispered over his shoulder. "Stop squabbling like women."

Alec glared at Samuel with narrowed eyes while Samuel innocently pointed at Alec, implying it was he that was causing the trouble. Alec briefly glanced back at the women to make sure they hadn't heard.

Akeim grabbed the purse with a sigh and left the troublesome pair, only to return an hour later with troublesome news.

"Is everything alright?" Sophia asked worriedly as she met him at the door.

"It is as I feared," Akeim spoke solemnly. "The mujahideen has been alerted to keep an eye out for two Englishmen fitting their descriptions."

"Oh, no," she groaned.

"There is also a reward, should they be found."

"What is it?" Genevieve came forward. "Is something wrong?"

"If who is found?" Samuel asked as he too joined them.

"You," Akeim informed him.

"Are you serious?" Samuel's brows shot up in surprise. "Why?"

"This is because of the map, isn't it?" Alec guessed as he looked over at Genevieve, who stood beside him. "We should separate. It will be safer for you."

"No," Genevieve responded quickly.

"In this case, I agree; besides, this is an easy thing to solve," Sophia said, looking at them speculatively.

"It is? How?" Samuel asked curiously.

In the dim light filtering through the many cracks between the boards and the open windows high above, Alec could see the expression on her face as she assessed them. "You should know," he watched her warily, "that we would make terrible women."

It didn't take long for both Alec and Samuel to be transformed. Sophia had seen to Samuel's disguise, while Genevieve worked diligently on Alec's.

"Do I want to know where this came from?" Alec asked as something that resembled a beard was attached to his chin.

"Probably not." Genevieve smiled sweetly.

When she was done with the false beard, she began wrapping a cloth about his head. As she wound the material, she ended up standing between his legs. He tried to keep his eyes off her anatomy, but with her breasts at eye level, it would have taken a saint. His thoughts were far from it, especially when she kept brushing against him as she moved.

She leaned forward to tuck in the last piece. "I believe you are finished." She looked down at him. The heated glance he gave her said otherwise. Though a blush rose to her cheeks, she didn't look away. In fact, she "accidentally" brushed against his thigh, sending scorching heat to his loins. A seductive smile played on her lips.

"Well, how do I look?" Samuel asked as he stood, interrupting them. Genevieve backed away, enough so that Alec could see the transformation.

"Let my people go." Samuel held up a staff, mimicking Moses as he assumed his character.

"Seems fitting." Alec laughed as he gave Genevieve a smoldering glance that only she could see as he rose to his feet.

Both Alec and Samuel wore black robes, donated from Genevieve's wardrobe. Their faces had been smeared with dark grease, and they both sported beards that resembled something off of a goat.

Sophia regarded the sinister looking pair critically. "You'll do."

Akeim coughed and rubbed his upper lip so as to hide the smile that threatened.

"You're certainly enjoying this," Samuel complained.

"More than you'll ever know." Akeim grinned. "I'm the one who collected the beards."

"That would explain the smell," Samuel replied.

"Is this really necessary?" Alec brought his hand up to rip it off.

"Only until we get to the boat," Sophia said, stilling his hand.

~*~

"Boat?" Samuel scoffed. "Is that what this thing is supposed to be?"

"Shh—" Akeim looked back at him as they crept around the small vessel, which looked to have seen better days.

"Who was the last person to sail it . . . Noah?" Samuel enquired scathingly before he turned to Alec and whispered, "I told you I should have negotiated for us." In an effort to give the ladies some privacy, both Alec and Samuel had followed Akeim outside while he waited for the governor.

"I have seen what happens when you negotiate, Samuel, and I, for one, am not looking for another wife," Akeim said as he suddenly reappeared from around the stern. "Besides, this is not the boat," he gestured across the water, "that is."

The ship was moored out in the bay, swaying gently as the water lapped against it. Its white masts shone brightly in the moonlight.

"Aahh, now that is a beauty," Samuel sighed.

"No, not that one, "Akeim pointed, "the smaller one next to it."

"Oh." Samuel was obviously disappointed.

"He does have a daughter, if you'd like me to bargain for the larger one," Akeim offered with an eyebrow raised.

"No . . . no, that one will do fine," Samuel informed him with a nod.

"I've heard tell that she is a *great* beauty," Akeim smiled, "as *great* in girth as the boat itself."

"No. Really, the *small* boat is an excellent choice," Samuel assured him.

Akeim merely lowered his head with a slight nod and disappeared around the boat again in response.

"He was kidding, right?" Samuel glanced warily over at Alec.

"You're asking me?" Alec eyed him critically.

"Right," Samuel nodded, "you'd probably love to see me married off to the bounteous beauty."

"It couldn't happen to a more deserving fellow."

Akeim reappeared from around the boat. "The omdeh is here. Go back to the women and wait while I take him to see the animals."

Alec and Samuel retraced their steps a few feet to a storage shed where the ladies waited for them. They knocked softly before entering. Not one sound was heard as they walked in and looked about the large storage shed for the women.

Alec was about to call for Genevieve when she suddenly appeared in front of him. She still had the unnerving ability to move soundlessly, but it no longer made his hair stand on end.

If he could only get a moment alone, he thought, looking at her in the light filtering through the slats in the shed. "Where is your mother?" he questioned softly.

"Behind you," Sophia replied.

Both men turned in surprise. Alec had to admit he might have become used to Genevieve's sudden appearances, but he still found it startling when her mother did it.

"Now I see where she gets it from," Samuel whispered to Alec.

"To what are you referring?" Sophia raised a brow.

"Ahh . . . her great beauty," Samuel supplied.

"I thought for sure you were referring to her catlike stealth." Sophia folded her arms across her chest.

"Ah, that too," Samuel amended with a quick side-glance to Alec.

"Try to remain quiet while we wait for Akeim to return," she admonished, returning to the place where she could see out into the street.

Alec had to smile at the quick putdown she had just delivered and mouthed "Ouch!", just to annoy him.

Samuel expressed mockery by pretending to laugh as Genevieve turned to leave.

Alec had better things to do than trade silent rejoinders with the simpleton. Genevieve had driven him to distraction earlier, and he knew how he'd rather be spending his time while they waited.

"He's a goner," Samuel sighed as he watched Alec disappear after her. There was just no saving the man from himself. He threw up his hands and turned away. Finding some dates in the food bags, he sat down on a barrel and started munching. It wasn't long before he was nudged in the shoulder by Cupid.

"Sure, now you're my friend," he said softly as the beast sniffed at his beard, then snorted. The camel, Samuel noticed, was suspiciously short one himself. The hair the animal used to have on its neck was missing.

"Well, at least it came from that end, and not the other." Samuel handed him one of the sweet fruits.

Alec followed Genevieve to a bench in the darkened corner. Rather than sit on it, as he thought she would have, she stepped up and boosted herself to a ledge higher up. Silently she swung herself up to the wood beam near the window.

Damn! Alec thought as he followed her. She wasn't making this easy. Try as he might not to make any noise, the beam creaked slightly with his weight as he settled onto it. "May I join you?" he whispered.

He could see the silhouette of her head as she nodded. She sat before an open window, watching the street below. Alec scooted over until his leg touched hers. Sitting back, he rested against the wall behind them, content to watch her in the moonlight.

She stifled a yawn, then smiled apologetically.

"It's been a long day." He smiled softly. "There is no need for both of us to keep an eye out. Why don't you lean against me and get some rest?" He waited, wondering if she would allow the familiarity.

His nose was filled with the scent of her hair as she leaned back against his chest, resting her head on his shoulder. He breathed her fragrance in, pressing his lips against her ear.

She tensed with a shiver, but instead of moving away, she nestled against him. He wrapped his other arm around her waist and let out a sigh as she settled deeper within his arms.

A peace settled over him as they sat together, one so great that he knew, without a doubt, that this was the woman he had waited his whole life for. It seemed a lifetime and not enough, by far, as he held her in his arms, and it was over all too quickly.

Chapter 15

"Akeim returns," Sophia whispered over her shoulder.

Samuel, who was stretched out on a sack of grain, yawned. "Oh, goodie." He stood, shaking out his limbs.

Genevieve and Alec climbed down from their roost. Alec came down first, reaching up his arms to assist her. He doubted she needed it, but he enjoyed the brief contact with her hips immensely.

The door opened, and Akeim stepped inside. "I have good news and bad."

"Let us hear it." Alec couldn't help but notice the change in his calm demeanor as he approached. He was now deadly calm.

"Bad news first, if you don't mind," Samuel interjected. "Matter of preference. I like my good news last. Always have."

"The boat is ready." Akeim scowled at him.

"Augh," Samuel groaned. "That was the good news, wasn't it?"

"What is the bad?" Alec asked as Akeim cast black, unreadable eyes on him.

"A few of the men that survived the fight today have made it into town and alerted the others that we are most likely here."

"I knew we should have killed them," Samuel declared.

Akeim gave him a weary glance. "As I said, I do not commit murder."

Alec pulled a hand through his hair. "How is it that those two made it here so fast without a horse?"

"From what I understand, there are three of them. We obviously missed one." Akeim spoke softly. "Their version is slightly different than the truth as well. They have accused the English of attacking them."

"That's preposterous!" Samuel snorted indignantly.

Ignoring him, Akeim continued. "Their leader has asked the omdeh for permission to search every house for us."

"And?" Sophia glanced over at the door.

"It is only a matter of time before they are here. We will have to make our way to the boat quickly and set sail under the cover of darkness."

"I thought he owed you for saving his life, and that of his family?" Sophia turned back toward him. "Does that not count for something?"

"It is why we are still here, and why they have started searching on the other side of town," Akeim stated flatly. "There is no other way for the omdeh to openly protect the English over the edicts of the mujahideen. This is our best chance." He looked over at the door. "After tonight, the debt has been repaid."

"Why are we standing here wasting time?" Samuel dropped the sack of dates back into the pouch. "Let's get a move on."

The trunk was reloaded onto Cupid's back, along with the food and a few other necessities. The tent was sacrificed in an attempt to reduce the noise the animal's hooves would make on the wooden dock. Akeim tore the fabric into long strips of cloth, which Samuel and Alec wrapped around the hooves of the animals.

"I hope this works," Samuel picked up the rear hoof of Akeim's horse, "otherwise, I just got pissed on for nothing."

Alec tied the cloth around the hoof that he held. "Your sacrifice is duly noted."

Once again they led their mounts through the narrow alley that took them to the dock. Akeim went first, then gestured to the others to let them know the coast was clear. One by one, they left the safety of the shadows and went out into the moonlit street.

"The moment of truth," Samuel said to no one in particular as they brought the animals onto the wooden boards. Their hooves were almost whisper silent, despite the strange way Cupid was walking. The animal's steps were awkwardly high and wide, no doubt in an attempt to rid itself of the bothersome boots.

It wasn't until it was Cupid's turn to walk over the plank onto the boat that it became a problem. Genevieve and her mother had already made it into the boat when the camel refused to go any further.

"Hold up there, Samuel," Alec whispered. "Let me get this horse over, and then I'll help you with that one."

"Fine by me." Samuel held onto the agitated animal tightly. "And to think I chose you over a horse," he complained to the camel at his side.

Alec returned quickly, but still the cantankerous beast refused to go up. "I've danced to this tune before. Here, you take the head, and I'll bring up the rump."

"Nice try," Samuel peered around the hindquarters, "but I'll take my chances with this end."

"Get him up, or leave him," Akeim cautioned them. "I think I hear someone coming." He mounted his steed and rode to the corner of the building.

"Ahh, you little bugger!" Samuel swore as he put his shoulder to its rear and pushed. Cupid took a few steps before rearing up slightly.

"Oh, no," Genevieve called out in a whisper. "Watch out for the trunk. Don't let it fall."

"Let's get the trunk down off him first," Alec whispered back to Samuel.

Even when Genevieve clucked softly, the animal still refused to go any farther. It took five different attempts to get him up to the plank. Bribing him with food eventually coaxed him partway up. The camel was halfway over the gangplank when he started to bolt, despite the fact there was food on the other side.

"I knew I should have taken a horse," Samuel grumbled.

Genevieve pulled on his reins, while both Alec and Samuel pushed. The camel did such a sideways skid that the boat started rocking, causing the gangplank to slip with it.

Akeim rode up behind and prodded it in the rear with a stick. The camel jumped forward onto the deck of the boat, bellowing and spitting all the way. Samuel barely had time to jump off of the plank before it fell, disappearing into the black water with a splash. . . . Alec wasn't as lucky.

"You could've warned us!" Samuel complained, dripping wet from the dousing.

"Shh, someone comes!" Akeim warned as he jumped down and tore off the wrappings from his horse's hooves. "Get that trunk out of sight," he said before he went back to meet the group.

Dripping wet, Alec hauled himself out of the water and helped Samuel to hoist the trunk up. They took off . . . in opposite directions. The trunk swung wildly between them before they caught it.

"This way," Alec whispered loudly, tugging on the trunk. They made it to a side street, then paused when they heard voices coming from that direction.

"No, this way." Samuel pulled him back.

Akeim returned, riding towards them. "They're coming!" He waved at them before disappearing farther down the street.

Heading towards the buildings behind them, Alec and Samuel found an opening and backed away from the entrance into the darker recesses of the alley. It was rank, filthy, and a dead end.

"This isn't good." Samuel looked down at Alec's wet footprints that led straight to them, and then searched around for an alternative exit. "There's not even a bloody door." He tripped over something in the dark. A cat hissed and ran from the recess. "That scared the—"

"Shhh," Alec whispered, "they're here."

The cat ran through the feet of several men who had appeared at the entrance of the alleyway. Alec and Samuel remained silent, waiting for them to make the first move. Just as the leader of the group commanded that they come forward or face the consequences, Akeim appeared on horseback behind them.

"Ah, shit!" Samuel groaned. Thinking fast, he walked forward. Speaking in Arabic, he called out to Akeim. "All clear, sayyid, no one here."

Akeim caught on to the ruse quickly. "Continue searching, and check the refuse pile," he ordered, turning his attention back to the men.

Samuel dutifully started to pick through the garbage, bemoaning his impulsive nature. "Of course he'd say the trash," he mumbled under his breath.

"We have searched here," Akeim asserted. "Why don't you continue on the other side of the street?"

Samuel continued searching through the foul-smelling remains until Akeim gave them the okay. "My thanks," he nodded toward Samuel, "I did not like the idea of having to kill them."

"I know. . . . You don't commit murder," Samuel parroted.

"Despite the fact they have been lied to, they are my brothers," Akeim said solemnly. "I thank you for your quick thinking."

"Like a fox," Alec said sarcastically as he emerged from the alley with the trunk over his shoulder. "If you two are through chatting, I could use a little help."

"I've got it." Samuel took the other side of the trunk and helped haul it over to the boat. "By the way," he looked up at Akeim, "nicely done with the rubbish. Remind me to thank you in kind."

Sophia had pulled the boat as close to the dock as she could, but there was still a gap where the plank used to be. Alec and Samuel had to toss the trunk across and then jump over a few feet of water.

It was obvious how the women had managed to keep Cupid quiet throughout the ordeal. The ornery beast was lying down in the center of the deck enjoying a whole sack of dates. Alec and Samuel had to step around the cantankerous animal as they boarded the boat.

"I wonder if he could have found a smaller one," Samuel criticized.

"*Ukaf!*" A voice shouted from the corner of the building.

"Oh, c'mon!" Samuel looked over his shoulder in exasperation, shaking his head. "They're on to us."

"Make way!" Akeim shouted over his shoulder as he drew his sword and charged toward the man, who took off running in the other direction.

Alec and Samuel worked the sails as the women dealt with the lines and the rudder. The wind buffeted the canvas as the fabric rose, causing both the ship and dock to creak with the stress.

"Hurry," Sophia called to Akeim.

The man Akeim had threatened disappeared around the corner, but his cry for help was raising the whole town. The distant shouts of men coming towards them were getting louder as they scurried to set sail.

Sophia loosened the line that tied the boat to the dock, and the felucca began to pull away. She glanced worriedly over to where Akeim had disappeared. "Akeim!" she called out. The gap between the ship and the dock was widening, despite the fact that Sophia held the line.

Akeim returned with a dozen men chasing after him. Several shots were fired from the group in their direction as he raced his horse down the pier. "Stand back!" he shouted as he charged his horse toward the boat, leaping off the edge in a dangerous bid to reach the ship.

Sophia let go of the rope as the stallion cleared the rail and landed just in front of Cupid. Jumping over the large camel, the horse skidded to a halt on the other side.

"If I hadn't just seen that with my own eyes, there is no way I would have believed it." Samuel's amused chuckle could be heard over the flurry of activity.

P-ting! Shots were fired, hitting the boat as the group of men rushed to the end of the pier. When the rope was released, the current pulled the ship away from the dock, though not as quickly as they would have liked.

"Take cover!" Alec looked back to make sure Genevieve was safe.

"This seems awfully familiar." Samuel glanced back at the angry mob. "We seem to have a knack for this type of departure."

A bullet struck the trunk at Sophia's feet, splintering the side. Akeim was off his horse, diving over her in the span of a heartbeat, covering her with his body.

Samuel and Alec worked the sails, giving them everything they had in order to take the ship further away from the flying bullets.

Genevieve crouched by the rail and loaded a musket. Taking aim, she fired; a man standing on the shore with his weapon raised ready to shoot grabbed his shin and started hopping on one leg in response.

177

Sophia's muffled voice sounded from under Akeim a moment later. He moved enough to uncover her face but remained where he was.

"I'm sure it's safe now," she repeated awkwardly.

With their noses a mere inch apart, he looked down at her with concern. "Are you alright?"

Surprised by his close proximity, not to mention their compromising position, she could only nod her head in response.

He stared into her eyes. "Did I hurt you, *Sitt* Hakeem?"

Sophia felt a blush rise to her cheeks. "I-I'm fine."

There was a glimmer of a smile on his lips as he looked down at her. "I should see to the sails." With that, he rolled from on top of her.

A flustered Sophia joined her daughter a moment later. The men standing on the end of the dock were running for cover. Genevieve fired again. This time, the bullet hit one of the men in the rear.

"That has to hurt," Sophia commented wryly as she loaded a musket beside her daughter. A moment later, another man who'd been hiding behind a crate was grasping his rear in pain.

"Nice shot!" Genevieve smiled.

"And you thought I was a pain in the arse," Samuel whispered over to Alec. "Remind me never to get them angry."

"That's the least of your worries, if you do," Akeim warned as he came up behind them. Checking the rigging, he trimmed the sails, doubling their speed with his efforts. Samuel looked over to Alec with amazement.

"Imagine that," Samuel whispered as he held the wheel against the strong current. "The lord of the desert knows his way around a ship."

"Imagine," Akeim remarked as he turned around. "Here, let me take the helm."

"Oh, no," Samuel protectively kept his hold on the wheel, "I had it first."

Alec rolled his eyes and went to the rear to help the women, who continued to fire at the men on the docks as they made their way toward the large boat.

"Then I guess you don't want this." Akeim retrieved a bottle he had stashed nearby.

"You make a hard bargain." Samuel gave up his post, taking the bottle from Akeim. He uncorked it. "Ahhh!" he sighed as he sniffed at the contents. His eyes closed. "There is a God." Putting it to his lips, he tipped the bottle back.

"We have company," Sophia shouted back to the men. Several boats had joined the chase, following in their wake.

"Help us return fire," Alec called to Samuel as the bottle in his hand shattered. The bullet wedged into the mast behind him.

"Oh, hell no!" Samuel swore. "I didn't even get a sip!" He licked his lips, sponging off what residue the bottle had left behind. He stared longingly down at the spilt liquid, most of which had been soaked up by the rags discarded from the animals' hooves.

Three ships were trailing them, the large one that had been moored alongside their own leading the pack. With its sails open, the large ship was steadily gaining on them.

"Oh, that is it!" Samuel yelled at their pursuers. "Now you've done it!"

"Does he always carry on so?" Sophia asked as she loaded her weapon.

"Afraid so," Alec replied while shooting his.

"I'll return fire, alright," Samuel threatened as he stalked over to the stockpile of weapons. Instead of a musket, he selected a bow and several arrows. Going back to the spill, he tore off a swath of the soaked cloth and wound it around the tip of the arrow. Using the flint-lighter from his pocket, he held it to the end. The spark ignited the alcohol, causing the fabric to burst into flame.

"This ought to be good," Alec remarked.

Samuel notched the arrow and pulled back the string. Raising it high overhead, he let it fly. They watched as the fire streaked across the sky, arcing down to hit the sails high up on the biggest ship that followed them. It didn't take long for the fire to spread across the fabric.

Samuel had quickly notched another arrow to his bow. Repeating the process, he hit the second sail, which went up in flames as rapidly as the first. The burning sails were brought down and put out by the crew, but not before the flames had spread to the decking. The large ship sat dead in the water with only the current to lend it speed.

Samuel sent several more arrows across the night sky, crippling the other two boats as they too lost their sails to the hungry flames. The glowing boats receded into the darkness as they sped away.

"By God, that will teach them." Without a target left to shoot at, Samuel let the bow sag to his side. Having singlehandedly stopped the pursuit, he looked over at Alec and the women, who had long since stopped firing and were now watching him instead.

Akeim started to chuckle.

"What's so damned funny?" Samuel glanced irritably over his shoulder.

"You have what I would call a fiery temper," Akeim announced.

"Great," Samuel said dully, "I suppose now you'll be calling me a phoenix, or maybe a dragon."

"No, you're still a sneaky fox," Akeim remarked.

"Super," Samuel sighed, "I'm forever the sneaky fox."

"Cheer up," Akeim handed him another bottle, "I believe you've earned this."

"What?" Samuel looked at the bottle in surprise. "You had another the whole time?"

"I'm not so stupid as to only get one and pass up the perfect bargaining tool," Akeim told him.

"Let me get this straight. . . . You're bargaining with something purchased with *my* money?" Samuel eyed him in disbelief. "I've underestimated you. . . . You are a snake." He saluted him with the bottle. "Well done."

This time Samuel wasted no time in uncorking the bottle and taking a big swig. "Augh," he sighed, wiping his mouth with the back of his hand. "Out of curiosity, how many of these did you get?"

"Let's just say you should keep that one out of target range," Akeim answered.

Samuel nodded, offering the bottle to the others. To everyone's surprise, Sophia took it. "Thank you," she nodded before taking a sip, "this has been quite the day."

"It will most likely be an even longer night," Akeim remarked. "We'll have to sail through it so that we can stay ahead of them. I'll take the helm for the first part of the night."

"I'll take it after that." Alec accepted the bottle Sophia handed him. He took a deep pull and passed it to Genevieve.

"Wake me at dawn." Samuel stretched.

"I'll stay up with Akeim and help him navigate." Sophia looked out at the dark water.

"I'll be the lookout while Alec is at the helm," Genevieve volunteered.

"Well, with that settled, you two should probably get some sleep." Sophia smiled over at her. "I'll wake you when it is time."

Genevieve paused as she passed the bottle back to Samuel. She didn't mean together, did she? Her eyes widened in alarm. "Where?"

"I suppose anywhere you can find room." Sophia looked around.

"I'm not touching this one," Samuel whispered to Alec. "I'm going to *sleep* up on the bow, if anyone needs me," he announced to the group. Raising the bottle in salute, he made his way to the front of the ship.

"Be careful of the mosquitoes," Sophia warned him. "Make sure you cover up."

"Will do, Mum," Samuel said with a nod of his head.

"Oh, and Samuel," Sophia stopped him. "Do you think you could take this . . ." She looked down at the camel that was in the middle of the crowded walkway, "this animal with you?" Cupid had long since eaten the dates and was licking the deck boards that had been splashed with the contents of Samuel's last bottle. "He is underfoot."

"C'mon, my pet," Samuel called as he came back for the camel. After Samuel let it sniff the bottle he carried, the great beast rose and readily followed after him.

"See if you can get it to go into the pen with the rest of the animals," Sophia called.

"I'll try, but I'm only human." Samuel made his way to the front of the ship with the camel trailing after him. They watched as he tried to get the beast to join the other animals that had been left in the penned area in the middle of the ship. It didn't appear that the camel was interested, as it ignored the opening and sought Samuel's bottle instead.

"Get in there, you batty ol' codger." Samuel attempted to shoo the animal inside. He even entered the pen but found that the wayward beast was fast on his heels and wasn't about to let him shut it inside. Lest it break the gate down, Samuel let it back out.

"Looks like Samuel's found a drinking buddy." Sophia watched as man and beast walked to the front of the boat. Her expression turned to one of horror as Samuel took a swig from the bottle and then offered Cupid a dose by pouring some onto his tongue. "Remind me not to drink from that again." She grimaced, turning away.

"Well, they both seem to be perfectly happy, but I, for one, can't wait to get this itchy thing off my face." Alec pulled at the false beard. "Ouch!"

Genevieve watched as several hairs came free. "Here, let me help you with that." She stood, collecting a few rags. "I'll just get some water in this bucket first."

Alec found himself the recipient of her full, if rather painful, attention. "Ow," he complained as she pulled at a few hairs left on his neck. "I liked it a whole lot more when you were putting it on," he smiled mischievously.

She blushed at the memory of her rather naughty actions. Brushing against his thigh had been quite wanton of her. "I'm sure you did," she added coyly, wiping at the spot.

"I most certainly did." Alec nodded with a grin.

"I've wanted to talk to you." Her tone was serious. "I think you should know that I may have led my mother to believe that we were married." She dared a quick glance at him.

He had to bite on his lip to keep from smiling. "I thought she knew of our marriage?"

"I meant afterward." A slight blush stained her cheeks as she tried to explain.

"Afterward?"

"Yes, after we decided to annul it."

"Ahh." He nodded.

"Don't worry," she rushed on, "nothing has happened to change it. We can still dissolve it by mutual consent, if you want."

"What do you want?" he asked her softly.

"Excuse me," Samuel came up to them with half of the beard in his hand, "but I'm having a devil of a time getting this thing off."

"Of course, I'll help," she readily agreed, using the intrusion to evade Alec's question. "Just sit here, and I'll get another rag."

Alec glared at him as she walked off.

"I'm sorry, did I interrupt?"

"If I said yes, would you go away?" Alec grumbled.

"And have this itchy thing attached to my face all night? Not on your life," Samuel said. "Besides, Cupid keeps trying to lick it off my face, and that's just not my cup of tea."

Chapter 16

Alec awoke before he was due at the helm. The moon was high overhead with wispy clouds drifting across the sky as he stretched. He looked over to where Genevieve slept on the other side of the boat. She was covered with a shawl, looking much the same as when he'd first encountered her.

He was immensely grateful now that he'd been so plagued.

Sometime during the night the winds had changed, and both Sophia and Akeim were working the boom, running off the wind, turning the sails into the wind, and then away again due to the strong headwind.

"Looks as though you could use another hand," Alec said as he came up behind them.

"Take the helm while I get this secured." Akeim strained against the rope as he maneuvered the sail. Sophia moved away from the yardarm, ducking as the sail came around. The boat changed its course, tacking in the other direction.

"Good morning." Genevieve came forward, rubbing the sleep from her eyes.

Alec couldn't help but smile at her. He didn't think she could be more beautiful, with her hair slightly tousled. She blinked her eyes and then stretched, arching her back as she yawned.

Though it had been completely innocent on her part, Alec was mesmerized as he watched her, forgetting even that he was turning the boat as it tacked from starboard to port.

She turned and smiled sweetly at him. "Are you ready?"

He nodded, not trusting his voice, especially in front of his in-laws, of all people. Unfortunately, there was a part of his anatomy that took it all literally. He turned back, noticing for the first time that both Sophia and Akeim stood watching him.

184

"Hum-mm," Alec cleared his throat as he focused on steering, placing all of his attention on the sail as it swung around. The fabric stretched taut as it filled with wind, lending speed to the boat as it jibbed across the water. Akeim shook his head and turned back around.

"Is something wrong?" Genevieve looked at her mother questioningly. Sophia shook her head and turned away with a smile. Puzzled, Genevieve glanced over at Alec, who looked to be quite busy.

"The river should turn towards the north soon," Akeim called over his shoulder. "Until then, we'll have to keep this up."

"Have you ever sailed before?" Alec asked the beauty at his side.

"Does being a passenger count?" Genevieve looked hopeful before admitting, "I've never actually worked the sails before."

He smiled at her. "We'll have you sailing like you were born to it before the night is through."

Weary, Sophia came forward. "Whew," she sighed, wiping at her brow. "I haven't done this since I was a child. I'd forgotten how much work it was."

"You do look tired, Momma. Why don't you get some rest?" Genevieve looked at her with concern.

"That sounds awfully good." Sophia smiled at her daughter. "Remember to watch out for sandbars, and make sure you keep a look out for any boats trailing us."

"I will." Genevieve kissed her cheek. "Now get some sleep. Everything will be just fine." She looked over at Alec after her mother and Akeim had walked away.

"I wonder if she will ever accept that I've grown up."

"Wait until you meet my mother." Alec chuckled. "She'll probably never accept that I've grown up."

Genevieve was struck speechless. He'd spoken as if she would actually meet her. He'd probably meant nothing by it. He was no doubt caught up in the role of playing her husband and hadn't thought of what he was saying.

"Here," Alec spoke softly at her side, "come and take the wheel. It's good to get a feel for it." He opened his arm, inviting her to stand in front of him.

She stepped forward and gripped the wheel with both hands while he kept one on it. She could feel his body as he stood behind her, his breath next to her ear.

"Can you feel that?" he asked softly.

Was he serious? Yes, she could feel it! Her body was alive with the awareness of him behind her. Every nerve was on fire as he whispered into her ear. "Feel that resistance?"

With difficulty, she remembered that they were talking about sailing the ship. "Yes." She tried to still the trembling.

"Are you cold?" He smiled, stepping forward, closing the gap.

Fire ignited between them. The heat from his body enveloped her as she stood before him. She could feel her own heartbeat as it pulsed through her veins. His free hand wrapped around her waist and settled just under her breasts. Her body reacted of its own accord. Her head pressed back into him as her back arched slightly with her indrawn breath.

His hand tightened beneath her breasts as he bent his head to nuzzle her ear. Her back settled against him as she moved, and he groaned in response when her bottom came into contact with his sensitive heat.

Alec hadn't thought to make love to her at the helm, but he should have known that he wouldn't be able to control himself so near her. She was like liquid fire in his blood.

Bam! Squee—eak. Everything was jolted forward as the boat struck a sandbar several feet below the waterline.

"Oh, hell!" Alec jammed his fist against the wheel to keep from crushing her as they were both thrown forward.

SPLASH!

"Bloody hell, damn it!" They heard Samuel's yell from off the side of the boat.

The ship was almost at a standstill as it moved over the silver white strip of land underneath them.

"Oh, dear," Genevieve gasped as she put her hand to her mouth.

"Get me out of the drink!" Samuel yelled.

Alec ran to the front of the ship to assist Samuel, who had been sleeping on the prow. Alec could hear splashing off the starboard side of the boat, and he leaned over to see Samuel treading water below, holding his bottle aloft.

"Man overboard!" Samuel yelled, hitting the side of the boat with his other fist.

"Grab ahold," Alec couldn't help but smile as he leaned over the rail, reaching out with his hand.

"What kind of horse's arse would run us aground?"

"What kind of horse's arse would sleep on the prow?"

"You did this?" Samuel sputtered. "What the hell were you thinking?"

"That you needed a bath." Alec leaned far over, grabbing hold of him.

"Is everything alright?" Akeim asked as he took Samuel's other arm.

"Just peachy," Alec replied as they pulled the soaked man up onto the deck.

"Do I want to ask what happened?" Akeim lifted a brow.

Alec cleared his throat as he looked over at the warrior, whose disapproving stare was making him feel like he was still in short pants. "I missed seeing the sandbar."

"You missed seeing it?" Samuel turned to look at the strip of gleaming white sand that stretched out in front of them.

The boat was still moving slowly over the sandy hill beneath them, creaking and groaning as it slid across the mud barrier.

"Let us hope that this doesn't rip the rudder off." Akeim turned away, heading back toward the helm.

Alec breathed a sigh of relief as he watched him go.

"Let me guess," Samuel stood staring at him with a look of incredulity, "you were distracted."

"I was at the helm," Alec replied slowly, evading his question.

"Was Genevieve anywhere near?"

"Actually, she wasn't—"

"Oh, Samuel," Genevieve she ran up to the prow with a blanket in her arms. "I'm so sorry, this is my fault entirely. Please say you'll forgive me. Alec was just showing me how to steer the ship."

Samuel looked over at Alec with his brow raised and his mouth pursed.

"Are you hurt?" she asked with worried eyes.

"It was my fault." Alec looked over at her. "You are not to blame."

"Now that I do believe," Samuel snorted. Looking back at Genevieve, he smiled. "Don't worry your sweet head about it, dear lady." He grinned. "Besides, it's not that easy to feed me to the crocodiles."

"Oh, I – I wasn't, oh dear." Genevieve lifted her hand to her mouth in dismay.

Watching both of their guilt-ridden faces, and the obvious reason for it, Samuel turned toward Alec with a knowing smile.

Ignoring him, Alec turned to her. "He knows, and he'll be fine."

Genevieve didn't know what else to do or say. She handed Samuel the dry blanket she was holding. "I'm glad you were not hurt."

"Don't think anything of it," Samuel said lightly, accepting her offering. "Besides, it was quite refreshing."

"You're too kind." Genevieve gave him a relieved smile. "Could I get anything else to warm you?"

"I've all I need." He held up the towel and the bottle. "We both miraculously survived the dousing." He grinned at her. "Besides, you forgave me for marrying you off to this big oaf. We're even."

"I'll leave you both to dry out, then." She smiled, casting an embarrassed glance toward Alec before leaving.

Samuel started to chuckle as he looked over at Alec. "I can't believe you actually ran us aground because you were so busy *steering the ship* that you couldn't see a sandbar that is as bright as a beacon and stretches for a bloody mile."

Alec knew he'd never live it down. Rather than try, he asked, "What the hell possessed you to sleep on the prow, anyway?"

"It was the only peace I could find with that animal pestering me." Samuel gave the camel a look of annoyance as he spoke.

"Ahh." Alec nodded in understanding. "If you need me, I'll be dealing with my in-laws," he commented dryly before heading back to the stern.

Luckily for him, the boat passed over the sandbar without damage. The worst of it was that they had lost their wind speed and would have to let the water's current take them downstream until they could take up sail again.

"I take it that Samuel survived his bath without any ill effects," Akeim commented when he joined Alec at the helm.

Sophia stood beside Genevieve, stifling a yawn. "I still can't believe you two missed—" she paused, listening.

Alec was spared the rest of what she was going to say by a low rumbling.

"What is that?" Genevieve stepped toward the rail as they listened to the noise throbbing in the distance.

"It sounds like an engine," Alec said, looking across the water.

"Let us take the sails down, so we are less visible." Akeim motioned to him as he walked to the first sail. Alec headed up front to take down the one by the bow.

Over in the shoals on the other side of the sandbar, they were almost invisible to the large *diahiyba* as it passed them. The houseboat was headed upstream, using the power of its steam engine, as well as its sails, to navigate the river.

"Someone's in a hurry," Sophia spoke softly to Akeim, who stood beside her.

"Yes." He looked down into her worried face. "They are probably just tourists hoping to make better time with the wind at their backs."

They waited until the boat had passed them before raising the sails again.

Sophia went to her daughter. "Goodnight, sweetheart."

"Goodnight, Momma," Genevieve looked guilt-ridden. "I'm terribly sorry."

"Nonsense, we almost did the same thing just before you woke."

Genevieve almost coughed. She highly doubted that! She thanked her lucky stars her mother assumed the accident was due to improper lookout and not improper actions of another sort. She glanced quickly over at Alec and felt a blush rise to her hairline.

"It's easier to see out if you stand closer to the front of the boat," her mother advised before kissing her on the cheek and heading off to bed.

Akeim looked at Alec before turning the helm over to him. "Is it safe to say that will not happen again?"

"I would like to think so," Alec replied uncomfortably.

With a nod of his head, and something that almost sounded like a chuckle, Akeim left him.

Genevieve came to stand a few feet away. She caught her lip in her teeth before looking over at him.

"Well, that was awkward." Alec rolled his eyes exaggeratedly.

She put her hand up to her mouth and did her best to suppress the giggle that threatened to overcome her.

"I didn't think he was ever going to trust me to take the helm," Alec whispered conspiratorially. Watching her in the moonlight, he winked. "I don't suppose you'd like to try again?"

"Not on your life," she whispered back. "I'm staying over here, where I can see clearly."

"As you wish, but you'll have to risk getting near me to take the wheel while I work the sails."

She looked at him doubtfully.

"Come, I promise to behave." He stepped back, smiling at her with that grin that showed the dimple in his cheek.

She stayed where she was as she considered his words. With his hair loose and a day's growth on his chin, he looked like a pirate straight from her wildest fantasies . . . and he seemed to know the effect he had on her.

"You have my word," he pledged, "but you'll have to hurry to decide since we are at risk of running aground again."

That had her moving quickly to grab the wheel. True to his word, he didn't close the gap between them as he stood behind her.

"Now," he said, "when I turn the sails, the resistance on the wheel is going to change to the other side. Just apply enough pressure to keep her steady."

"Aye, captain."

He treated her to another smile that made her pulse quicken before he left to work on the sail.

TREASURE OF EGYPT

What am I to do? Genevieve wondered as she watched him. He was the most handsome man she'd ever seen. The fact he exuded sexuality wasn't lost on her, either. He even made the long robes he wore seem masculine and exotic. She couldn't help the little thrill that ran through her as she remembered him standing against her. This husband of hers. . . . *A husband that intends to annul their vows*, she quickly reminded herself. Something she'd do well to keep in mind the next time he touched her.

~*~

The river, which had been flowing east, did indeed turn toward the north again. With the wind at their backs, they no longer had to tack across the river for momentum, reducing the risk of running aground.

Now that navigating the river was much easier, Alec was once again at the helm, while Genevieve elected to sit near the front of the ship where she could see the river on both sides. Not daring to get too close, lest she lose track of everything else again, she maintained a safe distance from him.

Samuel, who had been tossing and turning, finally gave up his effort to sleep. Sitting up, he saw Genevieve standing nearby. "I must have done something right, waking to find an angel watching over me."

"Good morning," she greeted him with a smile.

"Excuse me while I go find that no-good husband of yours, will you?" he said as he stood.

"Of course."

Samuel walked back to Alec, who stood at the helm. "Why don't you let me take over?"

"It's still early yet. Sure you wouldn't like more sleep?" Alec asked.

"Alas, I cannot. I keep having night terrors," Samuel replied dramatically. "I'm thrown overboard and lost at sea."

"Right," Alec scoffed.

"Actually, I thought I would let you help the little missus keep a lookout while I steer the ship." He winked conspiratorially at him. "It's the least I can do while the dragon sleeps."

Alec threw a brief glance back to where Akeim was sleeping.

191

"The other dragon," Samuel whispered with a slight nod of his head toward Sophia. "Besides, I owe you one."

Alec raised a brow.

"But, after this, I think we're even."

"You do, do you?" Alec replied skeptically.

"Oh, c'mon, man," Samuel said with feeling. "You can't keep holding the whole marriage to the *Plague of Egypt* thing against me, especially after throwing me to the crocs."

"I can't?"

"Take it or leave it." Samuel shrugged.

Alec joined Genevieve up in the front of the boat. She was sitting beside the sleeping camel but turned to watch as he approached.

"Samuel wanted to take the helm, so I thought I'd come and see if I could help you."

"Are you sure that's a good idea?" She eyed him warily.

"Well," he laughed, "now that we're sailing straight down the river, it's unlikely we'll run aground again." She looked a little nervous as he sat down beside her.

Trying to put her at ease wasn't going to be easy, Alec realized as she bashfully looked away. The sky was brilliant with stars. "Look there," he pointed, "that is Ursa Major, the Great Bear, and just below it is the North Star. It certainly is low on the horizon from this latitude."

"It has just barely become visible in the sky." Genevieve spoke quietly, hugging her knees to her chest.

"Really, you mean it completely disappears?"

"Yes, for three months out of the year. It reappears at the beginning of the rainy season. To the ancient Egyptians, its arrival heralds the inundation and return of the god Osiris."

"Osiris?" Alec noticed that she seemed more relaxed when she was talking.

"He's the god of the underworld," she explained as she looked over at him and visibly tensed.

"I thought Ptah was the god of the dead," he said quickly, hoping to keep her mind on the conversation.

"They both are. You see, every ancient city had deities that came into power when the Pharaoh did. Memphis, for instance, had Amun and a triad consisting of Ptah, the father, his consort, Sekhet, and their son, Imhotep. Ra, Osiris, Isis, and their son Horus held the same significance, only they were from Abydos."

"Ah, I see." Alec was watching her closely.

She caught his stare and quickly rambled on. "That is where Amun-Ra actually came from." She nervously swallowed. "Many gods eventually merged together."

"Really." He scooted closer.

She paused briefly, glancing over at him before continuing. "Since Osiris had been resurrected, the annual flood which made the dead earth fertile again was seen as his doing."

"I see." He breathed as he leaned closer still.

"Because of this, the North Star was also seen as his domain, the place where the Pharaoh's soul would be immortalized after he battled through the underworld." She paused to look at him. "In order," she lost herself in his eyes, "in order to live forever."

"Live forever," he repeated just before his lips touched hers. He started softly at first, gradually increasing the pressure of his mouth. His arm came up behind her, touching the small of her back.

Genevieve tilted her head back with a sigh, opening her mouth to his gentle assault.

He wrapped his other arm around her, pulling her more firmly against him as his tongue met hers. Unlike their first kiss, where he ended it as soon as it had begun, this time he fanned the flame that ignited between them. His mouth became hungry, demanding more as his hand moved to stroke her arm.

Disturbed from his slumber, the camel nudged Genevieve in the back, where Alec's other hand still rested. Genevieve jerked in his arms. With a sigh, Alec ended their kiss but wasn't prepared to let her go just then. He smiled lazily into her eyes. "Thank you for the lesson."

"Lesson? You probably weren't even listening," she said scornfully.

"Yes, I was." Smiling at the look of doubt she gave him, he kissed her quickly and set her free.

"Then tell me what I said."

"The North Star is to the Egyptians what Valhalla is to the Vikings."

She quirked her lips, giving him a look that said he'd confirmed her suspicions.

He laughed at her expression, nudging her gently with his shoulder. "I was listening." He smiled. "You know they call the stars in the North constant because they are always present, unlike the other stars. In fact, that is where the name constellation came from. . . . They are constant."

She lifted a brow at his attempt to change the subject as he continued.

"Because they were always there, the North Stars represented an eternal place, a place where the soul could live forever."

"Alright, maybe you were listening." She smiled.

"See." He hugged her tight. The camel groaned. Now he knew why Samuel had chosen the beast after all his complaining. They were kindred spirits bent on annoying him.

They sat together until the sun broke the horizon and other fishing boats joined them on the river. Nestled in his arms, Genevieve nodded off, and he too found the slumber he sought, secure in the knowledge that this woman was his. She just didn't know it yet.

Chapter 17

As she awoke, Genevieve became aware of several things . . . the rhythmic rise and fall of her pillow for one, and the feel of coarse hair against her cheek as she leaned against it for another. It didn't take long for her shocked senses to overcome her sleepy dreams.

She could feel the beat of Alec's heart beneath the palm of her hand as it rested against his bare chest. She opened her eyes and looked up, straight into his golden brown gaze, the warmth of which could challenge the glow of the sunrise itself. The slow smile he gave her almost made her toes curl as she watched him.

Her own complexion matched that of the pink morning sky as it dawned on her that she'd actually fallen asleep on top of him. She tried to ignore the fact that her legs were entangled with his and that her foot had ended all the way up between his knees.

Genevieve couldn't help but take a quick glance around to see if anyone else had witnessed their compromising position. Alec seemed to read her thoughts because a low rumbling chuckle shook his ribs. When she glanced up again, his eyes were sparkling with laughter.

"It's hardly funny," Genevieve said defensively. "If my mother sees us like this, she'll not let you off the hook easily."

"Maybe I don't want off the *hook*," Alec suggested as he hugged her to him, revealing that their arms were just as entwined as their lower halves before kissing her quickly on the nose. He sat up, an action which brought her up with him.

His revelation, as well as his swift movement, had her head spinning. Did he just say what she thought he'd said? Genevieve had to fight the sudden hope that sprang up within her chest.

He stood up in a burst of energy, offering her his hand as he did. "Come," he urged, smiling down at her, "let us see about breakfast." He leaned around the animal pen and looked down the deck. The smell of freshly grilled fish wafted past their noses from the brazier her mother was cooking on.

"Hmm, that smells good." He inhaled deeply. Taking hold of her hand he pulled her up. Not letting go, he drew her to him. "And I'm starved." His smoldering look told her it wasn't the fish he longed to devour.

Bashfully, she looked down and then raised her eyes again; her gaze stopped briefly at his lips before reaching his eyes.

"Hmmm," he sighed longingly, a slight grin playing on his lips as he watched her. "You are a temptation, young lady," he scolded, "and if you keep looking at me like that, you will never get your breakfast."

Her mouth opened in surprise. *Like what?* she wondered as he took her hand and spun her around. Laughing, he headed toward the stern, pulling her gently along behind him.

Samuel was the first to see them as he stood at the helm. "Good morning," he greeted them cheerfully.

"Good morning," Alec returned the greeting with gusto, clapping him on the back. Genevieve smiled shyly with a brief nod before continuing on to where her mother was.

"You seem awfully chipper this morn." Samuel was surprised by his friend's unusual mood. "I take it we're even then?"

Alec's only response was to smile as he headed toward the source of the delicious aroma.

"Good morning, dear." Sophia smiled when she noticed her daughter. "I'm so glad you're awake. I didn't want to disturb you earlier."

Alarmed, Genevieve looked over at Alec, who had come over to savor the fish her mother had cooked. "Earlier?" she questioned, trying to keep the nervousness she was feeling from her face and voice.

"You were sleeping so peacefully, I didn't have the heart to wake you." Sophia doled out a serving for Alec, who began wolfing it down as if he hadn't eaten in days, then handed

Genevieve a plate. "Why, is there a reason you wanted to rise earlier?"

Genevieve shook her head and took the fish. "Thank you," she murmured, glancing over at Alec. He didn't seem too worried that her mother may have witnessed their sleeping arrangement. In fact, when he caught her look. he returned it with an expression that was more comical than concerned.

Genevieve couldn't help but smile and shake her head. Didn't he realize that he was going to get them good and married with his antics?

Sophia turned to see his face. "Is your breakfast alright?"

"Delicious, thank you," he said brightly, giving her a brilliant smile. "Is there enough for seconds?"

There was nothing her mother loved more than a healthy appetite, Genevieve thought as Alec received another portion. Her mother was simply going to adore her new son-in-law, and if he didn't watch out, it was going to be a permanent arrangement.

"You're finally awake." Akeim walked up behind them with another fish dangling from a line.

Did everyone witness us sleeping together? Genevieve wondered with chagrin.

"Good," Akeim continued, "I want your help with the rigging."

"But of course," Alec responded as he popped the last piece of fish into his mouth. "See you later." He smiled at Genevieve before leaving.

Sophia noticed how her daughter bit her lip as she watched him go ... a sure sign that something was troubling her. "Is something wrong, dear?"

Her mother was watching her with more interest than Genevieve was comfortable with. She couldn't very well tell her the truth, especially since it was her mother to whom she had lied about her marriage. "No." She smiled weakly.

"Are you sure you don't wish to talk about something?" Sophia asked with concern.

Genevieve shook her head.

"You know, in marriage there will be many times—"

"Mother, I don't think. . . ." Genevieve quickly interrupted, afraid of what intimate advice might follow.

"You know you can always talk to me," Sophia spoke gently, "about anything."

"I know, and thank you." She kissed her mother on the cheek.

"Anytime, sweetheart."

Genevieve absently gazed out at the river behind them. Her mind filled with thoughts of her husband until she noticed a ghostly image on the horizon. She held her hand up to shade her eyes from the morning sun. "Mother, how long do you think it will take those ships to catch up with us?"

"It's hard to say. I can't imagine it'll be easy for them to replace the sails. It could take hours at the earliest, and that's if they have them available."

"I hope you're right." Genevieve looked over at her with concern. "But if I'm not mistaken, those are the ships that followed us last night." She pointed to three boats that had appeared on the horizon behind them.

"Akeim," Sophia turned to say over her shoulder, "I'm afraid we may have company."

All three men turned to watch the boats in the distance. Akeim lifted his telescope to his eye. After a moment, he passed it to Alec without saying a word.

Alec knew at once why Akeim had not said anything when he looked at the ships close up. Each one had their new sails standing full against the breeze. . . . Each one was filled to capacity with armed men. Alec passed the eyeglass on to Samuel, who let out a slow whistle when he too spied the small army.

Samuel slowly lowered the telescope. "It won't be long and they'll be breathing down our necks. I can ready the arrows and set their sails ablaze again."

"They will, no doubt, be prepared for that this time. Although it could stall them, it also puts us at risk for the same if they get too close." Akeim looked through the eyeglass once again. "I think it is best we keep our lead for as long as possible. I'm sure what they want is to board us."

"How much more speed do you think we can get out of her?" Samuel asked as he looked up at the sails above his head.

"Not much." Akeim's expression was grim. "We were able to take them by surprise last night. We will not be as lucky again."

Both Sophia and Genevieve came to stand in front of the men. By the look Akeim gave her mother, Genevieve knew it wouldn't be good news. He handed over the spyglass so that Sophia could assess the situation.

"Oh, dear heavens," Sophia breathed as she looked through the lens. "What can we do?" She slowly lowered the telescope.

"Last night," Alec spoke up, "you said they were looking for two Englishmen, right?"

"Yes," Akeim nodded.

Genevieve gently took the looking glass from her mother as Alec spoke. She placed it to her eye, glad that she could finally see what everyone else was talking about.

Alec weighed his next words carefully. "I think it would be best if we had the *Englishmen* that everyone is looking for make themselves very visible. It might give you a chance to get away."

A cold chill ran down Genevieve's spine, though whether it was caused by his words or what she had seen, she didn't know. "There has to be something else we can do." She looked over at him as she said it. The last thing she wanted was to be separated from him.

Alec looked at her, his own heart squeezing painfully in his chest. "I'm afraid it might be the only way to keep you safe." He looked over at Akeim again. "Didn't you just say we are almost to Aswan?"

Akeim nodded. "We could reach the dock within an hour's time."

"Good, it's settled then." Picking up his bag, Alec turned to Samuel. "Let's change and prepare to disembark quickly," he said, heading for the bow.

"Right-ee-oh," Samuel said, following close behind.

Genevieve watched them go, filled with mixed emotions. What did he mean it was settled? He hadn't even spoken with her.

Sophia placed her hand on her shoulder.

"Can't you stop them?" Genevieve asked her quietly.

"We may not have another choice," Sophia said softly to her daughter. She looked over her shoulder at the boats that followed. "I'm afraid we are going to have to trust their decision."

Genevieve turned away and walked to the stern. She stood looking back at the ships with a mixture of gut-wrenching fear and anger. A moment later, her mother joined her, saying nothing.

"How did you keep from hating them after they killed Papa?" Genevieve asked finally.

"Who says that I did?" Sophia answered soberly.

"Doesn't that make us just like them?"

"No." Sophia shook her head sadly. "It is how we behave despite our feelings that makes us different."

Genevieve remained in the stern while Alec and Samuel prepared to make a quick departure once they docked. Alec had glanced her way several times as the men tried to get all the speed out of the sails they could, but he hadn't yet approached her.

She watched him as he moved the yardarm and let out the sail. He had changed back into the clothing of an Englishman, reminding her of the first time she had laid eyes on him. She could still see him standing before the fallen tent after he'd sliced his way out, looking much like a conquering Viking warrior.

Her mind was filled with visions of him, the Greek god that had entered her tent the first night with moisture glistening on his wet skin. She thought of his face half lathered with shaving cream, laughter gleaming in his eyes. She remembered the way he looked at her when he'd first kissed her, the playfulness he had shown as he used the net to fish, and later the ferocity he'd displayed when defending her from attack. The pirate who, just the night before, had stolen her breath, as well as her kisses, would be hard to forget.

Genevieve's heart squeezed painfully in her chest as she took a deep breath to try to calm it, thinking of the words he'd teased her with only a short time ago. . . . *Maybe I don't want off the hook* . . . . She'd almost dared hope that it could be so.

She turned to stare out over the water again, taking a deep breath to fortify herself. She had known that this moment was bound to come, but still she couldn't believe it had arrived. . . . This was goodbye. Five days, it didn't seem possible that her whole world could have changed so much in such a short time. Genevieve found herself wondering if it would take the rest of her life to forget them . . . him.

"Genevieve, may I speak with you?" Alec asked softly, breaking through her thoughts.

She nodded, waiting for him to speak.

He gazed down into her beautiful eyes. "I can protect you better this way."

"And what if they find you?" she asked with concern.

"I have been a spy in Her Majesty's service." He grinned at the surprised look on her face. "Let us just say that it won't be the first time I've had to find my way out of a town where people are searching for me." He lifted her chin with a finger. She resisted slightly as he did, looking at him with her large, expressive eyes.

Genevieve closed her eyes as he placed a kiss on her lips, more in an attempt to keep the tears which sprang to them away than anything else.

"I'll be alright," he promised, hugging her to him.

She stilled herself against the feelings which threatened to surface.

"As long as I know you're safe, I'll be alright," he whispered.

She buried her face into his shoulder and hugged him tightly. The tears she fought squeezed past her lashes and slipped down her cheeks despite her efforts to stop them.

"I'll meet you in Cairo," he promised as he held her.

"It's time," Akeim called as the boat approached the dock.

Alec kissed the top of her head, then let her go.

She looked up into his eyes as he smiled reassuringly at her. She couldn't find her voice, not even to say goodbye as he left her.

Alec went to the side of the boat and tossed a rope to one of the dockworkers, who caught it and pulled it taut. He agilely hopped over to the wooden pier and tied it securely to a post.

Genevieve watched as the men hastily offloaded their mounts. As planned, they were off the boat quickly; even Cupid willingly stepped over to the dock without hassle. Throwing his pack over his shoulder, Alec turned to Genevieve and waved goodbye.

She lifted her hand and held it there.

Trust. Her mother had said she'd have to trust him, but it was a difficult thing to do, especially when she couldn't help but question whether she would ever again look upon his face, despite his promise.

Samuel paused on the dock and turned back to holler over to Akeim, who was busy casting off. "One more thing before we go."

Akeim waited, the rope in hand.

"That reward you mentioned for our capture."

"What of it?"

"Was that wanted dead or alive?"

Akeim let the line go slack in reply, waiting until the boat had separated from the dock before saying, "Yes."

"Which one?" Samuel called out in frustration as Akeim cupped his hand over his ear and shook his head to imply that he could no longer hear him.

"You enjoyed that a little too much," Sophia admonished as she came to stand beside Akeim.

"Guilty as charged," he admitted as he took the helm and guided the boat through the other vessels which clogged the waterway.

~*~

Alec kept eye contact with Genevieve until she was out of range. She had stood at the rail until he could no longer make out her form. He watched as the boat moved off, feeling as though his heart was still on board and had just sailed off without him.

"Here they come." Samuel nudged him. "Look lively, man. We don't want them to miss us." He tried to get the camel to kneel, but Cupid was having none of that. "Again, what was I thinking?" he grumbled as he threw down the reins.

Coming from the other direction, the large sailboat loomed nearer.

"Mind if I borrow your horse?" Samuel sighed in exasperation. "I'm having difficulty with my mount."

"Now there's a surprise," Alec remarked as Samuel climbed up on his horse and started shouting.

"You there," Samuel pointed to an old man who was fishing off the dock, "could you tell me where I can find the British Consulate?"

The man disregarded him as he scurried away from the abrasive foreigner. Speaking in Arabic may have earned a different response, but that wasn't his objective. Samuel wanted to be both seen and heard as an Englishman.

Alec moved to a higher elevation further down on the dock where he was sure he could be seen. He waved his arms at one of the workers. "Where can I find the British consulate?"

The man eyed him warily, moving away.

Money, Alec thought with irritation. That was all that would have been needed to turn this situation around. Then he'd have all the help he could want. Alec kept his eye on the large sailboat as it came closer. He moved his arms again, calling out to the men who were working there. They turned to look at him as though he were half crazed.

The ship continued on, keeping its course despite the efforts of the *Englishmen* to be visible. Alec stopped what he was doing and watched the ship when it became obvious it was going to sail right past them.

What the bloody hell was going on? Alec's mind raced. He had thought they were after the *Englishmen,* that they were wanted men who would be hunted as soon as they set foot on the dock. Instead, he found that he'd have to commit a crime in broad daylight to merit a second glance.

At the very least he thought the men in the ship would slow down. He scanned the deck, looking over its crew. On the ship, one man held a telescope to his eye as he surveyed the dock. Alec waited until the man had the eyeglass trained on him . . . still nothing.

Alec stared hard at him, waiting until he removed the telescope, exposing his features. "Bloody bastard!" he swore. He'd never wanted to wring a neck with his bare hands before!

"I don't know about you, but I'm getting real tired of that bugger," Samuel spoke up from beside him.

They both watched as their former guide turned and spoke with the captain of the ship. He pointed down the river, directing him to sail on.

"That certainly answers a few questions," Samuel commented dryly. "At the very least, that bastard owes me some ammunition."

Alec remained still, silently staring after the boat.

"What do we do now?" Samuel asked, looking over at him.

"Whatever we have to," Alec's voice was deadly calm, "to stop that bastard."

~*~

Alec stood on the pier, watching the water where he had last seen Genevieve. He ran a hand through his hair in frustration. He had all but handed her over to them. "Damn!" he swore angrily, tortured by the thought of her at their mercy.

He looked over to where Samuel was haggling with one of the captains who had a boat for hire. Samuel briefly glanced over and shook his head in exasperation.

"Offer him twice what he wants. I'll pay anything," Alec told him, not caring about the cost.

Samuel sighed in frustration. "I'm sorry. He's still demanding the money up front."

"Can I be of service?" a man with a crisp English accent said from behind them.

They both turned to see a distinguished older gentleman in a brilliant white suit, more fitting for the English countryside than the Egyptian climate, standing before them. His crisp cravat stood at odds with the humidity. "I couldn't help but overhear that you are seeking passage."

"Yes," Alec said quickly.

"I believe I could offer a fellow countryman an assist," the gentleman offered.

"Spot on, my good man," Samuel exclaimed, clapping Alec on the back. "What say you, Alec?" He turned quickly back to the gentleman. "We're in desperate need of such assistance."

"Admiral Percival Dunham, at your service," the gentleman introduced himself.

"Admiral," Alec extended his hand, "I am Lord Alecsian Rothchild Brighton, and we could definitely use your help."

"Consider it done, then." The admiral waved one of the attendants that stood behind him forward. "See to these men's bags and have their animals brought aboard," he instructed. The servant bowed before seeing to the task.

"Lord Samuel Augustus George St. Clair, at your service." Samuel ended with a slight bow.

"Lords Brighton and St. Clair, you say?" the admiral asked with a raised brow. "The same Brighton and St. Clair who secreted the *informatique de sécurité* out of Europe?"

"One and the same," Samuel proudly exclaimed. "I'm surprised you know of it."

"Know of it! I'm sure there is not an admiral in the Royal Navy who hasn't heard of it," Admiral Dunham stated, clearly impressed. "It is a privilege to be able to help you."

"Thank you for your assistance." Alec nodded.

"Anything to help two of Her Majesty's own," he assured.

"To be entirely truthful, we are in a bit of a hurry," Samuel admitted. "My man's wife is aboard a boat we must catch. We fear that both she and her mother are in terrible danger."

"Your wife, you say?" The admiral glanced over at Alec in surprise. "Fear not, gentlemen, we shall endeavor to aid these two damsels in distress."

"It could be risky," Alec cautioned him. "They are being followed by a ship full of mercenaries."

"I've had my share of danger."

"I'll pay whatever it is that you would like for the use of—" Alec started to offer.

"Nonsense!" Dunham interrupted. "I'll simply not stand by and let this despicable act go unchallenged."

"Thank you, sir," Alec responded.

"Time is of the essence, my good men, especially with two women in mortal danger," the admiral stated emphatically.

Alec briefly looked down the river to where Genevieve had disappeared. *Please God, let me make it in time,* he prayed.

Chapter 18

"This way, gentlemen," the admiral said as they approached a large houseboat docked at the end of the pier.

The ship must have just arrived, Alec realized, since it filled the spot where they themselves had been put ashore. He watched as the admiral lifted his arm, presenting the ship to them.

"My ship is at your disposal." He waved his hand with a flourish.

"She's a beauty," Samuel whistled.

Alec couldn't help but notice an army of servants in white rushing around the ship as it picked up supplies. It seemed somehow familiar to him.

"I do hope that your ship is up to the speed which we may have to ask of her," Samuel commented as they boarded her.

"There is nothing faster!" Admiral Dunham defended. "Why, I have installed the latest in technology. She's streamlined, has eight sails and a steam engine. We'll catch up with them, no doubt about it."

Steam engine, Alec thought of the boat that had passed them in the middle of the night, wondering if it was one and the same. "What about her defenses?" he asked, looking across the deck.

"She has four cannon hidden below decks," the admiral boasted.

"You don't say!" Samuel exclaimed.

"And each of these men," the admiral motioned towards his crew, "has been handpicked for their lethal fighting skills. Those pirates will rue the day they thought to threaten Her Majesty's subjects, I tell you." He stood tall, puffing his chest out as he issued the edict.

"You certainly have come well prepared." Alec gave Samuel a sideways glance.

"Well," he coughed, "I have been seeing to matters of the Crown."

"Really?" Samuel asked in amazement.

The admiral seemed surprised. "Have you not noticed the state this country is in?" he questioned. "It was bad enough that Sa'id Pasha put this country into severe debt with the French over the Suez," he sighed in disgust. "I was afraid that, when Sultan Abdul Aziz changed the rule of succession and allowed Ismail to become the Khedive of Egypt, things would only get worse." He shook his head. "Even with the increased revenues from the Ottomans, the debts are almost insurmountable. The peasants are overtaxed, and the Sudan is clearly ready to revolt. You haven't heard of the uprising? The Zulus are threatening war, my good man."

"Actually, we had heard." Samuel gave Alec a wry smile.

"The Zulu king, Mpande, has asked the crown for support against the Afrikaners, as well as his other enemies."

Samuel's smile faded as he again made eye contact with Alec.

Alec raised a brow in response. He'd known the admiral was too well armed to be on a pleasure cruise.

"I have the responsibility of making sure Her Majesty's interests are secure," Admiral Dunham replied. "Please excuse me while I see to our departure." He again turned to one of his servants, who always seemed at hand. "See these men settled and get them anything they may require."

The man nodded and motioned for Alec and Samuel to follow. He led them to their rooms and promised fresh water for them to wash up.

A knock sounded on Alec's bedroom door about twenty minutes later. "Come in," Alec called as he finished drying his hair. Samuel entered, looking a little wet around the ears himself.

"What do you make of this?" Samuel asked as soon as he'd shut the door.

"We seem to have interrupted a mission."

"That's just it," Samuel whispered conspiratorially.

"What do you mean?" Alec questioned.

"From what I learned back in the bar at the hotel, the Zulu king's son, Cetshwayo, is rumored to have killed his own brother so that he could rule. Since then he has been buying arms and building an army that now threatens the power of the king himself." Samuel paused, waiting for a response.

Alec looked at him, a little perplexed. "I'm sorry, but I've been a little preoccupied with worrying over my wife. You're going to have to explain how the problems of the Zulu king, who is half a continent away, are relevant."

"I think Dunham has been dealing arms to Cetshwayo."

Alec stopped what he was doing with a sigh. "I don't know if you've noticed, but I couldn't care less who he's been selling them to. He can sell them to the whole damn family, for all I care. . . . And why here in Egypt?" Alec gave him a look of incredulity. "Zululand is on the other side of Africa, for God's sake; why not sail around the Horn?"

Samuel glanced cautiously back at the door. Ignoring most of what Alec said, he whispered, "Even if it makes him a traitor to the Crown?"

"Even then," Alec replied angrily. "All I care about at this moment is saving Genevieve, and if I have to sail with the devil himself to do it, then, by God, I will."

"I understand." Samuel held his hands up. "It's just that I believe there is more to it . . . and to answer your other question, sailing around the Horn takes months."

"For God's sake, man, I've enough on my plate. I'm of a mind to let the Turks handle it. After all, isn't the Ottoman Empire and their High Gate running the country?"

"Exactly."

Alec threw his arms up in confusion.

"Don't you see?" Samuel implored. "Ask yourself what is here that would inspire so much interest from so many powerful nations?"

"Samuel," Alec rubbed his temples, "I can't think of anything except Genevieve at the mercy of those men. Tell me what the hell you're talking about."

"Trade."

"Trade?"

"Not only the ongoing power struggle to control the Suez, but I'm talking ancient trade routes, to be specific." Samuel nodded. "We've seen it before. The Silk Road in China, the Poppy Trail.... Did you know that there is an existing route from Arabia, across the Red Sea to here?"

"No," Alec shook his head, eyeing him in disbelief, "and now that the Suez is being built, I doubt that anyone cares about those. Besides, what could be brought across that they could possibly want? I think the market for frankincense and myrrh died out with embalming."

"I believe that Cetshwayo is using these ancient trade routes to buy guns. I've heard he's in the Sudan recruiting for his army. It's not the only thing of value, however." He paused before adding, "There's also gold."

"Gold?" Alec rolled his eyes. "What gold?"

"This gold," Samuel said, pulling the map out of his boot. "It finally dawned on me as I was bathing."

"You think that old map has something to do with us being on a houseboat that is armed to the teeth, in a country controlled by Turks, overrun with the French, and what else? Oh, yes," Alec said in exasperation, "with an admiral who is illegally arming the Zulu king's son, chasing the misinformed members of the mujahideen."

"Yes, exactly. I'm glad you've been listening."

Alec threw his hands up in frustration.

"Like I said, it dawned on me while I was bathing," Samuel continued as he sat on the bed. "What is here, you ask? What was here when this map was made?"

"You mentioned gold, so I'll go with that," Alec sighed.

"Yes! By God, he's got it." Samuel slapped his thigh, "But whose gold, you must ask."

"Must I?"

"Only if you want to solve this puzzle as much as I do."

"What I want is to save Genevieve."

"So do I."

"You do?"

"Of course," Samuel declared. "don't you see?"

"No, I don't." Alec's expression conveyed his exasperation.

"The dragoman and his ilk are after the map," Samuel stated. "Can we agree on that?"

Alec nodded.

"And this map leads to the greatest treasure known to man, right?" He waited for Alec to nod again. "In a time when pharaohs, or, in this case, their wives, were buried in tombs filled with golden treasure. Correct?"

Alec raised his hand to his mouth and started rubbing his chin as he thought about it. "You may be on to something."

"Wait till you hear the rest of it." Samuel's eyes gleamed with excitement. "When I realized the trail went from here to the Red Sea and then across Persia, that was the clincher." He smiled as he turned the map over, exposing the circular map on back and its ancient cuneiform script. "I had thought, at first, that it pointed to one of Ramesses's Hittite wives."

Samuel gave Alec a quick glance to see if he was still listening. "The greatest treasure known to man," he repeated placing his finger on the "X". "King Solomon's mines," Samuel stated triumphantly. "The lost mines are located somewhere in Africa."

"He did have an affair with the Queen of Sheba," Alec slowly added.

"Holy hell! I hadn't even thought of that." Samuel looked down at the map in amazement. "S'ba . . . Sheba. By Jove, I think you've got it. You've found our elusive queen."

"No, but we can make them think we have." Alec spoke with more enthusiasm than he'd ever shown toward the map. "Those bastards won't touch Genevieve or her mother if they think we know where the treasure is."

Samuel shook his head as he continued to stare at the map. "How could I not have seen it?" He looked up at Alec. "You know it's even said that she came out of Africa, across the desert to become queen." He glanced down to the map again. "All this

time, right, there, ✗ S'ba, the Keeper of Wisdom," he said in wonder.

"I think it best if we keep this to ourselves for now," Alec advised.

"I agree." Samuel nodded, tucking the map inside his boot once more.

~*~

"Look lively, men!" Admiral Dunham commanded as he studied the three ships that loomed on the horizon through his telescope.

Alec's stomach was in knots as he looked out over the water. Borrowing the admiral's lens, he placed it to his eye. The sun was low on the horizon, making it hard to see in the dusky light.

"What do you see?" Samuel shaded his eyes as he peered ahead.

"Nothing yet." Alec adjusted the telescope to see further, beyond the boats. He could barely make out the sails of another ship. "I think it's them, but it's too far to see clearly."

"Here," Samuel motioned, "let me have a look."

Alec handed him the eyeglass.

"Yes, yes! It is them," Samuel cried excitedly.

Alec breathed the greatest sigh of his life as he heard the news. Genevieve was still safe.

"What do you know?" Samuel asked as he handed the lens back to Alec. "That black serpent could outsail the devil himself." He clapped Alec on the back. "We've got her now!"

Alec peered through the lens again in time to see a flickering light land in the water beside the ship. "Bloody hell!"

"Was that what I thought it was?" Samuel asked, squinting. "Are those bastards shooting flaming arrows at them?"

"It appears that way," Dunham said as he came up beside them. "Man the cannon!" he ordered his men. "Let's send these vermin to hell, where they belong!" he yelled as the crew ran to their battle stations.

Alec could feel his nails cutting into the palms of his hands as he stood there, wanting nothing more than to smash his fist into the dragoman's face for what he dared.

"Fire!" the admiral commanded. A cannon beneath their feet blasted, sending a plume of acrid smoke upward.

Samuel covered his nose and mouth with his sleeve. "Nothing like the smell of cannon fire to lend atmosphere to the chase," he coughed as the air swirled about them.

They watched as the cannonball splashed into the water far short of its mark. "They are still out of range," Dunham scowled, "but we'll catch them."

Samuel started checking his pockets and vest, assessing his weaponry. "Although it may appear that I'm dressed for battle," he motioned to his guns, "I don't suppose you have some extra ammunition we could use?" Samuel looked over at the admiral. "Perhaps some for this?" He held up his rifle with the chipped stock.

The admiral turned to another of his guards. "See them properly armed."

The man nodded and motioned for them both to follow him.

Alec shook his head. "I'll stay here. Just get me some ammo." He turned to the admiral. "Thank you. I don't know how I will ever repay you."

"The knowledge that I have assisted in the rescue of two ladies is thanks enough," Admiral Dunham told him.

Alec watched in anguish as another burning arrow flew through the sky, igniting a sail on Genevieve's ship.

~*~

"What has happened?" Samuel asked when he returned a few minutes later.

"I'm afraid they have done some damage to the ship the women are on." Dunham delivered the news solemnly. "They set one of their sails to flame and are steadily gaining on them. I only hope we can get to them in time."

Alec wore a tortured expression as he watched the black smoke rise up from the distant ship. *God, please keep her safe. Don't let me get this close only to let her—* he couldn't finish the thought.

"Look!" Samuel hollered. "They're abandoning the ship!"

"Indeed they are." Dunham peered through the lens again. "That may be the smartest move they could have made. If they've horses, they might elude capture yet."

They sent round after round as the admiral's ship steadily gained on the other's boats, damaging one and sinking another. They failed to stop the largest and fastest of the three, however, which continued on to where the burning skeleton of Akeim's ship was moored on the riverbank.

Alec watched as the men from the big boat boarded the ship. He knew Genevieve, Sophia, and Akeim had escaped, but he still stared, unblinking, as the men scoured their ship, searching for something.

Dunham handed him the telescope once again. Alec watched as several horses from the dragoman's ship were dumped into the water with their riders and carried to the shore by the current. He could almost make out the treacherous bastard as the men took off on horseback toward the eastern desert.

"It looks like they are headed toward those ruins," Samuel commented when Alec handed him the glass. "Hum, it also seems that the men who've stayed with the ship have taken Genevieve's trunk." Samuel watched as the men put the old trunk on their boat. "Damn! Sure wish I'd kept that little book now," he sighed regretfully.

"Keep firing!" Admiral Dunham ordered. "Spineless dogs!" he swore as the men on the large ship cast off in an attempt to get away.

Alec watched as they sailed past the smaller ship the admiral had targeted earlier. The sails of the sunken ship were still sticking out of the water, dragging the hull across the bottom. The men who had been on her had swum for the closest land.

"If you see any of those scallywags on the bank, shoot to kill," Dunham ordered his man-at-arms.

The houseboat came up alongside the ship he'd been on only hours before. . . . Alec found himself staring down at the prow, remembering the night he'd spent there with Genevieve in his arms.

"Get those animals ready!" the admiral ordered.

"Are you coming?" Samuel asked him when it appeared that he too would be joining them.

"I shall follow this until the end." Admiral Dunham spoke with finality.

~*~

"What are they waiting for?" Samuel glanced over at Alec as they took cover behind the remnants of a stone wall.

Alec continued to watch the group of men who had followed Genevieve into the ruins of Karnak. They had dismounted and were hiding behind an outcropping of stone . . . waiting.

They heard the sound of gunfire coming from just outside the temple. One of the men grabbed his backside as he fell to the ground.

"Never mind," Samuel whispered again. "Mystery solved. It seems your wife is a crack shot."

"Yes," Alec couldn't help but smile at the pun, "so it seems."

They continued to watch the men as they took cover from Genevieve's accurate, if not deadly, aim. A few returned fire, making Alec pull his rifle out; his eyes narrowed as he placed the dragoman in his sights.

"Hold up there." Dunham placed a hand on his shoulder. "Let's not let them know of our presence just yet. I think, if we take them by surprise, we will avoid a standoff. I am going to see if I can flank them. The bastards won't know what hit them if we come at them from two sides."

Alec released the lever he had been about to pull and looked over at the older man.

"We know that your wife is still safe." Dunham removed his hand. "Let's keep it that way."

Alec knew he was acting impulsively, but even if it was the wiser choice, waiting while the admiral maneuvered into position wasn't going to be easy. As it was, he winced at every shot that was fired upon the temple, wondering if Genevieve was safe, or if, this time, the bullet had found her.

"You two stay here and command these men." Admiral Dunham motioned toward twenty of his armed guard. "I won't be long." He looked directly at Alec. "Wait until we're out of sight before firing."

Alec nodded as Dunham clapped him on the shoulder again. "She'll be fine," he promised before leaving them. He went to speak with the highest ranking of his guards and then left with a handful of men.

"Have them divide themselves into three groups and watch for my signal," Alec instructed Samuel, who conveyed the order to the men the admiral had left behind.

Samuel looked over to Alec. "Ready when you are."

"Once the admiral is out of sight, we'll start firing; that should take the heat off Akeim and the women."

~*~

Genevieve had taken cover by one of the many ram-headed sphinxes that lined the walkway leading to the Temple of Karnak. The ruins, which had once served as the seat of power for the pharaohs of Egypt, lay partially buried in the sand behind her.

"We are running out of gunpowder." Sophia looked worriedly over at Akeim as she loaded her rifle. Spying something in the distance over the paws of the statue, she sighed wearily. "And now it seems there are more men joining them."

"But aren't those the men who were firing from the other ship?" Genevieve asked.

"In this case, 'the enemy of my enemy is my friend' may not apply," Akeim said grimly as he watched through his spyglass. "I cannot tell who they are. They have taken cover." He lowered the lens. "For all we know, they are jackals fighting over the spoils of war."

"Let us take refuge farther back where we can better defend ourselves." Sophia gazed up at the two giant seated statues of Ramesses that guarded the entrance to the huge, pillared hall. "Perhaps a little height might be to our advantage as well."

Akeim nodded his approval as he looked up at the large stones that crossed over the tops, creating a latticework above them.

They backed carefully away from the leonine statues into the large hall. The light was all but blocked out by the forest of stone trees that rose up to a dizzying height. The shadows from the setting sun cast stark patterns of light on the columns.

"Follow me," Akeim whispered. "Be careful."

A roosting bird flew from its nest high above, crying out against the intrusion, its eerie call summoning all sorts of demonic imaginings in its wake.

Genevieve couldn't help the ripple of fear that raced down her spine as she edged around the cold stone surface. The etchings of Ramesses in battle rippled under her fingers as she traced them along the pillar, following the path Akeim had taken toward the back of the ruins.

~*~

"Fire!" Alec shouted to the first group. The area around him exploded in a cacophony of sound as the men discharged their weapons. Surprised by the attack, the dragoman's forces took a few minutes to react. When they did, they turned to fire on their attackers, abandoning their assault on the temple for the moment.

Alec watched as Samuel reloaded his weapon. Timing was everything. Samuel emptied gunpowder down the throat of the musket as Alec signaled the next group.

Samuel slammed the rod down into his musket. "And here I thought the admiral said he had the latest in technology. There's not even a flintlock among us!"

Alec ignored his ranting, focusing on the remaining group of men. "Fire!" Again the sound of gunfire rang through the air.

"Take that, ye slimy bastards!" Samuel yelled in an Irish accent. "Let them try to make a move now." He chuckled as a constant stream of fire rained down on the dragoman's men.

"Fire at will!" Alec shouted as he aimed his weapon. "It's better than what we had before," he said as he lit the fuse of the rifle he held.

~*~

"Sounds as if the jackals are fighting amongst themselves," Sophia whispered. Distant gunfire reverberated through the stone cathedral as they stood before one of the crumbling walls. Akeim climbed a wall of uneven blocks that ended in a sheer drop several feet below the large stone stretching across the pillars joining them at the top.

He looked back at them and shook his head to indicate the way was impassable.

"Stay here." Sophia motioned to Genevieve. "I'm going to see if I can make some progress."

Genevieve nodded in response and watched as her mother climbed up to where Akeim stood.

"Could you lift me up there?" Sophia asked, indicating the twelve-foot ledge above them.

He glanced back at her and nodded. Rather than give her a shoe-up with his hands, as she thought he might, he placed his hands about her hips and lifted her off the ground. It might have been easy to dismiss the familiarity if they hadn't made eye contact.

Sophia hadn't thought to feel again after the loss of her husband, but the simple act gave way to a flood of sensations throughout her body. She watched as his eyes darkened with passion. Her eyes flared with something akin to shock.

"Mother," Genevieve whispered from above, "give me your hand."

Mortified, Sophia jerked her head around. "How did you get up there?" she gasped, taking the hand that Genevieve was holding out to her.

"I don't think you want to know," Genevieve stated as her mother climbed up to the ledge. She looked around her to see where her daughter had come from. She could see nothing but vertical drops.

"Honestly, Genevieve, you gave me a fright," Sophia whispered as they helped Akeim up.

~*~

"Where do you think he is?" Samuel leaned over to Alec. "Don't you think Dunham has had plenty of time to get into position?"

Alec scanned the desert, looking for any sign of the admiral and his men.

"I don't like it." Samuel's forehead creased. "We're starting to lose the light."

"Those men are headed for the temple." The guard pointed. Alec looked up to see the dragoman and his men move forward despite the shots being fired.

~*~

"Shhh." Akeim placed his finger to his lips. "I hear something."

They had made their way to the top of the blocks crowning the pillars. Lying down flat, they peered over the ledge. A shadow crossed the angular light on the floor below. In silence, Sophia trained her rifle on the shadow as Akeim did the same on the other side.

The same shadow emerged once again, coming closer. Sophia could see the shoulder of the man as he stood by the column. She pressed her finger against the trigger, waiting for a clear shot.

"Sophia, Genevieve?" the man called out in a hushed voice.

Sophia released her finger with a jolt of surprise. She hadn't thought to hear that voice again.

"Sophia, it is all right. You can come out now," the man called again.

Sophia almost questioned her hearing. "Percival?" She stared down at him.

"Thank God!" the man sighed in relief. "I thought I might be too late."

"Uncle Perry?" Genevieve peered over the edge.

"Dear God in Heaven, it is you!" The admiral smiled as he looked up at their faces. "When I was first told that you had been seen, I thought that it would be yet another wild goose chase."

"It was you in the large boat with the cannon?" Genevieve asked.

"Yes, indeed." Uncle Perry came forward. "How in God's name did you get up there?" He looked around curiously. "Come, we must hurry." He waved them down as he looked cautiously around. "I have men on the other side fighting, but it is only a matter of time before the infidels take advantage of the fading light and flood in here."

"We'll be right down," Sophia called.

~*~

"Was that cannon fire?" Samuel asked.

"I believe it was." Alec nodded as he glanced behind them in the direction of the boat.

"We cannot wait any longer." Samuel squinted at the fading sun. "It'll be too dark, and we'll lose them if we don't take action."

"I don't think that will be possible now," Alec said in a low voice.

"What do you mean?" Samuel looked over at him, surprised, at first, by all the rifles now trained on them. "What the hell is this?" he questioned.

"It appears that we've been set up . . . again."

"By whom?"

"The White Devil," it was Akeim who spoke up from behind them, just before he was thrown to the dirt at their feet.

The dragoman stood before them, his teeth gleaming in the light of the setting sun as he smiled down at them.

"You treacherous bastard!" Alec swore as he started for him, only to be struck by the stock of a rifle held by the guard he'd so recently called upon.

Knocked to his knees, he glanced over to Akeim. "Where are the women?"

"Percival has taken them," Akeim spat out in anger.

"What happened to protecting them with your life?" Samuel questioned.

"He tricked me," Akeim glared at their former guide as he answered, "by leaving me in charge of his men."

"Ahh." Samuel nodded in understanding. "Tricky bastard."

"Silence!" the dragoman ordered.

"Do we kill them now?" the admiral's head guard asked, pointing his rifle at Alec's head.

The dragoman grinned. "We're to make it look like an accident."

Chapter 19

"No one is going to believe this is an accident!" Samuel accused the dragoman while he wrestled with the bonds that held his arms against his sides.

"For once, would you stop helping them?" Alec swore as the guard who was securing his bonds tightened the rope at his wrists.

The dragoman sneered at them. "I don't imagine you will remain tied up for long." He motioned to one of his men, who held a canister. "Just long enough for this to take effect."

"What is it?" Alec eyed the clay vessel warily.

"Oh, that is a surprise," the dragoman smiled coldly, "one which you are sure to enjoy."

"You will never get away with this." Samuel narrowed his eyes at their former guide as another guard secured his legs.

"I already have," the dragoman replied confidently. "This tomb is one of many which have already been sealed for the season. By the time they check it next year, you will have long since perished in the cave-in."

"What cave-in?" Samuel's eyebrows shot up.

Alec groaned.

"How could you betray your people?" Akeim growled as he too strained against the ropes that bound him.

"Betray?" the dragoman laughed. "It is not I who has betrayed his people. It is you who have aided the Englishmen against your own."

"I have taken an oath to protect the S'ba."

"You actually think the Englishwoman is the S'ba?" the guide mocked him.

"Why do you think he took them, you fool?"

The guide's eyes lost their laughter as he stared at Akeim. "It is you, old man, with your misguided loyalties, who is the fool."

"And your loyalties obviously lie with the White Devil," Akeim sneered contemptuously. "Or is it just that you've been bought by the Englishman's coin?"

"Enough!" the dragoman shouted. He turned to his guard. "Place that over there," he ordered the man who held the canister. The space he'd indicated was right between Alec and Samuel. One of the dozen men who had followed them into the tomb gave the dragoman a long reed.

"Wait," Samuel spoke up. "We can tell you where to find King Solomon's gold."

The dragoman paused before looking over at Akeim. "You see my point."

"What?" Samuel responded to Akeim's angry look.

"Out!" the dragoman ordered his men as he stepped closer to the canister. Using the long stick, he tipped the lid, which balanced precariously on the edge of the container.

"Don't make any sudden moves, gentlemen," the guide told them. "They don't like sudden movements or loud noises. It aggravates them."

They watched as something pushed from inside, making the lid rock on the edge.

The heavy iron door used to seal the tomb creaked on its hinges as the dragoman left. A moment later they were plunged into darkness as the heavy door closed, blocking out the light.

"That went rather well." Samuel's attempt at levity was lost in the darkness.

The door opened briefly, and a stick of dynamite was thrown inside.

"Perhaps I spoke too soon," Samuel commented sourly as the glowing end of the fuse burnt away in the darkened corridor. They heard the heavy iron bar on the other side of the door slide into place, followed by a second thud closer by.

"Was that you?" Samuel questioned.

"No, it wasn't me!" Alec struggled against his ropes as the lid hit the floor. "Damn it, I hate snakes!"

"There is a small cut out over here," Akeim called from across the room, "follow my voice."

Scuffling sounds and heavy breathing mingled with the hiss of the fuse.

"Bloody damn!" Alec swore again. "Watch your boot!"

"Oh, sorry," Samuel apologized as they scooted across the dirt floor. "I didn't realize that was your head."

"Hurry!" Akeim shouted from far off.

"Is he serious?" Samuel grumbled. "How did he get so far away?"

"He must have figured out a way to st-a-a-a-n-d," Alec called out as he rolled down an incline.

Thunk!

Crash!

"God, would you watch your boot!" Alec swore again as Samuel joined him in a heap at the bottom of a rather steep corridor.

BOOM!

The noise of the percussion reverberated in their ears as tremors tore through the ground beneath them. Dust blasted down the narrow passage in a thick layer, covering them

Cough, cough, and *cough.*

"Ah—Ahh—Choo," Samuel sniffed. "Augh, I'm allergic to dust."

"And yet you still chose to come to Egypt." Alec remarked.

"Keep your faces covered," Akeim cautioned as the dust settled.

"Damn it, Samuel!" Alec swore.

"What now?"

"Move your boot!"

"What are you talking about?"

"I suppose you're going to tell me that it's not you rubbing against my leg."

"It's not me."

"Oh hell!" Alec's voice was muffled.

"Ahh, the poisonous canister of snakes. . . . How could we forget?" Samuel commented.

"I didn't forget," Alec gritted out.

"Be quiet!" Akeim whispered. "You must lie perfectly still. I cannot do anything until I get out of these bindings."

"Ahh—ah—ah . . ." Samuel tried to stifle a sneeze so as not to *aggravate* the situation.

"Oh, hell," Alec groaned.

"I caught it," Samuel sniffed. "Ah-Choo-oo!"

~*~

"Prepare to cast off," the admiral ordered his men as he stood on the deck of his ship.

"Wait." Sophia turned worried eyes toward him. "Akeim has yet to come aboard."

"I'm sorry, dear, did I not tell you?" Her brother-in-law turned to her. "He was delayed and said to give you a message."

"What is it?" Sophia's brow knitted with concern.

"He had something of importance to take care of and said he would meet up with us in Cairo."

"That isn't like him." Sophia looked back to the temple in the distance.

The admiral sighed as he watched her. "I didn't want to say anything, but I believe he wanted to," he paused as if to spare her delicate nature, "*interrogate* the villain who was chasing you. He asked that I keep you safe until his return." When she still looked undecided, he continued, "If there is one man that can take care of himself, it is that one." He smiled at her reassuringly.

Sophia nodded in agreement.

"I'll have my man here," the admiral summoned the servant behind him, "show you to your rooms if they are ready."

"Of course." She smiled in gratitude.

The servant bowed with a nod, then indicated they were to follow him. "We have just aired them out."

"Good, then." The admiral nodded. "Let us get you safely away from here, shall we?"

"Yes . . . and Percival?" Sophia looked up at him.

"Yes, my dear?"

"Thank you."

"I have never given up my hope of finding you," Percival said with a slight misting of the eye. "My prayers have been answered that you and Genevieve have been safe all these years."

~*~

"Be prepared to act quickly, Samuel," Akeim advised as he knotted a piece of cloth around a piece of wood. "The light may startle it."

Samuel gripped his knife, ready to fling it once the light flickered. "Is it still against your leg?"

"Yes, it's against my inner thigh," Alec whispered.

"Really that must be. . . . How high?" Samuel asked curiously.

"High enough," Alec said meaningfully.

The flint lighter sparked but didn't light the cloth. Another try brought a brief flicker of light before it too was gone.

"Third try is the charm," Samuel said as Akeim struck the flint again. A small, but steady, glow of light permeated the darkness.

"Well?" Alec whispered in frustration as he waited. Being trussed up like a Christmas goose with a poisonous snake near his groin wasn't his idea of a holiday. "Can you see it?"

Samuel came nearer, squinting in the darkness. "Yes." The head of the thing had risen above Alec's leg. He tipped back his wrist, then paused.

"Kill it!" Alec hissed. What was taking him so bloody long?

"Hold still, it's too risky." Samuel slowly came closer. "I'm going to grab it with my hand."

"What?" Alec cried in alarm. "No!"

Samuel made several attempts before he seized the piece of twisted wood that rested between Alec's legs. He made a grand show of grappling with it as Alec wilted with relief.

Alec's eyes narrowed on him when he realized what it actually was.

Akeim came forward to cut Alec's bindings with a look on his face that suggested he was tempted to deal with the idiot. "I could secure his bonds again, if you'd like."

"Watch out, Alec," Samuel warned. "There is another piece of wood behind you."

Alec sat up, rubbing his wrists. "I'm seriously reconsidering my threat to kill you."

Akeim gave Alec another look that said it would be his pleasure to do so, as Samuel continued to laugh.

224

"That won't be necessary." Alec stood, brushing the dirt from his pants. Considering the quantity of dust, it was a wasted effort. Their hair and clothing were covered in a thick layer.

"Ah-ah-choo," Samuel sneezed.

Alec stood over him as he shook his hair out for good measure.

~*~

"Genevieve, dear," Sophia said as she entered her daughter's room aboard the ship, "I just thought I'd check on you. Are you settled?"

Genevieve had been looking out the window, watching the ruins of Karnak fade away. Everything reminded her of Alec, the smell of the pillow she held, even the comb at the washbasin. Her imagination was certainly playing tricks on her. "Yes," she sighed with a slight nod.

Sophia could tell something was troubling her daughter. "What is it, dear?"

"So much has happened," Genevieve said.

"Eight years is a long time." Sophia nodded.

"I meant with Alec," Genevieve sighed. "I just can't help but wonder if I'll ever see him again."

"Of course you will," Sophia said comfortingly.

"You don't understand," Genevieve said, at a loss, turning away.

"Then why don't you explain it to me."

"He didn't come for me." Sadly, Genevieve sat down on the bed. "I thought that, once he saw that the ship still sailed after us, he would come for me." She looked back to her mother with troubled eyes. "I believe he's had enough of this."

"Oh, I don't know about that," Sophia came forward, sitting beside her on the bed, "he is probably doing his best to do just that. I'm sure he's on his way."

"I don't think so," Genevieve said with a heavy heart.

"Didn't I hear him tell you that he would see you in Cairo?" Sophia questioned. "After all, he is your husband."

"Oh, Momma," Genevieve sobbed, "we agreed to annul it."

"Oh," Sophia put a comforting hand on her shoulder, "I see."

Genevieve turned to her with tear-filled eyes. "I'm so sorry I lied to you."

Sophia patted her shoulder in understanding.

"It's all my fault. If I hadn't lied, then we never would have been . . ." Genevieve paused. "I put us all in great danger."

"Nonsense," Sophia said matter-of-factly. "It is I who put you at risk. I should not have left you alone." She paused. "I'm sorry. Never in my wildest dreams did I think the sheik would dare to marry you off."

Genevieve inhaled a shaky breath at her words.

"Sweetheart," Sophia soothed, "I'm not sure what you and Alec agreed to, but sometimes actions speak louder than words."

Genevieve looked up at her. "What do you mean?"

"I believe that your husband will come for you," her mother replied softly.

"You really think so?" She sniffed.

"I think I know a man in love when I see one." Sophia nodded insightfully.

"You think he loves me?" Genevieve looked at her mother with troubled eyes. "Oh, Momma, what have I done?" she sighed. "I let him go and never told him how I felt."

"He knows." Sophia smiled.

Embarrassed, Genevieve looked away. "Was I that obvious?"

"Yes." Her mother squeezed her.

~*~

"How long have we been digging?" Samuel asked tiredly.

"Three days," Alec replied.

"I'm so thirsty," Samuel sighed as he settled back onto a dirt mound to rest. He retrieved the bottle from his pocket and eyed it skeptically. Finding the contents entirely unappealing, he returned it without taking a sip.

Alec pulled another boulder from the debris at the front of the tunnel and sat back on his haunches to wipe the sweat from his brow. "At least we have a little ventilation." He looked up at a few cracks of light which could be seen above the door they had finally unearthed. He motioned back at Akeim, who was turning one of the snakes on the small fire he'd built from the fallen timbers. "Not to mention food."

Akeim came forward and offered them each a morsel of the meat he had cooked.

"Thanks," Alec mumbled as he accepted the meager fare.

Samuel eyed it skeptically. "Augh, I'm tired of these too. They are most disagreeable to my system."

"We know," Alec said, while Akeim raised a brow in response.

Choosing to change the subject, Samuel asked, "What is the plan once we're out of here?"

"It should not be hard to track them," Akeim responded as he crouched down beside them. "I know a man in the next village that will loan us a horse."

"*A* horse?" Samuel questioned. "As in *one*?"

"It is one more than we have now," Akeim replied briskly, ripping a bit of the tough meat from the stick.

Samuel rolled his eyes and looked at Alec with disbelief.

"What do you know of this White Devil?" Alec asked Akeim, speaking aloud what had remained unsaid. "Will he hurt them?"

"He will not hurt them as long as he needs them." Akeim tore off another bite with his teeth.

"What does he need them for?" Samuel asked. When his question remained unanswered, he asked another, "What did you mean when you said that you protected the S'ba?"

"Nothing." Akeim stood abruptly. "Hurry up, we haven't time to waste."

A puff of air blew in from one of the cracks above the door, silencing any other questions Samuel might have had. All three men remained perfectly still as the light, which had been streaming through the fissures, was blocked by something on the other side.

Akeim, closer than Alec and Samuel, slowly made his way forward. With great caution, he approached one of cracks. The sound of sniffing was followed by a snort and another puff of air as he looked out.

"Samuel," he whispered as he climbed back down the mound of dirt, "I believe you have a visitor."

"Really?" Surprised, Samuel wiped his fingers on his pants before climbing up to look out. "Hey there, fella," he said softly after looking through the small fissure. The air above his head swirled with a puff of dirt as the animal on the other side sniffed at him.

Samuel fought back a sneeze, then turned back with a smile. "Can you believe that? Now, there is a loyal pet." He laughed. "I knew there was a reason I chose you!"

Cupid, standing above the earthen mound, started to paw at the earth after hearing Samuel's voice. The action revealed how thin the earthen layer must be now that the dynamite had blasted the area. Dirt started raining down from the ceiling next to the door.

"You'd better move," Alec warned as a huge clump of dirt fell on top of Samuel's head. He rolled forward just as a hoof broke through, followed by the rest of the camel.

"Augh, get him off me," Samuel groaned as the animal frisked his body until he found his bottle of spirits.

"Well," Alec said as he watched them, "I don't know about loyal, but he is certainly spirited."

"Or in need of spirits," Akeim corrected.

Samuel fended off the animal. "At least he has good taste."

"I can truly say I've never been happier to see him." Alec breathed deeply as sunlight and fresh air poured down from the hole.

Making their way past Samuel and his *loyal pet*, both Alec and Akeim climbed to the top of the dirt mound and looked around.

"Hey," Samuel called to them, "help me out here."

It took quite an effort to get the large animal up out of the steep hole, but they managed by adding a few stones to the hill and tempting him with libations on the other side. Once out, Akeim whistled for his own faithful steed, which appeared almost instantly.

"Well," Samuel said good-humoredly as he draped an arm across Alec's shoulder, "it appears that you have no other solution but to double up with one of us or walk."

Alec didn't seem amused.

"Look at it this way," Samuel smiled, "at least you got the girl."

Alec gave him a sharp glance before turning to Akeim. "Didn't you say you knew a man with *a horse*?"

"Indeed."

Cairo, Egypt, three weeks later

"You're still up?" Sophia asked from the door to Genevieve's room. The house Percival had rented in the city was beautifully designed in the Moroccan style. The haremlik, where the women stayed, was opulently decorated with Persian rugs and silk trappings.

"I couldn't sleep," Genevieve said quietly from her perch next to the window. The large harvest moon was just rising on the distant horizon, lending a golden glow to the city. She sighed as she gazed at it; thoughts of Alec were never far away, especially on a night such as this.

Sophia stepped closer. "I'm going out for a while."

"Out?" Genevieve turned to look at her. "Now?"

"I have just learned that there is a possibility the artifact might be in jeopardy."

"You mean," Genevieve stared in disbelief, "*the* artifact?"

Her mother nodded. "I can hardly believe it myself."

"How can that be?"

"Do you remember when we first came to Egypt? We met a man by the name of Auguste Mariette, who was starting to excavate the temple."

"I thought he'd given up when he realized the enormity of the task."

"Apparently, he didn't," Sophia sighed.

"I'm going with you," Genevieve said as she started to scoot off the cushion.

"No," Sophia shook her head with regret, "it's not safe."

"All the more reason that I should be going with you," Genevieve said stubbornly.

"I need you to stay here to cover for me," Sophia whispered, "just in case one of the housekeepers notices I've left."

"It's late. They won't know."

"In case I get back late tomorrow." Sophia glanced cautiously back at the door. "You can tell them I'm not feeling well and not to disturb me."

Genevieve shook her head.

"I'm just going to see the temple for myself," Sophia explained, "to see if there is cause to worry."

"Why can't we both do that tomorrow?"

"It is my understanding Monsieur Mariette has his workers there during the day. I must find out if they have unearthed anything of importance. If they have, then you know that it is only on a night such as this that the temple can be opened, and I can't risk anyone asking questions," Sophia added meaningfully.

"But I thought Uncle Perry knew?" Genevieve moved from the silk cushion she'd been sitting on. "Don't you trust him? After all, he did save us from those men."

"Of course I do," Sophia whispered, "but he is only aware of some things. It's safer for everyone if we keep it that way."

"Momma," Genevieve grabbed a shawl, "I'm going with—"

"Genevieve," her mother interrupted her, "I must do this alone. Should something happen," she paused, "we cannot let them have both of us. Don't you understand?"

"Yes." Genevieve nodded, she did understand. She wasn't going to win this argument. She was, however, going.

"Good." Her mother smiled. "I should only be an hour or two at the most. I will, no doubt, be back before you're even awake."

As if she could sleep. Genevieve smiled sweetly as her mother kissed her on the cheek.

~*~

"Coast is clear. . . . No, wait. There's another servant coming this way," Samuel whispered to the bushes as he peeked around the corner.

"What is this, Waterloo Station?" the bushes asked. "That's the second within the last five minutes."

"Shhh," Samuel hushed the shrubbery as he too moved back out of sight.

The servant, who carried a basket on top of his head, passed by where they were hiding without noticing the large man dangling from the trellis several feet off the ground.

"Alright, it's clear now." Samuel signaled the go-ahead.

"Next time, you climb up the damn trellis," Alec grumbled as a twig snapped under his weight.

"May I remind you that it's *your wife's* bedroom window?" Samuel whispered.

Alec smiled at the surprise he was about to give *his wife*. It had taken almost all of his strength to climb the exterior of the building to the upper floor, but thinking of her gave him the stimulus he needed to push on. He felt power surge into his limbs as he reached for the wooden parapet just over his head.

Taking hold of the edge, Alec swung beneath the *mashrabiya* that decorated the window. The lattice shutter was no match for his weight and snapped off in his hand. His body went swinging as he held on with his fingers. He tossed the wooden shutter to Samuel, rather than let it clatter to the cobblestones below.

"Easy there," Samuel whispered as he caught it.

Alec pulled himself up to the window ledge and climbed in. Inside, there was nothing but silence as he waited, listening to the sounds of the room. He crouched low, moving to a darkened corner. Silently, he crossed to the bed, imagining the kiss he would place upon her lips to wake her. Standing briefly before the bed, Alec slowly raised his hand to the silken cloth that draped it. He took a deep breath before gently parting the sheer fabric. . . . It was empty.

"Damn," Alec swore softly, looking around. This had to be her room. After all, he had stood watching her from below as she looked out at the night from the very window he had just come in through.

Alec quickly checked the other rooms in the women's area. All of them were empty. He crossed to the window and looked down at Samuel. He shook his head. "They're not here," he whispered down to him.

"No?" Surprised, Samuel looked up at him. "Then where are they?"

"Good question." Alec disappeared from view, appearing a few minutes later around the corner.

"Why did you even bother with the window if you were going to use the stairs?" Samuel threw up his hands.

"I didn't think they'd notice," Alec replied, "since the whole house is empty."

Akeim joined them a moment later. "Where are the women?"

"Good question." Alec ran a hand through his hair in frustration.

"Only the admiral and a few guards left out the front as I watched." Akeim looked back from whence he had come. "Did you see anyone else leave?"

"There were a couple of servants, but they didn't leave together," Samuel answered.

"That had to be them," Akeim replied.

"Where the hell could they have gone?" Alec swore. How could she have walked right past him? He could hardly believe it as he stood looking at the corner where they had disappeared.

Unbelievable!

Chapter 20

Alec wasted little time chasing after Genevieve and her mother. He rounded the corner at an all-out run, colliding with the basket that one of them had used as part of their disguise. "Genevieve," he called out as he continued running.

"Alec, Alec.... Wait!" Samuel called as both he and Akeim ran to keep up with him.

Alec turned with a look of vengeance on his face when he reached the river's edge and had to stop. "Where the hell have they gone?" He pointed his finger at Akeim. "Tell me! I am tired of these secrets."

Akeim was taken aback by his wrath. "I do not know."

"If you cost me her life because of some lost treasure, I will personally dismember you!"

"I do not know," Akeim repeated.

"Tell me what you *do* know then," Alec growled. "Who is it that you are sworn to protect . . . the S'ba?"

"Just because I'm sworn to protect the S'ba does not mean I know the secrets."

"You know more than I do . . . Start talking," Alec demanded.

If it was anyone besides Alec, they may have been in danger from such a request. Akeim nodded with a sigh. "My people have protected the Keeper of Knowledge for thousands of years."

"Knowledge of what?" Alec asked.

"A history of a people."

"That's it?" Alec looked at him in disbelief.

"And their knowledge."

"So all of this is about the history of . . . Egypt?" Alec scoffed.

Akeim drew himself up. "I am Sabean."

"So it is a history of the Sabeans." Alec again looked at him as if it was inconsequential.

"Again, I am sworn to protect the S'ba. I do not know the—"

"Secrets," both Alec and Samuel reiterated with a nod.

"I thought the Sb'a was the Queen of Sheba?" Samuel puzzled aloud.

Akeim remained silent.

"How is it that this involves my wife?" Alec watched him closely.

"The knowledge has been passed down from mother to daughter, generation after generation," Akeim explained.

"So what you are telling me is that my wife is being hunted by the admiral because she has this knowledge?" At Akeim's nod, he continued. "Do I need to tell you how farfetched that sounds?"

"Regardless, it is the truth." Akeim stood taller.

"How does the admiral fit into this?" Alec asked.

"He is Sophia's brother-in-law."

Alec pondered this for a moment. "And Lord Langston?"

"The old man is Genevieve's grandfather," Akeim answered.

Alec raised his brows in surprise. "So the uncle, as well as the grandfather, betrayed them?"

"That's rough," Samuel commented.

"Whose side of the family do they come from?" Alec questioned Akeim. "Sophia's?"

"No," Akeim said. They are both on her late husband's side, although I believe the uncle married into the family."

"Some family," Samuel muttered.

"Is there anyone else I need to know about?" Alec asked in frustration, feeling as though he was prying the information from Akeim. "I'm tired of blindly running into their traps."

Akeim nodded in understanding. "It is one of the reasons I took them to live among the Bedouins where I could better protect them."

Samuel snorted at that information. "I don't know if I'd admit to that if I were you. One might question where you were when Genevieve was married off to my good man here with, I might add, the tribe's blessing?"

Akeim eyed him angrily. "That had much to do with you and your conniving tongue, from my understanding," he accused. "Convincing the sheik that it was your *king's* destiny to protect her was rather cunning of you. When I returned from patrolling the southern border, the ceremony was already over," he added meaningfully.

Samuel was quick to respond when both Alec and Akeim trained dark looks on him. "Let us remember what is important here." He held both hands up as if to stave them off. "We were talking about Genevieve and her mother and where they could have gone. . . . Right?"

Alec ran a hand through his hair and took a deep breath to calm himself. Akeim folded his arms across his chest and stared at him.

"Right," Samuel continued. "So that begs the question: What is the Keeper of Wisdom doing here in Cairo? Are they running *from* something or *to* it?" He looked around at the docks and the city beyond.

Alec rubbed his jaw with his hand as he considered the question.

Akeim shook his head. "I do not know. I wish now I still held the map."

"You mean this map?" Samuel quickly retrieved yet another copy, holding it up.

Akeim raised his brow at the map that Samuel had so easily procured.

"Oh, alright, so I kept a copy." Samuel rolled his eyes in response. "Perhaps the Egyptian writings might give us a clue," Samuel suggested as he held the map up for them to see.

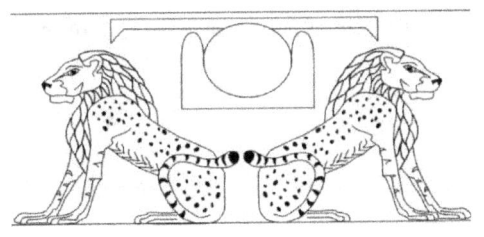

In the light of the full moon, they each studied the drawing before them. The double lions facing away from each other dominated the page.

"There has to be something here that will shed some light on this." Alec came closer. "What are the clues, again?"

"On this side of the map, it tells of a temple belonging to a goddess, or the revered one, before the sacred land of the west." Samuel then added, "And let us not forget my personal favorite. . . . Where the cat arches over the door."

"The sacred lands of the west are the deserts on the western side of the Nile," Akeim remarked.

"*Before* the sacred lands of the west," Alec contemplated. "What is this here?" he questioned, pointing to a large disk between the lions. The sphere was nestled between two large mounds.

"It's reminiscent of two large breas-" Samuel started.

"Mountains," Akeim clarified.

"There are several depictions of the ankh," Samuel pointed out.

"What of this symbol?" Alec said, pointing to the large Egyptian eye drawn beside one of the lions. "Isn't that the all-seeing eye?"

"Yes." Samuel nodded thoughtfully. "I wonder what it means in this instance?"

"It is the eye of Horus, the left eye of Ra," Akeim added helpfully.

"Well, that's insightful," Samuel said sarcastically.

Akeim gave him a baleful glance in response.

Alec turned from the map and assessed the city before him. Close to the water, he could see across the river to the pyramids, which stood like white granite beacons in the moonlight.

"How many tombs are there in Cairo?" Samuel wondered aloud.

Akeim shook his head as he considered the question. "Thousands."

"More importantly," Alec exclaimed, "how many have lions which guard them?"

Samuel paused to consider the question. "I don't . . . wait, you think?"

Alec nodded with a smile. "The Sphinx!"

"Damn!" Samuel swore. "I was sure the treasure map led to the tomb of Sheba."

Akeim extended his hand, silently asking for the map. Samuel sighed as he handed it over.

"If it's any consolation," Alec said, "they have never found the treasure buried in the pyramids."

"My only consolation is that now," Samuel separated his coat, revealing his revolvers, "I'm properly armed!" The weapons he displayed glinted in the moonlight.

~*~

Sophia walked in front of the temples that stood before the Sphinx. She cautiously looked behind her before entering the Valley Temple. The excavations had unearthed the ruins down to the large stones that stood at the base of the walls. Twenty-four megalithic columns, which rose to the open sky, were topped with large stones creating a wall of square arches.

"I find it hard to believe that this is a coincidence," Genevieve said from behind her.

"Oh." Startled, Sophia grabbed her heart and turned towards her. "Genevieve," she whispered loudly, "you gave me a start. . . ." She paused, taking a breath. "What are you doing here? I told you to stay home."

"I have come to help," Genevieve replied matter-of-factly as she gazed at the temple, which had been detailed in the old book that her mother now carried in her bag. It was the only one they had removed from the trunk.

"What do you mean 'a coincidence'?" Sophia's brow knitted with concern as she looked at her daughter.

"Don't you find it odd that we have come out of hiding at the same time that this has been unearthed? It is almost as though we have been summoned," Genevieve said prophetically.

"How perceptive of you." A deep voice sounded from behind them.

They both turned to see the admiral standing at the entrance of the temple. Several of his guards peered over the walls.

"You," Sophia said with an indrawn breath as she turned. "It was you who betrayed us?"

"Betray is such an ugly word, Sophia," Percival stated coldly, "especially when all I have done is try to protect you from this."

"You killed my father?" Genevieve's expression was one of horror.

"It was most unfortunate that you did not listen to your mother and stay at home." He didn't even look at her as he wiped a speck of dust from the sleeve of his coat.

Protectively, Sophia stepped in front of her daughter. "You will not harm her!"

"Of course not, dear," he looked up again with a bored expression, "as long as you do as I ask."

"What is it that you want?"

"Come now, Sophia, do not play with me." He narrowed his eyes on her. "I have known that the artifact lies within this temple for some time now."

"If you know, then what do you need us for?" Genevieve took a step towards him as she spoke. Her mother placed her hand in front of her to stay her.

"I also know that it can only be retrieved by someone with your knowledge, or it will be lost forever," Percival sighed again. "I grow weary of your games. . . . Open the temple, and you and your daughter can go free."

"That is it?" Sophia eyed him suspiciously. "And what if I don't?"

"Isn't it obvious?" Percival glanced up at the men who remained on the walls of the temple.

"If you hurt us, then you will never have it," Sophia warned.

"I have never wanted to hurt you or your daughter, Sophia," Percival replied, "but I think you should know that you are not the only one with the knowledge."

"What do you mean?" Sophia questioned.

"I grow weary of this." Percival heaved a great sigh. "Do it or not . . . It is your choice, but I am tired of waiting."

The silence stretched as Sophia watched him. He signaled to his men with a wave of his hand. The men on the top of the walls trained their weapons on the women as he turned to leave.

"I will need help," Sophia finally spoke up.

"That is a wise decision." With another wave of his hand, the men eased up on their weapons. "What kind of help?"

Sophia slowly let out a breath, visibly shaken by the incident. "I will need water."

"Water?" He looked mildly surprised by the request. "Certainly." He motioned for a water bag to be brought forward.

Sophia shook her head. "I will need much more than this."

~*~

"What are they doing?" Samuel asked as he waited for Akeim to look through the lens. "I've got to get myself one of those," he grumbled when Akeim finally handed the telescope over to Alec.

"They are filling the pool with water." Alec peered through the lens. Unfortunately, he could still only see a partial view of the temple.

"Really? I wonder why?" Samuel strained to see for himself.

Alec looked at him with an expression that stated the obvious before handing over the lens. "As if anyone of us could answer that."

Samuel chose to ignore him as he looked through it. "If only we could get a better view," he complained while he adjusted the telescope.

"If we go behind the temples and then follow that wall," Alec pointed to the sloping walkway which went up to the Great Pyramid, "I believe we could get closer without being seen."

"You and Samuel do that while I take the place of that last guard." Akeim motioned toward the distant sentry beyond the temple.

"That's it?" Samuel looked from one to the other with disbelief. "That's the plan?"

Irritated, Akeim turned to him. "What do you want?"

"Something with a little more clarity would be nice," he watched as Alec shook his head, "and a happy ending."

~*~

"I will have the book and the map that you carry as well," the admiral ordered Sophia, motioning to the guard closest to them.

"Mother," Genevieve whispered, "are you sure you want to do this?"

"What other choice do I have?" Sophia looked at her daughter. "He knows I would not risk losing you. We will just have to stop him some other way," she whispered before she turned to give both items to the guard. She watched as he handed them to the man that she had once thought of as family.

The admiral scanned the map, looking up. "I must warn you that, if you attempt to deceive me, there will be dire consequences."

"I will not," Sophia replied with a lift of her head.

~*~

"Are you thinking what I'm thinking?" Alec whispered over to Samuel. They were lying across the top of the wall, spying over the edge at the back entrance of the temple on two guards who had just emerged from beneath the archway.

"I don't know. Are you thinking about whiskey and women?" Samuel smiled at his own joke. At Alec's frown, he sighed, "I'll take the shorter one. He's more my size."

~*~

"You there!" the admiral commanded one of his guards as he stood before the Valley Temple. The walkway had been built up with stone, creating a shallow area beside it. "Shore those sides up!" He pointed to where some of the water was threatening to spill out. "Make sure that it will hold water."

The guard immediately knelt and began piling sand where the rock had crumbled away.

The water in the pool was dark against the white stone. Genevieve watched as another bag was emptied, creating ripples in the otherwise mirror-like finish.

"Will this be enough water?" Percival asked from his position beside the reflection pool when the last bag had been emptied.

Sophia shook her head, pointing to several dry spots. "The surface must be unbroken."

"You are not just attempting to delay this, are you?" he accused.

Sophia returned his cold, unwavering stare.

"Because, if you are, you should know that neither Mariette nor his men will be here tomorrow . . . I lied." He smiled. "Work here has ceased until next season, and I assure you we will be quite alone."

"I am not delaying," Sophia replied evenly.

"Then tell me, why must we fill this pool with water?"

"In order to reveal the door," Sophia answered simply.

Skeptically, he looked down at the pool. "And how will this reveal it?"

"You are questioning my understanding of the ancient knowledge?" Sophia lifted a brow.

"I want proof that you are not impeding our progress needlessly." The admiral's features were hard as he watched her.

"The proof is there before you." Sophia pointed to the scroll he held. "Look at the map."

Percival opened the parchment once again and studied the page.

"Where the cat arches over the door . . . Sekhmet, the lioness." Sophia waited, then added disparagingly, "Wadjet, the all-seeing eye."

He looked up at her angrily. "I warned you about playing games."

"You will have to see with new eyes what has always been before you," Sophia replied calmly, unwilling to let him rile her.

"I am losing my patience with your riddles," he warned, wrinkling the parchment in his fist.

"This pool was used to reflect the image of the great goddess Sekhmet, the guardian of the underworld," Sophia explained evenly.

"The Sphinx?" He turned to look at the great stone beast that could be seen in the distance. "How could that be? It stands in the opposite direction behind the temples."

"On the map above each lion are the words 'horizon' and 'sky'." Sophia waited as he smoothed the page out, studying it carefully.

He looked up at her impatiently. "I'm not here to play your games." His eyes narrowed on her.

"She is there," Sophia pointed to the large golden disk that was reflected in the water, "in the moon."

"The moon?" He looked over his shoulder at the golden orb in surprise.

"The ancients held this land as sacred long before the pyramids were built because of the outcropping of stone which bears a striking resemblance to the face they so revered in the heavens."

"But I thought the Sphinx was carved by Khafre as part of the pyramid complex."

"The body was carved out and the face retooled, but the head has always been prominent in the landscape. This place was chosen by the great architect Imhotep because it had always been revered by the people as the entrance to the underworld."

"I still don't see it."

"It may be easier to see her reflection in the pool since her image is upside down. It isn't until she sets in the west that her image rules the night."

"I see it!" Percival exclaimed. "Amazing, I would never have thought." He gazed up at the sky in wonder.

"I take it that I have your permission to continue," Sophia said.

"Of course, by all means." Percival nodded.

Genevieve watched as the guards filled the pool. She was momentarily distracted by the one who was repairing the sides. He was working only a few feet away from her, but instead of packing the sand, he was tracing an image with his finger . . . a heart.

She stared as he traced the contours again. The turban he wore concealed his features until he looked up, revealing his face. *Alec!* Genevieve couldn't believe her eyes. He smiled before smoothing the sand away with his hand. She moved closer to her mother, bumping into her. At Sophia's questioning glance, she motioned with her head, but before she could say anything, the admiral spoke up.

"What is next?" His eyes were filled with excitement.

"We will need to stand as if coming from Abydos, in order for the door to be revealed." Sophia indicated a point just outside the temple.

"Abydos?" Percival looked over the desert. "Why?"

"That is the direction that the pharaoh's procession would have entered from."

The admiral nodded, motioning for them to follow him.

Genevieve briefly glanced at Alec before going with her mother and the admiral. Her heart was racing. She could hardly believe it. He was here. He had come for her . . . and now he was in terrible danger. *Oh, dear God. Please protect him.*

Genevieve made note of how many men were working for her uncle as she walked, scrutinizing each one as she went. There were at least five on the walls above them. Several men had been working to fill the pool, and others guarded the surrounding area. She guessed there were twenty in all.

As she passed, the last guard tilted his head slightly. Her eyes widened briefly as she made eye contact. *Akeim!* She quickly looked away as she followed her mother up the hill.

"What are we looking for?" the admiral asked as they walked to a knoll just east of the temple.

"Do you see on the map, the disk between the two lions?" Sophia asked. "The lions, as well as the disk, are below the symbol for the sky."

Percival once again looked down at the map.

Genevieve nudged her mother while he was distracted. Sophia looked at her questioningly, as Genevieve motioned with her head toward the guard.

"Yes, I see it," Percival said, looking up.

Sophia quickly turned to the admiral. "Just as the disk lies between the mountains, we must stand so that the head of the Sphinx rests between the two pyramids."

A cloud drifted across the moon as they waited.

"I cannot believe that after all this time—" Percival began. His voice stilled as the clouds parted. From their vantage point they watched as a beam of light reflected off the pool and lit the entrance to the temple. "There!" he shouted, pointing to the northern entrance of the Valley Temple. In his excitement, he ran ahead of the women.

"What is it?" Sophia quickly asked.

"They are here," Genevieve whispered. "Akeim and Alec are em—" She broke off when the admiral stopped.

"Ladies." The admiral turned back towards them. "After you," he invited.

As they walked toward the entrance of the Valley Temple, Sophia gently tucked her arm within her daughter's. "We should prepare ourselves for anything."

They entered the narrow corridor, where the reflection of the moon had pierced the darkness. The walls were high on each side with an archway on the right leading into the interior of the temple. The passage continued further back into a darkened alcove.

"What is the next step?" The admiral stepped beneath the archway and looked around. Several guards followed them inside.

Genevieve looked up at the men who remained on the top of the walls. Their number was now three. She counted again, noticing, as she did, the guard at the far end. *Samuel!* He winked at her before she quickly looked away.

"I'm not sure," Sophia replied, buying time.

"What do you mean you're not sure?" the admiral asked sharply.

"These twenty-four columns represent the hours of the day and night, whereas these twelve niches," she pointed to the indents in the floor, "used to hold statues of the goddesses that represent the twelve hours of the night."

"Twelve goddesses?"

"Yes," Sophia nodded as she considered the indents, "the guardians of the gates through which the pharaoh must pass in his journey through the underworld."

The admiral walked around the columns. "Is this a lunar clock, then?"

"It might help if I was able to read from the book." When it looked like he would decline, she added, "This has not been done for several thousand years."

He reluctantly handed her the book. Sophia's voice echoed through the structure as she opened the book and read from it.

> *I have come, bound to rocks and plants,*
> *men and women, rivers and sky.*
> *When the cat arches over the doorway, think of me.*
> *I am there, speaking to you.*
> *When you look up, know that I am there,*
> *Sun and moon, woman, cat or lotus.*
> *All these things I am,*
> *And though apart, I am part of you.*
> *The same god breathes within everybody.*
> *You and I together are a single creation.*
> *Nothing stops my love for you. . . .*

"What does it mean?" the admiral asked, watching her closely.

"I'm not sure." Sophia continued to study the page.

"It mentioned both the sun and the moon," Percival said, looking over her shoulder.

"Yes, the earth god Aker is portrayed by two lions, one at each entrance to the underworld." Sophia continued to look over the page. "The lion is a symbol of royalty. In this case, the double lions represent the seats of power of the supreme rulers of the sky, where the sun and moon rise and set."

The admiral stepped away from her, tracing the angular shadow of the moon across the stone floor with his boot. "It is said that this temple was built to worship the sun." He turned back to her as he spoke. "Perhaps we wait for the light of day for the rest to be revealed?"

"I am waiting for a sign." Sophia briefly glanced toward the heavens above.

Samuel swooped down on a rope from the upper wall as she spoke. He rammed into the admiral, sending him flying backwards. The momentum of his descent wasn't stopped, however, only deflected, as he crashed into the wall with a thud.

"Oomph." The air escaped his lungs on impact. "That's going to leave a mark," Samuel moaned as he slipped the rest of the way down the wall.

Chapter 21

In a flurry of activity, Alec took out the guard who was standing next to the women while Akeim fired both of his revolvers, hitting the guards who stood above them on the wall. Akeim then stepped protectively in front of Sophia.

Alec moved Genevieve behind him, fighting against several attackers.

"Kill them!" Percival screamed as he struggled to stand.

From his position on the ground, Samuel fired off a shot at one man charging towards him. Scrambling to his feet, he drew his sword, blocking an oncoming blow from another of the guards. The man stepped back, slashing the deadly blade in his hands through the air threateningly. Samuel rolled his eyes as he waited.

Backing away, Alec, Akeim, and the women entered the hall. The alcove to the right was a dead end, leaving only the opening they had come through on the left.

Gunfire echoed through the passage as Alec approached the entrance. A piece of stone shattered off from the blast just inches from his head. He ducked, stepping back. "We've a better chance of getting out the other way."

Just as they turned back, Samuel dove into the passage from the other opening. Rolling to the side, he fired his gun into the temple. "They have more men coming in from the rear."

Alec looked back at the entrance. "We're trapped!"

"Cover me," Akeim called out as he headed for the opening.

"Wait!" Sophia yelled over the sound of gunfire. "There is another way."

"That's what I like to hear," Samuel said as he fired another shot, making several guards take cover on the other side.

"The secret door." Sophia pointed to the alcove at the rear of the hallway. A small niche had been built at the end of the passage.

Samuel did a double take as he looked up at the depression near the top of the wall. The image of Sekhmet shimmered on the rock surface from the reflection of the moon. "Well! I'll be damned; it does reflect the moon. . . . Where the cat arches over the door."

Sophia knelt beside the wall and started feeling the groove between the stones with her fingers. "Genevieve, look around for the lock. It should be near."

"Isn't the key something to do with the symbol of life?" Samuel wondered aloud. ♀ ∼ ⊜ "We have used water. ∼∼∼ I don't suppose you have a placenta on you?"

"A what?" Sophia stopped what she was doing, turning to look at him oddly.

"A ball of string, perhaps?" Samuel amended, speaking of the round ball.

"He means the moon in all its phases," ⊜ Genevieve corrected as she felt along the stones on the other side of the wide corridor.

"I do?" Samuel glanced over to see Sophia's expression. "Of course I do."

"Honestly." Sophia shook her head. "How did they get *that* so confused?"

"I'm not sure." Genevieve slid her knife along grooves between the stones, stopping when she encountered a niche in one. She scraped the sand away with the blade, being careful not to put the knife in too far. The hole became deeper as she worked. "I think I've found it."

"Let's see." Sophia came forward, examining the small crevice between the large stones. She unhooked a necklace, withdrawing the pendant that she wore beneath her clothing. It was in the shape of a large ornate teardrop, an ancient symbol of woman. ◊

Reaching beneath her skirt, Sophia withdrew a dagger, the hilt of which resembled a cross, † the symbol of man. She joined the two pieces together, creating the shape of the ankh, ⚲ the symbol of life.

"So it literally was the ankh. . . . I knew it," Samuel nodded triumphantly. "Well, not exactly, but I was close."

Alec regarded him skeptically. "Right."

"I hope this still works," Sophia breathed as she inserted the ankh into the depression. As the key slipped into the lock, she looked over at the door expectantly.

Nothing.

"I don't know how much longer I can hold them," Akeim hollered over his shoulder as he reloaded his gun. "We must hurry!"

"Perhaps if you turned it," Alec offered.

Sophia grabbed the end and jiggled it, but it wouldn't budge. She looked up at him. "I think it's stuck."

"Great," Samuel muttered, "now what?"

Shots continued to be fired into the passage from both directions. Alec left his position by the entrance so as to lend some assistance. Sophia stepped back from the key and motioned for him to try.

Alec grabbed the handle and tried to turn it with little effect. Wrapping his hand with cloth from his robe, he tried again.

Genevieve stood watching him. "It could be a lever. Try pulling up on it or pushing down, instead of turning it."

"Yes," Sophia nodded, "that's a good idea."

Alec found himself yanking on the handle, while both women continued to add constructive advice. He looked briefly over to Samuel, who was now decidedly minding his own business. *The coward!* Alec thought with derision as the women continued to direct him.

It didn't take long for Alec to stand up in frustration and use his boot to kick the protruding handle down.

"I didn't mean like that," Sophia criticized sharply.

Alec threw his eyes heavenward in mute dismay.

"Oh, look!" Genevieve cried excitedly. "It moved."

"Do it again," Sophia urged.

He kicked with all the force he could muster. The handle of the knife broke away from the pendant that was still buried within the wall.

"Step back." Sophia placed her hand protectively in front of him before picking up the twisted blade. "Whatever you do, do not touch that again."

"You did it!" Samuel exclaimed. "It's opening!" From his position nearest the alcove, he could see the stone as it moved back, revealing a dark passage behind it. "Damn! If we could only get that rope back." He stared longingly at the rope that still dangled from the archway he'd tied it to.

"I think it might be better if we improvise," Alec said, looking out at the armed men who stood in the way.

Samuel was about to respond when Genevieve ran at her mother, who flipped her up to the ledge high above. She had become a dark blur of movement, so fast was the undertaking. "I told you they could fly," he whispered under his breath.

Stunned, they both watched in amazement as Genevieve unwound her head covering and lowered it down to her mother, who climbed it with ease.

"I'll never doubt you again," Alec said as he watched.

Akeim pulled back from the entrance. "Go." He motioned to Alec as he took up his spot. One-by-one, they climbed the rope and entered the opening to the tomb.

"Can we close the door?" Akeim asked as he climbed up to the ledge.

Sophia started to feel the wall just inside the door. "There is a lever somewhere along here."

"Is this it?" Samuel asked as he placed his hand on it. "Whoa!" he said in surprise when it moved.

"Watch out!" Alec yelled as he pulled Samuel away from the spot. A counterweight slammed down where he had been standing only moments before. Akeim dove inside as the stone slid into place, sealing them inside. Plunged into darkness they waited, listening to the sound of muffled gunfire.

"That was too close." Sophia breathed a sigh of relief.

"We can open that back up again, right?" Samuel's voice held a note of regret.

"Not from here," Sophia answered him. "We will have to follow this passage. But, Samuel, do try not to touch anything. The way is fraught with disaster."

"Great," Samuel muttered under his breath. "Good thing we didn't fall into another trap."

Alec, who was standing next to him, whispered back, "At least this time it was one of our own making."

"Now why is that not a comfort?" Samuel muttered in the darkness.

Akeim used his flint-lighter to light some cloth he'd torn from his robe and wound around his knife. Pressed against the walls of the ancient stairwell, the cramped space seemed even smaller in the dim light as they looked around them.

"Look here," Samuel said as he reached for a torch on the wall beside him.

"No . . . don't touch it," both Genevieve and her mother called as he raised his hands to pick it off the holder.

Akeim raised his flickering knife higher. Sharp, pointed spears hung down from the ceiling above.

Samuel swallowed hard as he stepped from beneath them. "Holy hell! The map said nothing about daggers of doom."

"As I said, there will no doubt be many such dangers along the way," Sophia reminded him.

"In the *Amduat*, there are twelve hours, each signifying a different rite of passage that the pharaoh will have to overcome in his journey through the underworld," Genevieve explained.

"There are twelve of these booby traps?" Samuel asked in disbelief.

"At least," Sophia reemphasized the dangers.

Leaving the torch where it was, Samuel used his own sword instead, wrapping it tightly with fabric. He then lit it from the flame that Akeim carried. Pleased that it produced an even brighter light, he held it up, looking around the narrow passage for more sharpened spears.

"What now?" Alec asked.

"We walk." Akeim started to descend the steep stone steps. Sophia followed closely behind him.

Genevieve took a step towards them but was stopped when Alec reached out and pulled her into his arms. "Miss me?" He smiled, hugging her to him in the tight space. "Thank God you are all right," he breathed as he started kissing her cheeks over and over until he found her lips.

Samuel, trapped behind them, chimed in, "I've missed you too."

After he set her lips free, Alec looked over his shoulder at him. "No one asked you."

"But 'tis true, I avow," Samuel pledged.

Genevieve laughed. "I've missed you both." She smiled as Alec reluctantly released her. Quickly catching up with Akeim and Sophia, they slowly navigated the treacherous path that twisted and turned like a coiled snake.

"You do realize this is the entrance to the underworld," Samuel commented as they descended. "We are headed straight to Hell."

"Does this mean you're not coming?" Alec asked hopefully.

"Of course not," Samuel replied. "I'm right behind you."

~*~

"Hold your fire," the admiral ordered. When it was silent, he called out, "Surrender, and you will live. Continue this, and you will all perish." When no one responded, he ordered one of his men to walk into the entrance hall where they had fled.

Nervously, the man approached the opening, mumbling a prayer as he went. Entering the hall, he quickly returned. "It's empty," he yelled. "They have vanished!"

"Nonsense!" the admiral shouted. "Search the area!"

The guards scoured the grounds. "Look!" one man called out in fear as he stood beside the reflection pool. "The water—it too has vanished," a whisper of fear threaded through the men. "Evil djinni," the man accused as he cautiously stepped away from the dry pool.

Enraged, the admiral stood before the temple. "She must have opened the door." He turned to his first in command. "Search that hall." He pointed to the entrance the moon had shone into earlier. "There must be a way in through there. Find it!"

The guard nodded.

~*~

The stairs were rutted deeply from the groundwater which had run down the incline at one time. Alec held onto Genevieve where the steep, rubble-strewn path looked especially dangerous.

It was doubtful she needed his assistance, but he couldn't help it. He'd lived every day for the past few weeks in turmoil over her safety. It was a balm to his soul to have her near. Besides, it felt too damn good when he touched her.

He held onto her waist while she bent to find her footing. Before letting her go, he slipped his hand into hers. He lost himself in her eyes when she glanced up and smiled at him. . . . He would go anywhere, face anything . . . fight the devil himself to be with her.

~*~

"Yes?" the admiral asked the guard who approached him.

"We've found something, Sayyid." The man bowed his head respectfully.

"What is it?"

"A hole in the wall that looks as if it was recently cleared of sand," the guard answered him.

Admiral Dunham followed him to an area where scratch marks marred the rock around the small hole. Bending down, he sifted through the pile of sand at the base of the rock. "It appears they used a sharp object," the admiral commented as he examined the slit.

"What would you have us do?" The guard stood behind him.

The admiral stood up, dusting his hands off. "Open it."

One of the guards produced a slim dagger. The admiral stepped back, allowing him access to the hole. He slipped the knife inside the opening, and then pulled it back out. A murmur of appreciation ran through those nearest as he held up a tear-shaped pendant. He handed it to the admiral and then bent to the task once more.

The admiral held it up. He recognized it, having seen it around Sophia's neck. He turned it in his hand as the man on the ground slipped his knife into the opening again.

"No wait!" the admiral called, but it was too late. A fine spray of acid salt blew out from above the hole, exploding in the man's face and coating several others beside him.

"Ahh-hh!" the man screamed, covering his face with his hands.

~*~

"Are you going to stop at every boulder to fawn over her?" Samuel sighed as they slowly picked their way down to the bottom. "Because I, for one, would like to get a move on."

"In a hurry to get to Hell?" Alec inquired with a backwards glance. "Don't get your knickers in a twist."

"For your information, I do not even possess a pair." Samuel harrumphed then paused. "Shhh, do you hear that?"

"It sounds like a soft roar." Genevieve looked back worriedly.

"It's almost like the story revealed on the stele between the Sphinx's paws." Samuel's voice was hushed. "The one where the young man was napping under the head of the beast when he heard it whisper to him, telling him that, if he uncovered the great lion, he would one day be the pharaoh." He looked above them warily. "We must be somewhere under the great lion."

"What is the voice telling you now?" Alec asked sarcastically.

The noise suddenly became louder as the ground itself started to tremble. "To run!" Samuel shouted.

"Dear God! Percival must have tried to open the door," Genevieve shouted.

Alec jumped down to the base of the stairs, lifting Genevieve with him. The passage widened considerably at that point, providing enough room for Genevieve to run at his side. Samuel leapt down the rocks after them.

"Keep coming this way!" Sophia called from up ahead of them. Genevieve stumbled as they ran. Alec reached down and pulled her up, keeping her hand within his as they went. They quickly came upon Sophia and Akeim, who had stopped where the passage split in two.

"Which way?" Samuel asked as he skidded to a halt.

"North." Sophia looked from one passage to the other, unsure of which one to take.

"That would be this way." Samuel headed off, disappearing around the corner. He immediately returned at an all-out run. "Not that way!" he yelled. "The other north, the other north!" he shouted as he passed them, running down the opposite corridor.

The noise, which had been loud before, became deafening. They turned to see a wall of water coming toward them from the corridor that Samuel had narrowly escaped. Running as fast as they could, they followed closely behind him.

Samuel skidded to a halt, balancing precariously on the precipice of a black hole in the middle of the passage. Swinging his arms wildly, he tried to overcome the inertia of his reckless flight.

The water swept the rest of them from their feet, the current carrying them forward as they fought it. Akeim's light was extinguished as he sank below the surface for a moment before finding his footing.

"Augh!" Samuel screamed as the swirling wet fingers pulled at him, pushing him towards the abyss.

"Stay here!" Alec shouted as he left Genevieve clinging to one of the timbers bracing the roof. Running forward, he slammed into Samuel with enough force to send him hurtling forward across the expanse of the hole. Alec's toes touched the other edge as he fell with Samuel, but his foot slipped, sending him scrabbling for the side.

The flaming sword that Samuel held flew from his hand, sticking into the ground a few feet away. The flame sputtered, threatening to leave them in the dark as water spilled around it. The fabric higher up on the blade caught fire as it burned toward the handle.

Sophia joined her daughter as Akeim braved the waters to get closer to Alec. The turbulent flow surged forward. Some of it crossed the boundary to the other side, but most of it spilled into the abyss, creating a churning spiral of water that pulled at Alec as he clung to the edge.

Samuel crawled forward, reaching out his hand. Alec lost his hold just as Samuel dove at him, catching his wrist. Alec reached up and tried to seize Samuel's forearm with his other mud-slickened hand, but it slipped off. Struggling, Samuel pulled with all of his might, hanging on for dear life to Alec's hand, which was slowly sliding from his grasp.

Akeim dove across the expanse, rolling onto the ground beside Samuel. He shrugged his robe off, tossing one end toward Alec. Samuel's grip failed just as the fabric hit Alec in the face. Falling backward, he grabbed at it.

"ALEC!" Genevieve screamed in horror as his head disappeared beneath the torrent of water.

Alec grabbed the cloth with both hands as he held his breath against the water, which pummeled him without mercy. His weight jerked the makeshift rope as he fell, pulling Akeim towards the edge. Samuel grabbed hold of the fabric that was stretched to a thin cord, adding his strength to Akeim's. With all their might, one hand at a time, they slowly drew Alec up.

When his head broke the surface of the falling water, Alec drew in a huge gulp of air, greedily sucking it into his lungs. Akeim reached forward, pulling at his shoulders, dragging him up over the edge to safety.

Breathing heavily from the exertion, Samuel collapsed where he was. Alec crawled forward, coughing to clear his lungs of the water he'd been forced to swallow.

"We have him!" Akeim called over the noise of the water as he sat back.

"Oh, thank God!" Sophia whispered.

Genevieve hadn't stopped praying. She let out a sigh of relief and closed her eyes when she heard the news. She hadn't been aware she was crying until her vision cleared, and she blinked the tears away. "Thank you, God," she whispered.

Alec looked over to Samuel. "Thanks, I thought I was a goner there."

"So did I." Samuel gave him a wry smile before looking around with considerable displeasure. "This place is a bloody death trap!"

"Well, you did say," Alec coughed, "you were in . . . come hell or high water."

Chapter 22

"Who would put a large, gaping chasm of death in the middle of a passage?" Samuel stood, looking over the edge of the deep hole. The flood had receded, leaving a mud slurry in its wake. Moisture continued to drip from the ceiling, the sound echoing through the passage.

"Someone who obviously didn't want us to get past it," Alec commented dryly as he stood. Having lost his turban, he vigorously shook the water from his hair.

"What kind of sinister mind are we dealing with?" Samuel eyed the tunnel suspiciously.

"What is it about Hell that you didn't understand?" Alec asked as he came to stand beside him.

"It does mean we are on the right track," Sophia spoke up from the other side of the void.

Samuel peered down the black hole again. "You're telling me this is a good sign?"

"Yes," Sophia said matter-of-factly. "This chasm of death, as you have so aptly called it, is actually a well which links the tomb to the primordial waters."

"Well . . . now that that's cleared up," Alec winked at his wife, "can we offer you ladies some assistance across the chasm?"

Genevieve tossed Alec the end of the rope that she had made earlier. "I thought you'd never ask." With very little notice, she sprang across the abyss, clearing the hole with room to spare.

Alec couldn't help but move so that she ended up in his arms. He held her for a moment, not wanting to let her go. To his surprise, she held on when he released her.

"I thought, for a moment, I might have lost you," she said softly, looking up at him. Her eyes went to the wet lock of hair that fell rakishly across his brow.

"It's not going to be that easy for you to get rid of me." He grinned widely. "Haven't I told you that?"

Samuel, who was standing beside them, shrugged nonchalantly. "I believe I've mentioned it." He unwound his turban, looping it around his shoulder as he spoke.

"So you did." She smiled before spinning around and tossing her mother the end of the rope.

~*~

The admiral stood before the temple, staring at the entrance where his sister-in-law and niece had vanished. "Whatever you do," he raised his voice in anger, "do not let them get away again."

The dragoman nodded in response.

"If they do manage to find their way out," he looked over at his trusted servant, "bring the women to me, along with the artifact."

"What of the men?" the dragoman asked.

The admiral gave him a baleful glance. "Do not let them leave here."

The dragoman nodded his understanding before turning away.

~*~

"This appears to be a mock city." Samuel looked around the large room they had entered. "There is even a pretend door cut into the wall."

"Interesting." Alec poked his head through several openings along the hall that appeared to be storefronts.

Sophia stood before one of the many carvings along the wall. "Everything you could want in the afterlife."

Samuel turned to her. "But it's empty."

"Not for those who dwell in the underworld." She pointed out a hieroglyph beside her. "They believed that everything that has been depicted on the walls would be available to them, along with what they were actually buried with."

"I don't know about you, but there is nothing here that would make me want to call this Heaven." Samuel leaned closer to Alec.

"It's decidedly vacant of two very important commodities . . . wine and women."

Despite the fact her head was turned away, Sophia answered, "We haven't yet found the actual stores of goods."

"As to the women . . . here you are." Akeim handed him a small figurine.

"What is this?" Samuel turned the wooden statue in his hands.

"A woman," he stated with a slight raise of his brow before turning away.

Samuel watched the warrior walk away. "He's really taken a liking to me."

"A real shine. . . . It's obvious." Alec nodded.

"Here," Genevieve laughed at them, "let me see that." She turned it within her hand. "It's a *shabtis*."

"A what?" Samuel viewed it with renewed interest.

"It means one who answers," Genevieve explained as she handed the statue back to him. "They buried these figures in the belief that they would come to life and be of service."

"I don't know which is more unsettling," Samuel whispered over to Alec, "the idea that this figure would come to life, or that Akeim is playing cupid with it."

"That *is* unsettling," Alec agreed. "I wouldn't be too eager for the wine, either, if I were you."

"Why is that?" Samuel asked.

"I'd be leery of anything over four thousand years old." Alec grimaced. "It no doubt went to vinegar long ago."

"Why must you spoil everything?" Samuel gave him a look of irritation as Sophia spoke up.

"I believe I've found it." She stood before a wall depicting a boat with nine Egyptian gods within it. Below the depiction, the writings had crumbled away.

"Found what?" Alec walked over to her.

"How to enter through the first gate," Sophia replied.

"Wait a minute; I thought we had already *entered*." Samuel followed behind him. "You mean we haven't even started?"

"Afraid not." Nonplussed, Sophia continued her study of the wall.

"What does one have to do to get to Hell?" Samuel whispered under his breath.

"This is considered to be an interstitial space, before the actual underworld." Genevieve thought to add. "Much like the ferryman who rows the dead across the lake. Only, in the Egyptian belief, you must pass through a gate, which is guarded by Urea."

"Urea?" Alec asked in alarm. "You mean we have more snakes to contend with?"

Genevieve was surprised by his reaction. "We have yet to see any."

"That was in the last tomb," Samuel informed her.

"In the last tomb?" Genevieve looked over at Alec again.

"Your uncle had us entombed when we tried to rescue you the last time." Samuel threw his hands up dramatically. "Well, perhaps 'rescue' is too broad a term since all we managed to do was aid him in capturing you."

Noting her questioning glance, Alec shrugged. "We followed you to the ruins of Karnak. Unfortunately, we believed we were fighting against the men who had sailed after you."

"You mean you were there? I had thought," she paused, turning a little pink over the confession, "that you didn't come."

Alec smiled at her. "As long as I draw breath, I will always be there for you." He would have pulled her towards him, but Samuel stood between them.

"This is awkward." Samuel looked painstakingly over at Alec. "Please leave me home on your next honeymoon."

"Believe me, I will."

"Will what?" Genevieve looked around him.

"Avoid unfortunate traps in the future." Samuel turned back to say with a smile. He was quick to change the subject. "Tell me about these snakes which guard the door."

"The cobra goddesses of ancient Egypt?" Genevieve warmed to her subject. "Some stories say, much like the Sphinx, that they too ask a riddle, and if you do not know the answer, they will devour you. Other stories say that you must be pure in order to pass, and that only by speaking their names will you have power over them."

"I've heard of this name-calling." A glimmer of excitement lit Samuel's eyes. "Wadjet!" he yelled out.

Both Sophia and Akeim turned to look at him in surprise.

"Amaunet! Tefmet!" he yelled again. "Open sesame!" He shrugged when nothing happened. "It was worth a try."

"Where did you get that?" Sophia asked him when she noticed the figurine he was holding.

"The doll?" Samuel raised the statue in his hand. "Why, Akeim gave her to me." He couldn't help but grin as he held it up.

Akeim gave Samuel a black look before Sophia turned to him. "Where did you find it?"

"I will show you." Akeim led her over to another wall where the plaster had long since fallen away, leaving only the false door that had been cut into the stone and a small shelf beside it.

Samuel examined the stone for cracks. "I say, how does one open a pretend door?"

"By turning the pretend handle," Alec responded with the obvious answer.

"Funny," Samuel replied.

"Samuel, may I see that statue?" Sophia stood looking at the rubble at her feet.

"By all means." He handed over the figurine. "Do you think she's the key?"

"I'm not sure. The hieroglyphs speak of the door being guarded by Sekhmet." Sophia turned it in her hands, wiping the dirt from its crevices. "Hmm, it does appear that she has lost the rest of her headpiece. It must have broken off."

"But isn't Sekhmet a lioness?" Samuel asked as everyone else started shifting through the debris around the area where Akeim had found the statue.

"What of this?" Alec held a piece of wood that looked like two fingers.

"I have found something too." Genevieve cleaned the dirt from what looked to be a round disk that had once been orange.

Sophia took the two pieces and fit them together. "That's what I thought, this is no ordinary *shabtis*."

261

"Is that a good thing?" Samuel strained to see over her shoulder.

"It is if it opens the door," Alec replied.

"Would you look at that!" Samuel exclaimed when she held up the figure. "It's just like the drawing on the map."

"This is a statue of the goddess Hathor, Mistress of the West." Sophia looked over at him. "You see, Hathor and Sekhmet are one and the same."

"No kidding. So our girl went from servant to goddess lioness just like that?" Samuel snapped his fingers. "I knew there was something to that hat."

"Ah, yes, the feather in one's cap," Alec noted.

"Out of curiosity. . . . How can you tell that it's Hathor?" Samuel pointed to the statue. "Even Ramesses's queen at the small temple at Abū Simbel wore that headdress."

"His queen, Nefertari, was the high priestess of Amun," Sophia replied.

Samuel's expression was one of confusion as he looked over at Alec. "That explains everything."

"Considering we're going to need to work together to get through this," Alec appealed to her better nature, "wouldn't it be best if we understood more?"

"Even though this tomb has been compromised," Sophia said soberly, "this information is not common knowledge." Turning her attention toward Samuel, she continued, "to make it so could put us in mortal danger."

"I shall guard it with my life," Samuel pledged.

"What I need is your silence," she said prudently.

"Mum's the word." Samuel nodded.

She appraised them critically. "Alright, I shall explain." She held the figurine up. "The feather in her cap is actually the double-plumed crown of the god Amun."

"As in Amun-Ra." Alec winked at Genevieve, who had told him this.

"This could take a while," Sophia sighed. "You see, Ra represented the sun, whereas Amun was worshiped, in part, for his association with the moon. Combining Ra and Amun together joined the two most powerful deities that the Egyptians worshiped . . . the sun and the moon, essentially fusing the aspects of female and male together into one."

"Ah, like Pharaoh Akhenaton." Samuel nodded.

"I'm sure that is where he got the idea, but before we get too distracted," she held up her finger, "let me explain your first question. You see, it was Amun's association with the night that gave him knowledge of the underworld. The double-plumed headdress depicts the two lands which the moon travels through—day and night, the lands of both the living and dead."

"Ah, I see. That explains the feathers, but what of the horns of fertility around the sun disk?" Samuel used his hands to draw an imaginary headdress.

"For one, that is not the sun," Sophia sighed yet again. "It is the moon, or harvest moon, to be correct. It represents a woman in her prime, fertile and pregnant." She paused. "After all, the symbol for woman is the half-moon. ⌒"

"And here I thought that was a loaf of bread," Samuel said under his breath.

"This is a loaf of bread." ⛉ Genevieve pointed to a wall, which depicted a table piled high with food and wine.

"What of that symbol in the ankh. You said that was the moon as well? The one I thought was a ball of string?"

Sophia raised her brow. "You mean the one you thought was a placenta," she corrected. "It is the moon in all its phases. ⊜ Much like life itself, it represents the stages of a woman from her birth to death. The waxing of the moon is her adolescence. The full moon is her birthing years. The waning of the moon is woman in her maturity. It is the full circle of life."

"I thought Champollion had this all figured out." Samuel tapped a finger against his lips. "Why is this still so misunderstood?"

Again, Sophia appraised him before speaking. "It was no doubt due to the role of women within the temples. You see, the priests in the temples of Amun were dedicated to the burial of the pharaoh's body, and it was their duty to see that the pharaoh was guided by these writings. It was the priestess, however, who was ultimately in charge of his resurrection."

"I thought that was Anubis?" Alec spoke up.

"Many do." Sophia nodded. "He is the god of embalming. Have you heard the story of the god Osiris who was killed by his jealous brother, Seth?" She turned toward the false door as she asked the question.

"I was afraid it would turn biblical," Samuel commented under his breath.

"Isis brought the body of her dead husband to Anubis to prepare, but it was she who brought him back to life," Sophia explained as she studied the wall.

"Ahh, the fertility cults." Samuel raised his brows suggestively.

Alec nudged him, giving him a warning glance.

"Fertility is another word," Sophia stated, nonplussed by his behavior, "describing not only the act of creation, but also the power of birth. In this life, and in the afterlife, it was the female who was bestowed with this most awesome of gifts."

"That explains why so many warriors carried amulets of fertility goddesses into battle," Alec remarked. "They were seeking life after death."

"Just so." Sophia placed her hand on the small shelf and brushed the dirt away. "It was a common practice in many different cultures of the day."

"So that's it?" Samuel said, deflated. "It was all about rebirth."

"Yes," Sophia replied simply.

"Well, the afterlife just got a lot more boring," Samuel said under his breath. "Next she'll tell me they did away with the forty virgins too."

"Considering that belief comes from a different country altogether, I think it's safe to say they're history," Alex told him.

"There are plenty of women in the Egyptian afterlife," Sophia commented, despite the fact she had her back to them.

Samuel looked only slightly chagrined at being overheard. "I say, remind me that she has the hearing of a hungry bat chasing a mosquito in the wind."

"Alright, I will." Genevieve, who had been standing behind them, smiled before joining her mother.

Before Samuel could comment, Alec leaned over. "I think, in this case, silence is golden."

Samuel nodded in response, his mouth pursed and eyebrows raised.

"What have you found?" Genevieve asked.

"I'm not sure." Sophia blew at the rest of the dust. "Akeim, could you bring that light closer?"

With a nod, the warrior held his flaming knife blade overhead so she could see as she brushed the rest of the dirt off with her sleeve.

Samuel held his flaming sword up, as well, studying the ceiling. "No sign of any spears."

The shelf had a groove in the bottom that matched that of the figure. Taking a deep breath, Sophia placed the statue in the niche that had been carved for it.

"Should we duck and cover?" Samuel anxiously looked around. "Hold our breath?"

"Yes, you should hold your breath," Akeim answered him.

Samuel gave Akeim a sour look as they waited for something to happen. When nothing did, Samuel whispered, "What now?"

"I wonder." Alec stepped closer, running his fingers around the shelf itself. "It appears to be a separate stone." He pressed gently on it and felt it move. "Stand back everyone," he said before pushing on it.

"Up there!" Genevieve pointed to a stone high above the false door. "That stone is moving." It slid back a few inches, accompanied by the sound of grinding within the walls.

They watched as the stone continued to move, revealing a small opening above the false door.

"Still no sign of spears." Samuel diligently continued his search of the ceiling.

"Nicely done." Sophia stepped back to get a better view. "We just might make it out yet."

Samuel's brows shot up in surprise. "Might?"

Sophia ignored him as she assessed the opening. "It looks awfully small. It appears as if we're going to have to crawl."

"Like the riddle?" Samuel nodded. "What has four feet when it's born, two when it's an adult, and three when it's old."

"Actually, that was only written on the map in reference to the Sphinx," Sophia told him, "not as a note on how to proceed."

"Oh." Samuel looked over with obvious disappointment.

"But you never know, now do you?" Sophia smiled back at him. "It was, after all, part of the ancients' advice. Can you give me a boost?"

"No offense, but I believe one of us should go first," Alec said, indicating one of the men.

"Of course," Sophia said with a smile, "but one of us should follow directly after . . . just in case of booby traps."

Samuel looked over at Alec in alarm. "You first," he invited.

Alec rolled his eyes. "Give me a lift."

Samuel handed Genevieve his torch while he cupped his palms together and offered the required assistance. Once Alec had climbed up, he reached down to assist Genevieve. Giving Samuel his torch back, she took Alec's hand and climbed up after him.

Alec smiled at her as he pulled her inside with him. The space was so tight that she had to slide across him until they were nose-to-nose. She held herself up, hovering above him until her foot caught in the folds of their clothing. The stumble caused her to press herself against the length of him.

"Hmm," he whispered, "I think I like exploring tombs."

"Me too." Samuel's head appeared over the edge.

"As always." Alec placed a quick kiss on her nose before scooting back. Unable to turn around in the small space, they moved deeper into the tunnel, making room for Samuel to climb up to the ledge.

Akeim handed Samuel's torch up next.

"Watch out," Samuel hollered as flames spread across the ceiling. "I believe I've just singed my eyebrows off. Ow!" He rolled the sword across the stone to extinguish it. "Bloody thing makes a good branding iron."

"Here," Akeim's voice sounded from below, "see if you can manage this one."

"As if I couldn't handle a wee little knife," Samuel grumbled under his breath. Gingerly, he passed it over to Genevieve so that he could help Sophia climb in. "It's getting a might close in here." Samuel looked over his shoulder. "Mind moving up a bit? I feel as though I'm in a tin of sardines."

Alec slowly crawled away from the opening so the others could have more room, clearing cobwebs from his path as he went. Genevieve followed right behind him. The shaft went for another twenty feet before an opening appeared.

"Take this." Genevieve passed Alec the light.

Looking over the edge, he held the small torch aloft. Before him was a room almost identical to the one they had just left. Genevieve scooted up next to him and peered out.

"What do you think?" Alec looked over at her. "Is it safe?"

"Unfortunately, there is only one way to find out." Shoulder-to-shoulder with him, she looked down at the floor. "Lower me down."

"Not on your life." He shook his head. "I'll not watch something happen to you."

"Where does that leave us?" She lifted her chin stubbornly. "Because I most certainly am not going to watch something happen to you."

"I'm glad you care." He grinned at her.

"Did I mention that I'm claustrophobic?" Samuel said from behind them. "Someone had better move. I have a hot poker, and I'm not afraid to use it."

"Perhaps you would like the honors, then?" Alec handed him back the small torch. Sliding partially out of the opening, he dangled his upper torso out into thin air. "Grab hold." He rolled over, reaching a hand back toward Samuel. Twisting into a sitting position, he scooted far enough away to get a leg out. When the other was free, Samuel let go of his hand, dropping him to the floor.

"Is he still there?" Samuel crawled forward curiously.

"Thank you for your concern." Alec gave him a disparaging glance as he assisted Genevieve to the floor. "Your morbid curiosity warms my heart."

"I say, it's almost exactly like the room we just left." Samuel dropped down beside them. "That is, with the exception of that cobra-shaped torch, the different drawings on the wall, and all these little balls covering the floor." He held the light up as he turned around. "And let's not forget the scary passage leading down that dark hallway."

"In other words," Alec gave him a sideways glance, "it's completely different."

"Exactly." Samuel smiled as he picked up several round pebbles, which were curiously scattered across the floor. "I wonder if this is some type of child's game?"

"I'm having a hard time seeing children at play here," Alec moved a few of the stones with the toe of his boot, "even the ones in the afterlife."

Samuel walked over to the dark hallway. Holding the flickering knife up, he peered across the threshold. The mummified heads of a jackal and a ram, which had been skewered on either side of the opening, greeted him. "Good God, I hope this is not a common theme." Samuel took a step forward.

"Actually," Genevieve put her arm out, blocking his progress, "it would be safer for you not to go any farther."

"Right." Samuel nodded, backing away. His retreat sent several of the small stone marbles rolling down the incline of the darkened opening. Within the span of a heartbeat, sharp spikes shot up from the dirt floor, covering every foot of the passage.

"Holy hell!" Samuel swallowed hard as he stared at the deadly forest of spears. "I almost walked over that."

"How did you know that would happen?" Alec asked from behind them.

"I've been told stories of the journey through the underworld since I was a child," Genevieve answered as she took the light from Samuel's frozen grasp. She carried it over to her mother, who was studying the hieroglyphs on the wall.

"That's grim," Samuel commented, "even grimmer than Grimm." He smiled at his own joke. "You know he just died?"

Alec gave him another sideways glance. "Then you should look on the bright side."

"And what is that?"

"Perhaps you'll get a chance to meet him while we're down here," Alec replied dryly as he turned away.

"That's hardly funny." Samuel gave the deadly spikes one last glance before following him.

"This appears to be the litany of Ra." Sophia studied the many names scrolled across the wall.

"And what of this?" Samuel looked at the wall Genevieve was standing in front of. Two sets of nine baboons were drawn on either side of the god Ra and his two companions. Below them were a number of otherworldly beings, including twelve cobras that bordered the scene.

"This is the Pharaoh with the Path Opener and the Guide of Boat," Genevieve read the wall for him. "The baboons are here to sing to him as he's greeted by the collective dead."

Samuel's eyes shot down the darkened passage. "Good God, we're not going to be greeted by the collective dead now, are we?"

The corner of Alec's mouth lifted at his concerned expression. "I would imagine that would depend."

"On what?" Samuel quickly turned his head back to him.

"Whether or not you are living or dead." Alec's smile broadened. "Considering we are still among the living, I doubt we're invited to the celebration."

Samuel looked away, ignoring him. "So what are the baboons singing about?"

"It speaks here of a goddess whose job it is to light up darkness," Sophia read further down.

"Which goddess?" Samuel perked up with interest.

"That is part of the puzzle," Sophia responded.

"Perhaps the cobra sconce over there has something to do with it?" Alec wondered aloud. "That would light it up."

Genevieve considered that for a moment. "It has to be Wadjet."

"Of course." Sophia nodded.

"Why, exactly, does it have to be that goddess?" Samuel looked curiously from one to another.

"Wadjet is also known as the all-seeing eye," Genevieve explained. "The left eye of Ra."

Samuel shook his head in confusion. "Am I missing something?"

"You need ask?" Akeim punctuated his words with the raise of an eyebrow.

Samuel gave him a baleful glance in response.

Sophia walked toward the sconce. "The image of the great lioness Sekhmet is not the only one on the moon."

"You're telling me that there is yet another image on the moon?" Samuel asked in amazement. "How is that possible?"

"I assure you it is," Sophia promised.

"Why is it I've never seen them?" Samuel looked over at Alec. "Have you ever heard of this?"

When Alec shook his head, Genevieve left them to retrieve the book her mother carried. Opening it, she turned it for them to see.

On the page, was a drawing of the moon. "There are many ancient cultures which have seen them as the ancient Egyptians did. The Chinese, for instance, also saw the likeness of a dragon when they gazed at the moon. It has been there from the beginning, rising in the east. The tiger and the dragon . . . yin and yang."

Genevieve traced the ancient symbol of light and dark with her finger. "As you have already heard, when the moon sets in the west, it is Sekhmet who rules the sky." This time she traced the silhouette of the great lioness' head with her finger.

"When the moon rises in the east, however, it is the image of Wadjet, the cobra goddess, who rules the heavens."

She turned the book upside down, displaying the same picture. "Besides, she is also known as the Opener of the Way." Genevieve couldn't help but smile.

Chapter 23

"Simply amazing." Samuel moved to get a closer look at the image. "May I see more?"

"I'm sorry," Genevieve gently closed the book in her arms, "there is much here that is not for the viewing of . . . well, you know." She smiled before returning the book to her mother.

"Touché." Alec grinned when Samuel looked over at him. "Perhaps you should have shared the secrets of your diary."

"I doubt that would have been wise under any circumstances," Samuel snorted. "But I was right," he smiled triumphantly, "she does know how to read it."

"So it appears."

"Speaking of which, did you notice the writing in that book? I told you it was the same as the ancient script on the other side of the map," Samuel said in a hushed tone. "Even Champollion's expert couldn't translate the cuneiform text. He said it was from a dead language." Looking briefly around, he added, "No pun intended."

Alec groaned. "You never stop, do you?"

"Well, aren't you in the least bit curious about it?"

"No!" Alec gave him with a look of disbelief. "I'm fairly certain we have enough to contend with."

"You mean, with being in the Egyptian equivalent of Hell?" Samuel indicated the space around them. "Well, how much worse can it get?"

Alec sighed. "Would you like to know the true meaning of Hell?"

"Is this a philosophical, or rhetorical, question?" Samuel asked suspiciously.

"Hell, I believe, is what happens when you have the same conversation over and over again with the same outcome."

"Are you implying that I am incapable of a new argument?"

"I'm glad you see my point," Alec commented dryly as he walked away.

"Alec, I believe you were right about this sconce." Sophia looked over the ornate handle of the cobra. "It was meant to light the way." She moved to take the sconce from its holder, but Akeim stopped her.

"Sitt Hakim," he said as he bowed his head respectfully before placing his own hand above hers. He then waited patiently for her to back away.

"Of course." Sophia smiled at him before moving.

The rest of them waited as Akeim slowly removed the sconce from its holder. There was an audible sigh as soon as he held it within his hand. Their relief was short-lived, however, for the bracket fastening the holder to the wall moved several inches up without the weight of the sconce.

"Now what?" Alec breathed in the silence as they waited to see what the trigger might unleash upon them.

"We're going to be crushed, that's what!" Samuel hollered as the exterior walls started to move towards them.

The edge of Akeim's kaftan became trapped beneath the stone as it slid forward. He wasted little time tugging on the fabric, choosing instead to slice the garment free using his sword. He then pulled several spears from the edge of the corridor and braced them between the walls.

"I was really hoping those little balls were part of a child's game," Samuel lamented as he pressed against the stone. "Now it appears they are the grease behind this little torture chamber."

Alec pushed against the other side to no avail. "Moving a stone that weighs several tons is hardly child's play."

"And they said the Egyptians didn't have wheels," Samuel scoffed.

The spears snapped like toothpicks as the walls continued to close. The only escape was the dark passage that Samuel had almost taken earlier. The remaining spears jutted up from the floor, looking like the sharp teeth of a beastly creature in the flickering light.

"We must go forward," Sophia called out as she headed toward the passage.

"Wait. . . . Are you sure?" Samuel's eyes darted quickly over to the yawning mouth of the beast. "It's an obvious trap." He looked back at Genevieve. "Isn't there another way?" He took a step toward the opening they had come through. "What about going back?"

Just as he spoke, the large slab of rock above the opening crashed down, sealing off the passage. "On second thought, that passage looks quite welcoming." Samuel turned back to the spear-filled opening.

"Are you sure?" Alec raised a questioning brow.

"Quite," Samuel said with a nod. Despite his new attitude toward the death trap, he paused at the threshold while Alec and Genevieve wove through the forest of spears.

"Samuel, come on!" Alec called from the other side. "Hurry!"

Samuel remained where he was, unwilling to brave the short distance until a chunk of plaster crashed to the floor behind him.

"Glad you could make it," Alec said when Samuel joined them on the other side.

"I wouldn't stand there if I were you," Akeim said from behind him.

"Why is that?" Samuel jumped back, looking all around for the next booby trap.

"You're casting a shadow in my light." Akeim stepped forward with his knife held high. The flame he carried shed light upon the wall that Sophia was studying.

Samuel narrowed his eyes on Akeim's back as he passed.

"You had to see that one coming," Alec chuckled as he joined Samuel.

Out of sorts, Samuel reached inside the waistband of his kaftan and retrieved a small bottle. Prying the cork out with his teeth, he took a healthy sip. "I'm not going to be the same after this."

"Sure you will." Alec clapped him on the shoulder. "We've been in worse scrapes."

"Yes, but I've a bad feeling about this," Samuel replied, trying to shake his feelings of doom.

Alec looked at his expression of gloom. "You said that in Amsterdam, and that turned out alright."

"For you." Samuel glared at him. "If I remember correctly, I awoke to Helga the hairy." He shivered for effect. "'Twas enough to make me want to gnaw off my own arm rather than risk waking her, I tell you."

"Waking who?" Genevieve inquired as she joined them.

Samuel took another sip, leaving Alec to play dumb until he had to swallow. "Aaugh," Samuel sighed exaggeratedly, "sleeping demons." He cleared his throat. "Uh-um, I, for one, will be glad when this nightmare is over, I tell you. Which brings me to ask, what can we look forward to in the next hour?" He looked over at the wall, which depicted a boat with several gods within it.

"The second hour is devoted to granting land rights to the grain gods," Genevieve replied.

"That sounds fairly hair—I mean harmless," Alec quickly amended.

"Nothing is ever harmless." Samuel's eyes narrowed on Alec, then darted behind him. "Speaking of which. . . ." He quickly sidestepped Alec. "Are you sure that is a good idea?" he asked as Sophia lit the sconce she held.

Holding the torch high, she looked over at him. "I'm fairly certain that it is how to light the way."

"What if it explodes?" Samuel asked in alarm. "Is it possible to vote on actions of this nature in the future?"

"No," Akeim said flatly.

Sophia chuckled at his remark. "I did not expect you, of all people, to become so skittish."

"Skittish?" Samuel practically snorted. "I have almost been crushed, skewered, drowned, and flattened," he defended, "and have no idea what is to happen next."

"And yet you're still here," Akeim remarked.

"Here, hold this." Sophia stepped between them. "I need your keen artistic eye to help me translate some of these writings." For a moment, it looked as if he might refuse. "You see how these have deteriorated?" Sophia focused on the wall beside her. "Perhaps you could help me make out the images."

Samuel looked at the sconce in her hand as if the cobra she held might come to life and strike him at any moment. With a sigh, he did what he could under the circumstances . . . he took the torch from her hand, though not before pulling up a spear from the entrance. He followed behind her, poking the ground as they proceeded down the ever-sloping passage.

"You see here the barque that the god Ra sails in during his journey through the underworld." Sophia pointed out the longboat that the scene depicted.

"I am more concerned about what is happening here." Samuel used the spear to indicate a group of mummies floating above the souls of the damned.

"It appears they are waking the dead."

"I was afraid you would say something like that." His trepidation was obvious as they continued further down the passage, finally stopping before a huge image of a serpent, which dominated the scene.

"Ah, here we are." Sophia pointed to the large snake coiled around the boat. "Our first run-in with the god Apophis."

"That doesn't sound like a favorable thing," Alec said as both he and Genevieve joined them.

"In this case, I'm afraid it is not," Sophia sighed regretfully as she started to walk down the passage again. "He could strike at any moment."

Samuel remained rooted where he was. "What do you mean strike?"

"It is the eternal quest of the god Apophis to destroy the sun god as he travels through the underworld." Sophia turned to look back at him when it appeared he would go no farther.

"You're telling me that a giant snake is about to attack us?" His voice was suspiciously higher than normal. "How, exactly, would he destroy the sun god?"

"By swallowing him, of course." Sophia waited patiently. "Metaphorically speaking, that is."

"Metaphorically?" Samuel repeated in alarm.

"What of this?" Alec pointed to an area of blue water with figures floating within it that had been drawn as a border across the bottom.

"It depicts the ambivalent lake of fire." Genevieve stepped closer, studying the wall. "Where the damned will meet the flame."

"Ambivalent?" Samuel eyebrows shot up. "What the hell is that supposed to mean, it can't make up its mind?"

"They are opposing elemental forces," Akeim supplied.

Both Alec and Samuel turned to look at the warrior in surprise.

"Whatever it is," Sophia said, "it appears that it also comes in the form of a test."

"A test?" Samuel's ears perked up. "What kind of test?"

"A test of purity." Genevieve indicated a symbol of a foot with a pitcher where the knee should be, pouring water out over it. "It also warns," she turned back to look at them, "of the fires of damnation."

"Oh, is that all?" Samuel replied sarcastically. "And here I was worried."

"What of this test of purity?" Alec came closer to the wall. "Does it say how it is passed?"

"Perhaps all we need to do is wash our feet," Samuel considered the symbol a moment, "metaphorically speaking, of course."

"Although washing of the feet did signify purity, most purification ceremonies within the temple involved the priests pouring water over a stone altar," Genevieve clarified as she continued her study. "Look here," she referred to the upper register, "it shows Maat, the goddess of purity, with the blessed, who are provisioned from the flame."

"How are they provisioned?" Alec leaned over her shoulder.

"It, it doesn't say," she stammered slightly as his breath caressed her cheek. His grin was enough to tell her that he was aware of the effect he had on her. Without a word, he took her hand in his and squeezed it.

"Isn't Maat the goddess who presides over the weighing of the heart against a feather in the judgment hall?" Samuel asked as they moved down the incline.

"Is this the judgment hall, then?" Alec looked around with interest.

"Yes, she is, and, no, this isn't," Genevieve responded to their questioning.

"What have we here?" Samuel stopped in his tracks. The light he carried revealed an ornate archway that held him enthralled.

"The Gate of Passage," Sophia announced as she stood beneath the elaborate carvings. Fantastic snakes with human heads on either side of the opening were entwined with serpents with wings across the top.

"So this is Hell." Samuel looked up at the beastly creature in the center, which stared down from its many heads. "Finally."

When Sophia moved to take a step forward, Samuel's arm shot out in front of her. "I'm not sure we should just enter." As a precaution, he withdrew several stones from his pocket and rolled them across the floor. They scattered across the room. When nothing happened, he threw a few more for good measure. Holding the sconce as far as he could reach without actually entering, he stood on the precipice and looked around.

"Is there a time limit to this excursion?" Alec waited, with arms folded across his chest, for Samuel to finish.

"It's possible," Sophia said with a shrug of her shoulders.

"Great," Samuel bemoaned before stepping across the threshold.

"So what exactly is the Gate of Passage?" Alec watched Samuel walk in a large circle in the center of the room.

"It is the entrance taken by the dead," Genevieve answered.

"But we're not dead." Samuel stopped what he was doing at that revelation.

"Details, details," Alec sighed as he stepped inside the room. "You might get an invite to that party yet." He chuckled as he walked across the floor. "It looks fine to me."

"How would you know?" Samuel's expression was one of annoyance. "Did you even notice how this floor is flat compared to the slope of the rest of the passage?"

"Yes," Alec answered simply as the others joined them. "I also noticed that the drawings are in relief and richer in color."

"We must be getting closer." Sophia turned around, looking at the opulent designs within the room.

"To what?" Samuel's eyes widened in alarm.

"To the burial chamber, of course," Sophia supplied.

"We are definitely getting close." Genevieve stood before a large portrait of the god Osiris. "The priests of Amun are bestowing Osiris with the two divine forces of will and mind."

Sophia walked to the opening on the other side of the room. Centered on the archway above her was a drawing of a goddess with two white spheres on each side of her.

"Those must be the two images of Sekhmet and Wedjat." Samuel stood, looking up at the drawing. "I still can't believe that they've been on the moon all this time, and I've never seen them." He shook his head with a chuckle. "At least now the Frenchman's love sonnet makes sense."

"The Frenchman?" Sophia raised a questioning brow in his direction.

"Yes, you know," he nodded as he peered into the room, "the man Alec won the map from. He had a little note tucked within the scroll that extolled the virtues of the goddess Hathor, the golden one." He held the flame aloft as he tossed a few pebbles across the threshold and stabbed the ground.

Sophia took the sconce from him as she spoke. "I'm surprised you didn't plague him to death with questions."

"It was too late for that." Samuel missed Alec's look of concern. "Someone else beat me to it."

Sophia turned the light towards his face. "Whatever do you mean?"

Alec rolled his eyes, gesturing with his hand for silence. Samuel might have seen him, if not for the bright flame.

"Why, yes, he was already dead." Samuel was more than delighted to inform her.

With her brow raised higher than before, Sophia turned the torch toward Alec. "And you didn't feel that this information might be pertinent?"

"I thought only to stick to the facts," Alec attempted to placate her. "If you will recall, I was being held at knifepoint by a man who had already seized my weapons and promised death for trespassing."

She turned to Akeim with a look of *I told you so.* "You see, people are much more forthcoming when not coerced."

Akeim gave both Alec and Samuel a look of extreme irritation before he followed behind her. Alec, in turn, gave Samuel a look of disbelief.

"What?" Samuel lifted his hands as if to imply his innocence.

Alec shook his head. "And you consider yourself a spy."

"It's not as if it was a national secret," Samuel replied as he followed after them.

A great hall, wider and longer than the one they had been traveling through, emerged in the dim light. "That must be where Wedjat belongs." Sophia pointed to an ornate holder on the wall.

"Wait," Samuel rushed to the front when it appeared she was about to set the sconce in the holder, "should we not vote on this?"

"Again with the voting," Akeim mumbled. "Does this look like the House of Lords to you?" He looked around meaningfully.

"Alright," Sophia intervened, placing a hand on Akeim's arm, "we'll vote." She turned to the group. "If we wait, we could wait . . . indefinitely." After a lengthy pause, she sighed. "The coronation of every pharaoh that has ever ruled over Egypt was held before the Temple of the Sphinx because of its unique access to the underworld. Unfortunately, Percival destroyed the passageway when he tried to open the door."

"You mean no one else has been through here?" Samuel's eyebrows shot to his hairline. "But I thought. . . ."

"Not through this area." Sophia shook her head. "Not since it was sealed." Her concern was apparent when she spoke. "I'm sorry, but if we do nothing, then we do not proceed." She took a deep breath. "The only way that I know of to go through to the other side is to follow the instructions left by the priests."

Samuel considered her words for a moment. "It's not for you to apologize," he sighed. "I realize that I've been a horse's . . . that I've been difficult."

"Is that what you call it?" Akeim assessed him critically.

Samuel chose to ignore him, addressing Sophia instead. "I don't suppose you would allow me the honors." He stepped over to her with an apologetic smile. Taking the flaming sconce from her hand, he placed it within the holder.

Immediately, the flame grew brighter, igniting a trough that had been cut into the wall above it. The flame spread out, tracing a line down both sides of the passage, where it wavered slightly before stretching across the back of the long hall.

The fire lit the huge corridor, highlighting the ceiling, which was decorated with white stars against a dark blue background. It also revealed that the floor had several deep holes in it.

"These must be the fire pits the drawing suggested." Genevieve peeked over the edge of the closest one.

"Right now they are just pits," Samuel warned. "Let's do our best not to add to the fire, shall we?" He looked meaningfully at Akeim, who still held his blazing knife.

Akeim raised a brow but extinguished the light, nonetheless.

"How would you suggest we proceed?" Samuel tested the edge of the first pit. Dirt fell into the deep hole, which stretched for ten feet and ran from one side of the hall to the other. Beyond it lay the next pit with barely enough dirt to stand on between them.

Sophia stood, looking up at the wall. "Perhaps we can use that ridge to our advantage." She smiled over at Samuel.

Akeim led the way, with Sophia close behind. Hanging from their hands, they used the lip of the small ledge to cross over the first pit. Once they were on the other side, Alec and Genevieve started across. Samuel slipped the spear into the sash at his waist and followed suit. Slowly, one-by-one, they crossed over the deep holes.

"I'm glad there are only two more to go," Genevieve said with a sigh. "My arms are getting quite tired."

"I'm curious as to why there are nine." Samuel jumped down, rubbing his hands together. "Why not ten, or twelve?"

"Or one," Alec replied sarcastically as he flexed his fingers.

"All numbers had sacred meanings to the ancient Egyptians," Genevieve explained as they watched Sophia and Akeim negotiate another ten-foot expanse. "Nine, especially, was a— Mother, hold on!" she gasped as the wall under Sophia's left hand crumbled away, leaving her to dangle by one arm halfway across.

Akeim attempted to climb back to her, but the wall threatened to crumble on the other side as well. "Can you reach me if you swing?" He watched closely as she tried, but the wall disintegrated a little more with her weight.

Samuel sprang up and crossed the distance, getting as close as he could without putting more stress on the wall. "I thought this might come in handy." He held on by one hand as he slid the spear across the trough above her.

Sophia reached up, taking hold of it. The wooden pole sagged slightly but held as it spanned the weakened space. "Oh, thank you." She gave him a weak smile.

"Sure thing, Mum, just do me a favor and make it to the other side." A crackling sound from the front of the chamber stopped Samuel from crossing behind her. "Uh oh," he groaned, "that didn't sound good."

KABOOM! The first pit they had crossed exploded, sending a ball of fire up to the ceiling.

The trembling almost cost Sophia her balance as she landed on the other side. The spear came away in Samuel's hand as the wall crumbled from the shock. He had no other choice but to swing back where Alec pulled him to safety.

"Hurry!" Sophia hollered over to them as they began crossing over the pit on the other side of the hall.

"There is no telling how long we have until the next one goes." Alec glanced back at the flames as he followed close behind Genevieve. "Perhaps I should tell you now that I love you."

KABOOM! The second pit exploded, sending another plume of smoke across the star-studded ceiling.

"What?" Genevieve paused, turning her head back toward him.

"I said. . . ." Alec swallowed.

"I hate to sound like a pessimist in the wake of hellfire," Samuel said as he came up behind them, "but perhaps you two could hurry it along."

Genevieve leaped across the remaining distance with Alec right behind her. After Samuel had passed, Alec turned her toward him, pulling her into his arms. "I said," he whispered softly, "that I love you." He touched his lips to hers.

She moved further into his arms as the kiss deepened. They stood in an embrace as the stars shone down from the smoky ceiling above. When the kiss ended, she looked up at him with a brilliant smile on her lips. "I love you too," she whispered.

Picking her up in a tight hug, he sighed as though a heavy burden had been lifted. "I wanted to tell you, but the timing always seemed to be off," he laughed. "I suppose Hell's fire isn't the most romantic scenario."

KABOOM! The trembling underfoot caused him to tighten his hold on her.

"I disagree. I would most definitely say your declaration has moved Heaven and earth." She smiled up at him.

"My plan all along." He winked as he set her down. "We'd better get a move on." He grinned as he took her hand.

The smoke had become dense, making it hard to see the fine etchings across the wall. Coughing, Alec held a cloth to his nose and mouth to cut down on the smoke. "What is happening?" he asked.

"This appears to be a dead end." Samuel turned away from the wall in frustration as Genevieve joined her mother, who was trying to make out the writing in the smoke-filled room.

"What does it say?" Alec walked up behind them.

"We must choose between two lakes." Sophia stood up wearily. "The Lake of Fire, which is guarded by jackals, or the Lake of Urea."

"That's a hell of a choice." Alec turned, dragging a fist through his hair.

"With the fires of Hell on our heels, I'd welcome either one," Samuel coughed, looking back at the flames. "Only one problem. . . . I'm not seeing any lakes."

KABOOM! The fourth pit blasted, making the floor tremble. Sophia stumbled backwards from the tremor, falling into Samuel.

"Whoa—" Samuel teetered on the edge, swinging his arms in great circles to keep from falling. He failed. Toppling into the hole, he hit the dirt and rolled awkwardly, slamming against a rock that protruded from the side. "Ouch! Bloody—" he swore. "I could have cracked my skull on this . . . this big rock."

"A big rock?" Sophia leaned over the edge, "Is it flat on top?"

"I'm fine. Thanks for asking." Samuel felt the surface of the stone slab. "And yes, the top is definitely flat."

"Is there a groove at the base?" Sophia knelt beside the pit.

"A groove? It's a little hard to see down here," he complained while feeling about. "Wait. . . . Yes!" Excitedly, he followed it with his fingers. "There is a groove that seems to lead to a basin of some type at the bottom."

"That's it!" Sophia wilted with relief. "I'm coming down."

KABOOM! The ground shuddered as the fifth pit exploded.

"Be careful, that first step is a doozy— Oomph!" For the second time, Samuel found himself knocked down as she stepped on him.

"Yes, you're right." Sophia cleared her throat apologetically. "Thank you for breaking my fall," she said as she stepped off of him.

"My pleasure," Samuel groaned as he sat up.

Crouching beside the altar, Sophia felt her way around the stone. Leaning back on her haunches, she looked up at the silhouettes above her. "We need water."

"Water?" It was a question that everyone asked in alternating tones of dismay.

"Where in hell are we going to get water from?" Samuel sank back.

"What if we were to wring out our clothing over the stone?" Genevieve spoke up. "Mine is still quite damp."

"That could take forever." Samuel threw his hands up in frustration. An action that was lost in the dark. "What if we spit on it?"

"And you think that would be quicker?" Alec rolled his eyes.

"What about this?" Samuel held up his bottle of spirits.

"That's a good idea," Alec remarked as he climbed down. "Let's add fuel to the flames."

Samuel ignored him. "How many more pits before this one goes up?"

"There are four more pits," Akeim informed him.

KABOOM!

"Make that three," Alec amended.

"Hurry! This *is* the lock that opens the next door." Sophia wrung her hands together. Her voice, normally so calm, was thickly accented in her agitation. "I hate to think of what might happen if we fail to open it."

"Where is this vast lake when you need it?" Samuel mumbled.

"Same place the ice water is, I imagine," Alec said dryly as Genevieve slid down into his arms.

"That actually gives me an idea." Samuel jumped up.

"It does?" Alec's voice held his surprise. "Do I dare ask?"

"Ladies, I implore you, please step back," Samuel cautioned.

"What are you doing?" Alec moved to stand beside him.

"Something that would get most people kicked out of Hell, I would imagine." Samuel responded. "I could use some help," he muttered while he fumbled with his clothing. "Damned dress!"

Alec took a step back when it became apparent what he intended. "Count me out."

"I meant with the amount of liquid needed," Samuel grumbled.

KABOOM! The seventh pit exploded, sending a fireball overhead.

"Bloody hell!" Alec swore, fumbling with his own clothing.

Silence ensued. Only the time passed slowly by as they waited.

Samuel rocked backward on his heels. "I can't seem to piss now that my life depends upon it."

"Shhh," Akeim ordered as they stood shoulder-to-shoulder. "Concentrate!"

"Yes, add to the pressure, why don't you?" Samuel complained. "That helps."

"Need I remind you that this was your idea?" Akeim asked as the sound of liquid splashing against stone reached them.

"Thank God!" Samuel shouted jubilantly.

KABOOM!

"Oh, hell!" Alec swore again as the ground beneath their feet dropped several inches. The area above their heads exploded as the floor broke away altogether, leaving them to plummet through midair.

"Aahh!" Their screams echoed in the air around them as they fell.

Chapter 24

With a splash, they were plunged into the deep pool below. The water over their heads sparkled with the reflected light from the fire spreading across the ceiling of the cavern. As they surfaced, firelight shimmered across the ripples of the water from the burning embers that still clung to the ceiling above.

"Is everyone alright?" Sophia called out when she surfaced.

All but one answered.

"Genevieve!" Alec spun around in the water, calling out to her again. "Genevieve!" When she still didn't respond, he took a deep breath and dove under.

Samuel and Akeim both followed suit, searching the water behind him.

Alec swam until his lungs felt like they were about to burst. Something inside him pushed harder. Forcing himself, he kicked out, swimming deeper into the dark water.

Samuel returned to the surface, gasping for air. "Any sign of her yet?" he panted as he looked over at Sophia.

"Not yet." She shook her head as Akeim came up beside her. She turned worried eyes toward him. Without a word, he disappeared beneath the surface once again.

"Don't worry, Mum, we'll find her." With that, Samuel took a deep breath and returned to the search.

Alec felt light-headed as he kicked out, going even deeper. When his hand reached the mud bottom below, he spun around, looking up through the dark water. Above, he could see Genevieve's silhouette floating, unmoving in the water. Reaching out, he pulled her close before kicking with his powerful legs for the surface.

"Oh, my God!" Sophia sobbed when he erupted from the water with Genevieve in his arms.

Akeim was behind him instantly. "There is land beyond those rocks," he called.

Alec's mind was numb to everything but the woman in his arms. A surge of adrenaline gave him the strength to push through the water to the mound of earth that could be seen in the flickering light.

He carried Genevieve's limp body over the boulders and placed her gently on the ground. He cupped her chin with his hand and turned her face to his. "Breathe," he whispered, begging. "Please!" He placed his forehead against hers. "Please breathe," he willed her as he touched his thumb to her lips.

Sophia rushed over to them. "Is she breathing?"

"No," he whispered hoarsely.

With a grip stronger than he knew she possessed, Sophia pulled Genevieve from his arms and rolled her over until she lay face down. With the force of her whole body, she pressed against her daughter's back with urgency. Fluid rushed out of her lungs. Again Sophia pushed until Genevieve gagged, throwing up the rest of the water.

Sophia sat back, wiping a shaky hand across her brow as Genevieve began coughing. Alec was on his knees next to her instantly, taking her into his arms and cradling her as she cleared her lungs.

"You've got her? Oh, thank God!" Samuel sighed in relief as he crawled up the embankment and sprawled across the dirt. "I don't know how you did it," he gasped, trying to catch his breath. "It's black as pitch down there."

Alec gazed down at the woman in his arms. He didn't know how, but he had felt her. Something within him had known she was near. "How are you feeling?" Alec asked gently.

She looked up at him and smiled weakly. "A little dizzy." She winced, rubbing the knot at the back of her head.

"Let me take a look." Alec leaned her forward, lifting her hair. "You've a good bump on your head." He tilted her head back, smiling gently into her eyes. "You gave me quite a scare. I'm not leaving here without you. You know that, right?" He kissed her forehead. "Thank God your mother knew what to do."

"Sitt Hakim," she whispered with a smile.

"What does that mean?" Alec asked her softly.

"It is what the tribe called my mother. It means 'honored lady doctor'." She flashed him an amused smile, "She was their savior, while I was their plague."

"A two for one kind of deal," Samuel commented wryly.

Genevieve sat up in Alec's arms, looking out at the black water beside them. "I'm almost glad I don't remember that."

"It reminds me of that pond we used to—Aaugh," Samuel yelped with a start as he rolled over. A gruesome stone face with fire spurting from its mouth stared back. "Geez!" He scrambled away from the broken statue that lay half covered in dirt. "That scared the hell out of me!"

"Something was bound to," Akeim replied as he pointed out three other statues bordering the mound. "I believe we've found the Lake of Fire." As he spoke, a splash from the other side of the pool caught their attention.

"I hope you're right." Alec watched the dark ripple in the water as it made its way towards them. The sinuous movement reminded him of a serpent. "Especially when considering the alternative."

Another burning ember fell from the room above, landing with a splash. Samuel watched the glowing cinders float down from the ceiling and land not far from where they sat. "We'd better get out of here before the whole roof comes down on us."

"He's right." Akeim looked up at the structure above them. "For once," he added when Samuel turned to look at him with surprise.

"There is an opening over there." Sophia pointed to a dark gaping cavity in the wall behind them.

"Not very welcoming, is it?" Samuel scoffed. "I mean, they could have cheered up the place." He turned to Sophia. "So where are we in the whole scheme of things? Is this still a part of the underworld?"

"This is the primordial mound." Sophia looked back over her shoulder to the water. "In the Egyptian creation myth, they believed that life began when a mound of fertile land rose above the waters of chaos." As she spoke, part of the wooden structure above them fell, crashing into the water. Huge cinders broke away, scattering across the ground where they were walking.

"Run!" Samuel yelled.

Alec scooped up Genevieve and ran with her towards the passage as another piece of the roof landed beside them. Using his robe to shelter Genevieve from the burning shards, he rushed forward. They ducked under the entrance just as a wooden beam smashed into the ground behind them, blocking off the passage.

"Whoa, that was a near thing!" Samuel backed away from the burning mass. The fire flickered to life, licking out toward them as air rushed from the tunnel they were in, fanning the flames.

Akeim took a piece of wood that was only partially burned and held it toward the ceiling. The glowing ember burned brighter as the air whispered past, igniting in the breeze. "There is a wind."

"It's a giant chimney flue." Samuel narrowed his eyes as he tried to see into the darkness beyond.

"The breath of the beast," Sophia whispered in awe as she began walking up the incline. As the flame grew brighter, the light revealed a drawing of the god Apophis stalking the royal barque.

"Have we been swallowed then?" Samuel's eyes darted to the scene as he hurried after her. "Metaphorically speaking?"

"Not yet." Sophia motioned toward the next drawing, which revealed the giant snake being fettered by several gods.

"This looks like a positive sign," Alec said, nudging Samuel.

"For those with rope," Samuel replied while contemplating the drawing. Immediately, he started removing pieces of his wardrobe, tying them together as they walked.

Alec watched him for a moment. "What are you doing?"

"Isn't it obvious?" He looked up quickly. "I'm making rope."

"Why?"

"You could say I'm reading the writing on the wall," Samuel answered as he wound the pieces together, adding them to the bit of cloth he already had looped over his shoulder. "Don't tell me you haven't noticed how everything that is written on these damn walls comes to pass?" He looked around the passage as if the devil himself might have overheard his whispered comment.

"You actually think there is going to be a giant snake that we're going to tie up with that?" Alec lifted a brow.

"Make a joke of it, then." Samuel shrugged. "I didn't believe we'd actually run into a lake," he added meaningfully as he knotted two pieces together and tugged at the knot. "Now I intend to be prepared," he paused, looking over at him, "for anything."

"Alright, then. Just supposing you're right," Alec removed his own robe, knotting it as they moved up the corridor, "I'll let you have mine, as well, if it makes you feel better." He handed the twisted garment over to him as they met up with the others.

"Ah yes, the proverbial burning branch," Samuel commented when he noticed what Sophia was studying.

"It's the symbol for sound," Sophia corrected softly.

"How is it that a burning stick could stand for sound?" Samuel's expression was one of puzzlement.

"First of all," Sophia whispered, throwing her eyes heavenwards, "it is not a burning stick."

"It's not?" He looked close. "Are you sure? It looks just like the symbol for a brazier." Samuel quickly drew the symbol in the dirt at their feet. "What are the triangles, if not heat?"

"Secondly," she bent over, adding a curling line to his picture, "it isn't fire without smoke, and the triangles represent heat radiating out." She turned back to the symbol for sound, tracing the drawing with her finger. "But here the stem represents a throat, and the oval above it an open mouth. The triangles, in this case, represent sound radiating out."

"Only one more question." At her look of disbelief, Samuel continued. "If it stands for sound, then why are we whispering?" he asked, leaning toward her.

"Because it warns not to make any." Sophia pointed to the sign for water ∼∼∼ before pressing her finger to her lips for silence.

"Oh, right, the zigzagged line implies the negative." His voice drifted off as he put his own finger to his mouth.

As they climbed farther, another archway could be seen ahead of them in the flickering light. A noise like a soft moan whistled in the wind as they approached. They stood before the opening, which was decorated with the goddess Hathor, who held her sacred instrument, the sistrum, up to the stars above her, the largest an eight-pointed star within a circle above her head.

They silently watched as the cobwebs that hung across the arch moved in the draft until Samuel spoke up, "This is most unnerving." His hushed tone seemed to resonate within the room beyond.

"Shhh!" Sophia put her finger to her lips once again.

Akeim brushed the dusty strands away from the entrance and walked inside, illuminating the room with the burning wood he held. A triangular cathedral rose high overhead, disappearing into the dark recesses above him.

Alec stepped through with Genevieve and looked around. The walls had been formed by stacking huge rectangular granite blocks one atop the other. The slight overhang of each stone created a steep, inverted staircase.

Sophia and Samuel joined them in the center. "What now?" Samuel muttered softly. The sound echoed through the chamber, turning into a groan which produced a creaking noise above them. Alec, who was standing nearby, elbowed him.

"O-w-w," Samuel mouthed, rubbing at his arm.

Silently they crept through to the other side, where they were forced to stop. The opening under the archway was blocked by a huge stone. Etched on the surface was the image of Pharaoh Khafre. Beside him was a woman of incredible beauty.

The goddess had been drawn wearing the headdress of a vulture with its vibrantly colored wings cascading down into her long, braided hair. Above it rested the horns of fertility around the golden disk of the harvest moon. She held an ankh up to the pharaoh's lips, breathing life into the newly resurrected being.

"Isis," Sophia whispered. Her words produced a whispered hum in the cathedral above. The stone blocking the door moved up an inch, revealing an opening beneath. "Isis!" she called out again. This time the room was filled with an echoed chant, sis . . . sis . . . sis . . . sis.

The creaking noise from above continued as the door crept slowly up, revealing a two-foot space at the bottom. The groan they had heard before returned, echoing through the chamber as the door ground to a halt.

Akeim wedged the burning stump beneath the stone and rolled to the other side. His hand reappeared in the opening as Sophia crouched down. Taking hold of her, he quickly pulled her through the narrow opening.

Genevieve followed behind her mother. As soon as she was clear, Alec motioned for Samuel to go, but he refused. High above them, the creaking noise became stronger, sounding as though a sizable piece of timber was about to snap.

Again Alec motioned, but Samuel shook his head. *Why does he choose now to be brave?* Throwing up his hands in defeat, Alec dropped to his knees and followed Genevieve under the door.

The creaking intensified, as did the loud popping as Alec crawled through. Samuel looked up at the ceiling warily. Whatever it was, it sounded as though it would be joining him on the ground soon. "Ah, c'mon," he breathed anxiously.

As soon as Alec cleared the door, Samuel started to crawl. He was halfway under the door when it dropped, falling to within an inch of his face. His eyes grew wide as Alec grabbed a hold of his arms, pulling him the rest of the way. Just as his boots cleared the threshold, the door slammed down, smashing the stump beneath it.

"Holy hell!" Samuel jumped up. "Is it me, or are these close calls getting closer?" A thunderous noise, accompanied by a tremor, shook the floor. He looked down at the dust billowing in from the crack beneath the stone. "Well, then." He turned around. "I'd say that way is definitely closed to us now."

Akeim stabbed one of the charcoal pieces of wood with his sword and held it up, blowing on it until it flickered to life.

"Oh, it's chilly in here." Genevieve rubbed her arms as she looked around at the chamber. Stone pillars surrounded the space they found themselves in. Sophia nodded in agreement as they followed Akeim farther into the room.

"Hell is just not what I expected," Samuel grumbled.

Amused by his comment, Alec couldn't help but ask, "And what were you expecting?"

"Fire, that is a given. Dry, perhaps. . . . We are in the desert, after all." Samuel gave him a look of disbelief. "I, for one, was under the impression that, in Hell, one would have to beg for water. I certainly never thought that drowning could be such a serious threat." He looked down at their wet clothing. "And now, I'm soaked to the bone and freezing my arse off."

Alec chuckled, clapping him on the back. "But we are alive." He smiled.

"Yes, I have my chattering teeth to remind—" Samuel stopped in mid-sentence as Akeim held up the light near the center of the room. "Would you look at that!"

In the middle of the chamber, surrounded by pillars, rose a dais crowned by a huge golden sarcophagus. The edges of the raised floor were decorated in golden lions with two-headed snakes coming out of their mouths. Around it was a shallow trench, reminiscent of a moat around a miniature medieval castle.

The golden glow of the torch reflected not only the pharaoh's tomb, but also the golden bands which collared each pillar. The ceiling above it was decorated with a goddess, her golden body stretched across the dark blue sky. The sun's journey through the night was elaborately drawn across her form.

"This is beautiful," Sophia whispered in awe as she stood before the shrine.

"It's even more impressive than the pyramid that rests above it," Samuel quipped. "They really need to add this to the tour."

Sophia gave him a disapproving glance.

"What?" he inquired innocently. "Have you seen the tour? I, for one, was very disappointed," Samuel joked as he walked to the edge of the three-foot drop.

"Be careful," Genevieve cautioned.

As he looked down briefly at the moat, Samuel's eyes sparkled with humor. "I think I can handle this one, even if I do fall in."

"Don't be so sure," Sophia warned. "This is where the pharaoh and the god of the underworld become one. His throne is on a raised dais, signifying not only the primordial mound, but where he, as the god Osiris, sits in judgment."

"So this is the judgment hall?" Alec looked around curiously.

"Yes." Genevieve nodded. "This is where the goddess Maat presides over the weighing of the heart. Only if it is lighter than the feather of purity, can you be received by heaven." She paused, looking over at him. "Unfortunately, if it's heavier, you will be fed to the goddess Ammut."

"And who is this Ammut?" Alec grinned at her dour expression.

"She is the devourer of the dead, a demon with the head of a crocodile and a body that is part hippo, part lion," Genevieve explained.

"So, in other words, she's not very attractive," Samuel chuckled.

"She was most feared by the ancient Egyptians," Sophia replied seriously with a look of dire warning.

Samuel smiled at her words as he walked over to a chest that had been enshrined between two columns. The square box had an open shelf on each end that housed stone vessels with square lids. Walking around it curiously, he picked one up and opened the lid, sniffing the contents. "What are these?"

Sophia lifted it from his hand. "Be very careful," she admonished. "These are canopic jars."

"Oh, hell!" he spat, wiping his mouth with his sleeve. "They should warn people." He eyed the containers warily. "What happened to the baboon and jackal that are supposed to protect them?" He looked mildly offended by their lack of decorum. "These don't even look like the ones I've seen in the museum."

"You have to remember that this tomb is from a much earlier period. Pharaoh Khafre ruled during the old kingdom." She shook her head as she explained.

"What, exactly, does that mean?" Samuel asked.

"Everything in the underworld wasn't set in stone, per se. Their beliefs evolved over several hundred centuries."

"So what did I just inhale?" Samuel curiously peered over at the vessel she held. "Brains?"

Sophia looked down at the jar in her hands. "Intestines," she read before placing it back on the shelf. "The Egyptians didn't keep the brain."

"You're kidding." Samuel did a double take. "They kept the intestines, but not the ol' thinker?"

"The Egyptians believed that the heart was the center of wisdom and place of the soul," Sophia left him and went to the first column as she spoke, "whereas the brain was essentially thought of as useless."

"Wait a minute, I've heard that the ancient Egyptians operated on the brain." Samuel trailed behind her. "Now I find that they didn't even value it?"

"There were several maladies they thought to cure by drilling a hole in the head," Sophia explained, "everything from tumors to letting demons out."

"That gives me a headache just thinking of it," Alec joked as both he and Genevieve followed their progress.

"That too," Sophia nodded. "In fact, in the embalming process, it was common practice to insert an instrument up through the nasal cavity and scramble the brain. Once they had pulled the tissue out through the nose, they would simply discard it."

"Augh!" Samuel grimaced. "Now you're pulling my leg."

Sophia gave him a look of reproach. "I would never . . . pull your leg."

Samuel shot Alec a silent plea for help.

Alec smiled at him insolently, enjoying Samuel's discomfort.

Samuel eyed him ruefully. Unwilling to risk her ire, he turned to Genevieve instead. "Didn't they weigh the heart on some type of scale?"

"Yes," she watched as his gaze circled the room, "why?"

"We seem to be suspiciously missing one in this rendition." Samuel's gaze came to rest once again on her.

"All the more reason to be careful," Sophia warned from where she was looking at a drawing of the god Osiris that had been carved in relief on the column facing the sarcophagi.

"Why is he green, anyway?" Samuel asked, noting what she was examining.

"Because he's been resurrected, his green skin symbolizes the divine power to create new life from death," Sophia answered before going to the next column decorated with beautiful carvings.

"And here I always assumed it was because he was moldy." Samuel looked over at Alec, who shrugged his shoulders. "So what is this telling us?" Samuel gazed up at the woman who stretched across the ceiling.

"This is the sky goddess, Nut," Genevieve answered him. "She was thought to swallow the sun god Ra every night and give birth to him every morning."

"That sounds rather bleak." Samuel's expression was one of aversion as he tilted his head back.

"After the primordial mound rose above the waters of chaos," she continued, ignoring his comment, "Ra created the deities Shu, the goddess of air, and Tefnut, the god of moisture. They, in turn, gave birth to Nut, the sky goddess, whom Tefnut lifted up to take her place above the heavens." Genevieve motioned to the ceiling. "She was separated from her mate, the earth god Aker, who is portrayed here as the golden lions at each corner of this raised platform."

"A story of unrequited love," Samuel mused.

"Not exactly." Genevieve pointed to either end of the goddess. "But it was only at the edge of the earth, where the sun rose and set, they did meet." She then motioned around the room at the other gods portrayed on the walls in vibrant colors. "Along with Osiris, Isis, Seth, and Nephthys, they create what the Egyptians called the *pesedjet*, the group of nine."

"Ah, the number nine," Samuel remarked. "Now it begins to make sense."

"What makes sense?" She raised a questioning brow.

"The gods in the boat, the baboons, even the fire pots, were nine in number."

"The number nine has special significance," Sophia added as she moved to the next column.

Curious, Samuel walked behind her. "So it seems."

"You see, a triad or trinity, according to the Egyptians, consisted of a god, a goddess, and their son and heir." Sophia drew a triangle with her foot on the floor. △ "The Benben stone, or obelisk, is an important Egyptian symbol for," she paused, looking slightly uncomfortable, "a man's . . . ah, how do you say?"

"Ah, I see." Samuel nodded in understanding. "It's a phallic symbol."

"Exactly," Sophia rushed on. "You see, three triads placed together represent a very powerful symbol of strength." She drew another triangle beside the first and placed the third on top. "The pyramid." She looked over at him. "But notice that there is another triad that has been created by doing so."

"Would you look at that, right in the middle," he whistled softly as he considered it. "So who does this represent?"

"Who do you think?"

He pondered this a moment. "Amun and his merry men?" He received a sour look for his levity. "Wait, the women." She gave him a look that said he might be redeemed yet. "The missing daughters from the triad are actually still there." He looked down at her drawing as it dawned on him.

She nodded, retracing the middle symbol with her foot. "This one is another ancient symbol for woman."

"Amazing." Samuel studied her drawing a moment longer before looking up at the column she was studying. The colorful etching depicted the god Osiris with a large orange disk on his head. "So is this the moon too, then?" Samuel pointed to the crown.

"No, that actually is the sun." Sophia glanced up briefly before walking to the next pillar. "It is the two aspects of one god. When he was living, he was the embodiment of the sun god. He was to inherit his father Ra's kingdom until his brother Seth killed him."

"Yes, I remember you told us that one." Samuel nodded as he followed behind her.

"On his death, he became the god of the underworld, and his son Horus took his place," Sophia explained as she stepped around the column. "The solar disk is symbolic of his resurrection and connection to his former self. He is restored."

"Ah." Samuel nodded in understanding as he followed behind her. The image of an animal with a long snout, pricked, blunt ears, and canine body with forked tail confronted him on the other side. "Isn't this the god Seth?" He looked the beastly creature over. "Why is he here? Is he to be judged, then?"

298

"Actually, no." Sophia glanced up. "Even though he is a murderer, he is also the Egyptian god of war." At his look of confusion, she continued, "His might is needed to battle Apophis, so that his father, Ra, will be able to rise again."

"So he has been forgiven his sins for the greater good," Samuel gave the god's hideous form a last glance, "despite his appearance."

"Many people think that he is the first depiction of Satan." Sophia turned towards the next column, depicting the goddess Maat wearing the feather of purity on her head as she enfolded Pharaoh Khafre in giant wings. "Perhaps they are right." After taking only a few steps away from the pillar, she paused.

Samuel turned to follow her, but stopped short. The floor in front of him had risen by a foot while it had sunk the same amount where Sophia stood. A large piece of the granite had separated from the floor with Sophia on it.

Moving slowly, Sophia tried to retrace her steps on the sloping surface. The block of granite continued to move, increasing its angle despite her attempt to right it.

Samuel jumped on the other end of the block in an effort to balance it. His weight sent the giant teeter-totter rocking back the other way. It quickly passed level and started to dip on his end, sending Sophia up on the other side.

"I think we've found the scale." Samuel held out his arms for balance. Unwinding his rope, he tossed the end of it to Alec, who had come up behind him.

Akeim came around the side, reaching for Sophia. "No." She shook her head as she stepped farther toward the edge in an effort to balance their weight. "We'll lose Samuel if I get off."

For a moment, Akeim looked as though he considered the loss an acceptable trade. He jumped onto the middle of the stone, balancing there a moment before he began slowly walking toward Sophia. The slab of granite slowly started to tip back the other way. "Sophia, I want you to step off as I walk out to you."

She nodded, stepping off the end to where Genevieve waited. The scale rocked back toward Samuel without her. Akeim slowly stepped to the end until the stone started to level itself once again.

"Let's step off at the same time," Samuel suggested. At Akeim's nod, he continued. "To the count of three. . . . Ready?"

Akeim raised a brow but nodded all the same.

"One . . . two . . . three-e-e-e-e!" Samuel hollered as the marble slab fell, taking both men with it.

Chapter 25

Samuel and Akeim both jumped for the edge. Akeim was able to hold on, but the rope around Samuel's shoulder pulled against him, ripping him from the ledge. The stone plummeted into the darkened pit below, taking him with it.

"Oh-h, No-o-o-o!" Samuel's voice echoed up from the hole.

The rope that Alec held was almost pulled from his hands. "Bloody hell!" He braced himself against the weight of it while Genevieve and Sophia pulled Akeim to the top.

"Samuel, can you hear me?" Sophia called down into the pit.

"Do you think he's trapped under it?" Genevieve peered over the edge.

"Augh, of all the rotten!" They heard Samuel's voice from far below.

"Samuel," Sophia tried to see into the darkened pit, "are you alright?"

"Ah, Pic-plah-k!" Samuel spit.

"What did he say?" Sophia looked up at Alec.

"Pull me up!" Samuel yelled from below. "Hurry! Ah, Plah-k!"

"This weighs a ton." Alec strained against the taut fabric.

Genevieve came to stand behind him, followed by her mother and Akeim. Together, they hoisted the disagreeable wretch up. The smell hit them before he actually emerged from the hole. The creature that came over the edge was hardly recognizable as human, let alone Samuel.

"Oh, hell!" Samuel rolled onto the floor, covered in foul-smelling slime. Sophia put a rag to her nose as she bent to wipe his face with a piece of cloth.

"Who would have thought that bat guano and beetle dung would be so lethal a weapon?" Alec took a step back, holding his nose.

"Oh, God!" Samuel moaned. "Where is the water when you really need it?"

"You should probably keep your mouth shut," Sophia advised him as she wiped at the mess, smearing it all the more.

"Oh, this really is Hell!" He shook his head, rolling to his side. "Water," he begged.

Exasperated, Sophia tossed him the rag. "Here, you do it."

"Next time," Akeim stood with his hands crossed over his chest, watching as Samuel struggled to stand, "we go on *one*."

"Sure, now you're the critic." Samuel stood, peeling off the heavy garment that was plastered to his body. "I feel like I've been to the bowels of the earth!" Dropping the offending garment to the floor, he stepped out from the pile, wearing only his pants.

"You certainly smell like it." Alec tore a swath from his own clothing and handed it to him.

Samuel liberally coated it with the contents of his bottle of spirits and wiped at his face and hands. "Tell me that was worth it." He looked up hopefully. "Did it open the next door?"

"Not exactly, but I believe you have shown us the way." Sophia pointed to the wall, where a large scarab beetle was enveloped in the body of a five-headed snake. "The god Khepri is the god of transformation."

"Exactly how does this show us the way?" Alec followed behind Genevieve as she walked back to the hall where the hieroglyph was located.

"The scarab beetle is also known as the dung beetle for its penchant for laying its eggs in manure." Standing before the carving of a beetle, she looked back at him. "Essentially causing new life to spring from the decay, the very definition of resurrection."

"I hardly feel reborn," Samuel commented as he tried to sponge the filth from his hair. It was a useless endeavor.

"Hmm, this is interesting." Sophia examined the wall.

"How so?" Genevieve leaned over her shoulder.

"There are five snakes, yes?" Sophia considered them. "Are they for the remaining hours? Or . . ." She went to the next register. A rendering of a baboon holding an ibis was on the adjacent wall. A five-pointed star with a depression in the middle was above him. $\bigstar$ "Is it a reference to the Keeper of Knowledge?"

"I think Thoth, the god of wisdom and writing, is definitely hiding something." Genevieve's smile faded when Samuel joined them. She wrinkled her nose as the aroma hit her.

"How so?" Still rubbing at his arms, Samuel came around the side to see.

"It was his role to found a city for the gods and rulers of Egypt," Sophia answered him as she reached above her head and pressed the tip of her knife into the hole. Air burst from the edges of the slab as it rolled back, revealing a passage.

Samuel jumped in front of them. His heroic effort only succeeded in blowing the debris clinging to him back towards the rest of them.

"Oh my," Sophia coughed, waving her hand in front of her face. "Thank you ever so much." She stepped around him, peeking inside the entrance. "Let's see what kind of city the gods have created, shall we?" Excitement danced in her eyes as she looked back at them.

Akeim stepped in front of her with the torch. "If you will allow me." He nodded politely before taking the lead. A narrow passage rose steeply above them.

Samuel glanced up at the ceiling cautiously as he followed behind them. "Watch out for spears." The stairway continued for another fifty feet before opening up into another room. "And be sure and roll something across the floor," he instructed from his place at the back of the line. "Oh, and stab the ground with something as well."

Akeim's sigh was audible as he threw a few pebbles and poked the ground with his sword. With a nod of satisfaction, he entered, his light held high.

The room was square, with a cone-shaped ceiling. Sophia and Genevieve immediately went to the wall where the hieroglyphs began. A scene of a great harvest emerged in the flickering light. On the border, a giant cobra had been drawn with a double-twisted cord being unwound from its throat.

Samuel stood behind them as he assessed the drawing. "Looks as if we'll be needing more rope."

Sophia looked up to see what he was referring to, pointing out another symbol. "It is merely the symbol for time."

"More time, then?" Samuel wondered aloud as she covered her nose, looking back at him.

Noticing her glance, he stepped back. "Oh, sorry." He smiled apologetically. "I'll just go have a look from over there." Leaving them to their studies, he ambled around the room, meeting up with Alec on the other side.

"What do you think of this?" Alec stood before a drawing of the royal barque with the god Ra and his entourage. His enemies were shown being decapitated and lassoed with a rope by the gods who sailed with him. Unfortunately, it also depicted the boat sailing right into the waiting jaws of the god Apophis, who waited on the next register.

"We're definitely going to need rope," Samuel said with certainty.

"If you'll recall, that didn't work out so well the last time." Alec pointed to the snake, which was being held at bay with forked poles. A rope, which looked suspiciously like a hangman's noose, hung around its neck. "Suppose next time it gets really ugly?"

"What do you mean?" Samuel looked slightly askance at him. "If I hadn't had rope, I could have drowned down there!"

"You wouldn't have been down there in the first place," Alec reminded him, "if your rope hadn't been caught."

"Well, talk about unappreciative." Samuel raised his chin a notch.

"It's a hard thing to appreciate, if you get my drift." Alec thumbed his nose.

"Well," Samuel harrumphed as he left, joining the ladies once again. "What have you found?" He made sure to stand a gentle nose distance away.

304

"Here in the upper register are two groups of the blessed dead," Genevieve pointed up at the pictographic cornucopia that covered the wall, "one with baskets of grain, and the other with baskets of feathers."

"They will exist until the end while sheltered by the goddess Maat," Sophia read, "while the damned below are consigned to their place of annihilation."

"Just annihilation?" Samuel replied with a high degree of levity. "Glad it's nothing too drastic."

"Let's just say nothing has reared its ugly head." Sophia gave him a sideways glance.

"Yet," Samuel warned with a note of ominous portent. "I think you should see what is on the other side. It may change your mind."

"Really?" Genevieve turned to him. "Show me."

Just as she said it, Alec, who was walking across the floor, stopped in the middle and looked up.

"What is it?" she asked as he brushed a sprinkling of dust from his shoulder. When it was immediately replaced, Genevieve grabbed him by the front of his kaftan and pulled him roughly to her. His eyes opened in surprise as she turned and ran, dragging him with her.

Alec had only taken a step when he felt a sharp sting on his back. An immense weight pressed down on him as a torrential downpour of petrified grain fell from the ceiling.

"Watch out!" Samuel covered his head with his hands for protection as he dove out of the way, rolling to the edge of the wall as the room filled up with a billowing cloud of dust.

Akeim joined Sophia next to the wall as the wheat cascaded down from the giant hill to the outer edges of the room, shielding her with his body.

Alec looked over his shoulder at the mountain of partially disintegrated grain that had fallen where he had stood only a moment ago. "You saved my life." He turned back to Genevieve, who still had a grip on his collar. She let go of him, smiling apologetically for her rough handling. "Thank you." He kissed her briefly.

"Keep moving!" Sophia yelled. "Don't let it bury you!"

"Oh, why couldn't it have been feathers?" Samuel grumbled as he passed in front of Alec. As he ran knee-deep through the bountiful harvest, his pants legs quickly became caked as the granules stuck to him everywhere they touched. He stumbled, falling headfirst into the grain, only to emerge a moment later completely covered in the tiny particles.

Alec gave him a hand up. "Steady there."

"Easy for you to say," Samuel said as he stood. "You're not fast becoming a rolled-oat loaf." Alec laughed as he righted him. They were suddenly plunged into darkness when the light that Akeim held was extinguished.

"I'm sure you'll manage." Alec set him free. Taking up Genevieve's hand, they circled the room, keeping to the edges as much as possible. A fine dust filled the air as the wheat separated from the chaff. Around and around they went, getting higher and higher as grain poured in through the hole in the center of the roof.

"Good heavens!" Sophia exclaimed as the flood trickled to an end and the dust cleared. "I feel as though I've been in a giant-sized hourglass."

Exhausted, Samuel once again fell to his knees, landing face-first in the pile. "I feel as though I've been rolled in offal and baked in the fires of Hell." he complained as he rolled over.

When Akeim relit the torch, Genevieve found herself facing Samuel; she took one look at him and opened her mouth in surprised laughter. "Oh, I'm so sorry." She covered her mouth in dismay. One more glance in his direction caused another giggle to escape, despite her effort to hold it in. "I can't seem to help it." She smiled apologetically as the others glanced over.

Samuel tilted his head up at the remark. His eyes were the only things visible as he blinked back at them. With his hair on end, it looked as though he were wearing a giant rooster's tail on his head.

Alec started to laugh, while Sophia tried to stifle her own mirth at the sight.

"Humph!" Samuel huffed as he rolled over and sat up. The action only increased the bobble of his crown. "Alas, my worst nightmare has arrived."

"Hoh-hoh, ho." Akeim's deep booming laughter filled the remaining area of the room. In shock everyone, turned to look at him.

"I was wrong," Samuel dropped his head, "now it's my worst."

"Oh, come now." Sophia went to him, offering him a hand up. "If you could see yourself, I believe you'd find it amusing as well."

Samuel sighed, "At least now I smell more like a ripe barnyard than just the pigsty." He stood, brushing the pieces from his face and body. "I feel that it's only fair to tell you that the city of the gods is a bit lacking, in my estimation." Samuel critically assessed the hill they were perched on. "I still wouldn't call this Heaven."

"I understand." Sophia nodded sympathetically.

Akeim held the light up towards the hole in the center of the roof. Alec came to stand beside him. The ceiling was still several feet above their heads at the top.

"Here," Alec folded his hands together, "I'll give you a lift."

Akeim gave him a nod before stepping up to look through the opening. "There is a door." He climbed up into the room above, taking the torch with him. Holding out a hand, he drew Sophia up. Genevieve followed next.

"Jump on," Alec motioned to Samuel, "I've got this one."

"Alright then, if you insist," Samuel scrambled up. His rooster tail appeared in silhouette as he leaned back over the hole and offered Alec a hand up.

Alec climbed through until he sat on the edge of the opening, looking around at the new room. It was larger than the one below it, with a much higher ceiling. Unfortunately, it wasn't the only thing that soared above them. Alec stood, looking up at the opening located near the top of the wall.

"Any ideas?" Samuel asked, noting the direction of his gaze.

Sophia sighed as she too gazed up at their only means of escape. "It's so high."

"I suppose we know now how they filled this room with so much grain." Samuel followed Alec as he walked to the wall. "How did they get these things so close?" Samuel bent to examine the cracks between the stones in the otherwise smooth wall. "It's completely useless," he stepped back with his hands on his hips, "there is nothing to climb."

"Don't be too sure about that," Genevieve said from behind them.

"Do you mean the grain?" Samuel gave the floor a quick glance. "I suppose we could give it a try," he scraped his toe through the wheat which still remained on the floor, "although I doubt there is enough here to pile up."

"Actually, I was going to suggest that we stand on each other's shoulders." Genevieve looked up at the opening. "I believe I could reach the ledge."

Surprise registered on Samuel's face. "Has that knock on your head made you addle?"

"Are you sure?" Alec looked over at her with concern.

"There is plenty of grain on the floor to break my fall should something happen." At his look of alarm, she smiled. "I'll be fine, truly."

"Should we give it a go, then?" Samuel rubbed his hands together. "There's no time like the present, I always say."

Alec sighed, resigned to his fate. "I'm the biggest, so I'll be the base." He walked over to the wall and braced his back against it.

Samuel grinned over at Akeim, who was the next in line as far as size went. "After you." He bowed with a flourish.

Alec stood on the ground with Akeim on his shoulders while Samuel climbed up. Samuel teetered as he stood, groping at the wall to steady himself. "Why is it that I suddenly feel as though I've run off and joined the circus?"

Sophia waited until he nodded before she quickly climbed to the top.

Genevieve smiled at Alec's concerned look. "I'm afraid you're the one who may be in traction after this."

"Maybe they have a rack?" His attempt at levity was followed by a grimace.

"I'll be quick about it," she said as she started climbing. Her mother's legs wobbled ever so slightly as Genevieve stood on her shoulders.

"Nearly there." Genevieve straightened up to her full height. The ledge was just below her shoulders. She climbed up and turned around, reaching down for her mother's hand. Their fingers barely touched as she bent over the edge. Sophia reached higher, threatening her balance.

"Whoa." Samuel teetered, rocking side to side as he tried to hang on to her. "Steady there, Mum."

"There's no way around it, we need rope," Genevieve called down.

"I knew it!" Samuel looked down. "Any rope?"

"Samuel, keep still." Sophia steadied herself on his shoulders.

"Here, take this." Akeim released Samuel's foot for a moment so that he could pull his turban off. Black hair fell into his face as he handed it up.

Samuel had to let go of Sophia's foot for a moment to take it from him. "Takes quite a bit of skill, doesn't it? Hold tight . . . steady . . . steady." Slowly, so that the movement wouldn't upset her, he held the cloth up. Sophia grabbed it from him, tossing the end up to Genevieve. "Well done!" he crowed as she scrambled up the rope to the ledge above. The little jig he did almost cost him his own balance, much to Akeim's consternation.

"We're going to need more cloth," Sophia called down when the end of it dangled a few feet above Samuel's hand.

"Ahh, the problem is . . . I've only my britches." Samuel looked down at Akeim. "What of you?"

"I have only the kaftan left," Akeim replied meaningfully, looking down at Alec.

"I have pants under mine," Alec said, avoiding looking up.

Akeim had to move his feet while Alec slid the kaftan off. Unable to step out of it, he ripped it down the front to free himself of it. He passed it up to Akeim, who tossed it up to Samuel, who then threw it up to the women.

Tying the new piece on, they were able to reach Samuel, who climbed up with ease. The new length reached Akeim, as well, but proved to be too short for Alec. He stood down below as they tied the last piece of available cloth.

Alec tied the flaming sword on next. The rope caught on fire as they pulled the flickering light up. Samuel grabbed hold of the handle when it reached him and cut the material away from the blazing sword.

"I will wear your soiled pants if you so much as take another inch off," Akeim threatened him. Samuel, who was about to hack off more of the burning fabric, chose to stomp the fire out instead.

Alec could hear Akeim grumble from down below. The rope that came back down to him was suspiciously shorter than the last time he'd seen it, and he had to jump for the end. Grabbing hold, he quickly climbed to the top.

Samuel was grinning at him as he reached the ledge. "Didn't I tell you we'd need rope," he laughed.

"Where is Akeim?" Alec asked.

"He is back there," Samuel motioned with his head, "in the dark." His grin broadened as he untied the last garment in the rope and held it up.

"Ahh." Alec nodded in understanding as he looked at Akeim's much shorter kaftan.

"I will not wear this!" Akeim yelled after Samuel tossed the much shorter robe to him. "Give me your pants."

"I've seen young men in robes that short," Samuel said reasonably.

"Young boys," Akeim growled.

"How bad can it be?" Samuel asked, his voice serious, though he couldn't erase the grin from his face as they waited for the warrior to don his new clothes.

"It is done," Akeim announced.

Holding the light, Sophia entered the hall, followed by the rest. Akeim stood in front of them wearing the short black kaftan. The cloth fell well above his knees while his boots started just below them. They stopped in stunned silence. With his long, dark hair loose, he looked more like a gladiator of old.... One prepared for battle, by the look on his face.

"Whew," Samuel whistled. "That is short!"

"I will cut your tongue out," Akeim warned as Samuel opened his mouth to speak again.

Sophia passed Akeim the light as she headed toward the next room. "Are you coming?" She looked back over her shoulder as everyone remained rooted where they were.

Akeim turned away first, following her to the opening.

"Touchy, isn't he?" Samuel chuckled softly.

"We've apparently found his Achilles heel." Alec nodded.

All thoughts of the warrior and his new wardrobe faded when they entered the next room. Sophia and Akeim stopped just inside the threshold in amazement. The room was filled with funerary items for the Pharaoh in his afterlife.

"This is more like it," Samuel whispered in awe as he stepped into the room and picked up a golden statue.

"Be careful." Sophia gave him a stern look. "These items do not belong to us."

"You actually think he's using them?" Samuel motioned toward a stone statue of the pharaoh.

"Don't be ridiculous." Sophia's tone was disapproving as she moved into the room. "I am saying that these things belong to the people of Egypt. It is their legacy, not ours."

"What about the artifact the admiral spoke of?" Samuel picked through the items curiously.

"That is different." Sophia stopped before a statue of the Sphinx. "It was placed here much later by the high priestess of Amun, and it belongs to the S'ba." She looked at the hieroglyphs written on the side before moving on. Akeim followed behind her with the light, while Samuel trailed behind, pestering her with questions.

"You're really going to leave all of this here?" Samuel asked in amazement.

She turned, looking back at him. "I am the Keeper of Knowledge. It is my duty to protect this, not exploit it."

"Unbelievable," Samuel sighed, looking around. "But—"

"No buts either," Sophia stopped before another lion-faced statue.

"Good luck with that argument," Alec chimed in as he and Genevieve made their way through the crowded aisle behind them.

Sophia stopped before a cat-faced goddess with a sistrum on her head in place of a crown. Two cobras had been carved in the middle of the sacred instrument. Again, she studied the inscription around its base. She then picked up a small wooden handheld version of the sistrum.

"That's like the instrument that the goddess drawn on the map is holding," Samuel said excitedly.

"Yes, it is." Sophia set it down.

Samuel looked at the discarded statue for a moment. "So it's not important to us?" he asked, picking up a small statue of an ordinary house cat from a table nearby. "What exactly are you looking for, a cat?" He flicked the golden nose ring that adorned it. "Is this it?"

When she didn't reply, he tried again. "Why is this artifact important, anyway?" He looked back at Alec and Genevieve when Sophia wouldn't answer.

Alec shrugged in response.

"Well, what can I know?" He raised his hands in frustration.

"That is the goddess Bastet you're holding," Genevieve said, indicating the statue he held.

Samuel gave her a look of exasperation as he set the statue down and turned away. He caught up with Sophia and Akeim as they entered the next room.

"But . . . what of the eight-pointed star within the circle?" Alec and Genevieve heard Samuel say as the trio disappeared from sight.

"How are you doing?" Alec turned to ask his wife. "Are you still cold?" He drew her closer to his bare skin.

"No," she whispered, though she shivered all the same as he enfolded her in his arms.

"Are you coming?" Samuel poked his head back around the corner.

"I'm no longer even surprised by his uncanny ability to thwart me," Alec sighed. "I suppose we should catch up. You never know what may be lurking around the next corner, or above."

"Or below," Genevieve added.

"Especially that." Alec smiled as he took her hand, weaving them between the aisles of the cluttered room and into the next.

The next hall they entered was enormous, with many storage rooms, like the one they had just left, on either side. They followed the voices, easily catching up with the others as they entered yet another room.

"But," Samuel was saying again.

"No!" Sophia gave him a look of exasperation.

Alec shook his head. "I cannot tell you how many times I've had the same conversation." He laughed at Samuel's disgruntled expression as Sophia uncovered another statue. This time it was of a seated woman, whose bent knees created a flat surface. A seven-pointed star was inscribed on the front.

"Who is this?" Samuel couldn't help but ask.

"You are worse than a child," Akeim growled.

"Alas," he sighed, "but at least I'm not the one in short pants." Samuel stared pointedly at the warrior's knees.

Akeim's eyes narrowed as he stepped forward menacingly.

"It is Seshat," Sophia placed a hand on Akeim's arm to stay him, "the goddess of writing."

"Really?" Curious, Samuel came closer, "But—"

"No," Sophia, Alec, and Akeim responded all at once.

"No?" Samuel lifted his hands innocently. "I was merely going to point out that I thought that the goddess of writing was the Keeper of Wisdom, the S'ba," he paused, studying the statue, "but this one has a seven-pointed star, rather than a five . . . wait. The star on the back of the map had seven points." He looked up at Sophia. "That's why you uncovered it, isn't it?" When she didn't respond, he laughed. "That's it isn't it? They are the same."

"If I tell you, will you let it be?" Sophia sighed as she left the room with him on her heels.

"He knows no bounds," Akeim said as he watched Samuel follow her.

"Tell me about it." Alec nodded in agreement.

They entered another storage room, containing many vessels piled to the ceiling. Samuel picked one up and eyed it warily. "What does this contain?"

Sophia briefly looked back at it. "Soap."

"So cleanliness really is next to godliness," Samuel chuckled as he opened the lid and sniffed the contents. "Augh!" He winced. "Are you sure? It smells of something else entirely."

"It was for washing wool, not humans." Sophia shook her head. "The Egyptians used scented oils to bathe."

"Ahh," he said, brushing at his wheat-caked limbs. Rather than set the jar aside, he tucked it under his arm and followed them to the next room, which was filled with an array of stone-working tools. Samuel picked up two half-round blocks joined with leather straps. "What is this?" He moved the pieces, weighing each in his hands.

"Be careful with that," Sophia sighed. "It is what they used to strap onto a square granite block in order to make it roll up an incline."

"So they did have wheels," Samuel said curiously as he folded it together to form a circle.

"Would you stop messing about? It's very old." She took the piece from him, looking at him sternly. "We should leave everything as we found it."

"Does anyone else hear that?" Genevieve stood at the entrance to the room, looking down to the other end of the long, dark hallway. "Listen. . . . It sounds as if something is hissing."

Akeim moved past her into the hall, holding the light high as he walked to the end of it. A giant statue of a snake emerged from the darkness, looming above him as he neared it. The open mouth alone was large enough to fit a man inside.

"Apophis," Sophia whispered as they approached the menacing creature.

"Does this remind you of anything?" Samuel looked meaningfully over at Alec as he fingered the rope wound about his shoulder.

They watched as Akeim crouched, holding out his hand. He lifted it to his mouth and looked back at them. "It is water."

"There is a God!" Samuel ran forward to kneel before it.

"What about your desire to slay the beast?" Alec raised a brow as Samuel cast the rope aside and knelt before the small pool.

"To hell with the beast." Samuel opened the jar of soap and stepped into the small pool. Filling the container with water he poured it over his head.

Sophia cleared her throat. "We'll give you some privacy, then." She turned, lighting one of the many sconces along the wall and taking it with her as she entered one of the many rooms along the hall.

"Let us know if we are needed," Genevieve added before following her.

As soon as they left, Samuel stripped the rest of the way down and scoured himself thoroughly.

"What do you suppose this is for?" Alec walked to the side of the fountain, studying it. "It's doubtful they meant to flood this area." He looked back at the pharaoh's wealth.

"That's a good point," Samuel agreed as he rinsed his pants. "It also appears to be under pressure." He felt where the water was spraying in through a small hole at the base.

"Maybe it's some type of water wheel?" Alec continued his study of the structure while Samuel slipped his wet pants back on.

"This soap has the consistency of molasses," Samuel complained, dousing himself again with the water. "I'm having a devil of a time getting it off."

"It could very well be a gear." Akeim stood back as he considered the head of the viper. All three men looked up as they contemplated the possibility.

"Oh, hell!" Samuel exclaimed when he looked back down. Bubbles had started to form and were rapidly filling the pool with frothy white suds. "Something tells me the priests of Amun didn't see this one coming." He chuckled as he climbed out of the slippery pool.

It didn't take long for the area to be overwhelmed by foam. In remarkably little time, there was a veritable mountain of suds. "Now what do we do?" Samuel walked about, stomping at the bubbles in a futile attempt to keep them at bay.

"We?" Akeim raised a questioning brow as he stood back with his arms folded across his chest.

"Yes, *we*. . . ." Samuel asserted with a look of irritation. When Akeim still refused to yield, Samuel sighed with exasperation, "Oh, alright. . . . I apologize deeply for the short dress."

"It is not a dress," Akeim insisted angrily.

"It is where I come from," Samuel snapped. "And a damn short one too!"

Chapter 26

"What on earth is that commotion?" Sophia looked up from the papyrus she was studying. Both she and Genevieve stared in amazement at the wall of bubbles beyond the doorway of the room they were in.

"Don't get your short pants in a twist," they heard Samuel say, followed by the sound of a fist meeting flesh. "Oomph!" Samuel stumbled from the white foam wall as they watched. Rolling to within a few feet of where they stood, he grinned up at them.

"Hello there, Mum," he said as he rubbed at his jaw.

"Good heavens!" Sophia's eyes widened in surprise. "What has happened?"

Akeim erupted from the frothing mass with a crown of bubbles atop his head.

"Got to run!" Samuel scrambled to his feet, laughing. He tossed a statue at the angry warrior and dashed into another room.

"Akeim!" Sophia cried in alarm as he ducked. "What are you doing?"

"What I should have done long ago!" he roared, charging after Samuel.

Alec emerged from the bubbles, casually wiping them from his face.

"And you?" Sophia eyed him critically.

"Me?" Alec started in surprise.

"Why didn't you stop them?" She pointed her finger at him before going after the two.

Alec threw his hands up in dismay as he watched her walk away. He looked over to Genevieve, who was biting her lip to keep from laughing.

"Come here." His eyes gleamed as he smiled mischievously. Taking her hand, he led her back into the bubbles. The sconce above cast a golden glow through the bubbles, lighting them softly. Tunneling through them he made a small niche, then turned to grin at her.

"It's like being in a cloud," she whispered.

Alec nodded playfully as he drew her near. "It's like being in Heaven with an angel." The dimple in the side of his cheek deepened.

Genevieve felt a thrill run through her as he took her hand, guiding her further into the bubbles. She gazed at his muscular chest, glistening with moisture. The light cast a golden glow across his form. The shadows played across his skin, accentuating the muscles that rippled across his belly.

She watched, spellbound, as he lifted his hand up to her shoulder. His fingers grazed her skin as he slid them down her bare arm, leaving a trail of soapy bubbles. His other hand skimmed her hip as he stood watching her with his smoldering gaze. She shivered from the effect as he pulled her to him.

"God, you are beautiful," he whispered huskily as he bent to kiss her.

His kiss was a soft caress. Opening her mouth with his tongue, he explored gently before tilting her head back, nuzzling her ear. His hands claimed her waist as he trailed kisses from her neck to her collarbone, pulling her lower body more firmly against himself. She could feel the hard length of him against her.

"Umm," he groaned softly as he raised his hands, brandishing a path of heat as he brushed his palms against her sides. His hands continued up until they rested on either side of her breasts.

His tongue played across the flesh exposed at the top of her neckline. The tingling awareness of him seemed to resonate within her. She arched further back, wanting, needing his touch. Her hardened nipples pressed against the thin fabric. His thumbs grazed the tips as he cupped her full breasts.

"Ahh," she sighed as he claimed her mouth again in a heated kiss. He placed his hand on her lower back as he rocked his hips forward. The heat of him pressed into her. She was lost in a world of sensation as he raised his head. His eyes seared her very soul as she watched him.

"Mmm," he groaned, looking at her with longing. "How I wish I could touch you as I want." He hugged her to him. "Samuel will, no doubt, be running through here any minute. Not to mention Akeim and your mother." With regret, he released her.

On cue, Samuel darted past them, appearing a moment later in the niche Alec had carved out. "I'm not intruding, am I?" He grinned as he stepped inside the small area.

Alec stepped before Genevieve, shielding her. "Tell me you're not going to use that on him?" Alec asked, referring to the small statue Samuel held in his hand.

"What, this?" He looked over his shoulder. "What do you take me for. . . . A guileless ruffian?"

"I will have your head!" Akeim bellowed from somewhere in the foamy mass.

Samuel's grin widened as he put his fingers to his lips. "Shh," he whispered before tiptoeing away.

Akeim appeared a moment later in the opening that Samuel had left in his wake. Without a word, both Alec and Genevieve pointed in the direction that Samuel had taken when he'd left.

"Will they be alright?" Genevieve asked softly.

"Of course." Alec smiled at her concern. "They are just blowing off steam. As you can plainly see, the guileless ruffian, as it were, is enjoying himself immensely."

Samuel emerged from the bubbles once again as Sophia stood watching. Her face registered surprise when she looked at the figurine in his hand.

"Samuel, you've found it!" She rushed toward him.

"I have?" He gazed down at the figure in his hand before slumping to the ground. Akeim stood behind him with the butt of a revolver in his hand.

"He had it coming," Akeim said as Sophia raised a brow.

Alec and Genevieve followed the path through the bubbles that Samuel and Akeim had left behind. They found Samuel flat on his back with the warrior standing over him.

Sophia took the statue of a woman he was still holding in his hand.

"He found it?" Genevieve looked at the figurine in wonder. A five-pointed star with two cobras on either side crowned the statue.

"And a lot of thanks I get for it too." Samuel sat up, rubbing his head. "Damn, what did you hit me with?"

Akeim said nothing as he tucked his gun back into his belt.

"You coldcocked me?" Samuel glared up at him accusingly. "I should have known."

"I take it we can leave here now that we have the artifact?" Alec reached out a hand to Samuel and pulled him up.

Sophia looked around them. "Unfortunately, I haven't a clue as to how." She looked over at Genevieve. "Did you notice anything in the writings before these bubbles overwhelmed us?

"No," Genevieve stifled a yawn as she shook her head, "I'm afraid not."

"Why don't we get some sleep while we wait for them to subside," Alec suggested.

"It doesn't seem we have any other choice." Sophia covered a yawn of her own.

~*~

An hour later, Alec found Samuel in one of the storerooms, sitting in a throne-like chair he'd pulled up to a table. Pieces of a game were scattered across the top, while on either side he had placed the statues of Thoth and Anubis. "What are you doing?" Alec came forward.

"Having a bit of sport with my two chums here." Samuel held out his bottle. "Care for some?"

"No, thank you." Alec shook his head. "I know where that has been."

"Ah . . . right," Samuel glanced down at the bottle with mixed feelings. Shrugging, he took a healthy sip. "Aaugh!" he sighed, wiping his mouth as he eyed Alec thoughtfully. "Couldn't sleep?"

"No." Alec ran a hand through his hair as he looked around.

"Then you'll be excited to see what I've found." Samuel reached over, picking up the rope he'd hung from the stiff member of a statue of the god Amun.

"We obviously have differing opinions." Alec raised a brow at the huge phallus.

"What?" Sitting at eye level to the appendage, Samuel chuckled. "Oh, you mean this. Yes, well, apparently there is something in the afterlife worth getting worked up over after all." Amusement danced in his eyes as he looked up. "I'm thinking I'll get a replica for my foyer. I believe it would make an excellent umbrella holder."

"I think you might be shunned by polite society. Not to mention your mother may disown you."

"You think so? Then I'm definitely getting one." He laughed as he pointed to the hieroglyphs etched lower on the statue. "Look here."

"What have you found now, the secret to male potency?"

"This is the symbol for gold."

"Not this again," Alec groaned.

"No, this is different," Samuel promised as his head bent under the huge projection. "Just listen."

Alec shook his head as he watched the spectacle. "If you could only see yourself."

"I believe this is talking about the land where the gold came from. See this ship with the sails? It implies that it's traveling against the current, in this case south." He pointed to another. "And this tells of cataracts." He looked up at him. "We were so close."

"Samuel . . . we weren't close."

"You mean to tell me you're not the least bit excited about it?"

Alec gave him a wry smile as he shook his head.

"C'mon, man, a map to the pharaoh's gold, to the same mines as that of King Solomon?"

Alec chose to change tactics. "Aren't you forgetting one important fact?"

"What's that?"

"We're not going anywhere while we're stuck here."

"I've been thinking about that too." Samuel grinned as he stood, maneuvering around the statue's protruding anatomy. Stepping further into the room, he returned with a forked pole.

"Remember this?" He jabbed the floor with the end and tossed Alec the rope. "Perhaps all we need to do is hold Apophis at bay?"

"Let's get this straight. . . . Your plan is to lasso and hold an immovable statue at bay?" Alec's voice was incredulous.

"Don't look so damn skeptical." Samuel scowled at him. "I'm thinking it could be the key." He went back again, returning this time with a net. "We might need this as well."

"Yes," Alec said sarcastically. "It might put up a struggle."

"Your cynicism is misplaced." Samuel tossed the old piece to him. "You yourself pointed out the hieroglyph that showed several gods using a magical rope against him."

"A magical rope?" Alec raised an eyebrow. "And just how do you know it was magical?"

"C'mon," Samuel sighed, "what do we have we to lose?" He watched as Alec lifted the net, eyeing it skeptically. "Are you willing to give this a go or not?"

"This is falling apart." Alec watched as small pieces fell away as he handled it.

"Well, it's like you said," Samuel passed him on the way out, "it probably won't put up much of a struggle."

"If it's all the same to you, I'd rather not wake the others for this," Alec tiptoed across the hall where they slept.

"Nothing to it." Samuel grinned as he stood under the giant serpent. "We'll just lasso this beast and be on our way." He made a small loop on one end of the rope and tossed it over the hood of the cobra. "Hold tight," he whispered, motioning for Alec to catch it.

Alec cast a quick glance toward the others before taking up the dangling rope. He shook his head as he watched Samuel jump on and swing over the pool in a wide arc. The rope slipped through Alec's hands, threatening to land Samuel in the foam again.

"You're doing it all wrong," Samuel whispered, giving him a harsh look.

Alec briefly thought about letting go of the rope as he watched Samuel try to gain a foothold on the slick stone.

"You're going to have to pull harder," Samuel instructed as he reached up higher. "Put your toe in that loop at the end."

~*~

Akeim woke to the sight of Alec and Samuel dangling awkwardly from the head of the snake, above a sea of foam. They bobbed upside down on each side, looking like a mismatched pair of earrings. He blinked, rubbing his eyes.

"Now look what you've done," Samuel accused his partner in crime as he struggled against the rope which bound both his ankles together.

"Whose bright idea was it to put my toe in the loop?" Alec retorted in a whisper.

"At least it only captured one of your feet," Samuel pointed out.

"What happened to voting?" Akeim stood with his hands folded over his chest.

Alec groaned.

Samuel smiled brightly. "Oh, hello." Dangling upside down, his head was on the same level as the warrior's. "Just what we need, another hand."

"Why, so he can be strung up like a goose as well?" Alec had crossed his booted feet, as well as his arms. Upside down, he swayed gently back and forth on his side of the impromptu swing.

"Here, give me your hand." Samuel reached out.

Akeim remained unmoving. "How have you survived this long?"

"Fine then, don't help lasso the beast with the magical rope," Samuel replied loftily as he bent at the waist. Reaching up, he grasped his foot, trying to untangle the knot that held him there.

"A magical rope?" Akeim lifted a brow.

"What's this about a magical rope?" Sophia asked.

Alec groaned again, looking up to see both Sophia and Genevieve watching the spectacle they made. Genevieve smiled at him, her eyes dancing with merriment.

Samuel fell back, swinging in an arc. "Back in the torturous bottom half of the hourglass, just before it was filled with grain, we noticed a drawing of Apophis being fettered by the gods with a magical rope."

"Why didn't you say so earlier?" Sophia asked in surprise.

"I had forgotten, myself, until a few minutes ago." Samuel reached up again.

"Explain to me exactly what you saw." Sophia took a step back, eyeing the beast.

"Well there was—" Samuel started.

"Wait," Alec interrupted him, "you mean this idea of his actually has some merit?"

"It may." She nodded.

With a groan, Alec bent at the waist. Taking hold of the rope above his feet, he pulled himself upright.

"You mean you've been letting me dangle here like a worm on a hook when you could have done something about it?" Samuel asked, incredulous.

"Yes, yes I have," Alec replied evenly as he climbed the rope until he straddled the head of the huge serpent. Holding the rope taut, he started pulling Samuel up.

"As I was saying. . . ." Samuel frowned, which looked oddly comical upside down. "The gods were standing on top of Apophis, who was wrapped in a net with a magical rope around his neck."

"Like this?" Sophia drew the shape in the fading bubbles at her feet.

"One and the same." Samuel nodded as Alec gave him a hand up.

Akeim, would you do the honors?" Sophia indicated the net beside the pool where Alec had left it.

It didn't take long for the great statue to be fettered by the dilapidated net and magical rope. "What now?" Alec asked. Other than the decorations, nothing had changed.

"The triton!" Samuel pointed to the forked pole.

"And you think that will be the deciding factor in this asinine idea of yours?" Alec asked, shaking his head.

"Yes, yes, I do," Samuel replied, mimicking Alec's earlier tone while he waited for Akeim to tie the staff onto the end of the rope.

Alec held onto the hood of the great cobra, while Samuel stood on the head, stabbing the stone with the end as the picture had portrayed. "I don't understand," Samuel paused, "why is it not succumbing?"

"Maybe it already has," Alec replied. "It looks pretty dead to me."

Samuel stopped and looked over at him. "Why don't you give it a try, then, if you think you can do it better?" When it appeared he would refuse, Samuel held out the pole. "I insist."

"Alright." Alec climbed up to stand on the back, taking the forked staff from Samuel. "The picture did show the beast being fettered by the gods as Ra sailed on. In this little reenactment, we want to be in the position of Ra, correct?"

"He sailed on to the next register," Samuel replied sarcastically.

"Exactly," Alec said as he tied the magical rope onto the end of the triton.

"I didn't see the next register." Samuel looked over at him.

"I did." Alec smiled before drawing back his arm and letting the makeshift harpoon fly. It embedded itself into a wooden crate that stood against the wall with a resounding thud.

"What are you doing?" Sophia asked from down below.

"The sun god sailed past the fettered snake, transforming into a creature with a scarab body, a falcon head, and great wings," Alec said as he tested the rope with his foot. "Like the one above you."

They all looked up to the ceiling above them. In the center was a winged creature like the one Alec had described.

"Of course!" Sophia exclaimed. "Why didn't I see it before?"

Alec cut a piece of rope from the end and used it to slide down to the trident. Prying the staff from the wood, he went to stand before a statue of a winged man with the head of a falcon. "And this fellow was on the other side of that."

Alec examined the statue while he waited for the others to join him. Samuel remained on the great snake, supervising from his perch high above. "Look at his hand. It's as if he's supposed to be holding something."

Alec slipped the end of the staff he held down through the statue's curled fingers.

"Shouldn't you untie it first?" Samuel fingered the rope, which was still connected to the giant snake.

Alec stood back to survey his handiwork.

"I really think you should—" Samuel began.

"He was connected to the others by your *magical* rope," Alec cut him off.

"Well, it's not as if it's mine," Samuel said defensively, "although I was right about needing it." He smiled.

Akeim came forward and pressed down on the arm of the stone statue. To everyone's surprise, it rotated down until the staff hit the base it stood upon.

"Hey, what about voting?" Samuel lost his grin.

"Listen," Genevieve whispered. "The hissing has stopped."

The silence was deafening as they waited.

"I think I'll join you." Samuel tested the line with his foot, had as Alec. When it appeared it would hold, he swung down, lowering himself hand-over-hand. He'd only gone a few feet before a deafening groan filled the chamber and the huge snake rocked forward. Samuel looked over his shoulder at the open jaws of the snake that threatened to swallow him. "Aaa-aagh!" he screamed as the head crashed to the floor, taking him with it.

"Samuel," Genevieve called as dust billowed out from the wreckage.

Alec ran forward to clear broken rock and bubbles from around the fallen statue. "Samuel, can you hear me?" he called, rolling a large chunk away.

"Aaugh-choo!", came the answer as Samuel crawled from between the open jaws of the snake.

"Oh, thank God!" Sophia sighed.

"Tell me that was worth it. Did we find the door?"

"Indeed," Akeim replied as he held a torch up, shedding light on an opening where the snake had once stood.

Samuel brushed himself off, looking over the debris before turning to Sophia. "Do you think they might guess someone was here?"

"Samuel," she shook her head, "what am I going to do with you?"

The stairs were long and steep, twisting and turning as they climbed higher. The walls were oddly vacant of any markings. "Are you sure we're on the right path?" Samuel asked as he followed behind the others.

"How many other ways do you think lead out of there?" Alec glanced over his shoulder at him.

"Good point," he murmured.

"Here we are," Sophia sighed as she rounded the next corner. Above her, the winged disk that was on the map spread across the archway.

"Where is here, exactly?" Samuel asked as the stairs ended.

"These are the wings of Isis, the gates of Heaven," Sophia said, looking up at them before stepping into the small, square room on the other side. Though small, it was decorated from floor to ceiling with hieroglyphs on every wall.

"Didn't think I'd miss these," Samuel remarked as he stood in front of a rendering of Ra being towed by twelve snake goddesses.

"Why is the boat so different?" Alec asked as he too looked at the scene.

"It's the solar boat." Genevieve smiled. "We're getting close."

"To what?" Samuel asked looking around.

"To the end, of course," Genevieve laughed.

"That is entirely too subjective for my taste." Samuel leaned closer to Alec, whispering. "The end is near. . . ."

A cow was depicted walking out of tall grass wearing the headdress that Hathor wore. "So our girl becomes a cow now, is it?"

"The cow is a revered symbol of fertility," Sophia stated as she glanced over it, "and yes, it is yet another symbol of Hathor."

"Well, it does make the hieroglyph for 'revered' much more understandable." Samuel pointed to the symbol on the wall.

"Ah, yes, the bovine pâté," Alec remarked, earning an odd glance from Genevieve, who smiled at him.

"Oh, look," Samuel pointed to the grasses where it bloomed like a flower amongst the reeds, "here is that eight-pointed star again." ✸ His expression was somewhat confused. "Wait, I thought that was a symbol of Isis."

"It is," Sophia chuckled, "as well as a symbol for the planet Venus."

"I—" Samuel started, "I'm not even going to ask."

Everyone stopped to look at him in surprise.

"What?" He lifted his hands.

"What are you smiling about?" Alec asked when everyone else turned to study the opposite wall.

"The eight-pointed star," Samuel whispered.

"What about it?" Alec shrugged, looking at the symbol in the grasses.

"It's on the other side of the map in one of those little circles." He grinned like the knowledge of the universe had just opened up to him.

"Really?" Alec shook his head with a sigh. "We just went through Hell . . . correction, are still in Hell, and you're—"

"Alec," Sophia spoke up from across the small area, cutting off his next words. "Was there anything else that you noticed in the hieroglyphs after Apophis was fettered?" she asked.

Alec took a moment to consider her question. "Yes, there was a round, speckled disk."

"Speckled?" Her brow rose.

"Like this." ◉ Alec drew it in the dirt at their feet.

"Ah," Samuel nodded, "the sieve."

"That is not a sieve," Sophia sighed.

"A polka-dotted moon, then?" Samuel asked.

She smiled, shaking her head. "It is the Aten, the solar calendar."

"Why is that one lost, as the others were?" Genevieve went to stand in front of the symbol on the wall. "It has nothing to do with the moon."

"To expose one would have caused people to question the other, I suppose," her mother said. "Besides, it had fallen out of use after Pharaoh Akhenaton died." Sophia came closer to look at the symbol. "He had closed the temples of Amun, replacing them with his monotheistic sun cult."

"And here I thought it was because of the art. Now there was a bizarre figure of a man," Samuel replied sarcastically.

"He wanted to be portrayed as both female and male." Sophia glanced over at him.

Samuel looked positively horrified. "Why?"

"For the usual reasons, most likely." Sophia looked back to the Aten.

"What usual reasons could there be for that?" Samuel snorted.

"Corruption and greed by those in power, I would imagine." Sophia replied. "It was his attempt to reclaim the power that the pharaoh had once held. Placing himself at the center of the new religion, as the only one who could speak to the gods, proved to be quite effective. Until he died, of course."

"What happened then?" Alec asked.

"His temples were desecrated, and everything that had been used to represent him fell out of use. Even though his young heir went so far as to reopen the temples and change his name to Tutankhamen, which means the living image of Amun, he died tragically young, under suspicious circumstances."

Sophia sighed, shaking her head. "His young queen was forced to marry the former general, and then she too disappeared." She looked over at him. "In fact, all of Akhenaton's descendants quickly died out and were replaced by a new dynasty that eventually gave birth to Ramesses the Great."

"All's fair in love and war," Alec said cynically.

"So it seems." Sophia nodded. "As for this symbol, it has rarely been used since Akhenaton's sun cult perished. Who knows? If it hadn't been used to mark the regnal years of the pharaoh, it may have fallen out of use completely." Sophia reached up to insert her knife around the outer edge of the disk.

Akeim moved forward before she could do more. "Allow me," he said, pushing on the seal.

Slowly, the center block at the top of the wall moved back. "It looks like we'll have to crawl again," Alec commented.

"Yes, it does, doesn't it?" Sophia grumbled.

One by one they emerged from a tight, narrow hole into yet another square room.

"This looks exactly like the other room," Samuel remarked when he emerged from the opening. "Except for those drawings and that spooky, dark hallway."

"Don't start," Alec replied as Samuel jumped down.

"There aren't any small, round balls on the floor, are there?" Samuel quickly assessed the ground around his feet. He bumped into Akeim, who raised an eyebrow in his direction.

"Sorry." Samuel cleared his throat, turning around. "So were we swallowed, then?" he asked, looking back at the hole where they had emerged.

"Actually, no," Genevieve replied. "Symbolically, we have been reborn."

"So we've come out the other end, per se," Samuel chuckled.

Alec nudged him.

"You know, you are absolutely no fun." Samuel gave him an accusing look. "Even in Hell, you are really quite boring."

"Actually, that is where you are wrong." Alec winked at Genevieve, who blushed in return.

Samuel shook his head before moving to the front of the line. He found a few bits of rock on the floor that he cast across the threshold. "Just checking." He smiled over at Akeim, who grunted in response.

The passage continued for several yards before it ran into another, teeing off into two different directions. "Which way?" Samuel looked back at the others.

"West," both Genevieve and her mother answered.

Samuel peered down one passage and then the other, undecided. "Ahh, is there going to be water involved in this?"

"Let me have your bottle," Akeim told him.

Samuel turned around in shock. "You want my whiskey?"

Removing a thin metal pin from his belt, Akeim held out the palm of his hand. "Pour some over my hand."

"Why?" Samuel eyed him suspiciously, holding the bottle close. "It's my last drop."

Akeim looked up with a raised eyebrow.

"Oh, alright," Samuel sighed as he poured out the last of the bottle.

Akeim rubbed the pin against his clothing, then settled it in his palm. They all watched as it turned toward his thumb.

"That's interesting. So which end is north on that needle?" Samuel asked.

Akeim indicated the hall on the right with a nod of his head.

"Are you sure?" Samuel eyed it warily. "What if it's like last time, and it's the other west?"

"Look, there is the all-seeing eye." Genevieve pointed to the hieroglyph marking a wall on the left side of the passage.

"So it's this way?" Samuel took a step towards it.

"No," Genevieve held him back. "The all-seeing eye always marks the east."

They traveled along the corridor until they came to a dead end.

"Are you sure this is it?" Samuel asked.

"Yes." Genevieve motioned toward another hieroglyph on the far wall. "It is Shu, the god of air." On the wall was the figure of a kneeling man who was holding the sky bar above his head. The scene also depicted two lions, as shown on the map, on either side of him.

"It is the god of air that seals the tomb as the pharaoh leaves the underworld and ascends to the heavens," Sophia said softly. "Be very careful."

"Oh look, he's wearing the same headdress as the Sphinx. I thought only the pharaoh could wear that." Samuel examined the folded blue- and gold-striped cloth on the rendering.

"I'm not an authority, but even I know that a god's wardrobe preferences would be above that of the pharaoh's," Alec said sarcastically.

Genevieve laughed. "The pharaoh wore that because it is a symbol of the sky god. It is the rays of both the sun and the moon shining down on the land across the sky."

"Here we are," Sophia said as she held her hand over the symbol of Horus. "Are we ready?"

"Are we actually voting?" Samuel raised his brows in surprise.

"No," Akeim replied. Stepping over to Sophia, he placed his hand on the falcon. "Now we are ready."

Sophia stepped away as he pushed on the symbol. The moment he did, Samuel ran over and tackled him to the floor just as a huge stone fell down where the warrior had been standing. They rolled across the ground, ending in a heap against the wall.

"I had a feeling it was just like the entrance we first came through." Samuel rolled off him. "I suppose you now owe me your firstborn child." He smiled a big toothy grin. "Forever in my debt."

Akeim stood, brushing himself off.

"Not even your everlasting gratitude?" When he still didn't respond, Samuel sighed. "Alright, how about we're even with the marriage thing and the short dress, and the—"

"How about your silence?" Akeim replied as the stone below that of the god Shu moved back, revealing another passage.

"Would you look there," Samuel said as he gazed down the passage. Light could be seen filtering in through the gaps between the stones. "Finally," he sighed, "there is light." A breeze stirred the air as he spoke.

Cautiously, Sophia glanced around as the wind picked up, whistling past them. "We must leave here quickly." It wasn't but a few seconds after they passed over the threshold that the block moved back into place, sealing off the passage.

"I think I might just miss it," Samuel replied as he stood watching.

"What, Hell?" Alec lifted a brow, looking over at him. "It's probably only a matter of time before you find your way back."

"Your opinion of my final destination in the afterlife is truly inspiring," Samuel remarked sarcastically as he pushed on a small stone in the crumbling wall. It broke free, rolling down the steep incline of the Great Pyramid. "This looks like the area where Belzoni tried to blast through. It's remarkable how close he actually came to finding the tomb," he said as he climbed up, poking his head out.

"We need to be careful," Sophia whispered.

"Ah, this is more like it," Samuel sighed. With the morning sun shining on his face, he inhaled deeply, filling his lungs with the fresh, crisp morning air. "We've done it!"

A shadow crossed above him as the legs of a man straddled the opening.

"So you have," the dragoman said.

"Ah, c'mon!" Samuel swore in disgust. "You've got to be kidding me!"

Chapter 27

Samuel hit the stone block with his fist, "Bloody—"

"It's about time you showed up." Akeim climbed up beside him. "Is everything ready?" he asked, receiving a nod from their former guide, as well as a hand up.

"What?" Samuel's mouth hung open in surprise. "You're a part of his—"

"He," Akeim turned around, offering Sophia a hand up, "works for me."

Samuel's mouth worked a moment before any sound came out. "What about the cave-in?" he finally said.

"We escaped," Akeim pointed out.

"The poisonous snakes?"

"Harmless." Akeim shrugged.

"The attack?"

"Unavoidable," Akeim sighed.

"And what of the ammunition?" Samuel was indignant.

"That was an oversight," Akeim replied as he turned away from him.

"An oversight!" Samuel sputtered, pointing a finger at the dragoman as the two walked away. "You owe me some ammunition!" he yelled as they joined three other men. "Of all the dirty tricks." He shook his head. "Can you believe it?" he asked, looking over at Alec

Alec clapped Samuel on the shoulder as he climbed past him, offering his hand to Genevieve. "I'm just relieved he's on our side, at the moment."

"And he calls me a sneaky fox," Samuel muttered to himself as he climbed out. "That . . . that snake!"

Sophia smiled. "He is known to his enemies as the Black Serpent."

Samuel eyed her with disbelief. "You knew as well?"

"The White Devil knew too much, and we too little." A haunted expression passed across her features as she glanced over to where Akeim stood. "He felt it would be best to place some spies of his own."

"So we were never in danger?" Alec asked.

"Those men in the town, in the boat, were his?" Samuel spoke up at the same time, his expression clouded with suspicion.

"Yes and, no. We were in peril." Sophia looked over at Alec. "Only a few men know Akeim's true identity."

"And what would that be?" Samuel looked back at the men. "Is he their king or something?" When she didn't respond, he harrumphed. "That actually explains so much," he muttered. "Arrogant bloody—"

"Samuel," Sophia interrupted.

"Yes?" He quickly turned to her.

She gave him a high brow before taking the statue of the S'ba from her pouch and handing it to him. "Help me with this."

"What do you want me to do?" Samuel puzzled as he held it.

"Hold it upside down while I open it."

"It opens?" He turned it upside down curiously. It looked solid to him.

Sophia slipped her knife along the edge, loosening the base. Gently, she removed the false bottom to reveal an opening containing a small wooden box.

"Whew!" he whistled as she opened the box. Inside was a diamond the size of a goose egg. "Would you look at that?" he questioned. "What do you think it's worth?"

"Considering it's only crystal, I'm sure it's quite worthless, monetarily."

"What?" He looked at her in disbelief. "Tell me we didn't just go through Hell, passing up the greatest treasure known to man, for a worthless rock." When she didn't respond, he threw up his hands. "Well?"

"Well, what?" She placed a piece of granite from the pyramid inside the statue.

"Tell me we didn't just pass—"

"We did not." She silenced him with a look.

"But. . . . Augh, that's just . . ." He sighed. "Wait! There is another one, isn't there?" Samuel slapped the bottom back on, holding up the statue. "Another treasure, even greater?" He grinned widely when she didn't answer. "I knew it!"

"If we act now, we may be able to stop them both," Akeim said as he joined them, taking the statue from Samuel. "We will need this."

~*~

"Whose idea was this again?" Samuel looked over at Alec and then back at the dragoman, who was tying his hands together. "Ouch! Why so tight?"

"They will check it," Akeim replied as he stripped him of his guns. "You remember Ahmed," he glanced over at the dragoman, "my eldest son." He lifted a brow as he turned back. "Tell me again why I should give you my firstborn?"

Ahmed laughed as he relieved him of his other weapons.

"Great," Samuel commented dryly as he jerked his hands away. "Not the knives!"

"They will check for these as well." Ahmed tucked them into his own belt. "And I will make sure to tell my cousin who owns the mutton shop you destroyed that you said hello." He grinned widely.

Samuel looked over at Alec. "I don't know about you, but my enthusiasm towards this plan just dropped considerably."

"They will not let you anywhere near the admiral if you are a threat." Akeim tugged on Samuel's rope, making sure it was secure.

"Considering you're not being trussed up like a goose," Samuel assessed him critically, looking over at his white uniform, "are you going to be the one that cuts us free?"

"None of us will be able to go in with you," Akeim answered. "Only his close personal servants are allowed near him."

"Whoa." Samuel stepped back, turning away from him. "I've changed my mind. Let's go with Plan B."

"This is Plan B." Alec rolled his eyes.

"Let's go back to A, then."

"We can't just charge in with both barrels blazing," Alec reminded him.

"Then C." Samuel whirled around. "Anything is better than being a pigeon."

"We're not the pigeons," Alec stated.

"Are you sure?" Samuel held up his tied hands.

"I'm not letting Genevieve go in there without me," Alec stated emphatically.

"Don't you think there might be a better way to protect her than going in as vulnerable as a newborn babe?" Samuel shook his bound hands for emphasis.

"You're welcome to join Akeim and his men on the outside."

"Augh," Samuel sighed in vexation. "Fine. Plan B it is. Let's just hope it's not 'b' for 'botched'," he grumbled.

~*~

"The artifact, Sayyid." The admiral's head guard held out the statue to him.

The admiral took the statue, gazing at it in awe as he held it in his hand. "The S'ba," he whispered triumphantly.

"The women have also arrived," the guard informed him, "but they are not alone. The two Englishmen are with them."

The admiral assessed him gravely, scooting his chair back from his desk. "And why is that?"

"From what I was told, they have information that you may want."

"I see." The admiral stood, setting the statue reverently on a bureau next to where the trunk rescued from the deserted ship stood open. "Send them in."

The guard bowed before leaving the room.

The admiral walked back to the desk and removed a gun from the drawer. "Apparently, I will have to see to this myself," he said to the empty room.

Akeim stepped away from his son once they boarded the *dahabiya*, slipping unseen behind the wheelhouse. It wasn't until the prisoners were turned over to the admiral's guards that he surreptitiously moved into position, signaling his men.

~*~

Alec was shoved into the admiral's cabin with Samuel stumbling through the door after him. "Watch it." Samuel yanked his arm away from the guard who held him.

"And to what do I owe this pleasure?" the admiral asked from his place behind the desk.

Alec raised his head, glaring at him. "What kind of evil bastard are you?"

The guard next to him slammed the butt of a rifle into his gut, doubling him over with the blow. Alec glared up at the man, recognizing him as the same one who had hit him upside the head the first time they had been captured. His eyes narrowed.

"I was told you have some information for me," the admiral said.

"Alec," Genevieve cried as she entered the room, rushing over to him. "Stop it," she turned to her uncle, "stop this at once!" Genevieve slipped a small blade into Alec's hand as she spoke.

"I'd love nothing more," her uncle replied coldly, leveling the gun in his hand at the couple.

"Percival." Sophia stepped into the room, followed by another guard. "You will never be able to use that artifact without us." The cannon on the main deck blasted as she spoke.

Without a word, the admiral signaled his head guard to find out what the disturbance was about. The man nodded, slipping from the room. "Then it would appear we are at an impasse," Percival remarked, turning his head toward Sophia. "What do you propose?"

"Let them go, and I will assist you." Sophia lifted her head a notch.

The admiral's laughter filled the room. "Ahh, Sophia," he chuckled. "You surprise me. Do you actually think I'd believe that?"

~*~

The head guard left the cabin to walk to the prow of the ship, where Akeim stood beside the cannon he had fired. The guard unsheathed his sword, opening his mouth to speak. The dragoman stepped behind him, quickly silencing him.

A black coach pulled up on the pier next to the large boat. The two footmen who stood on the back rail rushed to the door.

One opened it as the other fixed the stair for the passenger who was waiting to alight. A black cane with gold trim emerged. The hand that held it was adorned with a signet ring on the pinkie.

They were met at the plank by one of the admiral's men. "This way." Akeim bowed his head, motioning for them to follow.

~*~

"What do you intend to do with us?" Sophia demanded as she looked over at the two remaining guards.

"Unless these gentlemen can give me some useful information," Percival answered in a bored tone, "they will have to be dispatched."

"What do you mean 'dispatched'?" Samuel's head shot up. "Don't you think that's a bit extreme?"

The admiral narrowed his eyes on him as he came around the desk, pointing the barrel of the gun at his stomach.

"Apparently not," Samuel sighed. "You run a tough bargain." He looked over at Alec, then back to the admiral. "Alright then, I'll make you a deal. Release us, and I will turn over the map to King Solomon's mines."

The admiral chuckled, pointing the revolver at him. "Is that what you think this is about?"

"It's no use trying to fool him," Alec said. "It's the location of the tomb of Sheba he wants, and I'm of a mind to give it to him."

"Alec, no!" Genevieve gasped, turning pleading eyes towards him.

"I will not let this madman harm you for some ancient knowledge." Alec kept his eyes on the admiral as he spoke, slicing through the last of his bonds while Genevieve shielded his actions from sight.

The admiral's expression hardened as he cocked the gun, pointing it at Alec. "Stand back, Genevieve. I wouldn't want to harm you unnecessarily."

"I will not—," Genevieve started as the guard behind her pulled her roughly back.

Alec charged at the guard who held her.

Samuel dove in front of Alec as the gun fired. He hit the floor and rolled. "Holy mother of," he gritted out between clenched teeth, "I'm shot." Blood oozed from the hole in his thigh. "The bastard shot me."

Alec stopped in his tracks and turned toward the admiral.

"Now that we all know that I'm serious." The admiral aimed the gun at Alec once again. "What information do you have?"

"What is the meaning of this?" Lord Langston stood in the doorway.

Alec lunged forward, slamming his fist into the admiral's face as he twisted the gun from his hand. Akeim disarmed the two men who had escorted the old lord, while Genevieve left the guard that held her rolling on the floor gasping for air.

With lightning speed, Sophia flipped the guard standing next to her across the room; he landed with a thud against the bureau. The statue above him toppled from its place, the heavy base striking his head. The man slouched over, knocked out from the blow. The base of the statue broke open, releasing the brown rock that had been placed there.

The admiral stared in horror as it rolled across the floor.

BOOM!

Lord Langston held a revolver in his hand. "Cease this at once!" Smoke swirled from the end of the gun in his hand. The warning shot had shattered the window.

Alec stepped protectively in front of Genevieve as he eyed the new threat. Akeim moved closer to Sophia when the admiral pulled out a small pistol from his jacket. Another shot rang out. The admiral dropped the gun, grasping his hand.

"Don't think for a moment that I won't kill you," Lord Langston said as he held the gun on him. "I've the blood of honorable men, whose only crime was to fight for their country against mine, on my hands." He gave him a look of pure hatred. "You murdered my son and kept his wife and child from me." His finger tightened on the trigger as he stared at his son-in-law. "I would gladly go to hell just to make sure you suffer for an eternity."

"You think that this is the end?" Percival said venomously. "It is merely the beginning," he warned. "You have no idea who you are dealing with."

A dozen armed men wearing British uniforms entered the room. "Take him away," Lord Langston ordered, releasing his finger on the trigger. Two men hauled the admiral out as the old lord turned his attention to his granddaughter. "Genevieve," he whispered hoarsely.

"Grandpapa," she cried, running into his arms.

He looked over her head at Sophia. "Forgive me, I had no idea."

Sophia nodded with tears in her eyes.

"Hmm-hum," Samuel cleared his throat, holding up his bound hands. "Could someone cut these?"

~*~

"Aahh, aah, watch it." Samuel winced as Sophia ripped his pants leg open to inspect his wound. "Ow, not so hard. . . . Ouch!"

Sophia rolled her eyes. "Samuel?"

"What?" He opened his scrunched eyes.

"I haven't even touched it."

Samuel grimaced. "Dear God in Heaven, just give me a drink!"

"Oh, honestly," she sighed.

"Here," Alec came forward with a bottle of scotch, "this looks like it's from his private stock."

"That's better." Samuel took a healthy sip. "Augh!" He wiped his mouth. Looking up at Alec, he said, "Turns out the 'b' was for 'bullet'."

"Samuel?" Lord Langston came to stand in front of him.

"Sir!" Samuel immediately sobered.

"Looks as if you've taken a hit." He eyed the wound.

"Just a scratch, sir." Samuel straightened up, causing Sophia to lift a brow.

"From your note, I presume you have the evidence." The old lord waited.

This time it was Alec's turn to raise a brow.

"Yes, sir. You will find all the marked guns in his armory. He was definitely the one selling illegal arms to Cetshwayo."

"I see." Lord Langston turned to one of his own men and gave a quick order, dispatching him to find the evidence. He turned back to Samuel. "Good work." He nodded before leaving the room.

Samuel looked up to face Alec's anger. "It's not like it sounds."

"You mean to tell me that, all this time, you have been on an assignment?" Alec didn't allow him to respond. "That, even when we were on the ship, chasing after Genevieve, you were snooping around?" Alec pulled the bottle of scotch from Samuel's fingers and glared down at him.

"It's not like it sounds," Samuel pleaded. "And, in my defense, nothing was as it seemed. If you'll remember, the bad guy we were chasing was actually on our side, and the good guy was deceiving us by lending aid."

"All this time, and you didn't tell me?"

"I was sworn to secrecy!"

Alec gave him a look that lowered him to the level of a gnat.

"By the queen herself," Samuel defended himself. "Remember the night that you won the map?" He looked hopeful. "Well, I was with the queen."

"Are you implying that your new mistress is the queen?" Alec folded his arms across his chest.

"God, no," Samuel responded. "You've met the queen . . . but, let me tell you, she is nothing if not relentless."

"Unbelievable!" Alec shook his head as Akeim joined them. "I knew it was more than just a coincidence that we had the map and somehow managed to find the keeper as well."

"Lord Langston did ask that I look for his granddaughter," Samuel admitted. "Ah c'mon, it was brilliant," he added. "We walked out of there with Genevieve when everyone else he'd sent failed."

"I could remove that bullet." Akeim smiled as he pulled out his knife.

"Trust me, it's tempting," Alec replied.

"Alec," Samuel looked up at the leering warrior, "I took this bullet saving you. For God's sake, don't leave me alone with him."

"Stop it, both of you." Sophia took the bottle from Alec and handed it back to Samuel. "I will remove the bullet."

"NO!"

Alec walked over to Genevieve, who smiled at him despite Samuel's outburst.

"How is Samuel doing?" She glanced over at him in concern.

"Aahh!" the man in question screamed.

Alec smiled. "He's going to be just fine."

"How did you know it was Sheba's tomb that he wanted?"

"How did you dispatch that guard so easily?" He smiled as she blushed. "It doesn't matter now that you're safe."

"But I still protect the tomb." She watched him with concern in her eyes.

"Correction," he smiled at her, "we protect the tomb."

Chapter 28

"Samuel, what are you still doing here?" Alec crossed the lobby of the Shepheard Hotel in Cairo. The man in question was sitting between two brightly dressed ladies. The feathers in their hats bobbed, making them look like fantastic birds of paradise.

"Oh, hello there, Alec." Samuel grinned up at him from his place at the table. "I'd like you to meet Ladies Chastity and Amelia." He moved his eyebrows up and down as he spoke. "They are twins."

"Yes, I can see that." Alec nodded stiffly as he stood next to the table. "Samuel, may I have a word with you," he cleared his throat, "in private?"

"Of course." Samuel stood, excusing himself with a slight bow. "Ladies." He kissed their hands before walking over to Alec, who had stepped out of earshot, though he could still hear the twins twitter as Samuel turned and waved.

Alec noticed his limp was more of a swagger as he strolled toward him. "Well?" he asked.

"Well, what?" Samuel turned to look at him. "They are twins, booked on the same passage that we—"

"You know damn well what I'm talking about." Alec glared at him.

"Oh, that." Samuel looked back at the ladies. "I left Akeim in charge of the decorations."

"Oh, hell," Alec groaned.

"Don't worry about a thing," Samuel said as he waved again. "It's handled." He turned back to Alec, "Trust me."

"That may not be the best term to use to increase my confidence," Alec commented dryly.

"It's going to be fine," Samuel chuckled, changing the subject. "Speaking of Akeim, the Ol' Lord of the Desert's son, Ahmed, sends word that his cousin, Omar," he smiled, "you remember him? He's the owner of the mutton shop that you destroyed."

"I didn't destroy it," Alec replied testily.

"The last we saw of it, there was smoke billowing out the sides and flames shooting out the back," Samuel reminded him. "What would you call it?"

"Well-needed ventilation."

"At any rate," Samuel continued, "he has received your most gracious gift and will now stop cursing you as a filthy son of a pig, and he sends his blessings for restoring his livelihood."

"That's always comforting, but what about the packages?"

"The packages?" Samuel responded, distracted by the ladies who were waving back at him.

"Yes, the packages!" Alec ran a hand through his hair in frustration.

"Being delivered as we speak."

"What? Both of them?"

"Both of them." Samuel nodded absently. "What?" He looked back at Alec. "Oh no, of course not," he laughed. "I almost forgot, here you are." Samuel withdrew a box about the size of his fist from the inside pocket of his jacket. "It was almost like cracking a safe to get it, let me tell you."

Alec sighed, visibly shaken as he took it from him.

"Oh, c'mon, man." Samuel clapped him on the shoulder and turned him toward the door. "It's all been taken care of. Relax. Everything will be perfect."

"It better be!" Alec warned.

"Well, it won't be if they see you," Samuel continued in a calming voice as he ushered Alec toward the entrance. "You had better leave before you blow the whole thing."

Alec took a deep breath and let it out slowly. "Right."

"If you want to change your mind," Samuel offered as he waved back at the twins.

"Samuel!" Alec's look was one of extreme irritation.

"Alright, alright, just checking." Samuel grinned. "You'd better get a move on," Samuel looked up the grand staircase of the hotel, "they'll be down any moment."

Alec nodded, taking another deep breath before walking away.

As soon as he was out the door, Samuel returned to the table. "Ladies," he smiled, "have I told you yet about the time I took a bubble bath in Hell?"

"Oh, Samuel." Chastity tapped him on the shoulder with her fan. "The things you come up with are simply scandalous," she giggled.

Amelia batted her eyes. "You're absolutely incorrigible."

"Yes, but delightfully so." He winked in response to their delighted peals of laughter.

~*~

A knock sounded on the door. "Just a minute," Sophia called as she went to open it. She returned with a package. "It's from the dressmaker."

"I thought we had all the items she made for us already." Genevieve looked up curiously as her mother opened the box and gasped in wonder. "Oh my goodness!" she breathed as she uncovered a white gown. The tiny pearls sewn onto the bodice shimmered against the fabric. "There is a note," she smiled as she held it out, "with your name on it."

"For the keeper of my heart and soul," Genevieve read, "love, Alec."

"It's simply gorgeous." Sophia lifted it from the box. "It's a bit much for traveling. We should probably pack—"

"I'm wearing it." Genevieve smiled as she took it from her mother; holding it against her body, she twirled around the room.

~*~

"You're a vision of loveliness." Samuel grinned as he met them at the bottom of the stairs. Dressed in the latest fashion, both mother and daughter raised quite a stir as those in the salon turned to stare at the pair.

"Thank you." Sophia inclined her head, as Genevieve looked over the crowd.

"Where is Alec?" she asked.

"Oh, I'm sorry," Samuel held out his arm for her, "he had some things to attend to and asked me to escort you ladies to the ship."

"Oh," Genevieve said. Her entire demeanor deflated.

"Are these your trunks, then?" he asked, indicating the baggage being carried out by the porters. "I'll just see to their loading, and we'll be on our way."

The ride was a surprisingly short one. Sophia looked out the window at the cathedral as they came to a stop. "Here we are." Samuel opened the door and offered his hand up to Genevieve to assist her down. "There is something here that I'm sure you will want to see," he said with a grin.

Once inside, they were met by Genevieve's grandfather. "I would like very much to see you happy, young lady." He smiled warmly at her as he held out his arm. She accepted it as he escorted her further into the chapel.

He turned to face her, looking at her with tenderness. "There is a certain young man who has asked me for your hand in marriage."

Patting her hand as he spoke, he moved so that she could see what awaited her at the end of the aisle. Alec stood before the altar, holding a single white rose. The light from the stained glass window filtered down, casting him in an ethereal glow.

Her grandfather once again extended his elbow to her as music began playing softly. As they approached, Alec bent to one knee. She walked on shaky legs until she stood before him.

"Genevieve," his voice cracked, reminding her of the first time she'd heard it. He smiled nervously as he took a deep breath, extending the rose out to her. "Will you marry me?"

Love shone in his eyes as he gazed up at her. It moved her to the core that he would allow himself to be so vulnerable. He'd never been stronger, or more beautiful, in her eyes. "Yes." She nodded, taking the rose that he offered with trembling fingers. She blinked at the tears that had formed in her eyes. Alec stood, wiping them away with his thumb as he cradled her cheek.

"You have my blessing," her grandfather whispered, as he transferred her hand from his arm to Alec's and stepped back.

A priest stepped forward from the podium, smiling kindly at the couple. "Dearly beloved, we are gathered here," he began.

The ceremony was a whirl, much different than the first time. Alec smiled down at his bride as he took the box from his pocket. Opening it up, he withdrew a diamond ring, slipping it on her finger.

"I now pronounce you man and wife." The priest smiled at them. "You may kiss the bride."

Alec scooped his wife up into his arms and kissed her, to the applause and cheers of their family.

Genevieve was laughing with joy as he set her back down. He winked at her as he took her hand. "Are you ready for the rest of our lives together, Lady Brighton?"

"Yes." She nodded happily as they walked together down the steps.

Lord Langston turned to Samuel as they watched the happy couple. "What do you intend to do now that your business here is completed?"

"I was thinking about some rest and relax—" Samuel looked over at him, noting the sharp eyes that appraised him. He knew that look. "What did you have in mind, sir?"

Sophia met the bride and groom at the bottom of the steps. She hugged her daughter as Samuel came up to Alec.

"Congratulations!" Samuel vigorously shook his hand. "See, I told you it would be perfect."

"So you did." Alec smiled as he looked over at his bride. She and her mother were happily talking together. "Oh, that reminds me." He pulled a note from his pocket. "Deliver this to my mother upon your arrival, will you? She would probably like to know she has a new daughter-in-law before we arrive from our honeymoon in Venice."

"Ah, about that," Samuel's voice was somewhat hesitant, "your mother may not have been quite as zealous in her pursuit of a bride as it may have appeared."

"Samuel," Alec narrowed his eyes, "what did you do?"

"I may have sent a few sketches to the newspapers and expounded on a few rumors."

"You what?" Alec opened his mouth in disbelief as he remembered the cartoon in the paper and the whispering of his upcoming proposal. The fact that he'd pointedly avoided his mother probably hadn't helped him.

"I needed the cover," Samuel was saying when he turned his attention back to him. "All in the name of God and country, I assure you."

Alec tipped his head back and laughed heartily.

"You're not angry?" Samuel looked at him oddly.

Alec clapped him on the back. "Angry?" He smiled. "How could I ever be angry about getting the greatest treasure known to man?" He looked over at Genevieve, who had turned at his laughter. "Quite the contrary, I'm forever in your debt."

"Oh, well, that's a relief," Samuel said, then added conversationally, "I hear Venice is perfect this time of year."

"You're not coming," Alec stated flatly.

"I wasn't suggesting," Samuel snorted. "I'll have you know I have a new assignment."

Alec turned to him in surprise, "What of the leg? Are you sure you're up to it?"

"Of course." Samuel grinned. "It fits nicely into my plans, in fact."

"And how is that?" Alec asked.

"I'll be babysitting a spinster who is firmly on the shelf," Samuel replied. "In fact, you may know of her, Miss Constance Applegate." When Alec shook his head, Samuel continued. "I'm posing as her aged butler." He winked. "I'll be reviving my role as Higgins."

"Aren't you concerned she'll recognize you?" Alec raised a brow.

"From what I understand, she rarely goes out in public." Samuel smiled with a wink. "The twins will be in London, and I will have a lot of time on my hands. What could go wrong?"

"What, indeed?" Alec raised a brow.

~*~

Alec picked up his bride and opened the door, carrying her over the threshold of the honeymoon suite.

"Oh, Alec," Genevieve gasped as he moved to close the door. "You thought of everything."

Alec turned to see the room decorated with sheer drapery across the bed, rose petals scattered across the floor, and a bubble bath already prepared. A chilled bottle of champagne sat beside a platter of fruit, while candlelight lent a soft glow to the room, which looked like something straight out of *Arabian Nights*.

Alec grinned, silently claiming credit for the *decorations*. The Ol' Lord of the Desert apparently knew a thing or two.

Alec gently set her on the floor, turning her in his arms so that he could look into her eyes. "I love you," he whispered, grinning from ear to ear.

"I love you too." She smiled up at him as he bent to kiss her.

The End

Sneak Peek
Treasure of the Emerald Isle

Chapter 1

London, England, 1863

"Oh, there ye are, luv," Gurtie cheerfully said as she opened the back door for Constance. She watched as the young woman made her way up to the steps, the packages she carried threatening to topple at any moment. The plump cook took the basket from the top of the heap, uncovering the young woman's face. "I was thinkin' I'd have to go out and find ye for a moment."

Constance blew at a lock of hair that had fallen from her tight bun. "At least that's over with," she sighed as she entered the kitchen.

"You look all done in, dearie," Gurtie fussed as she lightened the load further. "Why didn't you wait for Iain to help with those?"

"I didn't want the eggs prematurely scrambled." Constance gave her a meaningful glance as she set the rest of the packages on the table.

"Well now," Gurtie chuckled, "seein' as how he's not blown the laundry up in over a month, I consider us lucky indeed."

"You have a point." Constance nodded as she inhaled the aroma of fresh baked bread. Her stomach rumbled in appreciation. "Oh, that smells good."

"Did you not eat breakfast again?" Gurtie looked up at her as she went about emptying a basket of vegetables. When Constance didn't reply, she tsked, "Shame on ye, yer too thin as 'tis."

Constance glanced down at the worn servant's dress. It did nothing to enhance her figure, but that had been the point in wearing it in the first place. The last thing she wanted was to attract attention while acting as her own maid.

"Where's the brisket an' the fish?" Gurtie asked, looking through the goods.

"Augh," Constance groaned yet again.

"That fishmonger didn't try to manhandle ye again, did he? Because if he did. . . ."

Constance smiled as the older woman picked up a particularly large stalk of celery and wielded it like a club. "No." She plopped down in a chair. "Our money didn't stretch as far as I'd hoped, but there are plenty of turnips."

"'Tis a shame, 'tis, but why you still insist on doin' the shoppin' is beyond me, especially when Betsy--"

"I'll not be swindled again, that's why," Constance replied. "Our coin is scarce enough as it is."

"That bein' the case, why don't you ask our kind benefactor for a wee bit more next month?"

"And have to explain that my teetotaling, nearsighted, elderly maid has a weakness for dice?" Constance arched a delicate brow. "Even if I were to tell him that she was taken by a charlatan, I don't think Lord Langston would be very understanding, do you? He might even increase his efforts to watch over us."

"Speaking of which," Gurtie gave her a knowing look, "you'd better get out of those rags. He's already had the agency send another butler around." She shook her head with a sigh. "As if we didn't have enough to contend with."

"Oh no," Constance groaned, "I thought we'd have more time?"

"They filled the post right quick, they did." Gurtie nodded. "But don't ye worry none, I've it all worked out." She looked back over her shoulder. "That reminds me . . . don't drink from the teapot in the salon."

"You didn't? Poor Mr. Crabbits is probably still recovering from your treatment of him."

"Now I did him a favor, I did." Gurtie's pin curls bobbed as she spoke. "Even now he's restin' in the country on a fine pension, instead of toilin' away as someone else's butler . . . and in fine health, I might add."

Constance couldn't help the smile that Gurtie's reasoning brought to her lips. "I suppose there's no help for it," she yawned. "We certainly can't afford someone spying on us."

"He'll be sleepin' like a wee babe is all," Gurtie assured the exhausted young lady. "Which is what you should be doin', rather than traipsin' around all hours of the night."

"You know why I have to," Constance replied tiredly.

Gurtie shook her head with a sigh. "I'll just send up a new pot for ye, then. A nice spot of tea will do ye good, an' I'll just put a wee nip in it to put the pink back in yer cheeks." Gurtie winked as she turned away to put the kettle on to boil.

"Maybe just a little." Constance picked up one of the freshly baked rolls and smelled it appreciatively. "I've got to go out again tonight."

"All this runnin' around, I hardly think it would be what your mum would want, God rest her soul. I don't think this is what she intended when she asked me to look after ye." Gurtie frowned as she turned back around. "Oh no!" She shooed Constance away from the steaming hot bun she was about to bite into.

"No?" Constance eyed the freshly baked morsel dubiously.

"Those are for the new butler," the cook warned. "I'm thinking he'll be stayin' close to the loo tomorrow, he will." She nodded with finality. "Ours are still in the oven."

"Just don't kill the poor man." Constance set the sweet back on the plate with the others, scooting them far across the table from herself.

"Well, I would never!" Gurtie looked positively innocent in her cap and curls. "I'm just helpin' him on his way to his new post is all." She rolled her eyes when the servant's bell rang. "Though this one will be a pleasure, I tell ye," Gurtie huffed as she placed the plate on a tray.

"Why is that?" Constance raised her brow curiously. "Is he a threat?"

"Gorr's no," Gurtie snorted. "But our Mr. Higgins is a cheeky one, he is. He's already rung that bell a dozen times. You'd think he's the comp'ny, rather than the 'elp, ye would." She lifted the tray as the bell rang again. "A positive nuisance!" she muttered, looking over her shoulder. "Don't be long, Connie, luv. I'll send Betsy in t' pour."

Constance shook her head with a sigh. "Poor Mr. Higgins." She couldn't help but smile to herself. The butler would, no doubt, be wearing most of the tea with Betsy pouring, not to mention seeking a new post before the night was through. That was, if he knew what was good for him.

~*~

Samuel stood before the mirror in the salon. The image reflected back was hardly that of the young Lord St. Clair. The only thing that looked remotely familiar was the blue of his eyes. He moved the bushy white eyebrows up and down as he straightened his withered grey beard that made him look like the ancient man he was pretending to be. "Perfect, if I do say so myself." He smiled, inspecting his false teeth.

"Good day, madam," he said, altering his voice to that of a gravely one. "Hmm," he cleared his throat and practiced it again. "Good day, madam." With a satisfied nod, he turned towards the window. Affecting the posture of a much older gent, he walked slightly bent over with an obvious limp, which was only partially an act. The injury he had sustained on his last assignment was acting up. Must be the weather, he decided as he looked out at the crisp autumn day.

With a sigh, he withdrew his pocket watch. Affixing a round lens to his eye, he scrunched his cheek to hold it there. It was always best, he'd found, to remain in character. Quarter past four. He sighed yet again, returning the watch to the pocket in his waistcoat. He'd already been waiting an interminable amount of time. He'd drained the teapot an hour ago and was starting to have a powerful need to relieve himself.

He went to the bell cord, pulling at it in frustration. He then moved towards the chair by the fireplace, where he sat down, stifling a big yawn. At least he'd have plenty of rest during the day so that he could continue his usual pursuits at night. He grinned. "A piece of cake."

"What's this 'bout cake?" Gurtie asked as she bustled into the room.

"Excuse me, Madam McPhee." Samuel cleared his throat. "I wasn't—"

"Now none of that. I've told ye t' call me Gurtie, and good news I have too," she continued. "Our Miss Constance is back from shoppin' and will be down t' see ye soon. I've just brought some of these sweet rolls fresh from the oven for ye till she arrives." She placed the tray next to the pot of tea.

"Ay, Mum," a young lad walked into the room.

"Well, there you are Iain. Come meet the new butler, Mr. Higgins." The boy that entered couldn't have been any more than ten or eleven. "This is my son, Iain. He's the best footman hereabouts, he is," Gurtie beamed proudly. "An' he even pulls the weeds in the garden, he does."

"Sir." Iain bowed.

"Hum, hum," Samuel cleared his throat, "Iain."

"You're not goin' t' get sick like the last butler, are ye?"

"Och now," Gurtie shooed him out of the room. "Run along like a good lad and take Mr. Higgins's trunk up t' his room." She turned back to the new butler with a bright smile on her face. "A bit of an imagination on 'im, but a good boy." She busied herself by plumping a few cushions. "Go on now, eat up," she encouraged as she checked the teapot beside him. "I make the best cakes from here to 'olandary, I do."

"Don't mind if I do," Samuel said as he sank his teeth into a hot bun.

Bump, bump, bump, thump, sounded from outside the room. "I'm alright," Iain called from the stairs.

"I'll just go see about a fresh pot of tea." Gurtie smiled brightly. "Oh, Betsy's finished with the laundry, she 'as, and will be in t' pour. Careful though, she 'as an eye for the gents, she does." She winked, smiling as she left. "What she can see of them, that is."

Samuel barely heard her parting comment as he chewed. He wasn't left long to ponder on it, however, as the spinster he'd been sent to babysit walked into the room. She was about as dull as the wallpaper in her crisp white cap and high-necked day-gown of grey. The spectacles she wore were perched high on her nose, and her complexion was most peaked.

Samuel slowly rose from his chair as she approached. "Good day, Miss Applegate." Bent over as he was, he almost toppled over as he bowed.

"Good day, Mr. Higgins," Constance replied in the most somber voice she could affect as she watched him straighten. "I trust you haven't been waiting long. I was unaware that the agency would be sending anyone around."

"Of course," Samuel's gravelly voice intoned, "Mrs. McPhee has been most gracious." He indicated the hot buns as she seated herself on the other chair. "Would you care for one?" he asked, picking up the tray.

"Oh, no thank you," Constance replied, almost too quickly. "I wouldn't want to spoil my dinner." She watched as the tray wobbled. The poor man's hand trembled so badly, she reached out to help him set it back down. She waited until he seated himself before continuing. "Your services here, I'm afraid, will be few and far between.

Samuel nodded as she continued.

"There is the women's reading club I go to every Tuesday, and the ladies auxiliary, but that is only once a month."

Samuel shook his head. There was a definite buzzing in his ear, and he found himself needing to stifle a yawn on several occasions as she spoke.

"And then there is Mrs. Crosby's tea." Constance looked over at him. "Mr. Higgins, are you listening?"

"Yes, yes," Samuel replied as he refocused on her face. He was afraid her monotone voice was putting him to sleep.

"Actually, Mr. Higgins, no one ever comes to call. I'm afraid the only one that comes and goes by the front door is myself," she sighed, "and even I use the servant's entrance most the time."

Samuel felt sorry for the girl. It wasn't her fault she'd been born with that complexion, or those looks. Maybe if she just did something with her hair? Unfortunately, it was red, which made two strikes against her already. And, if that wasn't enough, it appeared she had a slight harelip. She looked down most of the time, so it was hard to see her eyes past her spectacles. Poor girl, there was no hope for her, and he had an eye for that type of thing.

His taste ran more towards buxom blondes. Samuel's mind drifted away for a moment as her voice droned on. *Take the twins, for instance*, he thought, *now there was a pair that had been doubly blessed.* The ladies he'd recently met in Cairo, and had the pleasure of entertaining on the voyage home, were fair indeed. He sighed.

"Mr. Higgins?"

Her grating voice cut into his thoughts. "Yes?"

"Are you alright?"

"Quite." Samuel cleared his throat, looking at her once more. Green, he noticed with surprise. Her eyes were green with gold flecks in them.

"I was saying that, although you receive your pay from Lord Langston, I will not allow any disruptions," she droned on in a colorless voice. Samuel fought the urge to yawn as she continued. "My household runs as smooth as clockwork."

Before he could reply, Gurtie burst into the room. "Here we are, then." She placed a new pot of tea down on the service. "You'd probably like a fresh cup."

Samuel wanted to groan. If he had any more tea, he might float away. He'd never understood why it was so popular, anyway. He much preferred a rich cup of coffee, and if it was enhanced with a liberal dose of whiskey, it was all the better.

"Now where is that Betsy?" Gurtie sighed. "I'll just go see what's keepin' her."

"You were saying?" Samuel asked the young lady seated so stiffly across from him.

"Betsy!" Gurtie yelled from the hall. The volume she used was enough to shake the rafters. "What's keepin' ye?"

Samuel's eyes widened in shock at the lack of decorum.

"I'm not deaf," the maid yelled in response. "I just was wantin' to freshin' up, seein' as how I'm meetin' the new butler'n all."

Gurtie returned. "She'll be right down." She smiled brightly.

Samuel was further amazed when Betsy appeared a moment later. The glasses she wore magnified her eyes, giving her an owlish appearance. Her grey hair sprang from under her cap at every angle, and when she bobbed a curtsey, he was sure he detected the smell of whiskey and lye soap in the air.

"Hello there, Mr. Higgins." She batted her big eyes at him.

Samuel cleared his throat, "Madam."

"Oh, that's 'miss'." She batted her eyes again. "I'm not married."

"You don't say," Samuel coughed.

"Would ye care for a nice hot cuppa' tea, then?" She leaned over the service, "One lump or two?"

"Two," he replied as she handed him his cup, without the tea. She then proceeded to pour as he chased the stream of liquid from the pot with his cup.

"You can call me Betsy," she replied.

Samuel looked up to see her eyes on him, rather than the task at hand. Scorching hot liquid seared across his lap as she continued to pour. "Ah-Ah-Ah!" he yelped.

"Oh, dear!" Betsy put the pot down and grabbed her apron. Leaning over him, she dabbed at the spill. Her efforts only succeeded in pressing the scalding cloth against his skin, however.

"Augh!" Samuel did his best to stand as he brushed her hands away.

"Oh my." Betsy stepped back, wringing her hands in dismay.

"Mr. Higgins." Constance stood leaning over the two. "Are you alright?"

"No, madam, I am not!" Samuel asserted.

"Betsy," Constance replied calmly. "Could you see Mr. Higgins to his room, where he can change his trousers?

Samuel snorted indignantly. He seriously doubted she could see anything!

"Yes, ma'am." Betsy bobbed. "Right this way." She smiled.

Samuel had seen wolves with that expression. He followed behind her, his posture bent. The only difference, this time, was that he wasn't faking it.

"Here ye are." She led him into his room, where his trunk lay broken open, the contents scattered across the floor.

"How nice," Betsy claimed as she turned large eyes on him. "It seems Iain has brought your things up."

"Indeed," Samuel commented, far too concerned with the burning in his nether region to worry about the pile of clothes spilt on the floor.

"Would you like some help?" The owl blinked up at him.

"No," he blurted out as she winked. "No, thank you," he crisply repeated as he ushered her out the door, turning the key in the lock.

He had barely managed to get his pants off when a knock sounded.

"Mr. Higgins."

It was Gurtie. . . . Standing in nothing but his shirt and stockings, Samuel felt out of sorts.

"I've come to tend t' ye," she called.

"That's quite alright." Samuel stole a brief look down. His flesh was scalded and bright pink. He watched in horror as the key in the door fell to the floor, pushed through from the other side.

"Oh, pish!" Gurtie retorted, turning her key in the lock.

"Madam, you will kindly stay on that side of the door." Samuel looked around frantically for something to cover himself. He grabbed the sheet off the bed just in time.

"There's nothin' you have that I no' seen before." Gurtie pushed the door open, carrying a hip bath. "Now, off with that, and let me have a look."

"I will not!" Samuel blustered, wrapping the sheet around him.

Betsy appeared in the doorway with a bucket. "Good thing the iceman came today."

Before he knew what was happening, Gurtie pushed him backward. The movement caught him so off guard that he fell into the tub. Unable to recover, he sat there while Betsy followed right behind her, pouring freezing cold water across his lap.

"Ahh-hh!" Samuel leapt out of the tub. As he moved, the wet sheet slipped from his fingers, parting in the front. He quickly turned away from Gurtie's view, right into the owlish eyes of Betsy.

"Oh my!" Betsy's eyes grew even larger as Samuel jerked the sheet up.

"Well, what's it look like?" Gurtie asked her.

"It's all pinkish," she replied.

"And?"

"Well there's nothing much there," Betsy said. "It's shriveled up to a wee thing. We may have burned it off."

358

"It's . . . It's not been burnt off." Samuel blustered. "It's been frozen."

"Are ye goin' to let me see it, then?" Gurtie asked.

"Not if it's the last thing I do!" Samuel stood by the door with the handle in one hand and the bunched up sheet in the other.

"Suit yerself then," Gurtie sighed as she turned to leave. "Come now, Betsy. How 'bout a nice spot of tea?"

"That sounds nice." Betsy nodded, following her out the door.

He shut the door behind them, throwing the bolt home, "Holy hell!" Samuel rested his head on the door. "What kind of household is this?" He turned, bracing his back against the frame. "Runs like clockwork, indeed," he scoffed. "It's a bloody madhouse!"

~*~

"Works every time," Gurtie chuckled as Samuel slammed the door behind them.

"I think we're getting better at it." Betsy nodded.

"It's a fine art," Gurtie agreed.

"He did have quite a bit of fight in him," Betsy commented. "Did ye give him enough laudanum?"

"He's not as frail as he looks," Gurtie replied thoughtfully. "I'll have to up the dose, I suppose."

"Well?" Constance asked from the table as they entered the kitchen.

"He'll be packed and out the door as soon as he gets his britches back on." Betsy giggled as she set a plate of untainted rolls on the table.

"Only one problem," Gurtie took one of the three cups Constance had poured. "I'm afraid that Iain is catching on."

"Oh, dear." Betsy blinked as she sat down, taking a cup.

"We'll have t' mix it up a bit." Gurtie nodded. "We'll start next time with the itching powder ye make, Connie, and perhaps forgo it altogether on this one."

"Umm," Betsy blinked, "too late."

"Ye've already powdered his britches?" Gurtie asked in surprise.

"Well, what did you think I was doin' when ye called?" She snorted with laughter. "It's not as if I was gettin' pretty for the ol' codger."

Their laughter filled the kitchen.

"All in a day's work," Gurtie sighed.

TREASURE OF EGYPT

I love a book that takes me far away . . . to a time and place when the world was filled with mystery. Throw in some humor, nonstop action, a little romance and I'm pretty much hooked. Add to that an ancient mystery and I'm yours forever. . . . Well, at least until the book is finished. Hahaha!

My series Treasure of the Ancients delves into the greatest mysteries of the Ancient world. I have spent years researching ancient cultures and their languages. To me, understanding their ancient beliefs as well as their writing is not only fascinating, but essential to writing a solid book.

My new series, *Paranormally Yours*, gives me the freedom to take a few more liberties with the myths I am so fascinated by. You could say I jumped into the paranormal world with both feet in writing these lighthearted stories. We are still exploring the ancient mysteries of the world, but in this series everything of fantasy, myth, and legend can and probably will pop up.

I have spent years as a professional artist, (please see my blog or website to view art) but it wasn't until a late blessing came into my life, which magically transformed my oils into finger paints, that the opportunity to write the books I've dreamt of finally came.

Barbara Ivie Green

I am blessed to have the most amazing supportive husband and family. I also have the best dog in the whole world, (see his picture in the dictionary next to "best dog ever") and his sidekick, Mr. Widdle, aka Wiz-man, whose name has been changed to protect the little bugger. Let's just say that it's a good thing he's cute because he has a few issues that were worse when he first came to us. He's getting better, but at this time nothing is safe in the yard whether it's edible or not, and the carpet is . . . well, soon to be ancient history!

Contact Information

Barbara Ivie Green loves to hear from readers!
Visit her blog or website to see what is new and in the works for both her
series and art.

Email: barbaraiviegreen@aol.com

Twitter: http://twitter.com/Biviegreen

Facebook: http://www.facebook.com/barbaraiviegreen

Blog: www.barbaraiviegreen.blogspot.com

Website: www.barbaraiviegreen.com

www.ingramcontent.com/pod-product-compliance
Lightning Source LLC
Chambersburg PA
CBHW070800180626
46818CB00001B/34